ARE YOU GAME?

THE COMPLETE SERIES

RHIAN CAHILL

Are You Game? The Complete Series
By Rhian Cahill

For more information visit:
www.rhiancahill.com

7 MINUTES IN HEAVEN

ARE YOU GAME? BOOK 1

DEDICATION

For all those afraid of the dark, it doesn't always hide monsters.
For the man I'd gladly get in the closet with. Mr.C, you don't need seven
minutes to rock my world, you do it every second you love me.

1

Cassie clamped her jaw and clenched her fists. She would not rise to the Neanderthal in front of her. Lil had been gone only an hour and already this giant was throwing his weight around. Lillian McDermott may be her best friend and done Cassie a huge favor when she agreed to be the first to host the new line of adult parties run by Are You Game?, but that didn't mean Cassie, or her team, could be anything except professional. This was still a job.

A job that could break her company's good reputation or send it skyrocketing. She'd do anything to continue the success of Are You Game?, and if it meant putting up with the head of McDermott Security—aka Mr. Muscles—then Cassie would suck it up and deal.

Taking a deep breath, she focused her mind on her job—on making Lillian McDermott's farewell bash the party of the year. Calmer, Cassie tilted her head up and met eyes as black as coal and just as cold. It made her pause, the darkness lurking in that piercing gaze. He stood almost a foot taller than her, and if she were a simpering female, she might actually be afraid of the menacing giant. But Cassandra Moreland had never been simpering or particularly female. Growing up with five older brothers had fixed that.

She drew in another deep breath and let it out slowly. "Look. I know Lil left you and your team to oversee the rest of the night, but it's me and my team that are in charge of this event and the cleanup. I'd appreciate it if you and your men stay out of our way."

"Cassie."

Her eyes narrowed. Oh, how she hated that placating tone men used when they were trying to reason with a *difficult* woman. "Don't take that tone with me." She stepped closer.

His eyes flashed. Fire lit up the dark depths for a split second before he blinked and cut the emotion—if that's what it was—off. Not one to back down, Cassie pushed to her toes and got as close to in his face as she could without getting a stepladder. Her chest brushed his and the zing that shot through her system couldn't be mistaken for anything but desire. Cassie's breath stalled in her lungs and whatever words she'd been about to blast him with died on her tongue.

Holy shit!

She sank back to her heels, but before they touched the floor, he shot out his hands and grabbed her elbows.

"Oh no, don't back down now, Cass." He used his grip to pull her back against him. "Not when things are just getting interesting."

They eyed each other for long moments, and Cassie had the impression he was sizing her up—testing her mettle—before making another move. She wasn't sure what to do or think. For a start, he was manhandling her. That hadn't happened since she was in the eighth grade and Malcolm Birmingham had gotten a little too fresh on their first date. But unlike then, she didn't bring her knee up to rearrange the giant's groin. No, she wanted to reach down and cup it.

Oh boy.

He leaned closer, his lips a breath from hers. "Do you really want me to stay out of your way?"

Oh God.

Cassie's mouth went dry. The man held her spellbound, and she didn't even know his name. She darted her tongue out to wet her lips, except he was so close the tip slid over his full bottom lip before retreating into her mouth. They both sucked in a sharp breath and

Cassie's eyes widened, her heart thudding as his dark gaze bore into hers. His nostrils flared and air streamed across her face as he inhaled and exhaled in a gusty breath.

He smelled of peppermint, and she was reminded of when she was little and her grandma would sneak her chewing gum when her parents weren't looking. It made her feel safe—loved—and didn't that just blow her mind.

"Cassie?" Her head snapped around to find Dan standing beside them. "Everything okay?"

"Um…" She had no clue what to tell her second-in-charge.

"No problem," the giant said as he lowered her feet to the floor and set her away from him. "We were just trying to hear each other without yelling."

Cassie's eyes met those breath-stealing dark orbs once more and a frisson of heat arrowed through her belly. "Ah, yeah, um, just sorting out the remainder of the evening."

"Right, well we're out of scotch, vodka *and* tequila. Oh, and the last of the finger food is being circulated as we speak," Dan said.

"We're out of food?" she asked, turning her attention back to Dan.

"Not quite yet." Dan watched a waiter pass by, the silver tray he carried half-empty. "But it won't be long."

"That's okay. We're winding things down anyway." Cassie turned back to face Mr. Muscles. "We'll start shutting down the bars."

He crossed his arms over his massive chest and Cassie tried really hard not to ogle the mouth-watering pecs hidden beneath his tight black shirt. When she brought her gaze up to meet his, it was to find one dark brow arched and a look on his face that clearly said he was pleased he'd gotten his way.

Damn the man. She hated to give an inch to anyone, and if it weren't for the prospect of being in the house with no food or alcohol and a bunch of demanding partiers, she'd never bow to his demands to shut the party down and usher everyone out. The plan had been to allow the evening to come to a natural end, only now it appeared as though he'd be getting his way.

With no small amount of frustration and anger, Cassie added,

"We'll start cleanup, you and your men stay out of our way." She spun on her heel and, spine and shoulders straight, marched off, praying no one could see her shaking. The giant specimen of seething testosterone set her on edge, the least of which was the blade of arousal she felt for a man whose name she didn't know.

Lucas Wilhelm watched Cassandra Moreland walk away. The word 'run' slid through his mind, but Cassie wasn't the type of woman to run from anything—or anyone. Hell, if he didn't know better he'd think she actually had a set of balls in those sexy black pants of hers.

A smile tugged at his mouth and it took more than the usual effort to keep his face impassive. He was going to enjoy tangling with little Miss In Charge. Surveying the crowd, Luc doubted she'd be getting anyone out of here anytime soon. Not without pulling the fire alarm and starting the sprinkler system. Eyeing the couple in the far corner, he wondered if a drenching wasn't exactly what this party needed.

There were sweaty half-naked bodies all over the house. All gyrating to the pounding beat of the music thumping through the wireless speakers in a very adult bump and grind that was more sex than dance. Luc shook his head and moved through the room toward the front of the house. He spotted two of his men and motioned them over to give them orders.

"Where do you want us, boss?"

"I need the backyard and deck cleared. Herd everyone into the house and close the doors behind them." If they could slowly push everyone out the front door it would help Cassie, not that he expected her to be happy with him lending a hand. His lips curled. He looked forward to the argument they would surely have in the next little while. "And when you're done out there, start moving everyone into the front rooms."

"On it, Mr. Wilhelm."

Luc hated it when his men called him Mr. Wilhelm. It always gave him the urge to look over his shoulder for his father. Stifling the action, he nodded at the two men and continued through to the front door. Two more of his men stood either side of the wide-open double doors as though they were sentries stopping anyone from escaping, except he *wanted* the guests to get away.

"You two, upstairs. Start clearing out all the rooms. And check the closets." Lord knows what games people were playing up there. So far he'd seen more than one he'd played himself back when getting a hot piece of ass was all he was about. Of course, those days were long gone. In fact, he couldn't remember the last time he'd wanted to get his hands on any ass. Well, not before one pint-sized brunette went toe-to-toe with him, anyway.

Another smile tugged at his lips, and Luc marveled at the emotion one small woman could drag out of him when men twice her size couldn't make him so much as twitch.

He glanced at his watch. Two minutes after two. Time to put party shutdown into overdrive. Stalking through the downstairs rooms, Luc found each of his men and sent them out to move the crowd along. It was similar to herding sheep. En masse, they surged into the front of the house, filling the areas to breathing room only.

In twos and threes, sometimes more, they began to disappear out the front door and into the night. By the time Lachlan McDermott barreled into the living room, steam shooting from his ears, the place was down to half the number of occupants there had been when Luc first arrived.

The boss wasn't happy. And the silence that filled the house when Lachlan yanked out the DJ's power cables hurt Luc's ears. He swiftly made his way over to the man who personally signed his paycheck.

"Where's Lucas?" Lachlan growled at one of McDermott Security's men.

"Right behind you, boss," Luc answered.

Lachlan spun around. "Where's Mac?"

"He took Ms. McDermott off site about an hour ago. Maybe

more." Luc steeled himself. He had no doubt Lachlan wouldn't be happy with Mackenzie and Lillian's whereabouts.

"Off site? During a party Lil is responsible for?"

Luc nodded and kept his expression bland. He didn't want to give Lachlan McDermott any reason to stop signing those checks. "Mr. Harris arranged for my team to take charge. I've been monitoring the situation."

Numerous emotions flashed across Lachlan's face while he glanced around the room. Bringing his gaze back to Luc he said, "Get 'em out. All of them."

Inclining his head once more, Luc gave the only reply he could. "Consider it done, boss."

The fact Lachlan turned and strode from the room without a backward glance told Luc that not only was his pay safe but he was trusted to do the job given him. Breathing a little easier, he turned to the man on his right. "You heard the boss. Get 'em out."

His employee spun into action and Luc went in search of Cassie. She would not be pleased when he informed her they were shutting down effective immediately. He'd be a liar if he said the swirling in his gut wasn't excitement. But going toe-to-toe with Cassandra Moreland had more than his stomach churning. The tightness in his pants hadn't escaped his notice either.

And wasn't that an interesting development. He didn't usually go for bossy, confrontational females. Or ones that didn't even come up to his chin. Luc scrubbed a hand over his stubbled jaw. This evening was turning out to be far more entertaining than he'd ever expected.

Cassie was loading empty bottles into a recycling bag when someone grabbed her arm and propelled her across the kitchen, forcing her to jog or fall on her face. "Hey!"

"We need to talk."

Great. Mr. Muscles was manhandling her again. Yanking on her arm proved ineffective in gaining freedom from his vise-like grip, so she swung her full weight to the left and slammed into his rock-hard chest. Air burst from her lungs. *Holy shit.* The man was made of steel. Her brain rattled and any protest she might have uttered vibrated right off the thought train and into the fog this man's presence seemed to bring.

Dammit. She was a highly intelligent woman who ran her own business. Why the hell couldn't she think of anything other than exploring the slab of muscle she was currently plastered to? And it wasn't just her hands itching to wander new territory either.

Before she could ponder that thought any further he'd maneuvered them into the walk-in pantry and closed the door. For a heartbeat, the room remained pitch black, then he bumped his shoulder against the wall and eye-straining fluorescent brilliance flooded the area. His hands spanned her waist and it took her a second to realize he'd carried her the last few steps and still held her off the floor. She was eye level with his mouth.

The very mouth she'd inadvertently caught a taste of earlier. The one she wanted to take a bigger sample of now.

Cassie swallowed, her throat dry, and fought the urge to lean in to seize the kiss she craved. She moved her gaze up his slightly crooked nose and met those dark, dark eyes. Her heart kicked. How had she ever thought his eyes were cold? Heat turned the brown—not black as she'd previously thought—irises into molten pools of hunger that flared hotter as their gazes connected. She gasped. The beat of her heart stepped up double-time and she went soft in places she hadn't thought about in a long time. Who *was* this man and what the fuck was he doing to her?

"W-who are you?" Her voice came out a timid whisper, but she couldn't summon the energy or desire to be offended by her sudden lack of backbone.

"You know who I am."

His deep voice rumbled in her ears and sent shockwaves of sensation skittering over her skin. A shiver slid down her spine as warmth flickered into flame in her belly. She licked her lips. "No. No, I don't."

"Cass," he whispered as he moved closer. "I'm the man who's going to bring you to your knees."

Oh God.

He brushed her lips with his, the move slow and steady, allowing plenty of time for her to turn away. Only she didn't. Instead, she moved into him. Met him halfway and took as much as she gave.

They didn't ease into the kiss—they dove deep. He thrust his tongue against hers, caressed and teased until she was panting for breath and thinking they had way too many clothes on.

Cassie tilted her head and moaned when he took advantage of the better angle. The kiss went on and on. Each slide, each lick, each nip, drove her further into the sexual haze surrounding them.

He dug his fingers into her waist as he tightened his grip and crushed her against him. Her breasts pressed into solid muscle, her nipples going taut on contact with the hot wall of his chest. She tore her mouth from his and gasped for breath only to lose any hope of breathing normally when he trailed his lips over her chin and down her neck. He sucked and nibbled, devouring every centimeter of skin left bare above her collar. Every nerve ending buzzed until her blood hummed with the all-consuming lust flooding her system.

Cassie tangled her fingers in his hair, the silky strands curling around them as though tying her to him. She didn't remember wrapping her arms around him. Didn't remember hooking her legs around his waist either, but she couldn't deny she was currently covering him like shrink-wrap. He bucked his hips and his very impressive erection pressed into her sex.

There was no stopping her hips from thrusting back, from grinding her clit on the hard length of his cock in her search for relief. For more. With a growl, his mouth came back to hers and she lost herself in the sublime talent of his tongue.

He slid his hands up her sides, his thumbs coming to rest on the lower curve of her breasts, and another growl rumbled through his chest as she wiggled in an attempt to move his hands higher. He didn't disappoint.

With skill, he maneuvered those big hands between them and

cupped her full mounds in his palms. Her nipples throbbed and she arched her back, pressing her breasts deeper into his hold. She needed more. So much more. Cassie sucked his tongue into her mouth and then slowly let it out, raking her teeth along the sides as she did. The pounding of her heart echoed in her ears and through her body, thumping with a bone-jarring intensity.

He tore his mouth from hers and growled, "Fuck."

She couldn't catch her breath, couldn't fathom the change when he tried to push her away. "What?"

His dark gaze met hers, his chest heaving as he dragged in air. "There's someone banging on the door."

"What?"

He lowered his forehead to rest it on hers. "There's someone knocking on the door behind me."

Cassie's lust-fogged brain took another second to comprehend the meaning of his words, but when it did mortification swamped her. She was in a client's pantry making out with a guy she didn't know. With a groan, she closed her eyes and dropped her head to the side, butting her brow against his shoulder.

How could she forget where she was and what she was supposed to be doing? And why the hell was she still wrapped around this stranger like a wet Speedo on a Bondi lifesaver? A shiver rolled over her.

Oh, *so* not the right analogy to be thinking. She should be concentrating on getting herself off. Another shiver rippled through her. Oh God, not *off* off. Cassie dropped her legs and tried to unravel her arms from the giant's neck. But her feet didn't touch the floor and his large hands on her waist held her prisoner against him. Her heart raced with residual arousal and the embarrassment of her recent behavior, while her mind spun in circles in search of what to say.

"Cass."

Damn. The man knew how to use his voice to make her sit up and take notice. She never knew her name could render her senseless with desire. Except the way he said it, in that deep, gravely tone, made her insides not only sit up but dance a little jig too. Cassie swallowed over the lump in her throat and blurted out the first words that came to mind.

"I don't even know your name." Heat scorched her face. She'd spent the last few minutes locked in a pantry making out with a stranger. It was the one game she hadn't put on tonight's list—not that it had stopped some of the guests from playing it.

7 Minutes in Heaven.

Only seven minutes was nowhere near long enough with the man who held her in his arms. And altogether too long for her peace of mind.

2

Luc relaxed the muscles in his arms and did the one thing he really didn't want to. He set Cassie on her feet. Whoever had been hammering on the door had stopped, but the damage was done. Regret was written all over her pretty face. Scrubbing a hand over his stubbled jaw, he drew in a deep breath and let it out slowly.

"Luc," he said

Cassie's gaze met his, one delicate eyebrow arched.

"My name. It's Lucas Wilhelm. I'm head of McDermott Security, a position I've held for ten years." Luc added the last part in the hope of reassuring her.

"Oh. Um, well..." She lowered her eyes, hiding the uncertainty swirling in their honey-colored depths.

Placing two fingers under her chin, he tipped her head back until her gaze met his once more. "Don't back down now, Cass. Where's the woman who's fought me for control for the last couple of hours gone?"

She shook her head, dislodging his fingers. "She just had common sense kissed right out of her."

The small smile tugging at the corner of her mouth pulled at his gut and eased his mind. He hadn't been sure at first, but now he didn't doubt she'd bounce back from their mind-numbing lip-lock. Luc had expected they'd be explosive, he just hadn't realized how unstable their chemistry was. He'd have to keep his hands off her until they were in more suitable surroundings or they'd find themselves sans clothes. There was one sure-fire way to keep her at a distance though. Strip her of control.

"As of now, this party is over."

"What?" Her eyes narrowed to slits.

If looks could kill, the one she aimed his way would slice him to ribbons, and Luc figured she'd used it to de-ball many a man before him. Good thing he'd spent years developing a tough exterior. Although she'd found a way under his skin already, he wasn't about to cower before her hostile stare. Luc embraced the hum in his veins. The zap delivered courtesy of her returning ballsy attitude. He'd never gone looking for a fight. Sure he'd been in plenty, but he'd never started one. Except now. With Cassie. And there was no denying the thrill thrumming in his blood. He was more than looking forward to their combat. He was eager for it to begin.

"As you can hear, there's no longer music blasting through the house and that's thanks to Lachlan McDermott ripping out power cables. If I were you, I wouldn't be surprised when your DJ files a damage report and insurance claim." Luc smiled as a growl rumbled in her throat. He'd never heard that particular sound from a woman, and he'd certainly never found it a turn on coming from any man, but there was no mistaking the tightening of his sac or the hardening of his cock.

"Damn men." Cassie shoved past him and flung open the door, using it to push him out of the way.

Before he got his head in gear and made it out from behind the door, she'd disappeared into the kitchen. With long strides, Luc followed only to witness her sexy ass vanish through the far doorway. Covering the distance in seconds, he found his men doing as he'd ordered. Between them and Cassie's staff, the guests were quickly being ushered from the house in a tidal wave of drunkenness.

His search for Cassie was hindered by the surge of bodies moving toward the front door. With his chances to spot her zero he let himself be swept up in the tide. When he reached the front yard, hire cars and drivers lined the street. Inebriated partiers tumbled into backseats, car doors slammed and departing vehicles were quickly swallowed up by the night.

With the party down to the last few stragglers, he turned back to the house determined to find Cassie while his men dealt with the remaining guests. He found her back in the kitchen. Leaning his shoulder against the doorframe, he folded his arms, crossed one ankle over the other and watched as she gave orders while packing box after box with glasses.

The image of efficiency, her movements were economical and fluid, her speed and accuracy proving she'd done this a thousand times before. Luc relaxed and enjoyed the view. His pants grew snug and he had to shift his stance to alleviate the pressure on his hardening cock.

She turned and stared straight at him. Her gaze traveled from his face to his toes and back again, the slow survey like a physical caress, and a shaft of heat speared his groin. A knowing smile graced her mouth and more fire exploded in his crotch as he remembered the taste of those lips. He pushed off the wall and angled his body so the evidence of his arousal wouldn't be so blatant. Cassie's gaze dipped and her smile grew, sending the heat in his groin licking along his veins until he burned from top to bottom—inside out.

The woman was dangerous, she poked at every nerve he had and flayed them raw without trying. Luc couldn't wait to have her beneath him.

"Are you going to stand there all night scaring my employees or are you planning to make yourself useful?"

Luc jerked at her words. He'd thought for sure she'd continue to ignore him, and he smiled as he stepped toward her. Her next words stopped him in his tracks.

"Oh wait, that's right, you don't take orders. You *give* them."

His gaze narrowed, the burst of anger he felt a total overreaction, but then every emotion involving Cassandra Moreland was exaggerated. The smart-aleck grin on her face didn't help either. Nor the fact she was just as averse to taking orders as he was. It wasn't as though he couldn't take them. It was more that he normally delivered them. He could take direction just as well as the next guy. He'd taken an order from Lachlan McDermott, hadn't he? And Cassie definitely couldn't talk. She was exactly the same if their recent interaction was anything to go by.

"Pot, meet Kettle," Luc mumbled.

Her shoulders straightened. "What did you call me?"

"You heard." He walked closer. "We're two peas in a pod, Cass, and you know it."

"Bullshit." She slammed the plastic lid on the tub in front of her and snapped the locking handles into place with unnecessary force. "I can take orders."

"Really?" Luc leaned on the bench that separated them. "Prove it."

Cassie's eyes widened before they reduced to narrow slits and his insides clenched. God, why did her anger get him off? And why the hell did he continue to poke at her? The suddenness of her smile didn't bode well, but Luc waited with bated breath for her next words. She didn't disappoint him.

"On one condition."

"What?"

"You do the same."

Oh, this was going to be good. Inwardly he smiled, but he didn't let any of his excitement at her obvious capitulation to his challenge show. "Deal."

"Wait, we haven't worked out the terms."

"That's the easy part. We'll each take orders from the other for twenty-four hours." Luc couldn't help it, he upped the ante. Leaning forward, he brought his face inches from hers. His gaze dropped to her lips and he watched as her tongue slipped out to slide along the plump pink flesh he wanted to taste again so badly he ached with it. "For a whole day, anything I tell you to do, you do and vice versa."

Cassie sucked in a breath. He couldn't be suggesting what she thought. "You don't mean…"

"Yeah, that's exactly what I mean."

She glanced around to make sure no one was listening. "You can't expect me to agree to this. You're basically propositioning me."

Lucas laughed. "Nice to know where your mind is, but I don't recall mentioning sex."

Damn. He was right, he hadn't mentioned sex, but he'd definitely implied it, what with the way he kept looking at her. Or was it because her mind had been on a continuous loop of imagined pleasure with Lucas ever since their kiss in the pantry? Fantasies of being naked with him had plagued her from the moment she'd walked away.

She couldn't help it, they might not have done much more than kiss, but her body had shot straight to overheated and stayed there. Her recent lack of a sex-life might have something to do with her fixation with the sexily muscled giant in front of her too. God, she couldn't remember the last time she'd had a man-delivered orgasm, and he'd promised to deliver one with only his lips.

Cassie took a calming breath—or at least she hoped the lungful of oxygen would be—and let her mind clear of carnal thoughts so she could at least weigh the pros and cons of being what effectively was this man's slave for twenty-four hours. If he had no intention of moving their little challenge into the bedroom then she could deal with any order he gave.

At least she thought she could. Hopefully he wouldn't get her to clean his bathroom. She didn't do boys' toilets anymore. She'd spent her teenage years sharing one bathroom with five brothers and not one of them had ever cleaned up after themselves.

Or aimed straight.

She studied the man on the other side of the counter. If he wasn't planning to take this arrangement into the sexual arena then what was his agenda? Could she trust him to keep his word if she agreed?

"What's wrong, Cass? You afraid you can't handle me telling you what to do?"

Hah! "I can handle anything you dish out. Question is, can you say the same?"

Cassie hoped he couldn't see through her tough-girl act, because in spite of a lifetime spent being scared of nothing, this man had her insides shaking and her nerves jittering with a healthy dose of fear.

It wasn't the thought of taking orders that had her worried either. Her brothers had bossed her around for as long as she could remember, so she knew she was capable of putting up with Lucas telling her what to do. She was more concerned about her traitorous libido.

The electricity arcing between them was enough to light up the entire city of Sydney for a month. But she'd be damned if she'd let him get the better of her.

He chuckled. "No question. It would take more than some little woman to scare me."

A growl rumbled in her chest. "Did you just call me a *little woman*?"

Lucas shrugged. "If the shoe fits."

Oh boy. That did it. She'd spent her whole life proving her size didn't matter. She might be average height for a female, but in a household of extra-tall individuals that hadn't made a difference. As the shortest, she'd endured every tease imaginable from her brothers, and hearing Lucas refer to her as 'little' only tweaked her need to prove she packed as big of a punch as he did.

"Fine." She stuck out her hand. "When do you want to start?"

"Now's as good a time as any." His large hand engulfed hers.

"I'm in charge first."

He arched an eyebrow.

"I've got a job tomorrow, and Dan was going to help me but now you will."

His other eyebrow joined the first, his eyes widening. "A party?" he asked as he glanced around them.

"Don't worry. It's not an adults-only one." Cassie smiled. "I'm sure you'll be fine. It's a birthday party."

"Oh." Relief filled his face as he smiled.

Cassie had to hold back her laughter. She wasn't about to inform him he'd be spending six hours with a bunch of pink-tutu-wearing five-year-olds helping them make jewelry from tiny glass beads. "I'll give you my work address and you can meet me there in the morning to help me load up the supplies."

"I thought we were starting now."

"Oh, but I thought..." What had she thought? Cassie had just assumed they'd start in the morning; they were both still working after all.

"Okay, how about this." Lucas glanced at his watch. "We start the clock ticking when we finish up here. You get me for twenty-four hours, then I get you for twenty-four."

He held her with a look that sent shivers down her spine. "But when I finish here I'm going home to catch a couple of hours sleep before I have to prep for tomorrow's party."

"So will I." He grinned and Cassie's stomach fluttered. "You can get me to massage your feet before you hit the sack."

Cassie gulped. Good God, that wasn't all she'd like him to massage, and most of what she was thinking would be done *after* she hit the sack. "You're coming home with me?"

"Yep. Twenty-four hours is twenty-four hours." Lucas locked his gaze to hers, his stare and stance clearly telegraphing the words *I dare you to back out.*

She wasn't stupid by a long shot, but Cassie may have just made the dumbest deal of the century with a man who had already proven he could scramble her brain with a mere kiss.

Luc watched myriad emotions flicker across Cassie's face before she straightened her spine and yanked her hand from his. How either of them had forgotten to let go before now was a mystery. Then again maybe not.

His hand felt cold without hers tucked inside it and the heat her touch generated still zipped up his arm and through his body, hitting every erogenous zone he had. He slipped his thumb through a belt loop and shoved his fingers into his front pocket, which only made the fit of his slacks tighter and his semi-hard cock even more uncomfortable. He removed his hand and placed it on the counter, palm down, and leaned forward. The urge to kiss her fired his nerve endings and scorched his veins with molten lust.

What was it about Cassandra Moreland that sparked such an incendiary reaction?

Luc couldn't recall any other woman having such an instant or profound effect on him. In fact, he couldn't remember the last woman to have any kind of effect on him other than annoyance. He'd never been one to make close connections with anyone. It came with the job.

Being head of security meant he had to be available twenty-four-seven, and the women he met in his line of work were usually the shallow money-grubbing kind of individual, and therefore even if he'd found his interest piqued by a woman she was unlikely to want anything to do with a lowly bodyguard.

Of course, there were the few who wanted to take a tumble between the sheets with a dangerous man, but they tended to have their curiosity satisfied fairly quickly.

He'd left one-night stands behind him sometime in his twenties. At thirty-eight he was extremely discriminatory about his choice of bed partner. He wasn't in it just to get his rocks off. That type of dalliance left him unsatisfied and more often than not feeling selfish, used and disgusted with himself and the woman he was with. Might explain why he couldn't remember the last woman he'd had sex with.

If he had his way that dry spell was about to be broken, but not this weekend. Luc wouldn't use their challenge to get Cassie into bed. No. When he slept with her it would be because they both wanted it with bone-deep need, not because either of them had ordered the other there.

And the quicker they got this place cleared out, the quicker he could work his magic and have her panting for him. He wasn't delusional though, he knew full well that he'd be panting just as hard and looked forward to one very long weekend of temptation and anticipation with Cassandra Moreland.

"I'll get a couple of my men to give you a hand with the pack up," he said.

"What?" Cassie turned from the clipboard she was marking items off on. "My staff is more than capable of doing their job."

Luc smiled. "I didn't say they couldn't—"

"Then don't imply it." She squared her shoulders as though preparing for a fight.

He held up his hands. "Whoa. All I'm doing is offering to help."

"Then offer, don't order." Her mouth stretched into a straight line, her lips pressed together, and Luc wanted to lean over and tease his tongue along the seam until she softened and the harsh lines were plump and wet.

"Fine." He pulled his thoughts out of his pants and tried a different track. "It's two-thirty a.m., give yourself and your staff a break by allowing me and my men to help you finish out the night. I'm sure everyone is more than ready to head home. You've been here since two this afternoon."

Cassie's eyes narrowed and she crossed her arms over her ample bosom, drawing his gaze. "Could you not ogle me while we're arguing? And how the hell do you know what time I got here? Have you been spying on me?"

Luc brought his gaze up to meet hers. "We're arguing?"

"That's all you heard?"

"Well, no, but it was certainly the part that got my attention. As for the other, no, you aren't being *spied on*, but the McDermotts' security is the highest priority and therefore anything pertaining to them I know about."

"Anything?" She arched a brow.

"Yes."

"So you know that Lil quit modeling?"

"Yes." Luc quickly surveyed the space around them and judged the area safe. He knew he wouldn't be telling Cassie anything Lillian

McDermott hadn't already divulged. "I also know all about her children's clothing label, Lilli Pond, and next month's launch of her signature fragrance, Golden Lilli."

"Oh."

"It's my job, Cass. I take it and the safety of those under my protection very seriously." He placed his hands on the counter and leaned closer. "Now, will you let me and my men help you? You can give us orders and I won't even count the time toward our little weekend challenge."

She chewed the corner of her bottom lip. Her white teeth worrying the flesh until it turned a deep red caused Luc's groin to tighten.

"Fine. I could use some help loading these boxes into the back of the van in the driveway."

Luc smiled as satisfaction slid through his belly. She might not like taking his help, but she wasn't stubborn enough to refuse it to prove a point. He just hoped the rest of their time together would run as smoothly.

3

Cassie lowered the box to the van floor and tried to ignore the ache in her back. She didn't normally cart around the heavy equipment, usually she left the serious lifting for Dan or one of the other guys, so she only had herself to blame for any injury she sustained. Lucas hadn't actually challenged her competency, but after their earlier conversation her life-long compulsion to prove herself had reared its ugly head and she'd been compelled to show him she was more than capable of doing the job.

Unfortunately, that meant a sore back, and unless she treated the area with a heat pack when she got home, she was bound to suffer for the next few days. Cursing her stubborn need to demonstrate she measured up in every way, Cassie straightened and winced as a sharp twinge of pain lanced her lumbar region.

With a groan, Cassie reached around and pressed her hands against her lower back. Arching slightly, she stretched the muscles and kneaded with her fingers. Two large hands covered hers, warm strong fingers working along her spine with harder pressure than her own. She slipped her hands free and allowed the far more skilled ones to take over.

The ache eased with each caress and she couldn't stop the small moans of relief the soothing massage roused. Cassie didn't have to turn around to know who was behind her. Lucas. Heat radiated off him, surrounding her with the aroma of soap and man and a tantalizing cologne she couldn't name.

She'd know his scent anywhere. Funny how so little time spent in his presence could engrave him so deeply on her memory banks. She closed her eyes and took a deep breath. The heat and smell of him soaked in, curled inside her and drew her nerves taut until Cassie thought she might snap at any moment. She dipped her head forward with a groan as he hit a particularly tight spot.

It didn't take him long to weed the knots out of her stiff muscles. Concentrating on Lucas and his magic hands, she didn't hear anyone approach until Dan spoke beside her.

"We're almost done, Cassie. Just the walkthrough and letting everyone go left to do."

Her eyes snapped open and a gust of air burst from her lungs. She jumped forward, almost toppling into the rear of the van in her effort to move away from Lucas. Righting herself, she turned to Dan and thanked the darkness surrounding them. She'd hate for him to see her flaming-red face.

"You can let everyone go now. I'll do the walkthrough and fix anything we've forgotten, but I doubt I'll find anything. You always do a brilliant job on clear-out."

"Are you sure?" Dan asked. "I can do the walkthrough with you."

"No, it's okay, I can manage. If you let everyone know they can leave I'll get started." Cassie stepped around both men then stopped abruptly. "Oh, and you can have tomorrow off. I've found someone else to help me, and you already pulled those extra shifts this week so you deserve to have a full weekend free."

"I didn't think anyone was available for Saturday this week," Dan said.

Cassie glanced at Lucas. "Um, well, no, but Lucas has agreed to give me a hand."

"He has?" Dan looked Lucas over from head to toe with a critical eye. "Does he know what type of party it is?"

Not wanting Dan to let the cat out of the bag, she grabbed his arm and led him toward where her staff waited and away from Lucas. Cassie quickly changed the topic and pointed Dan in a different direction. "Make sure everyone has a ride home when you let them go. A couple of the guys are new to the team and I'm not sure how they got here."

He waited until they were out of earshot before pulling from her grasp and turning on her. "What the fuck is going on, Cassie?"

She didn't want to get into it with Dan right now, so she gave him the bare minimum of information. "Nothing is going on. Lucas and I got to talking and he volunteered to give me a hand sometime, and seeing how you really shouldn't have to do another shift this week, I thought tomorrow would be perfect."

Dan eyed her with suspicion, but she'd learnt long ago how to school her face. She wasn't the family poker champion for nothing.

"I know I'm missing something, but I'll take your word for it as long as you promise to ring me if anything fucks up."

Cassie smiled. Dan might sometimes behave like one of her overbearing brothers, but she could always rely on him to put business first. "Promise."

"I don't like it, but you're the boss."

"Honest, Dan, nothing is going on. Now go see to the staff and I'll catch you on Monday at the office. Don't forget we need to talk about bringing on another supervisor." Cassie gave his shoulder a little push in an attempt to nudge him into action.

Standing his ground, he studied her a minute longer before drawing in a big breath and letting it out in a rush. "Fine. See you Monday."

She watched Dan stride across the lawn to where everyone had gathered. Cassie knew he wasn't happy about her plans to bring in more staff. They'd argued about waiting to see how successful this new arm of the business was, but she could already tell the adult party theme would prove to be popular.

Besides, the children's party line had more than doubled in bookings over the last six months, so she'd already been contemplating employing a manager for that area. It would be nice to have a weekend free for once too. Movement beside her caught her eye, and she turned to find Lucas standing a few feet away.

He'd kept his distance while she'd been talking to Dan, but he quickly closed the gap when their eyes connected. He didn't say a word, just stared at her with that dark, penetrating gaze. It made her squirm, being under his scrutiny, and Cassie figured he'd spent years perfecting his silent treatment and using it to get his way.

Good thing she wasn't intimidated easily—also a good thing he had no clue as to how deeply he affected her. She had a feeling he wouldn't think twice about using any weakness he found to get what he wanted, and that included her traitorous libido. Shame she didn't have any idea what it was he was after.

A shiver stole down her spine as the summer breeze kicked up. At least she told herself it was the breeze that made her tremble. It wouldn't do to admit the man before her had her nerves vibrating with anticipation.

Breaking eye contact, Cassie turned toward the house and her final job of the night. She ignored the man at her heels. Ignored the heat emanating from his body. Ignored the enticing scent surrounding her. And would definitely ignore the burn of desire his presence delivered to every inch of her. Heading through the front door, Cassie cleared her mind of all smutty thoughts and began her walkthrough.

Luc followed Cassie as she made her way through every room of the house. He was surprised at her thoroughness. Then again, after only a few hours he shouldn't have been. She'd never do a half-assed job on anything. Speaking of asses, the one in front of him was world class.

She wasn't one of those super-skinny chicks and she wasn't what would be called full-figured either. Sleekly muscled, the firm globes of her ass seesawed up and down as she walked. Each step drew his gaze and made his pulse pound until every inch of him throbbed with need. Her curves were just the right size to fit in his hands. The urge to feel her backside pressed up against his groin shuddered through him, and without thought, Luc stepped forward and crowded her into the small bathroom she was checking.

"What—"

"Shh." He pressed her against the vanity, but their height difference meant that perfect ass met his thighs. His rapidly hardening cock nudged her lower back and Luc ground his pelvis into her.

"Lucas." His name slipped passed her lips on a sharp breath.

Cassie's protest was weak. Especially when he could feel her push back against him, felt her wiggle her rear end as though trying to get closer. His gaze landed on the mirror in front of them and he focused on their reflection. Luc studied them.

He towered above her, his body curled over hers, and he watched her face as he lowered his head and brushed his lips over the shell of her ear. Her eyes closed and her tongue darted out. The pink tip slicked across her bottom lip and left an enticing trail of moisture.

A groan rumbled in his chest as the memory of kissing her swamped him. In a split second, he grabbed her hips, spun her around and lifted her to the counter top.

He didn't give her a chance to protest. Not that she did when his mouth landed on hers. Luc forgot finesse, forgot gentle.

With a savage thrust, he drove his tongue between her lips and took what he wanted. What he craved. She gave all she had. Her mouth ate at his with equal demand, and Luc could only think it wasn't enough. It would never be enough. They had to get naked. Now.

So much for his plan of not taking her to bed this weekend. Tearing his mouth from hers, he struggled to pull oxygen into his starving lungs.

"I want you," he panted.

"Yes." She tangled her fingers in his hair and tugged his mouth back to hers.

Luc let Cassie take control of the kiss. Let her take her fill while he worked out the best way to have her naked beneath him. A noise overhead startled him and the fog of lust clogging his mind cleared long enough that he remembered where they were. Whose house they were in.

Shit.

He pulled away and stepped back. Cassie tipped forward and he reached out to steady her.

"What?" Confusion swirled in her dilated eyes.

"Not here." Luc gripped her waist and lowered her to the floor.

He saw the second comprehension dawned. Her face flushed red and her gaze dropped from his, her shoulders hunching forward.

"Oh God," she whispered.

If he wasn't watching her so closely, he wouldn't have seen her mouth move, wouldn't have caught the edge of embarrassment in her words. With the tip of his index finger he pushed her chin up and waited for her eyes to meet his.

"Don't." Luc moved his hand to cradle her jaw. "You weren't the only one lost in here."

"But—"

He placed his thumb over her lips. "No buts. And don't for one second think I was any less involved in this. I want you, Cass, more than I should I'm sure. But when I have you it won't be in the bathroom of the man who signs my paychecks."

"Jesus. I can't believe I forgot where we are. *Again.*" She smiled. "Thank you for not leaving me out on a limb on my own. I appreciate your honesty."

Luc cupped her face in both hands and leaned forward until his lips brushed hers. "One thing you can count on from me is honesty. I'll never lie to you. Now, let's finish your walkthrough and get out of here."

Cassie took a deep breath. "Um...maybe you should wait for me outside."

He chuckled. "I think I can keep my hands off you long enough to make it through the last couple of rooms, but if you think you can't..."

She grinned at him before she ducked under his arm and darted out of the bathroom. "Meet you by the front door," she called over her shoulder as she disappeared into the library across the hall.

Figuring Cassie might be right and they could do with some distance, Luc took his time as he made his way to the front door. He still hadn't told her she was his ride home.

Not that he was going home. As soon as she finished here their deal would start. Luc sighed. That meant he shouldn't take her to bed. There was no way he wanted her to think the bet they'd shaken on had anything to do with the two of them getting naked. Except he couldn't seem to keep his hands off her, and once he got his hands on her...well, nothing but getting her naked mattered.

He'd never been so taken—so out of control—with a woman before, and he had to make sure she knew this wasn't his usual behavior. He didn't ravish women within hours of meeting them. He leaned against the wall next to the door and waited for Cassie to finish. Luc didn't have to wait long. She was walking toward him as he thumbed through a news feed on his phone when a grainy photo popped up on the screen and changed his plans for the rest of the night.

"Son-of-a-bitch!" he growled as he straightened off the wall.

"Lucas?" Cass stopped a few feet away. "Is everything all right?"

Damn. How to tell the woman he'd planned to bed that he had to take a rain check.

―――――

Cassie watched emotions flicker across Lucas's face. It was the most expressive she'd seen him. Well, except for those few minutes in the bathroom. Watching his face in the mirror had been eye opening.

The man was not the cold giant he'd first appeared. He was madly swiping his fingers across his phone and whatever it was he was seeing didn't make him happy.

"I have to make a few calls. Can you wait while I do?" he asked, not taking his eyes off his screen.

She shrugged. "Sure. But don't you have Bluetooth in your car?"

His gaze snapped up. "I don't have my car. Mr. Harris took it when he and Ms. McDermott left earlier."

"Oh, so how were you... Oh." Cassie wasn't sure how she felt about him catching a ride with her. It made sense, what with their deal and all, but still. She'd be stuck with him. Anyone else wouldn't cause her insides to churn. Or her breath to quicken. No. Only the thought of being trapped in her van with Lucas could make her knees shake and her heart pound.

The man was far more dangerous than he looked, and to the average Joe he looked deadly.

He'd gone back to staring at his phone, his scowl becoming more menacing by the second. Sensing his need for privacy, Cassie moved toward the open door, but he stopped her with a hand on her arm.

"Just give me a minute." He didn't look at her, just tapped away at his screen.

Cassie didn't know what to do. On the one hand, she wanted to leave and let him do whatever it was he needed to, and on the other, she wanted to go back to when she was his single focus instead of the piece of technology in his hand. She sighed.

How selfish was that? He obviously had a problem, and all she could think about was she no longer had his attention.

"I'll wait outside."

His gaze met hers. The eyes she'd once thought cold probed hers for long moments. He nodded. "I'll only be a few minutes."

"Okay."

She made her escape and sucked in a lungful of cool morning air. Cassie wasn't sure what would happen when he finally came outside. Whether they'd pick up where they left off in the bathroom or if they'd remain caught in the tension of moments ago. One thing she was certain of was that Lucas Wilhelm was the first man in months to kiss her and the only man to ever render her speechless doing so.

Cassie headed for the van. Disengaging the locks, she hopped up in the driver's seat and shut the door. Only the confines of the cab were too small and she shoved the door open again. While warm, the night wasn't stifling enough to warrant turning the engine on and cranking the AC. Mind you, if Lucas heard the motor turn over he might think she was leaving without him, and that was the last thing she planned to do.

Jittery with nerves, she jumped from the van and paced to the rear and back again. By the time Lucas came out of the house and walked toward her, she'd almost worn a trench in the driveway and made what felt like life-altering decisions.

"All set. Ready to go?" Lucas asked as he reached her side.

"Definitely." What scared Cassie was just how ready she was to take this man home with her.

4

___

Cassie hadn't said a word since they'd pulled away from the McDermott house, but Luc didn't have time to worry whether it was a bad sign or not. He was too busy emailing and texting with his staff and the head of McDermott's PR division.

In the last thirty minutes, they'd managed to do nothing to stop the photos of Lachlan McDermott and Cameron Winters making out in a public park from hitting the news and every social media network on the planet. Luc would love to get his hands on Carl Holston for one minute. That's all it would take him to teach the scumbag photographer a lesson.

When the van finally stopped, Luc looked up. He'd barely taken notice of where they were going while Cassie drove, and it pained him to admit that if he hadn't known where Are You Game? was located he wouldn't have a clue where in Sydney they were. So much for his highly tuned observation skills.

He glanced around to discover they weren't at Cassie's work but in the driveway of a neat brick house with well-maintained gardens. Turning to ask her where they were, he found she'd already left the vehicle and was halfway to the front door.

Luc scanned the street as he climbed out, noted the quiet residential area and vaguely recalled Cassie lived in Seaforth. Although she could have driven him anywhere and he wouldn't have had a clue. Good thing she wasn't out to do him harm.

He chuckled at the thought of Cassandra Moreland being out to do anyone harm. She might be tough as nails and not take shit from anyone, but he knew enough to conclude she wouldn't hurt one strand of hair on his head. Instinct told him he could trust her and that beneath her prickly shell lay a heart as soft as marshmallow.

He'd delved into her life on more than one occasion during the years he'd headed up McDermott Security, and while he hadn't gone so far as to dig up any and all dirt, he did know she was financially secure and didn't date all that much. Luc grinned.

Cassie would be seriously pissed off if he revealed the extent of McDermott Security's probing into her life. And while he liked riling her up, he wasn't about to tell her he'd been poking around in her private affairs without her knowledge. He wasn't a complete masochist. Lengthening his strides, he caught up to her just as she swung the front door open.

"Sorry about the mess. I haven't had a chance to do more than breathe these past few weeks," she apologized as they entered a small living room.

Luc doubted her place would be all that messy. She didn't strike him as the type to be careless with her possessions. "Don't worry about it. I'm sure my place is worse."

She turned and looked at him with one eyebrow arched. "I highly doubt that. You're too in control to allow it."

He paused. How she'd pegged him so well when they'd barely gotten acquainted was a mystery. "You've got me." Luc held up his hands in surrender. "I'm a neat freak."

Cassie laughed. "More like control freak," she muttered as she headed farther into the house. "This way," she called over her shoulder.

Luc followed, his gaze dropping to admire the sway of her hips as she walked in front of him. Not that he could see that well. She hadn't bothered with lights, and yet she made her way through the living room and down the narrow hall with ease. Too busy checking out her ass, he almost stumbled into her when she stopped and pushed a door open.

"The bed's made up. And the bathroom is there." She turned and indicated the door opposite the one she'd opened. "Can I get you anything before we go to bed?"

Her question brought images of the two of them in bed to mind and his body instantly reacted. He'd been semi-aroused for hours now, and the explicitness of his imagination sent his libido skyrocketing. He moved closer and Cassie's breath hitched. Leaning over, he brought his mouth next to her ear and blew a stream of air over the delicate shell. She shivered and jerked back, causing Luc to smile and move closer still.

"I'm good, but seeing as I'm now on the clock is there anything I can do for *you* before we go to bed?" he murmured as he continued to crowd her against the wall.

In the dark it was hard to read her expression, but he could see her eyes widen and her lips part on a puff of air when he pressed his aroused body into hers. Luc wasn't planning to push for more than a kiss, but the second he brushed his mouth on hers all thought fled except one.

More.

Their height difference meant he had to bend his knees to mesh his mouth fully with hers. Widening his legs dropped his head a few inches and placed his thighs either side of hers while his straining erection pressed into her softness, sending blood, hot with need, rushing into his already throbbing groin. He flattened his hands on the wall beside her head so he wouldn't give in to the temptation of grabbing her and dragging her into the bed she'd offered him.

He'd be a fool to rush her. She'd never let him get closer if he used their sexual chemistry to win her over. How he knew that he wasn't sure, but he did. If he wanted to get to know Cassie, spend time with her, he'd have to tread carefully—needed to produce some of his legendary control and back away.

Only that wasn't so easy when her mouth ate at his like she

couldn't get enough. When she gripped the back of his shirt like it was a lifeline. Or when she came up on her toes, arched into him and rubbed against his straining flesh. With a growl, he tore his lips from hers.

"Fuck." Luc laid his forehead on Cassie's and tried to catch his breath. Pleased to note her breathing came in ragged gasps as well. "Damn, you're potent."

"Me?" She fisted her hands in his shirt and he couldn't recall when she'd moved them from his back to his chest.

"Yeah, you." He raised his head a few inches and met her gaze. "You scramble my brains without trying."

Cassie laughed and pushed him away. "Pot, meet Kettle."

Luc grinned. He liked that she wasn't playing coy or using his reactions to her against him. She was a breath of fresh air and Luc couldn't wait to saturate his blood with her. But not yet. Tonight they needed to get their balance, regain some sanity and think about where this was leading. Well, at least he did. "So, is there anything you want me to do? Unpack the van?"

Her smile faltered. "Ah, no. We'll do that in the morning when we get to the warehouse." She ducked her head, but before she could sneak under his outstretched arm and escape, he slid his hands lower down the wall, effectively trapping her.

"Look at me, Cass." He waited long seconds for her to comply. When she finally did, he could see the uncertainty swirling her eyes. "Make no mistake that I want you in that bed." Luc tipped his head to indicate the room beside them. "But I want far more than a quick tumble, and if you're honest I think you'll admit you do too."

She started to shake her head, but he stopped her by gripping her chin in his hand.

"You can lie to me, but don't lie to yourself, Cass." He brushed his thumb over her bottom lip and watched it tremble under his touch.

"I don't have time to get involved. Don't want to," she whispered.

Luc could understand her hesitancy, but he wasn't about to ignore the intense attraction between them. And it was between them, her body told him she was as equally affected even if her words didn't.

"I'm not sure what exactly it is between us but it's far more than one night of pleasure, and I'm willing to wait because I know we'll end up in that bed eventually."

A burst of air fanned over his thumb when she gasped, and a shudder rolled through him as he thought about how her warm breath might feel on other more sensitive parts of his body. Leaning forward, he planted a quick, hard kiss on her lips before he stepped back and broke all contact.

It was the hardest thing he'd done in recent memory, but Luc smiled and said, "See you in the morning."

He strode into the bedroom and closed the door behind him before he could change his mind and take her against the wall.

Cassie flopped face down on her bed and groaned. Her body thrummed with arousal. She felt achy and needy and empty. Sensations she hadn't experienced in a long, long time.

The last man to pique her interest had made it more than clear he didn't want to date a workaholic, and Cassie couldn't blame him. When she'd first started Are You Game?, her whole existence had revolved around making her business a success. And obviously Jared hadn't been enough of a draw for her to put that aside and satisfy his demands for more of her time. There was no doubt in her mind that Lucas was enough incentive to test her all-work-no-play schedule.

He'd already made her forget the job. *Twice*. Hell, she was pretty sure it would have taken her minutes to remember her own name if someone had asked after he'd kissed her. With another groan, Cassie rolled over and stared at the ceiling.

He was in the room next to hers and he'd made it perfectly clear he'd welcome her in his bed. Only he wanted more than one night tangling the sheets and she wasn't sure how she felt about that. Until Lucas had spoken his intentions she hadn't thought beyond the overwhelming desire he provoked, but now she was forced to examine what she wanted. And Cassie had the uncomfortable feeling she wouldn't like what she uncovered.

Lucas Wilhelm was trouble with a capital T. He'd managed to do what no other man had. Distract her from the most important thing in her life. Nothing and no one had been able to pull her focus from *Are You Game?* since the day she'd overseen her first event.

She couldn't afford to be sidetracked. Not now that she was launching the adults-only line of parties. Tonight had been a resounding success, but that didn't mean she could relax. Far from it. If anything, she had to be even more vigilant.

She'd taken a huge risk in diversifying in a direction that might offend future customers, especially those who booked children's parties or her corporate team-building packages.

Cassie sighed and brought one arm up to cover her eyes. Worrying wouldn't do her—or the situation—any good, and she'd never fall asleep if she didn't shut down her racing mind. She needed a shower. Needed to wash away the day's grime and hopefully the negative ions would clear her head as well. Sighing again, she rolled off the bed and padded over to her dresser to grab some PJs.

The idea of running into Lucas in the hall had her pausing at the door. Like a thief, she pressed her ear to the timber and listened before venturing out of her room. All was quiet, so she cracked the door an inch to see if he was using the bathroom. No light showed beneath the closed door and she wasted no time sprinting the two meters to the bathroom and safely shutting herself inside.

Although tempted to linger beneath the hot spray, Cassie made quick work of cleaning up and pulling her PJs on. Using the same caution as before, she snuck back to her room and closed the door behind her.

Breathing a sigh of relief, she switched off the light and climbed into bed. The house was warm, the residual heat of the day remained trapped inside, but it wasn't hot enough to turn on the central air.

It would be a waste anyway, she'd be leaving for work in a few hours and she wouldn't be home all day, plus she figured Lucas would expect her to stay at his place tomorrow night. She shivered.

Staying with him would be dangerous. He was already hard to resist, but Cassie got the impression spending the day with him would make it next to impossible.

The floorboards in the hall creaked a second before the bathroom door closed. Vivid images of Lucas standing beneath her shower, his body wet and slick as water cascaded down every ridge of muscle in his magnificent physique played through Cassie's mind like an X-rated movie.

Her pussy fluttered and moisture seeped out to soak her panties. She clenched her thighs, but the action brought no relief from the ache burning in her sex. Cassie couldn't remember any guy producing such an intense reaction, and Lucas wasn't even in the room.

His potent sexuality required no more than a thought to have her panting for breath and struggling to keep from marching across the hall and making him finish what he'd started.

Old pipes rattled as water rushed through them and another spasm gripped her lower belly. She was wound so tight it wouldn't take much to get her off. Her breasts felt heavy and her nipples puckered, throbbing to the beat of her racing pulse. Sliding a hand over her abdomen and into her pants, Cassie zeroed in on her clit and circled the protruding bundle of nerves she knew would bring her relief quickly.

Dipping lower, she spread her body's creamy essence through her folds and back to her clit. Her breathing shallowed—shortened—and she bit her lip to hold back the moans of pleasure bubbling in her throat.

Cassie's hips rocked with her hand as she inched closer and closer to orgasm. She brought her other hand to her breast. Pinched and pulled at her erect nipple and pretended it was Lucas delivering the delicious sensations screaming through her system.

Vaguely, she registered the water turning off and realized he wasn't showering, but she was too far gone to worry if he could hear her whimper and moan as she approached the jagged edge of release. Using a second finger, she pinched her clit and sent herself flying.

A cry tore from her chest, the sound of pleasure unmistakable in the quiet room—and probably the rest of the house—only Cassie didn't care. The hum of satisfaction settled over her, the discharge of tension softening her muscles until every limb—every cell—grew heavy.

Her eyelids drooped, her mind floating on a wave of bliss as the day finally caught up with her. With a smile curling her lips, Cassie thought of Lucas across the hall and wondered if he was seeking his own pleasure.

L uc stood in the dark and cursed. Barely in control, he fisted his hands and clenched his jaw. He'd come close to losing it in the bathroom. With Cassie's sweet scent surrounding him on the humid air, he'd known she'd showered only moments before, which had his imagination spinning visions of her naked in the glass-walled shower cubicle.

Add in the red lacy underwear dangling from beneath the hamper lid and Luc had to douse his head under cold water to cool off. And now, in the hall, with Cassie's cry of pleasure echoing in his skull, Luc knew nothing short of drowning himself in the Arctic Sea would cool him down. He still couldn't work out what it was about Cassie that set his blood boiling so quickly.

Forcing himself to move, he walked to the room she'd given him —not hers, even though a voice inside his head was screaming he should. After listening to Cass get herself off, he'd love nothing more than to go to her and slake his own lust, however, he had enough control to know that wouldn't get him the ultimate prize.

And at some point between going toe-to-toe with the diminutive Cassandra Moreland for the first time and now, he'd come to the realization that *she* was the goal, not the pleasure they'd find in bed together. Which meant he had to get his head—the one on his shoulders—in command of his body.

He stripped out of his clothes and crawled beneath the covers. His cock ached and Luc couldn't help palming his throbbing flesh. With a firm grip, he stroked from root to tip. A shudder rippled through him, and he closed his eyes and imagined Cassie's hand in place of his.

On each pass, he increased the pressure, sped up the pace and in an embarrassingly short amount of time, he found himself on the brink of coming. Stomach muscles clenching, balls drawing up tight, Luc let his orgasm take him and came in hard spurts over his hand and torso.

Cursing his lack of control and the arousal still humming in his veins, he got out of bed and stalked back to the bathroom. Uncaring of his naked state, he didn't even glance in the direction of Cassie's room. Didn't dare—she'd just proven, without being in the same room, she could get to him.

He'd never felt so out of control. Not with a woman, not with his job. Flicking on the water, Luc stepped beneath the cold shower and rinsed away the evidence of his weakness. She'd gotten under his skin—in his blood—and he didn't have a clue how to get her out or even if he wanted to.

With a groan, he closed his eyes and ducked his head under the spray. The water pelted his scalp, the sound drowning the voice in his head that told him to go to Cassie and finish what they both obviously wanted. He had no idea how long he stood beneath the cold shower, but he finally roused himself and switched it off.

Eyeing the only towel on the rack, he couldn't bring himself to use it, knowing she'd rubbed it all over her body first. Glancing around the room, he spied the cupboard tucked in behind the door and opened it to find shelves filled with female toiletries as well as fresh towels.

Grinning, Luc snagged one and ran it over his face only to have the smile die a quick death when he caught Cassie's distinct scent. With a moan, he buried his face deeper into the soft fabric and drew in a breath. Her smell surrounded him. It wasn't as pronounced as when he'd held her in his arms, but it was just as effective.

The erection he'd so recently satisfied re-emerged, and he wondered if he'd ever quench the thirst for Cassie his body seemed to have. One thing he was sure of was this wasn't your everyday run-of-the-mill kind of lust.

For a start, he respected her—admired her—and he could tell they held the same moral codes when it came to working hard and going after what they wanted. She wasn't hard on the eyes either. In spite of her lack of height, she wasn't what he'd call short, just shorter than his usual preference.

Of course, those preferences hadn't found him anywhere near the pleasure he'd found with Cassie, and he hadn't even fucked her yet. He had to assume there would be fireworks once he managed to get her beneath him.

Dry, Luc hung the towel on the free rail and made his way back to his room. The house remained quiet around him and he assumed Cassie had gone to sleep after she'd come loud enough to shake the rafters.

He chuckled. Hearing her scream when he made her climax would be music to his ears. A symphony he couldn't wait to conduct. With a smile, he climbed into bed once more and thought about tomorrow and how he'd win Cassie over. He expected her to fight him—in spite of their combustible attraction, they hardly knew each other—and he relished the chance to tussle with her again.

No doubt about it. Cassandra Moreland fired his blood and went close to driving him insane, but he wasn't about to walk away. Not until he'd explored every inch of her, discovered everything that made her tick and convinced her she wanted to do the same to him.

By the time their challenge was over, Luc hoped to have made inroads in his quest to not only win her over but to win her heart. He had the feeling she guarded that soft center with razor wire, but he planned to breach her defenses, because suddenly he wouldn't be happy with anything less than all of her.

5

Cassie rolled over with a grunt when her phone alarm blared from across the room. Burrowing her head beneath her pillow, she tried to ignore the offending noise, but that only allowed the voice in her head to remind her no one else would run Are You Game? or today's event. Just the thought of a lively bunch of five-year-olds made her want to weep. Of course, once she mainlined some caffeine and showered she'd be right to go. It was those minutes until then that were always the killer.

Eyes closed, Cassie tossed the pillow aside and all but fell out of bed. With her eyelids barely cracked, she staggered the few steps to her dresser and stabbed at the screen of her iPhone until the screeching stopped. Silence. Her lips tipped up on the ends while her ears sighed in relief.

Floorboards creaked beneath her bare feet as she made her way to the kitchen and the coffee pot. The aroma of coffee hung on the air and Cassie thanked the inventor of the humble timer mechanism. She also thanked herself for having the foresight to set the timer yesterday before she left for work so she woke to the much-needed kick-start to her morning today.

She grabbed her favourite mug from the dishwasher and filled it to the rim with the dark liquid that was her saving grace every day. Cassie had never been a morning person, and even after years of getting up at dawn, her body refused to be trained to enjoy the first light of day. With a sigh, she leaned against the counter and took a sip.

Hot, but not enough to scald, she rolled the coffee around her mouth and savored that first taste before she swallowed then proceeded to gulp down the rest of the cup. Warmth filled her chest and belly, and it would only take a few minutes for that initial shot of caffeine to hit her bloodstream.

Topping up her mug, Cassie resigned herself to the inevitable and headed back to her room. She had a lot to do this morning. Unpack last night's equipment from the van, repack ready for the bead party today's birthday girl had requested and do the last minute food prep. Dan would meet...

Cassie stopped mid step, the sip of coffee she'd barely swallowed catching in her throat. Standing in her hallway—naked—was the most gorgeous man she'd ever laid eyes on. Lucas Wilhelm was every woman's fantasy, and here he stood in all his bronzed glory. All she could do was stare. And drool. Definitely drool.

How had she forgotten he was in her house? He moved the bundle of clothes in his hand to cover his groin, but it was too late. She'd already seen his semi-erect cock, and her mouth wasn't the only thing drooling. Heat bloomed between her legs and moisture coated her folds, her body making it perfectly clear where she wanted that magnificent appendage.

And he was magnificent. Cassie had never seen one better. Or bigger. A shudder gripped her as her pussy clenched with delight at the thought of being impaled on his length.

She'd never been this affected by a guy before. Sex—while enjoyable—hadn't delivered this burning need to touch and be touched, and she wasn't all that happy about it. There was no denying the way he made her feel. Even if he couldn't see her dripping pussy he'd have to be blind to miss her nipples doing their impersonation of

Sydney Tower. They all but poked holes in her tank top they were that hard.

Lucas cleared his throat and Cassie's gaze darted up to collide with fiery black orbs. The flare of desire he aimed at her had heat washing up her neck and into her face. "Um…"

"I was going to grab a quick shower." His voice, rough and deep, skipped over her nerves and sent a shiver down her spine.

"Oh, right. Yes." She licked her bottom lip. "Go ahead. I'll go after you and we'll leave in about thirty minutes. Coffee's in the kitchen."

"Thanks." He didn't move.

Acutely aware of his every breath, Cassie sidled past him and escaped to the safety of her room. Only there was nothing safe about her bedroom. Not when she could still see him in her mind, and when the old house's plumbing rattled, she imagined him naked—wet. Sleek and hot as he stood beneath the falling water.

Her breathing stuttered and her lower belly warmed with arousal that dripped down into her core to remind her of what she was missing. There was no way she'd last through his shower. Yanking her bedside drawer open, she put her cup down, grabbed her ear buds and plugged them into her phone.

Within seconds, the pounding beat of the latest dance-floor tune filled her head and drowned out the sound of water rushing through pipes. Unfortunately, the music didn't erase the images her memory continued to play.

Sinking to the edge of her bed, she pressed her fingertips against her closed eyelids and tried to think of all the boxes she had to unload from the van. All the boxes she had to load. The cupcakes she had to bake before ten o'clock. A bunch of five-year-olds high on sugar attempting to sit still long enough to thread tiny colored beads on thin lengths of elastic to make necklaces and bracelets. But nothing seemed to remove the stunning pictures of Lucas in all his nakedness.

Frustrated in more ways than one, Cassie jumped to her feet and frantically gathered clothes to wear. Once that was done, she pivoted on her heel looking for something else to occupy her hands.

Spying her mug, she reached over and snatched it up, causing the dark liquid to slosh up the sides. She took a few quick gulps. Still warm, the coffee went down smooth, but like everything else she'd tried, it failed miserably in its effort to wipe her mind clean of one sexy man Cassie had the feeling she'd never be able to ignore no matter how much she wanted to. With her body humming and a sexy beat pounding in her ears, Cassie started to wonder why she even bothered.

Who said she couldn't enjoy all Lucas had to offer while he offered it?

A relationship was the last thing she wanted. The disastrous end to her last one had cured her of the notion she could have a successful business and a boyfriend. She wasn't the type to indulge in one-night stands, however, their challenge encompassed the whole weekend, which gave them more than one night. Of course, they'd kind of wasted a night already, but that didn't mean she couldn't make the most of the rest of their time together.

Cassie knew she was splitting hairs with her reasoning, plus there was that pesky problem of him wanting more to get around. Surely one weekend would satisfy him. Lust that sparked this hot couldn't be more than a flash in the pan. And what guy didn't want sex without strings?

Cassie smiled. She couldn't remember the last time she'd allowed herself to let loose and enjoy something for pleasure alone. Perhaps that's where all her previous relationships had gone wrong. Instead of trying to make the guy she was with into Mr. Right she should have been enjoying what they had and not worrying about the future.

If Cassie was going to have a fling with anyone it would be Lucas. Something about him said trustworthy. Maybe it was his job. Or maybe it was the guy himself. Either way, she wasn't going to let him walk away like he had last night. No. Next time they found themselves in a steamy lip-lock, Cassie would make sure they didn't stop there.

L uc scrubbed a hand over his stubbled chin. He needed a shave, but that wasn't happening until he went home. He'd been a twice-a-day shaver since he hit puberty, which meant he'd have to be careful around Cassie.

The sharp bristles would leave her skin raw, and while the thought of marking her in that way sent a thrill through him, he wouldn't risk hurting her. She might be a tough little thing, but her skin was soft as silk, and he had no doubt she'd end up with a severe case of beard burn.

He picked up yesterday's boxers and instantly changed his mind, dropping them back on the floor. He'd rather go commando than wear the pre-worn underwear. Snatching up his pants, he dropped the towel from around his waist and stepped into one leg.

With his other foot off the floor and both hands on his pants, Luc had no way of stopping the door from swinging open. Stumbling backward, he crashed into the basin and dropped his pants to catch his balance. For the second time today, Cassie stood in front of him staring at his groin.

Neither of them moved. Well, his cock did. That part of his anatomy knew exactly what to do around Cassie. Her shorts and top may have adequately covered her luscious body, but his libido didn't seem to care what she dressed in. It just wanted to get her undressed as quickly as possible, and at this point Luc couldn't come up with a good argument against getting her naked.

Now.

He noted he wasn't the only one affected by their close quarters. Cassie's breathing was shallow, her skin flushed and her nipples were hard beneath her thin shirt.

Before he thought about it, he had her in his arms. He spun around, hoisted her onto the basin and, using his legs, spread her knees until they were wide enough for his thighs to fit snugly between hers, his cock pressing into her belly. Luc lowered his head and took her mouth.

She parted her lips, and he took the silent invitation and thrust his tongue between her teeth to explore the hot recesses of her mouth. For seconds, she remained passive, letting him do and take as he wished. Then she exploded in a hungry surge that stole his breath. There was nothing submissive about her now. She stroked her tongue over his, past his teeth and into his mouth.

In moments, their kiss turned desperate. Blood rushed in his ears, his heart pounded in his chest and his cock throbbed where it lay trapped between them. He bucked his hips, rocked his length against her. He gripped the hem of her shirt and yanked it up so he could get his hands on the hard nipples that were digging into his chest.

Air rushed from his lungs when he cradled the soft globes in his palms. Luc pulled his mouth from hers and looked down. Cassie's top was bunched beneath her arms and his darker flesh covered her creamy skin. The sight sent an erotic spike into his groin.

He had to taste her. Had to feel her under his lips—his tongue. He lowered his head and trailed his mouth down her chin to her throat. Her pulse beat in a rapid tattoo and he lingered over it. Nipping and licking until her head fell back and she gave him free rein.

She gasped when he scrapped his teeth across her collarbone. Moaned when he moved lower and sucked one taut nipple between his lips. Luc loved the way she arched into him as he drew harder on the rigid peak. His fingers tugged at her other breast while he continued to feast on the one in his mouth.

Cassie curled her hands over his shoulders and pushed. At first he fought her, but she tangled her fingers in his hair and tugged to get his attention. Stepping back, he watched as she wiggled her pants out from under her ass and let them drop to the floor at his feet. He swallowed over the lump in his throat when she whipped her shirt over her head and tossed it over his shoulder.

Damn. She was the sexiest thing he'd ever seen, and he wanted to touch her everywhere. But his gaze was drawn to the valley between her legs. Her pussy hair was trimmed close and her pink folds peeked out to give him a flash of her glistening slit.

Luc fell to his knees and buried his mouth in her silken flesh. Gripping her hips, he pulled her forward so her ass sat on the very

edge of the counter and her legs were draped over his shoulders—
her heels bumping into his back.

Her smell and taste surrounded him. The tang of her desire
coated his tongue, flooded his mouth and sent sizzling need zipping
into his balls. She rocked against him, rode the rhythm he set with
his tongue and took what he offered and demanded more. He lapped
at her folds. Up and down. Back to front. With each swipe of his
tongue, Cassie moaned and thrashed above him.

She buried her fingers in his hair and held him close. His groin
burned with need and he had to wrap one hand around his cock and
squeeze hard in an attempt to stave off the orgasm barreling toward
him. He palmed her ass with his other hand, trailed his fingers over
her hot skin until they slid through the slick fluid flowing from her
pussy and drew a moan of pleasure from her lips. She dug her nails
into his scalp and her hips bucked, driving her wet slit into his face.

"Oh God." Cassie's words ended on a gasp as he drove two fingers
deep inside her.

Hot walls sucked at his fingers. Clamped down and held him tight
as her body convulsed in a bone-jolting climax. She writhed against
him, flexed and rolled with each wave of her release until she went
limp, spent as the last of her orgasm drained away.

Luc clenched his jaw, ground his back teeth and gripped his cock
in a punishing hold as he fought not to come all over the bathroom
floor. If he was going to lose his load it would be in the drenched
pussy that continued to quiver around his fingers.

He pulled back, glanced up to see Cassie slouched against the
mirror behind her, eyes closed, lips parted. She was the most erotic
image Luc had ever seen, and he surged to his feet to take her mouth
with his. Thrusting his tongue into her mouth, he matched the
rhythm with the fingers still buried in her pussy.

It didn't take long for her to be riding the ridge of release again.
His cock brushed the back of his hand and he pulled free of her
clenching channel to rub the swollen head through her dripping
folds.

"Condom?" he growled into her mouth.

"Huh?" Her eyelids opened half-mast.

Luc leaned back, separating their mouths. "Condom? Where?"

"What? You don't have one?" she panted, her hips rocking into his, dragging his length along her slit.

"No. Don't you?" *Please God let her say yes.*

"No." The word came out a sob.

Fuck! A sharp pain sliced through Luc's balls when his brain registered what no condom meant.

Cassie's eye's popped wide and she sat up. "You don't have one in your wallet?"

He shook his head. "I don't make a habit of..." He glanced down at where their bodies were pressed together.

"Neither do I." She lowered her head, laid her cheek on his chest.

Luc slid his arms around her and hugged her close. "Okay. No sex." He shuddered.

Cassie sighed and warm air flowed over his skin, sending a shiver down his spine. His heart pounded hard against his ribs in a bruising beat, an answering hammer vibrated through her breasts and into him. He gulped in air, his lungs struggling to keep up with his runaway pulse.

The heat surrounding his cock didn't help him rein in his lust either. Her cream coated him from root to tip, and Luc would love nothing more than to flex his hips and drive his length into her. But he wouldn't do that without protection.

He loosened his arms, made sure she was steady, and took a step back. "I'll just—"

She moved. One second she was on the counter in front of him, the next she was on her knees with her hand wrapped around his shaft.

"Jesus." Air hissed through his teeth as Cassie stroked him, her fingers curled in the tight grip he preferred.

Her tongue found the drop of pre-come leaking from the crown. She licked across the head, pointed her tongue and probed the small opening as though she were trying to find more of his seed. His groin tightened, his sac shrinking, his balls tucking up into his body. He looked down as Cassie slipped her lips over his head and sucked him deep. All the way to the root, she took him fast only to let him back out slowly as she lightly grazed her teeth over his entire length.

She sank down, took him to the back of her throat and swallowed. Luc's eyes crossed. Fire licked at his balls, blazed up his spine and set off a series of spasms that he hadn't a hope of fighting. And when her fingers teased the taut skin beneath his scrotum he went down for the count. He tried to hold still, but he couldn't. His hips thrust forward—backward, plunging his cock in and out of her pliant mouth as he spilled every drop of semen from his balls.

Shuddering, he held the back of her head in one hand as he locked his knees to keep from collapsing to the floor. Cassie eased back, licking his shaft and sending more darts of pleasure through his groin as she let his softening cock leave her mouth.

Luc gasped for breath, shook his head and tried to clear his vision of the sparks of light flickering in front of him. Too weak to remain on his feet, he dropped to the floor and pulled her into his lap. He pressed his mouth to hers. Thrust his tongue between her lips and tasted his own essence on her tongue.

He kissed her until they were both breathless and desire threatened to overwhelm them again. Panting, Luc broke the connection and tucked her head under his chin. His pulse slowed and his body cooled as he came back to earth. She'd blown more than his dick. She'd blown his mind. Luc couldn't remember the last time he'd had a BJ as mind-blowing or if he ever had. No woman had ever swallowed him as enthusiastically, that was for sure.

Cassie was the first to gather her senses. "We need to go."

"Go?" Luc didn't relax his hold.

"Yeah," she sighed. "As much as I'd love to continue—or finish— what we're doing, I have a business that won't run itself."

"Shit!" He untangled his arms and pushed her back to look into her eyes. "I'm sorry. I should never have touched you."

She laughed. "Don't you dare apologize for getting me off." Unconcerned by her nudity, Cassie crawled from his lap and got to her feet. Stepping around him, she turned the shower on. "You might want to rinse off."

Her words brought to mind another topic. "I'm clean by the way."

"Huh?" She glanced at him over her shoulder.

"You know, health wise. I'm clean and haven't been with anyone in months." He always found these discussions awkward, but it needed to be said.

"Oh, right. Me too." Her face flushed red and she turned away from him, giving him a glorious view of her sleek curves.

Luc watched as she ducked beneath the spray and began soaping up. He smiled where he stood, feet rooted to the floor. A shower with Cassie might not be the smartest move when he didn't have any condoms on hand, but he wasn't about to pass up the chance to feel her wet body sliding against his.

He'd probably end up with a bad case of blue balls by the time they were done. Because no matter what it took, he'd keep a tight grip on his libido and not make her late for work. She passed him the soap as he moved in behind her and he took advantage of her turned back to get his hands on her again.

Hands slick with bubbles, Luc worked his way from her shoulders to her ass. He gently kneaded as he smoothed his hands over her warm back. The water and suds made her soft skin even silkier. His fingers slipped and slid, and she shivered when he pressed a little harder into the muscles of her lower back. Remembering her discomfort the night before, he massaged the area until the tension beneath his fingertips eased. Cassie moaned and dropped her head forward.

"God, that feels amazing."

"Remind me later tonight and I'll give you a full body massage." He pressed his lips to her shoulder. "You'll be softer than jelly by the time I'm done with you."

"Damn." She moaned and arched against him when he dug his fingers into the muscles on either side of her spine. "Why do I have to be the boss?"

Luc chuckled. "I'm guessing that's a rhetorical question."

"Mmm..."

"C'mon." He slapped her ass lightly. "If we don't get out of this shower now we're never getting out."

She growled when he stepped from the shower and grabbed a towel. As much as he wanted to give in and spend the day naked with Cassie, he wasn't about to let her down when it came to helping with today's party. That didn't mean he wouldn't constantly remind her of what they could be doing instead of working.

A smile curled his lips and he turned away so she wouldn't see.

Today would be about anticipation.

He'd tease and inflame until neither of them would be able to deny the electricity arcing between them.

6

Cassie pulled up to the Are You Game? building and hit the button to open the dock door. Metal screeched as the oversized panel slowly retracted into the roof. She needed to get someone out to look at that. Dan had warned her on a daily basis for the last few weeks, but with the business calendar filled up she hadn't found the time to ring the repair company.

"That sounds like it needs oiling." Lucas leaned forward to peer through the windshield at the struggling door.

She sighed. "Yeah, one more thing on my to-do list for next week." Cassie inched forward when the door clanked into the open position. "Another reason I need to fast-track hiring a new supervisor."

Lucas turned her way. "You're looking for staff?"

"Now that the adult party line has launched I'd like to hire someone to work alongside Dan. We're running too thin at the moment, and we've got a full calendar of children's parties plus we've taken on a few baby showers recently that are keeping us even busier on the weekends." Cassie put the van in park and shut off the engine. "It's not fair to ask Dan to work six or seven days a week, and that's what I've been forced to do in recent months."

"I might know someone who'd be interested." Lucas opened his door. "Would it be all right if I gave her your business card?"

"Her?"

"Yeah." He smiled. "My sister. She's been out of the workforce for a few years but she used to manage a fast-food restaurant. Not sure if that makes her qualified for the job, but it couldn't hurt to interview her, could it?"

"No." Cassie thought about the staff scheduling and ordering skills Lucas's sister must possess. "It definitely can't hurt. I'd be grateful if you passed on my details."

"I could ring her now and organize her coming here during the week."

Cassie arched one eyebrow. Was he pimping out his sister? She grinned at the thought. "Being a little pushy, aren't you?"

"Sorry." He shrugged and one corner of his mouth tipped up in a sheepish grin. "It's just that she's my little sister, and even though she's over thirty and the mother of two teenagers, I can't help playing big brother."

"Ah, that explains a lot." She could totally relate to being big brothered and had a feeling she'd get on well with Lucas's sister. "Sure, give her a ring. I'll be in the office every morning except Wednesday and Thursday next week."

She climbed out of the van as Lucas pulled his phone from his pocket. Leaving him to make the call in private, she made her way to her office to grab today's run sheet. She'd get Lucas to unload last night's equipment while she got everything ready to go for today. The cupcakes would need to be in the oven in the next hour or they wouldn't be ready on time. With the murmur of Lucas's voice echoing through the loading area, Cassie took the stairs up to the office level two at a time.

Her desk, like the equipment downstairs, was meticulously organized. Everything had a place and was in it. The clipboard with today's run sheet sat on the top left-hand corner and Cassie scooped it up on her way around to her chair. With a quick glance, she checked her list and reassured herself that Lucas would be more than capable of helping her corral a bunch of five-year-old girls without resorting to duct tape.

She grinned. She'd never stoop to such drastic measures, but that didn't mean she couldn't imagine rounding up wayward children with something other than acceptable means.

"Cassie?" Lucas's voice carried up the steel staircase and echoed off the walls.

"Up here." She opened the bottom drawer of the filing cabinet behind her desk and removed a blank report sheet to fill out to add to the file for last night's party. If she was lucky enough to get ahead of schedule this morning, she might be able to finalize the file for the McDermott party before she took on twenty-four little girls and hundreds of beads.

"Jody said she can be here Monday at nine if that suits you." Lucas entered her office and stood just inside the door. His gaze took the room in with a quick sweep before he brought his attention to Cassie. "I said I'd send her a text if nine didn't fit with you."

She reached over and flicked the page on her open diary. "Nine's good. If we both like what we see I might get her to sit in on our weekly party review meeting."

He smiled. "I'm sure Jody will love this place. It'll just be a matter of whether she fits what you're after for the new supervisor."

"I haven't defined the actual role. I expect I'll utilize her the same way I do Dan. She'll be getting her hands dirty in all aspects of the business." She grinned. "Especially if she's in charge of the new adult party line."

Lucas frowned. "I thought you'd put her in charge of the children's parties."

"Why? Because she's a mum?" Cassie knew she was tweaking his big-brother nerve, but she couldn't resist.

"Yes. No. I mean, the adult parties are new and I figured you'd want to oversee them yourself until the line was established." His brows dipped in the middle, winkles forming above his nose. "I don't know—"

Cassie burst out laughing. He was adorable in caretaker mode.

He scowled at her. "What's so funny?"

"You," she gasped. "As a little sister myself I can almost hear your brain spinning with worst-case-scenario thoughts."

Lucas growled making her chuckle more. "You can't blame me. I was there last night. I saw what went on. Most of the guests were barely clothed."

"The guests, yes. My staff, no." Cassie stood and walked around her desk. "I'd never put any of my employees at risk, Lucas. And while the adult party theme might be a bit risqué, it's not illegal or dangerous. I have safeguards in place for every conceivable problem. You can go over the company's policies if you're worried, but I can guarantee you if your sister works for me she'll be well looked after."

He came toward her. "I'm sorry. I shouldn't question you. It's just that since she separated from her husband I can't help worrying about her and the girls more than ever."

"That's understandable." Now she felt bad for digging at his soft spot.

"Yes, but I still took it too far." He grinned. "It's not the first time and it won't be the last. I'd appreciate it if you didn't mention my lapse to Jody though. I promised her I wouldn't interfere while she finds her feet again."

"How long has she been separated?" Cassie had no experience with broken marriages. None of her relatives who were married had divorced, well, not yet anyway, and most of her friends were still happily single.

"Nearly two years."

"Oh."

"Yeah, overprotective older brother here." Lucas raised one hand. "If I remember right, the divorce will be final next month."

"Then she's probably on her feet already." Cassie laid a hand on Lucas's forearm. "How old are her kids?"

"Fifteen and thirteen. Both well adjusted. Actually, they're all doing great." He sighed. "It's hard to admit it, but they're better off without Colin in their lives. He was never a good husband or father."

"Well then, you're working yourself up for nothing. Besides, I haven't given her the job yet." Cassie grinned. "Speaking of jobs, let's go. You have to unpack last night's equipment while I get today's ready for you to load. And, you get to help me make and ice forty-eight cupcakes."

Not waiting for him to reply, she stepped around him and headed out the door only to remember the clipboard and papers still on her desk. With a sigh, she doubled back, grabbed the paperwork and turned to find Lucas staring at her with his mouth hanging open.

"Cupcakes?"

Cassie nodded, a Cheshire-cat grin spreading across her face. "Yep."

"*Cupcakes?*" He didn't have a clue why he was repeating himself, but he couldn't get his mind around that one word. He had a very bad feeling about what type of party she was running today. "It's a child's party, isn't it?"

Again, she nodded.

He closed his eyes. "How old?"

"Five."

"Shit." Luc opened his eyes and glared at her. "Boy or girl?" *Please say boy, please say boy.*

Her laughter did nothing to ease his mind. "Girl."

"You think it's wise to have a giant like me around a bunch of five-year-old girls?" Luc wasn't sure what had him panicking more. The idea of being surrounded by a bunch of little girls or keeping his contact with Cassie PG all afternoon.

"You'll be fine."

"It's not me I'm worried about. Most children are scared by my size, and I don't want to ruin the birthday girl's big day." That sounded good. Believable. Heaven forbid she work out his irrational fear of little girls and their frilly dresses. He remembered how awkward he was around his nieces before they hit double digits.

"As long as you don't scowl at them and flash those pearly whites with a smile or two, they'll be fine." She patted his chest. "*You'll* be fine."

He wasn't so sure, but Cassie didn't give him the opportunity to argue farther. She ducked around him and left the office. With no other choice, Luc followed, mulling over the fact he was willingly subjecting himself to hours of torture. If he were honest, he'd have to admit he was looking forward to every minute of his torment, especially if it meant he'd be with Cassie.

Shaking his head, Luc trailed Cassie through the ground floor. Rows of shelves took up one corner, plastic tubs, all clearly labeled and orderly filled every rack. She led him through a door and his step faltered at the sight of an industrial kitchen.

"You cater your own events?"

"Huh?" She glanced over her shoulder. "Oh, no. This is West's domain. He's Weston's Catering. His company does all the food I need plus he has his own customers."

"West?" He couldn't recall any mention of a guy named West in the years he'd known about Cassie.

"Yeah, he's my brother's best friend." She smiled before pressing buttons on the control panel of an oven that looked way too complicated for Luc to even think about using. "We've only recently added this kitchen. Before that I had to drive two blocks over to pick up all the prepped food."

"And now?"

"West staffs this kitchen when he's catering one of my events, and I use it when I need something as simple as cupcakes." She grinned at him. "C'mon, you can help me grab all the ingredients."

Luc wasn't sure how he felt about this West guy. Something in Cassie's voice made his gut clench. He'd never been jealous before, but he supposed that was the lead weight currently crushing his chest. He wanted to ask her if she had a thing for her brother's friend. Wanted to know if they'd ever crossed that line, and if they had, he wanted to find West and knock his teeth out for taking advantage of his friend's little sister.

He gave himself a mental slap. It was none of his business who

Cassie had been with in the past. Plus, he was fairly certain she'd hand him his balls on a platter if he went all Neanderthal on her. Unfortunately, it was a distinct possibility that he would. All these emotions were foreign and only reinforced his thinking that this thing with Cassie was far more than one night. Far more than a flash in the pan, even though the attraction between them fired hotter than the fireworks on New Year's Eve.

"Here." Cassie handed him a container and proceeded to load him up one after another until the pile reached his chin. "Take those over to the island while I get what I need from the cold room."

His phone beeped as he placed his load on the counter. He pulled it from his pocket and opened his email app, quickly scanning the latest update on the Lachlan and Cameron incident. Nothing new or requiring his attention. Thank God.

The last thing he wanted was to interrupt his time with Cassie more than his job already had. Although he was sure she'd understand, Luc didn't want to risk losing her attention before they'd forged a stronger bond.

"Problem?" she asked as she stepped next to him.

"No." He exited the mail app and stuffed his phone back in his pocket. "Nothing urgent or needing my input."

"I won't hold it against you if you have to bail on our deal." One side of her mouth kicked up. "Promise not to call you a welsher."

He wrapped a hand around the back of her neck and tugged her close. Lowering his head, he brought their mouths to within an inch of touching. "Oh, don't worry. I have no intention of reneging on our arrangement."

Luc pulled her in and slanted his mouth across hers. He didn't wait to be invited inside. Not when a little pressure had her opening to him with eager demand. Her tongue tangled with his. Their teeth bumped in the rush to take—to devour. It wasn't enough. This press of lips didn't satisfy the need, only inflamed it. Fire licked along his nerves, lashed at his groin and threatened to incinerate his thin grip on control.

Lust coursed through his veins and drove him to grab her ass and drag her in against his throbbing length. His hips flexed, rubbing his swollen cock on her belly. Her height limited their contact and frustration raked him. In a move that was quickly becoming habit, Luc picked her up and placed her on the counter beside them. He wedged himself between her legs, spreading them wide to fit his sex snug against hers. She thrust forward, hit the sweet spot and drew a strangled moan from each of them.

He tore his mouth from hers, trailed a line of kisses over her cheek to her ear. Her earlobe beckoned and he didn't resist. The delicate flesh was soft against his tongue. Sucking, he pulled it deep, nipped with his teeth then lapped at the sting to soothe the slight pain.

Cassie moaned, a sound barely more than air rushing over her lips, but Luc still felt it gut deep. It pulled and twisted, tightened his already taut nerves and flooded his cock with more heated blood. He'd burst from his pants at this rate, his clothing no match for the fierce need expanding inside him.

His lips found hers again, and he slid deep. Drew back to stroke his tongue over plump flesh before diving deeper only to retreat and do it again. And again. He made love to her mouth. Kissed her in a way he'd never kissed another and knew he never would. Cassie brought him to this.

To this all-consuming need to take while he savored.

How could he want to gulp and sip at the same time?

How did she understand what he needed and give it to him so willingly?

"Lucas," she breathed his name into his mouth.

A shudder rippled from his head to his toes, ricocheting from bone to skin and back. Jesus. He was going to snap. She'd break him into a million pieces before he ever got his cock inside her. She wrapped her arms and legs around him, clung like a vine, and he never wanted to be cut free. Wanted to stay surrounded by her forever.

Luc's breath stalled. What was he thinking? They barely knew each other. He shouldn't be thinking forever. Shouldn't be feeling the chaotic tangle of emotions bombarding him. Not yet. Surely not yet. It was too soon. Too much.

With a gasp, he pulled away, separated their mouths and stared down at her flushed face. Her eyelids hung heavy over her warm gaze, her breathing ragged in her throat. She was the image of rapture, but he couldn't bring himself to fall. There was no denying he would, no stopping the inevitable, except he needed to think. To breathe. To know that when he sank into the dark abyss she'd tumble with him.

Head over heels.

Cassie stared at Lucas. His eyes were alive. The dark-brown depths were anything but cold, and she couldn't get over how wrong she'd pegged him when they first met. She knew he held himself back—he had to in his line of work, except now it was like she'd been given the key to unlock the door to the hidden Lucas—the real Lucas.

She'd gotten behind his shields, past his defenses, and he either didn't want to stop her or couldn't. Both scenarios sent a chill down her spine.

The click and hum of a motor broke the silence as the compressor on the refrigeration units kicked in. Jolted from the haze of lust dulling her common sense, Cassie pushed Lucas away and jumped from the counter, shocked to find she'd been so consumed by him that she couldn't recall getting there.

Her gaze swept the room, avoiding him while she dragged herself back to rational thought. *Shit.* She'd lost her head with this guy so many times she didn't want to count. He wasn't the only one whose walls had been breached.

She closed her eyes and blew out a breath. If he hadn't pulled away they'd be...

Lord, she didn't want to think about where they'd be.

Opening her eyes, Cassie turned to meet his gaze. He stood in front of her, inches away. It would only take one step...a stretch of her arm... *Fuck! Enough!*

What was with her?

Her libido had never ruled her before. Sex was something she could go without easily. Except sex had never felt this good. And they hadn't even *had* sex. How lost would she be when they did?

Her heart pounded and warmth pooled low in her belly at the thought of sex with Lucas. She swallowed over the lump in her throat, licked her dry lips and tried to form words. Only there was nothing to say. No explanation for what they'd found themselves doing. Again.

"I..." What could she say?

One corner of his mouth curled up. "Yeah."

Gazes locked, they stared at each other until the chime on the oven dinged. "Oh." Cassie glanced behind her. "We should..."

Lucas sighed. "Yeah, we should."

He stepped away, taking his body heat with him, and Cassie shivered.

"Right." She needed to get it together. The cupcakes wouldn't make themselves, and the equipment wouldn't unload itself from the van either. "This way."

Cassie led Lucas back out to the dock. She unlocked the van and opened the rear doors. "I'll show you where to put the boxes from last night. By the time you're done I'll have the cakes in the oven and you can start packing the equipment for today's party."

"Yes, ma'am." He moved up beside her to grab a tub and Cassie fought the urge to jump back. With a box in his arms, he turned toward her. "Show me where these go."

His biceps flexed as he adjusted the weight and she took a deep breath as desire rumbled through her center. At this rate she'd be jumping him in the warehouse. Not something she wanted to do.

Okay, that was lie. She definitely wanted to jump him. But she couldn't do that here.

They needed distance. A few hours—possibly days—apart would be good. She'd have to settle for minutes though. With the deal they'd made she was lucky to get that much, so she'd grab what she could and hope it was enough to get her feet back on steady ground. And her mind out of the gutter.

"Over here." Taking a deep breath, Cassie headed for the storage racks. "Everything—shelves, boxes—are clearly labeled, so you shouldn't have any trouble putting it all away, but if you do give me a yell."

"I think I can muddle through."

She heard the grin in his voice and glanced over her shoulder. Not only was he smiling, but he was smiling while ogling her ass. Her step stuttered, a small pause that threatened to have him crashing into her back. Double stepping, she moved to the side and pointed to the first row of equipment.

"Glasses, china, platters and cutlery are in this aisle. Next is prep equipment and then sundries like napkins. Condiments are stored in the kitchen area, but leave those because I think they're all on today's list of requirements. Make sure you put everything in its proper place. The last thing I need is to have to search for equipment."

"Cass." He waited for her to look at him. "I've got it. Go make cupcakes."

Lucas strode past, a smile curving his lips, and Cassie wasn't sure if she was happy or sad that he could function so well after their kitchen encounter. With no time to dwell on her turbulent thoughts, she headed back to the scene of the crime and steeled herself against the memories of their scorching kiss.

Luc breathed easier as the echo of Cassie's footsteps faded. He wasn't sure how he'd kept his hands to himself. She tempted him in so many ways. The stunned look on her face when she'd jumped off the counter made him want to pull her in and hold her close. Soothe the alarm he'd seen in her eyes. Reassure her they'd done nothing wrong. Only they had. He'd all but screwed her on the job.

Would have if his own panic hadn't forced him to back off. Last night, he'd acknowledged their chemistry was volatile, but what he hadn't realized was his complete lack of control over his lust for Cassie.

He slid the box in his arms onto a shelf and with his hands free, drove his fingers through his hair. Today would be an exercise in restraint. One he figured he'd fail. Keeping Cassie at a distance, one where he couldn't get his hands on her, was impossible. Only he had to try.

Had to get the raging inferno burning between them under control until they were somewhere less public. Somewhere other than her place of work. Or his. He'd forgive himself for this morning in her bathroom but not the other times he'd dragged her against him.

Each time he'd been powerless to stop—a shudder ran through him—helpless in the face of his want for her. She was like lightning. Cracking hard and fast across his nerves. Sending his heart rate into overdrive and his mind blank in a flash of spine-bending need.

He'd never felt anything like it, and he couldn't bring himself to walk away from her. He knew they were bound to get burned. The flames between them were too hot to do anything else. And still he wouldn't take the cautious path. For once in his life, Luc was walking into something without knowing all the possible outcomes.

Shaking his head, he headed back to the van and got to work. He'd promised to be at her beck and call for twenty-four hours and he would be. Even if he had to sit with a bunch of five-year-old girls for most of the day. With any luck, Cassie would let him hang back and not get too close to the birthday girl or her guests. Somehow he didn't think he'd be that fortunate.

He worked up a sweat. The air inside the warehouse was still and as the sun heated the metal walls, the temperature rose to a stifling level. He'd rolled up his sleeves, undone the top four buttons on his shirt, but neither gave him much relief.

They'd have to make a detour to his house on the way to the party. There was no way he wanted to spend the rest of the day in yesterday's clothes. Not to mention he was commando since he'd refused to wear his boxers for a second time.

Luc climbed out of the van with the last box and was headed over to the racks when Cassie came through from the kitchen. She carried a tub that almost blocked her view. With a skill that spoke of numerous trips of a similar nature, she navigated around shelving and came toward him. He couldn't help but return the smile she aimed his way. Waiting where he was, he watched her as she sailed past and slid the tub onto the van floor.

"Oh good, you're almost done." She aimed that smile his way again and his knees actually went weak. "We're ahead of schedule so we can grab something to eat on the way to the party unless you'd prefer cupcakes."

This time her grin grabbed him by the balls. He wanted to see her smile like that all the time. It wasn't just a curve of her lips. Her whole face lit up. Her eyes sparkled and the little creases beside them told him she did it often in spite of the fact she'd never graced him with one this genuine. But it was the dimples that did him in. God, they were so deep. How had he not noticed them before? The urge to kiss them—lick them—pierced him and he leaned forward and took a step before he stopped himself.

She breezed past, a light fragrance that reminded him of sunshine and rain trailing in her wake. He drew in a deep breath, sucked in as much as he could before the enticing smell vanished.

Like a dog on the scent of a bone, he followed her. It wasn't until she looked at him, eyebrow raised, that he realized he'd been so mesmerized by her that he'd walked into the wrong aisle. Shrugging, he turned around and headed for the end row to put away the last box of equipment.

He took a moment to clear his head before he went back to Cassie. She'd already pulled three large plastic tubs from shelves when he returned. The rainbow of colors showing through the sides made him stop. Closer inspection confirmed his fears. Beads. Hundreds of thousands of beads.

He'd been here before. The one and only time he'd babysat his nieces overnight they'd been eight and ten, and they'd insisted he help them make their mum and grandma jewelry. Luc's palms began to sweat as he thought about those tiny things and the even tinier elastic he was supposed to thread them on.

"Please tell me you don't expect me to help make those—" he waved a hand at the box, "—things."

Cassie burst out laughing.

Luc narrowed his eyes and stepped toward her.

"Oh my God." She spoke between giggles. "The look on your face." More laughter followed.

He failed to share her amusement. Crossing his arms over his chest, he waited for her to regain her composure. Only she didn't seem to be calming down. Every time she glanced at him she sank further into the hilarity he didn't see.

With a growl, he lunged forward, grabbed her head and held her still so he could silence her the only way he could think of.

Her breath whooshed out as his mouth connected with hers. He drove his tongue between her parted lips and plundered. She froze against him and he was on the verge of pulling away when she tunneled her fingers through his hair and yanked him closer. The kiss exploded.

Luc backed her up until she met the rack behind her. His body ached to feel hers, but his height made it impossible to get close enough to satisfy the need. Tearing his mouth from hers, he gasped for air as he moved his hands to her waist.

"Wrap your legs around me." His demand was spoken on a ragged breath as he picked her up.

She didn't hesitate. Her slender limbs surrounded him, her thighs squeezing tight when she hooked her ankles at his lower back.

Face to face, their gazes locked and Luc watched as Cassie's pupils dilated until only a thin rim of brown remained. He wanted to dispense with their clothes. Wanted to feel her skin on his.

Tugging at her shirt, he slipped his hands underneath the soft fabric and palmed her back. Heated silk moved against his fingertips and he groaned, closing his eyes as he absorbed the pure joy of touching Cassie.

"Lucas." She gripped his shoulders, digging her fingers in.

He opened his eyes. Saw the raging fever he felt sweeping through both of them flash through her gaze. "God, I want you."

Her eyes widened, her hips flexing as her thighs clenched around him. Heat exploded where her sex was pressed against him. Did she like sex talk?

Luc leaned forward, nipped her lower lip before whispering, "I want to strip you bare. Drag every piece of clothing from your body and take you hard and fast."

She gasped into his mouth and he licked his tongue out to taste her.

"And when I'm done, I'm gonna start all over again. Only this time I'll go slow. I'll touch—taste—every inch of you before I drive my cock deep in your pussy."

"Oh God." She rocked her hips against him. Her sex rubbed on his straining flesh, their clothes doing nothing to mask the heat they generated.

He thrust forward, driving them both out of their minds and closer to release. Their breaths mingled as they nibbled at each other. The rock and roll of their hips grew faster, their urgency increasing with every surge of sex on sex. His cock throbbed, his balls tucking up as he dry humped the woman in his arms.

"Lucas." Cassie's cry urged him on. "Oh God, I'm gonna…"

She clawed at his back, digging her heels into him as she tried to pull him closer. He picked up the pace, shifted his hips and stroked his cock harder against her. She threw her head back and moaned. The arch of her neck drew his mouth and he suckled the pulse fluttering at hyper speed at the base of her throat. It beat against his tongue, the fast beat finding a similar rhythm inside him.

He moved his hands lower, squeezed her ass and ground their bodies together. Cassie's whole body jerked, her hips thrashing as she rode him. Her strength amazed him. Leg muscles tightened as she used them to grind herself to release. Luc watched as she took what she wanted. What she needed. And when she went over—exploded in his arms—like a flash of lightning, he did something he hadn't done even as a hormone-driven teenager.

He thrust against her and came in his pants.

Cassie collapsed forward, resting her forehead on Lucas's shoulder as she struggled to catch her breath. Heat and pleasure still rippled through her as the final waves of her orgasm ebbed away. He'd blown her mind. Again. They seemed to find themselves in this position every few hours, and each time they came together it was hotter. More intense.

His breath rasped in her ear and she couldn't help smiling. Lucas seemed just as affected by her release as she was. She unhooked her ankles and tried to slip her legs from around him, but he held her tight.

"Not yet," he panted. "Just need a minute before I let you go."

She knew she should be embarrassed by her actions, or at least a little ashamed for using him the way she had, but with all the endorphins flooding her system, she could only feel gloriously satisfied. He shifted, turned around until he leaned against the racks instead of her. Still wrapped around him, she tilted her head back and met his gaze.

"Wow." She licked her lips. "Guess I got carried away."

Lucas grinned. "Yeah, guess you did."

"Should I say sorry?"

"Not unless you're expecting me to say it too."

For a second, she didn't get his meaning, but when a flush rose up his neck and filled his cheeks the light bulb went on. She glanced down, leaned back farther and caught sight of the damp patch on the front of his pants. "Oh."

"Yeah, oh." He smiled. "Understatement of the year."

Cassie brought her gaze back to his. "You know, I don't feel sorry at all. In fact, I'm feeling rather pleased with myself." She grinned.

He laughed. A deep rolling rumble that vibrated through his abdomen into hers. "Keep hold of that thought, because now we're definitely stopping by my place for a change of clothes before we head out to work."

"I think we can manage that." She untangled her arms and legs and waited for Lucas to put her down. "We better get everything packed quickly then. The cakes are almost done. I was going to ice them here but I can wait and do them at the party. That might be better anyway. With the temperature predicted to be high they'd be melting before we got them on the table if I did them here."

"You know we really have to stop doing this." He gestured between them. "As much as I'd like to keep at it and go further, you're going to have to restrain yourself for the rest of the day."

"Me?" She gave his shoulder a shove. "I didn't start that."

"No." He gripped her chin. "But it's your fault for looking so goddamn edible."

He kissed her hard and fast. She was just leaning in when he pulled back and grinned at her. Spinning her around, he slapped her ass and said, "C'mon, let's get going. I want out of these pants."

Cassie laughed at his unintentional double entendre. "Hey, don't let me stop you from stripping."

A growl rumbled behind her, and before he could grab her, she darted down the aisle and headed to the kitchen. She was pretty sure the cupcakes would be ready to come out of the oven. Hopefully, she hadn't missed the timer going off while she'd been going off. Grinning, she raced through the swinging door as the oven buzzer rang. Perfect timing.

Her timing wasn't the only thing that was perfect.

The chemistry between her and Lucas was a thing of beauty. Of course, they blazed so hot it was possible they'd incinerate each other when they finally managed to get into bed. Then again, they'd more than coped without a bed so far. She bent to open the oven door and her slacks rubbed along her wet slit. Sensation fired, her flesh so recently satisfied oversensitive to the texture of her panties—the press of her pants.

Taking a deep breath, she willed her body back under control. The last thing she needed was to get excited again. There was no time to indulge in another hot and heavy session with Lucas no matter how much she wanted to. She glanced at the clock on the wall. Eight hours. It was at least that long before she could throw all thoughts of work out the door and concentrate on Lucas and the amazing sex they were going to have.

8

Cassie couldn't take her eyes off Lucas.

The last few hours had been mindboggling.

From the minute they arrived, the birthday girl had commandeered him to play the role of Prince Charming. She had to hand it to him. After his initial panic, Lucas had proven to be an excellent prince—crown and all. And it wasn't just the princesses he'd charmed either. There wasn't one mother present who hadn't at one stage or other found a reason to talk to him.

She'd never really dealt with the green-eyed monster when it came to a man. But Cassie couldn't deny that right now she wanted to go over there and stake her claim on Prince Charming.

"I can't believe how good he is with Prissy," Margo said as she stepped beside Cassie.

"Mmm." Cassie dragged her eyes away from Lucas and looked at the birthday girl's mother. "That crown does seem to fit him well."

"And I did notice there's no wedding ring on his finger. Is he available, do you know?"

Cassie looked away and rolled her eyes. Divorced from husband number three barely six months and Margo Fernwig Rothers Bennett was on the prowl for groom number four. She'd seen it before, or at least Margo's type, and while she had no claim on Lucas, Cassie wasn't about to give this woman a clear field.

"He's seeing someone."

"Shame. Still, without a ring I'd say he's fair game, wouldn't you?" Margo headed in the direction of her daughter and her latest prey without waiting for Cassie to reply.

Staring after the other woman, Cassie struggled not to follow. Lucas wasn't hers. She had no right to go charging over and drag him away from the female piranha no matter how much the voice in her head yelled at her to go get her man.

She watched as Margo leaned over to talk to Prissy, pressing her surgically enhanced cleavage into Lucas as she did. He shifted sideways. Margo followed. The frown on his face told Cassie that he wasn't any more impressed by the woman than she was. Smiling, she turned back to the food table and continued to top up the bowls of candy.

"Oh my God. I can't believe that woman."

Cassie jumped us Lucas brushed against her. She glanced up and almost laughed at the scowl on his face. "What woman?"

"The mother. She just propositioned me in front of her daughter."

"Ah, yes, well, she is without her usual accessory at the moment."

"What?" He arched one thick, dark eyebrow.

"She ditched husband number three. She's on the prowl for number four."

"Good God. And she's looking at me?" He looked over his shoulder as though he expected the woman to be right there, claws ready to sink into him.

Cassie laughed. "Relax. We're out of here in another hour or so. Besides—" she placed her hand on his chest, patting him twice, "—you're a big boy. You can handle her. After all, it'll take more than some little woman to scare you."

"That's not a woman, it's a damn shark." He stepped closer. "And there's only one woman I want to be handling at the moment."

She gasped when he dropped his head and planted a hard kiss on her mouth. "*Lucas.*"

"Relax." He grinned. "I'm just making sure you both know where my interests lie."

With that, he headed back to the row of tables where twenty-four five-year-olds were plying their skills as master jewelers. He squeezed his six-foot-five-inch frame into a child's chair and immediately helped the girl next to him thread her beads on the thin elastic.

Cassie's stomach flipped and her chest warmed. If someone had told her Lucas Wilhelm could hold his own in a group of tutu-wearing princesses she'd have laughed and called them a liar. Except now she knew firsthand that Lucas was capable of handling any situation.

Margo caught Cassie's attention as she headed back toward her. This would be interesting. From the look on the woman's face she was not happy about something.

"I don't think that man should be sitting so close to all those little girls." She put just enough inflection in her voice to have any one who overheard questioning Lucas's intentions.

A burst of laughter came from behind Cassie and she turned to see several of the other mothers within hearing distance. The pretty blonde that had laughed stepped closer. "Why, Margo, are you jealous?"

Margo stiffened. "I have no idea what you're implying, Sonia."

"I'm not implying anything. I'm stating a fact. Prince Charming just shot you down and then made it perfectly clear who his princess is." Sonia tilted her head in Cassie's direction. "Getting desperate if you're going after the hired help, aren't you, Margo?"

"Well, I never." Nose in the air, Margo flounced off.

Sonia put her hand on Cassie's arm. "Sorry you and Prince Charming had to be subjected to that."

"Oh, don't worry. I'm finding the whole thing rather amusing." Cassie turned to check on Lucas before turning back to Sonia and the other women gathered around. "And Lucas is a big boy. He can take care of himself."

The redhead on Sonia's left spoke, "Oh my, yes. He's definitely a big boy." Her grin was downright wolfish.

En masse, they laughed and Cassie couldn't help joining in. She shouldn't be laughing at the situation, not with Lucas looking all offended and Margo stalking off. Still, from her position, having her temporary employee sexually harassed at a child's party wasn't something she ever expected to occur. Now if it had happened last night...

Cassie glanced back at Lucas to find him engrossed with the beads as deeply as the five-year-olds. Another thing that made her smile. He was so cute sitting there surrounded by pink princesses. She slipped her phone out of her pocket and quickly snapped a couple of shots of Lucas.

Grinning, Cassie put her phone away and went back to work. They'd had the birthday cupcakes and presents earlier, and she'd packed up the remaining cakes in little bags for each of the princesses to take home. The party bags were lined up beside them ready to hand out, and other than the supplies being used she had nothing else to clear away once the party was over. She glanced at her watch. And that would be in approximately forty-five minutes.

Luc pocketed the bracelet he'd made for Cassie. He planned to give it to her later. Right now he had to pack everything away. The girls were pitching in to help close lids and stack boxes now the fun was over. Surprisingly, he'd had fun too. A lot of fun. He'd never own up to it, of course. But he had to admit, if only to himself, that little girls were unexpectedly amusing.

They'd squealed with delight when the colored beads were plunked down in front of them. There was more screeching when they managed to thread a few glass balls on the thin elastic to make a necklace or bracelet, and there were even more shrieks of joy when he'd helped them tie off their masterpieces and put them on.

Yep. He'd had a damn good time. Well, except for that one glitch...

Speak of the devil. Prissy's mother was heading his way. He was quite amused by little Priscilla's reaction to her mother's repeated attempts to get his attention. If he didn't know better, he'd think the little girl was jealous and territorial, but he figured it was more a matter of not wanting to share.

Prissy—who the hell named their kid Priscilla then shortened it to Prissy these days?—had told her mother point blank the last time the woman ventured near them that he was *her* Prince Charming and she should go find her own.

He smiled. Even saddled with a horrible name like Prissy, Luc didn't doubt that was one girl who would always get what she wanted. And right now that was her mother at a safe distance from Prince Charming. With shoulders thrust back, Prissy marched over to her mother, grabbed her hand and dragged her over to the table where Cassie had set out the take-home party bags and cupcakes.

"Bet you never thought you'd be rescued by a five-year-old pink-tutu-wearing princess." Cassie moved up beside him and began snapping the lids on the remaining containers.

Luc shook his head. "No, but then I never expected to be repeatedly propositioned by a woman at a kid's birthday party either."

"Have to admit, this is the closest thing to sexual harassment Are You Game? has ever encountered." She grinned at him.

He arched an eyebrow. "Sexual harassment?"

"What else would you call it?"

"Well." Luc rubbed his hand over his jaw. "Now that you mention it, perhaps I should put in a complaint."

Cassie chuckled. "Technically you're not an employee. Bit hard to make a complaint when you aren't on the books."

"Hmm...seeing how you're the reason I'm here, maybe I should sue you for emotional duress?" Luc moved closer to Cassie, bent his face next to hers and blew a breath over her lips. God, he wanted to kiss her. "Or maybe you can think of some way to ease my distress?"

Her gaze met his, lowered to his mouth before bouncing back to his eyes. "Um, maybe."

Luc had to stifle a groan when Cassie licked her lips. He also had to move away before he did something extremely inappropriate for a children's party. "You think about it and let me know what you come up with."

Before he gave in to the unrelenting urge to kiss her, Luc picked up a pile of boxes and headed for the van out front. By the time he got back Cassie had stacked the rest of the equipment ready for him to load and was busy talking with the mothers and girls as they collected their goodie bags.

Hopefully today's party drummed up some more business for her. Although he'd caught a glimpse of the huge calendar board in her office this morning and he'd noticed how many events Are You Game? had on the schedule. No wonder she needed to hire more staff. That thing was jam-packed full. Not one day was clear.

He gathered up another armful and made his way back to the van. As he turned around, he found two little girls with arms loaded. Both grinned from ear to ear.

"Why are the princesses carrying such heavy things when Prince Charming is here to do all the hard work?" he asked.

"My mummy says even princesses have to take care of themself," the little blonde—he thought her name was Michelle—said.

"Is that right?" He reached down to relieve them of their burdens. "Well, your mum's right. But when there is a strong prince around you should let him do all the work."

"Okay. C'mon, Cindy, let's go get our cupcakes." Michelle grabbed her friend's hand and they skipped away.

He secured the boxes in the van and went back to find Cassie rolling up the throwaway tablecloths. "Here. Let me get those."

"I've got this. I need you to take the cake-decorating equipment out to the van for me." She indicated two large plastic tubs by the back door. "Once those are loaded we're done and out of here." Her grin lit up her face, her dimples winking, and he was struck again by the need to put his mouth on hers.

Responding with a smile of his own, he said, "All right. I'll wait for you out front then."

Luc grabbed the tubs just as Prissy and her mother came out of the house. Not wanting to talk to the woman but wanting to say goodbye to the birthday girl, he called out as he walked away. "Happy birthday, Prissy. Hope you had a great day."

"Oh, yes, Prince Charming. Thank you for coming and making my day extra special." She raced away from her mother to bounce along beside him. "I wished for you when I blew out my candles at Daddy's house yesterday."

He glanced down at her. "You wished for *me*?"

"Yes. I wished for Prince Charming to come to my party, and you did." She clapped her hands.

Luc laughed. "I'm glad your wish came true."

"Me too." Prissy tugged on his T-shirt. "Can I give you a hug before you go?"

"Definitely. Just let me put these in the van first."

"Prissy!" her mother called out. "Stop bothering the man."

"She's not a bother." Luc put his load down and crouched to Prissy's eye level. "I really enjoyed your party."

The little girl threw her arms around his neck and whispered in his ear, "I love you, Prince Charming."

Luc panicked, his gaze darting to Cassie. She stood a few feet away next to Prissy's mother, a grin of approval on her face. Shame he couldn't say the same for the shark. No, she was shooting daggers at him. He disentangled himself and stood. Patting Prissy's hair he said, "Thank you for a wonderful day, Princess Priscilla."

She grinned up at him, a gap in her front teeth where one was missing, before she took off toward the house. "C'mon, Mum. I want to have a bath with my new princess bubble bath."

Not wanting to give Prissy's mother a chance to corner him, Luc quickly shut and locked the cargo doors and strode to the passenger side where he climbed in and slammed the door. He couldn't see what was happening from where he sat and he breathed a sigh of relief when Cassie slipped into the driver's seat and started the engine. Staring straight ahead, he thanked his lucky stars he hadn't had to rebuff another obvious come on before making his escape. Luc had a new understanding of what his boss went through after being the target of an over-zealous admirer.

"So what do we do now, boss?" he asked.

"We head back to work and you unload. I have some paperwork to fill out, but I can grab that and take it home to do later." Cassie took her eyes off the road for a moment and glanced his way. "I thought we could pick up some groceries and I'll make us some dinner."

He was surprised by her offer and would love to have her cook for him, but he had a better idea. "How about I cook dinner? I am working for you after all."

"You can cook?" She turned her wide eyes to him for a split second.

"I do okay. Do you have a barbeque?"

"No, only the grill in my oven." Cassie navigated them through the late-afternoon traffic with ease. "Will that do?"

Luc could work with that, but another idea appealed more. "Why don't we head to my place after we finish unloading? I've got everything I need at home to make us dinner and you can get your paperwork done while I cook."

The thought of having Cassie in his house sent a shudder down his spine and warmth into his groin. He could picture her sitting at his breakfast counter.

"Are you sure? I don't expect you to cook for me."

"I like cooking, and if I had any hope of doing the paperwork for you I'd offer." He studied her profile. Her mouth was drawn tight in a frown, and he wanted to lean over and kiss her until she smiled again. "You still have hours left to boss me around, Cass."

"I haven't really bossed you around." She chewed the corner of her mouth and he stifled a moan.

"Well, no, but you're definitely the one who's been in charge and you certainly took me out of my comfort zone in the last few hours." Luc smiled at the little white lie. Other than a few minutes here and there, he hadn't been uncomfortable at all.

They pulled up at a red light and Cassie turned in her seat. "Okay, you cook dinner, but I have to warn you I'm not much of a cook so if you expect me to feed you tomorrow when you're giving the orders you'll have to settle for take-out."

Luc laughed. "You can't cook? Didn't you make forty-eight cupcakes?"

"Well, yeah, but that's baking. I can bake better than most." She shrugged. "Just can't cook much of anything else."

"Can you make apple pie?" Luc had a weakness for fresh hot apple pie with vanilla ice cream.

"Sure." The car behind them honked. "Oops."

Cassie returned her gaze to the road and got the van moving again. She drove another couple of blocks before he asked, "So will you make me one?"

"What?"

"A pie. Will you make me one?"

"Oh, of course. I should have all the ingredients at work."

"What do you need? I might have them. If not we can go shopping. In fact, let's do that. We'll go in the morning." He rubbed his hands together and licked his lips. "I can already taste it."

"We can hit the supermarket near my house tonight. I'd planned to grab some things after work today anyway." She turned the van onto the street where Are You Game? was. "Sound good?"

"Yeah, I can pick up some fresh steaks instead of defrosting them." Luc mentally rolled through what he had in his fridge and decided it would be best to pick up everything fresh. He shopped regularly and rarely had to throw food out, but he'd prefer to be safe than sorry, and he planned to woo Cassie with his culinary skills tonight. The screech of metal blasted his eardrums as the garage door rolled up. That thing really needed oiling.

"Shit." Cassie braked hard. "I think it's stuck."

Sure enough, the door had only retracted three quarters of the way up. Luc undid his seatbelt and open his door. "Let me see if you've got clearance." He stood on the doorsill and discovered they had plenty of room to drive in without ripping the roof off. Hopping down, he slipped back into his seat and shut the door. "Plenty of room."

She eased the van forward and pressed the button to lower the roller door behind them. The grinding metal put his teeth on edge and Cassie stuck her fingers in her ears and leaning over, looked through the side mirror.

"Please go down. Please go down. Please go down," she chanted. When the door met the floor with a resounding crack, Cassie dropped back against her seat and sighed. "Thank you."

"Worried?"

"Yeah, I hate to admit it, but Dan's right. We need a new roller door." She turned off the van and pocketed the keys. "Let's get everything unloaded and I'll grab that paperwork."

Luc followed her out of the van to the rear doors where they got to work. They didn't speak, and he had to admit the silence wasn't uncomfortable. He didn't feel the need to fill it with mundane chatter, and he was immensely thankful that Cassie didn't either. He'd just picked up the final box when she spoke.

"I'll run up and grab that paperwork. We'll be out of here in five minutes."

She took off up the metal stairs, two at a time, and Luc stood immobile and watched her cute butt as she disappeared from view.

His cock stirred.

Not that the damn thing had been quiet all day. He'd kept it under control, but there was no denying he'd been semi-hard since last night, and Cassie was the reason for his embarrassing predicament.

That was something he'd never had to deal with before, an unmanageable libido. There wasn't any doubt that she was hot. But she wasn't the best-looking woman he'd hooked up with, so what was it about her that made his chest ache?

What did Cassandra Moreland have that made her irresistible?

9

Cassie leaned against her closed office door and sucked in a deep breath. It was becoming more and more obvious that she was in way over her head when it came to Lucas.

Her body wasn't the only thing wanting his attention.

She'd offered to make him dinner because she hadn't wanted the day to end. The more time she spent with him the more she liked what she saw. He was no longer just a hot body she could get her rocks off with. And that was the problem. She didn't need this kind of complication in her life.

Complicated didn't begin to describe what Lucas was. They'd known each other less than twenty-four hours and he was already the biggest distraction she'd ever faced. She couldn't stop looking at him. And when she wasn't looking she was thinking.

Like now. She'd come up here to collect the paperwork she needed to fill out before Monday's staff meeting and she was leaning against the door thinking about Lucas. With a sigh, Cassie forced herself to move.

She opened the filing cabinet and grabbed what she needed to finalize today's party. The folder from last night was still sitting on her desk, so she picked that up and headed back downstairs. A quick glance at the calendar for next week reminded her she had to be in the office early Monday to get everything together for Maggie and the Bernard job.

Luckily, she'd prepared all the documents earlier in the week so that job was ready to go first thing. Maggie was her top corporate consultant so she wouldn't need anything more than the agenda for the five days of team-building exercises.

Satisfied she had everything under control, Cassie closed her office door behind her and made her way downstairs. She found Lucas waiting by the van and her stomach and pussy clenched at the sight he made leaning back against the metal side, ankles and arms crossed.

He looked so different in his cargo pants and T-shirt. Easygoing and relaxed. Approachable. Mouth-wateringly sexy. The slacks and shirt he'd worn last night had given him an aura of cool detachment. An edgy, don't-touch, don't-come-close vibe that kept people at a distance.

This Lucas looked welcoming, and she couldn't help but be reeled in when he sent her a toe-curling smile.

"Ready?" he pushed off the van.

"Sure." Cassie wasn't all that confident she was ready to face the next part of their weekend challenge, but she wasn't backing out now. "My car's out front. I'll just grab my bag and clipboard from the van."

She flung open the driver's door, grabbed the board from the dash and retrieved her backpack from behind the seat. One thing was certain in her mind. By the time Monday rolled around everything would be different. It already was. From the second she'd gone up against Lucas something inside her had switched on. Something she couldn't get a handle of. She couldn't understand or comprehend how one person could change her in such an elemental way.

Cassie glanced through her lowered lashes at Lucas. There was no getting past how good looking he was or what her body's reaction was to him, but it had to be more than his looks that affected her so deeply.

For the life of her, she couldn't work it out, and that more than the intense physical reaction she had to him caused her alarm. If it were only lust she could deal with their attraction and move on.

But this whole need-to-know-him thing she had going on in her head just wouldn't quit, and Cassie knew she was treading on shaky ground, knew at any second she'd find herself sinking deep.

And yet she couldn't seem to stop from taking step after step toward him. The only other time in her life she'd felt this out of sorts was when she'd made the decision to start Are You Game?. And while that had turned out to be a roaring success, she'd still been on the brink of breaking on more than one occasion.

They reached her car and she hit the fob to disarm the locks. It was pointless to dwell on what might or might not happen. If she wasn't going to back out of their deal and end their time together now then she needed to let the cards fall where they may.

She was a firm believer in fate. Individual choices could change things to a certain degree, but if something was meant to happen it would—with or without her input. Regardless of the outcome or the traitorous path she walked, she'd made the decision to accept his challenge and she'd see it through to the end.

Cassie tossed her bag in the backseat as she got behind the wheel. They'd have to make a quick stop at her house so she could pick up some clothes and then they'd stop at the supermarket before going to his place. Lucas buckled his belt as she started the car, but before she could put the car in gear he grabbed her hand and wrapped it in both of his.

"Cass?"

She swung her gaze around to meet his, and in those mesmerizing brown depths, she saw concern as well as the banked need that had been shimmering there all day. She licked her suddenly dry lips —swallowed. "What?"

"We don't have to do this." He squeezed her hand. "Nothing will happen unless you want it to."

He was right. Nothing would happen without her consent but she couldn't stop this thing unfolding. No matter how much her mind protested, she found herself drawn closer to the inevitable—the two of them in bed.

It wasn't the physical aspect of their attraction that had her worried, and she had the sinking feeling that neither of them had control over the emotional side of this pull between them. She'd just convinced herself she'd follow through on their deal and now Lucas was giving her an out.

She had no intention of taking it. "I know."

Cassie tugged her hand free and shifted the car into drive. She released the brake and then eased out of her parking spot and turned toward home. The dread of a few moments ago was suddenly gone. In its place was a bubble of excitement—anticipation—eagerness to move their relationship to the next step.

Whoa.

Relationship? What the hell? Cassie glanced at him out the corner of her eye. Since when were they in a relationship? Hands curled tightly around the wheel, she squashed her thoughts and concentrated on getting them to her house safely. She needed to take this for what it was. A weekend of mutual pleasure. Nothing more, nothing less. No strings, no expectations.

Except all the lecturing in the world didn't stop her heart from skipping when he reached over and patted her thigh. Yep. Cassie was in trouble. Deep, dark, slippery sides trouble, and she had no intention of trying to find her way out. She just hoped come Monday morning her heart was still in one piece.

Luc cut the feta into cubes while sneaking peeks at Cassie. She sat exactly as he'd pictured her. At his breakfast counter, papers spread out around her, head bent, writing up today and yesterday's reports. He'd gotten a glimpse of the detail she went into and was amazed at her thoroughness.

Not that he should have expected anything less, but when she'd offered to show him her company's policies earlier he hadn't really thought about them—or her business—in anything more than general terms.

He'd sold her short and he had to give credit where it was due. The businesswoman blew his mind. She'd built Are You Game? from the ground up. And from what he could gather, she'd pretty much done it single-handedly. Oh, she'd surrounded herself with capable people to help, but she was the driving force—the focal point—they all took their cue from.

Dan had rung her twice since they'd left the supermarket. First time was to check on today's party and make sure Luc hadn't done anything nefarious with his boss, and the second to let her know one of their employees had called to say he'd be out of action for six weeks due to a broken arm.

They'd spent thirty minutes sorting out what needed to be done to cover the gap and it became clear to Luc that Dan was more than an employee. It had taken all his self-control to hold back the question burning his tongue.

Were they lovers?

He didn't think she'd hook up with him if she was sleeping with Dan, but that didn't mean she and Dan hadn't slept together in the past.

Luc didn't like the way that thought made him feel. She wasn't his regardless of what they'd done since that first kiss in McDermott's pantry. And she had every right to a sexual history, same as he did. Except it didn't matter how many times he repeated those words, they didn't stop the acid churning in his gut.

"Done." Cassie pulled all her papers together and stacked them neatly on the counter. "Need any help?"

"No. Everything's ready. I just have to fire up the barbeque and cook the T-bones." He pointed to the bottle of red on the counter. "You could pour us each a glass of that to sip while I cook if you want."

"Sure." She slipped off the stool and came around to his side of the counter. Her hip brushed his and he sucked in a breath as fire shot through his blood.

He cleared his throat. "Glasses are in the cupboard next to the fridge."

She took down two wine glasses and poured them each a half glass. "Probably best not to overdo on an empty stomach."

Luc dropped the cheese into the salad and covered the bowl. "I'll just put this in the fridge and grab the steaks. Mind carrying my glass out to the deck?"

With the salad in the fridge and the plate of steaks in his hand, he made his way outside. Dusk had settled over the yard and the heat of the day had eased, leaving the evening warm but not uncomfortably hot.

He'd built the deck himself last summer and he was pleased to finally have a guest—who wasn't family—to enjoy it with. Smiling, he pointed at the outdoor table. "Have a seat. I'll get the barbeque lit and have this meat cooked in no time. How do you like yours? Rare? Medium? Well done?"

"Medium rare, thanks." She pulled out a chair and sank into it with a sigh. "You have a beautiful set up."

"It's a work in progress." He indicated the hedge a few meters from the deck. "Behind there is a pool that's in desperate need of refurbishment. Luckily, the bushes hide that disaster area because I won't get to that until next summer at this rate."

"You're doing it yourself?"

"A lot of it, yes." Luc shrugged. "I like the manual work. It relaxes me, and it's more satisfying to sit out here knowing I had a hand in it."

"Wow." Cassie glanced around. "Did you do the decking?"

"Yeah, last summer. Convinced a couple of the guys to come over for beer and food one weekend and got the harder parts knocked out. Then it was a few hours here and there."

"I'm impressed. Really impressed." Her gaze trailed down his body. A slow perusal that had his gut clenching. "I guess those muscles aren't all show."

Luc's gaze connected with hers. Hunger burned bright and he took the two steps needed to close the distance between them. He curled his fingers around her upper arms, yanked her from her seat and plastered her body against his. Warmth bathed his neck as the air rushed from her lungs. He bent his head and brushed her ear with his lips. The simple touch drew a gasp and shudder from her.

Dipping lower, he trailed the tip of his tongue around the delicate shell until he reached her lobe. With a hard pull, he sucked the softness into his mouth and tugged with his teeth.

The moan that slipped from her throat left him with a desperate need to taste her. He slid his hand into her hair and tilted her head back so he could get at her mouth. Their lips collided, their breath mingling as he thrust his tongue inside.

She tasted of wine and Cass. Two intoxicating substances on their own—together they blew his mind and weakened his knees. He'd never understood how men could lose themselves in a woman. Never known this all-consuming need to have—to take. To claim.

He growled into her mouth and deepened the kiss. She dug her fingernails into his biceps, the sting an erotic shot to his blood that drove him higher. It pushed him further into the chaotic frenzy of want and need. His hips rocked, his cock throbbed and his balls ached. She arched against him, her stomach massaging his length. It wasn't enough. He wanted to feel the heat of her sex pressed to his. Naked. Skin on skin. Hard on soft.

Luc untangled his hands from her hair and skimmed them down her sides to span her waist. He dragged her closer, onto her toes, but it didn't give him what he wanted. Palming her ass, Luc lifted her feet off the floor and urged her thighs around his hips. She threw her arms around his neck and tore her mouth from his.

Their gazes locked. Her eyes were glazed with lust, her pupils dilated, rimmed with a thin line of caramel brown. They stayed locked together until the slam of a door caused them both to jump.

Luc's gaze shot to the house. He heard the voices before he saw his visitors. "Shit!"

Cassie unwound her legs and tried to pull from his grasp. It took him a second to collect his wits and set her free. He waited until she was steady on her feet before he headed through the sliding door to intercept his sister and nieces. Luc couldn't believe Jody's timing. Then again, it was a good thing she wasn't a few minutes later.

"Hey, Jody, girls, what are you guys doing here?" He'd have to have a word with his sister about using the spare key he'd given her.

"Hi, Uncle Luc," Leigh and Amy chorused. They ran toward him and gave him a bone-crushing three-way hug.

"I guess you didn't go into your laundry yet," Jody asked.

"No, why?" He turned his attention to his sister now that the girls had let him go and headed for his fridge and the cans of cola he kept in there just for them.

"My washer died this morning. I borrowed yours earlier today. We're just picking up the clean load that's sitting in your machine." Jody's steps faltered. "Oh, sorry. I didn't know you had company."

Luc turned to discover Cassie standing just inside the sliding door. "Cassie, this is my sister Jody and her girls. Jody, Cassandra Moreland."

"Oh." Jody took a step forward, hand out. "So pleased to meet you. We're still on for Monday, right?"

Cassie shook his sister's hand. "Yes, of course. I'm looking forward to seeing what you think of Are You Game?, not to mention the fact that as of today I'm down a staff member. I'm afraid if you like the job you'll be thrown in the deep end."

"Mum!" Amy yelled from the laundry room. "Leigh won't give me the basket."

Jody rolled her eyes. "Duty calls. I'll just grab the washing and be gone."

Luc watched his sister disappear before turning to Cassie. "Sorry, I forget she has a key and to be honest she's never interrupted…"

Cassie laughed. "It might be best that she did interrupt. We were getting a little carried away. Again."

He smiled. "We seem to do that a lot."

"I'll put the steaks on while you help your sister." Not waiting for him to agree, she went back outside.

Jody came out of the laundry with Leigh and Amy behind her,

each had hold of one side of the overflowing basket. "We'll leave you to your..." She glanced around. "Um, did she go?"

"No, she's out the back putting the steaks on the barbeque." He tried to take the heavy basket from the girls. "Here, let me take that out to the car for you."

"Na-uh, it's fine. Between the two of them they've got it." Jody stopped next to him. "Are you seeing her?" she asked in a whisper.

Luc tweaked her nose. "None of your business, little sister."

She scowled at him. "You don't think this will be a problem. You know, you and her. Me, the job." Jody looked behind and lowered her voice farther. "I really need this job, Lucas."

Instantly concerned, he asked, "Do you need money? Has Colin not paid again this month?"

"No, no, nothing like that. He paid, two days late but he paid." She wrung her hands. "I just really want this, Luc. The girls are getting older and I want to be me again. For so long I've been either Leigh and Amy's mum or Colin's wife. I want to be Jody again."

He pulled her close and wrapped his arms around her. "I promise not to screw it up for you if you promise not to do the same. So no sharing all my childhood secrets and I won't share yours."

Jody laughed just as he'd wanted her to. "Yeah, like I know any of your secrets, childhood or otherwise." She moved back, her gaze meeting his. "You really like her, don't you?"

Luc could lie or divert the question but he didn't. "Yeah, I really, *really* like her," he said with a grin.

"Then don't screw this up for you either." She stood on tiptoes and kissed his cheek. "I better go make sure the teenagers aren't killing each other out on your front lawn."

He let her go and followed her to the door. "Do you need the machine again this weekend?"

"No, we're good." She smiled over her shoulder as she opened the door. "No more interruptions."

Her grin told him she knew what they'd been up to, but before he could say anything to argue, Jody slipped out the door and closed it behind her. He cracked it open again to make sure they got off all right. As the taillights of his sister's car disappeared down the street, he shut and locked the door. This time he engaged the alarm, so if she did come back he'd have warning.

With a smile on his face, he made his way back to the deck and Cassie. He'd love to take up where they'd left off, but now that his jets were cooled he'd concentrate on getting food in their bellies. If that lip-lock was anything to go by they'd both need their strength. They'd be tearing each other apart before the night was over. He quickened his step. The sooner he got dinner on the table, the sooner he could satisfy the other hunger gnawing at his bones.

10

Cassie took a final mouthful and leaned back. The steak had been done to perfection and the salad and jacket potatoes had been just as yummy. She'd eaten too much but she couldn't resist when everything Lucas put in front of them tasted so good.

She couldn't recall the last time she'd eaten such a delicious home-cooked meal. Living alone, she rarely cooked, so unless she went to her parents for dinner it was something quick and easy most nights.

"Damn. That was good." Cassie reached for her wine glass and took a sip. "I can't remember the last time I ate a steak."

Lucas looked up, his fork stopped halfway to his mouth. "What do you eat then?"

She cradled her glass between her hands. "Frozen dinners, sandwiches, sometimes leftovers from work."

"That doesn't sound healthy." He popped a juicy piece of meat in his mouth and chewed. Cassie couldn't take her eyes off his lips. They were slightly damp, and a drop of steak sauce clung to the corner. She wanted to lean forward and lick it off. "You shouldn't compromise your health just because you're busy, Cass."

"Huh?" Her gaze darted to meet his. What was he talking about?

"Frozen dinners?" He shook his head. "The preservatives and additives alone are enough to make you sick."

Oh, right, crappy diet habits. She shrugged. "I'm lucky to remember to eat half the time so those preservatives and additives are probably the only thing keeping me alive."

He shook his head. "You should take better care of yourself."

Cassie understood where he was coming from, and when she had more time and energy she did cook, but lately those days had been few and far between. "I cook when I can. Are You Game? has been so flat out in recent months that I barely have time to scratch when the urge strikes." She smiled.

Lucas narrowed his eyes. "Good thing you're hiring more staff then. You need to slow down and look after yourself as well as you do your business."

She nodded. "Oh, I agree, and I will, once the adult parties are in full swing."

They should change the subject. She could see he wanted to say something else, so before he could she pushed her chair back and got to her feet. "Let's clear the dishes and then we can have dessert. I know it's not pie, but the raspberry ripple ice cream we bought at the shop will do for tonight. I'll make you your apple pie tomorrow."

Cassie began stacking plates, but Lucas stopped her with a hand on her arm. He wrapped his long fingers around her wrist, his dark skin stark against her paler tones.

Warmth flowed from his touch, travelled up her arm to seep into every cell and fill her with a need to be touched—everywhere.

Her breath stalled, her pulse raced and heat flooded her core. The cotton crotch of her panties grew moist as her pussy fluttered, clenched with want. She dragged her gaze to his and all the air was sucked from her lungs.

His eyes were black as pitch. They burned with a passion so hot Cassie's body caught fire with just a look. He rose from his chair and walked the few steps to her side without letting go of his grip.

She swallowed around the lump in her throat, licked her lips and watched as his nostrils flared, his eyes tracking the movement of her tongue. The small guttural snarl barely registered before his mouth crushed hers.

Lucas took them deep. Drove his tongue between her teeth and took everything in his path. The stroke of his flesh on hers, the press of lips, the slick slide of their mouths joining in a desperate need to get closer fogged her mind and drenched her system with desire so potent it could never be satisfied. She tore her mouth from his, gasping for breath while her mind reeled.

He didn't give her a second to catch her breath. His lips trailed over her chin, his teeth nipping at the curve of her jaw, his tongue licking at the slope of her neck on his way to the delicate skin beating frantically for him.

Cassie curled her fingers in his shirt, holding on to the only solid thing around her with a death grip that turned her knuckles white. Her head spun, her chest was heavy and her stomach flipped when Lucas took his lips lower.

Heavy and aching, her breasts tingled, her nipples puckering tight as she waited for that first touch. She cried out when he pulled away, her grip on him not strong enough to keep him close.

"No." The cry fell from her lips on a harsh breath as he pushed her to arm's length.

"Cass." Her name, said on a ragged groan, drew her gaze to his. "Not here."

She didn't have time to figure out what he meant. He pressed his shoulder to her stomach and tossed her over his back. Cassie grabbed his waist, slid her arms around until she cuddled the length of his spine. His strides were long—purposeful—as he made his way across the deck and into the house.

In no time, he flipped her upright and dropped her to his bed. Following her down, he pinned her body beneath his.

"Here." He brushed the hair from her face. "Here is where I want you."

Lucas kissed her then.

A slow, sweet, drugging kiss that left her breathless and craving more. She sank into the soft caress. Sank into the sensual pleasure that his lips delivered. Immersed herself in the most erotic kiss of her life as he took them straight into sinful delight. His tongue stroked hers. A swipe of wet heat that drew her in. Lured her deeper into the man surrounding her.

He slid his hands down her sides, curled his fingers around the hem of her shirt and pushed up. With a slowness that frustrated, he worked the fabric up her torso until it bunched under her arms. All the while he continued to feast on her mouth. He eased back, took her mouth in gentle nips before pulling away completely. She couldn't stop the murmur of protest. Couldn't prevent her fingers from clawing at his scalp to keep him close.

He chuckled. The sound was rich and rumbling and vibrated through her breasts where his chest lay pressed against them. "I'm not going anywhere." His gaze connected with hers. "Not for a very long time."

Tangling his fingers with hers, Lucas tugged her hands away from his head and over hers to press them into the mattress. He tightened his grip as he lowered his mouth to hers again. He brushed his lips back and forth, swept his tongue from one corner to the other, never pushing for more.

Even when she opened for him, he didn't take what she offered. Instead, he drove her mad with a kiss that could only be described as PG. After the carnal way he'd taken her mouth before, this maddening, unhurried slide of his lips over hers ripped away every last vestige of self-control she had.

"Please. Please." The plea fell from her on a panted breath.

Lucas withdrew, moved to brush his lips over her cheek, her eyelid, her temple and finally her ear. He breathed out, blew warm air across her sensitive flesh, sending a shiver down her spine, goose bumps breaking out along her neck. He scraped his teeth over her lobe and another shudder raked her.

"Don't worry, Cass. I plan to please you all night long." He rocked his hips, pressed his cock into her sex and sent sensation spinning through her. "All. Night. Long."

He punctuated each word with a thrust of his hips. Her clit

pulsed. Her hips bucked beneath his as her body tried to increase the pleasure—sought the ultimate satisfaction she knew he could give her.

Cassie wanted to touch him, pull him closer, but he still held her hands prisoner against the mattress. She fought his hold, tugged and yanked with all her strength. Except she was no match for Lucas. His grip was tight, not painful, but definitely firm, and he held her in place with ease.

Bringing his mouth back to hers, he nipped at her lips. "Tell me I can have you, Cass. Tell me this is what you want," he demanded.

There was only one thing she could say—wanted to say. "Yes."

L uc stared at the woman pinned beneath him. She'd given him the answer he wanted, so why wasn't he taking her?

And why did he feel like it wasn't enough?

Confused by his hesitancy, he shook off his thoughts and gave them both what they wanted. Cassie was on fire. Everywhere he touched her she burned. He unclamped his fingers and trailed them over her hands, down her arms. When he reached the scrunched-up shirt, he gripped it tight and tugged it higher until the garment slipped over her head.

What he'd revealed took his breath. Her breasts were encased in plain white cotton. Not meant to showcase, the white cups concealed her from him, only the look was anything but innocent. The underwear designed for comfort and support had his mouth watering and his cock throbbing.

It was the sexiest thing he'd ever seen, and he flicked the front clasp to expose the flesh beneath. No. *She* was the sexiest thing he'd ever seen. Clothed or not, she was a shot of desire straight to his bloodstream. His body reacted to her like no other—*knew* her without ever having touched her.

From the moment they'd met, she had him climbing the walls of desire, and now that he'd touched her—made her come—he couldn't get enough. He couldn't satisfy his need for her. With a growl, he sat up, straddled her hips and ripped his own shirt off. He tossed it across the room.

Next, he popped the button on his shorts, gave himself some necessary breathing room, before shuffling farther down her legs and going to work on her pants. The button and zipper gave easily, and he yanked the pants over her hips and down her thighs. Sucking in a breath, he gawked at the simple white panties stretched between her hipbones.

"Damn." Luc traced a fingertip along the elastic waist. "Just when I think you can't possibly get any sexier."

The shadow of dark hair hidden beneath her underwear drew his gaze. Dampness left the cotton see-through at the juncture of her thighs and his mouth watered with the need to taste her again. He remembered her flavor and he wanted to sample her once more.

Deciding they both had way too many clothes on, he jumped from the bed and shucked his pants. She lay still, her gaze trained on the hard throbbing erection he revealed. Her sharp in-drawn breath, the way she squirmed on the bed pleased him, and he smiled.

He leaned over her, slipped his fingers into the waistband of her undies and slowly eased them down. He'd seen her naked before. Touched her. Tasted her. Except this slow reveal teased him and worked him up more than ever before.

Maybe it was the fact that he knew he'd be buried inside her soon. Buried deep and thrusting hard until they both lost control and let the bliss take them. Her dark curls glistened with her cream, her flesh, flushed pink and swollen, was slick with her need, and he let his thumb skim the crease of her sex as he stripped her panties off.

She shuddered, a moan slipping up her throat, and Luc couldn't wait any longer. He climbed back onto the bed, slid his body over hers and found a home for himself between her legs.

"I want to taste you again. Want to eat you until you scream my name, but I can't wait another second to get inside you."

Luc flexed his hips, rubbed the head of his cock in her wetness. His balls tightened, his cock grew harder and he angled his pelvis while spreading her legs with his own. Settled between her thighs, he lined up with her opening and pushed in. Tight wet heat surrounded him.

She rocked against him, rolled her hips to line their bodies up better and Luc's eyes crossed as she took more of him inside. Cassie slid her hands down his back and grabbed his ass. She dug her nails in and thrust up, driving his cock deeper, taking him completely.

Her pussy walls scorched him from root to tip, and he prayed he wouldn't embarrass himself by coming right now. He locked his jaw and concentrated on not feeling the delicious sensations bombarding him. She wiggled under him, dug in her nails and heels to try and make him move. But he wasn't giving in.

Not yet. Any second now he'd lose control and all hell would break loose, but for right now he wanted to savor the moment. Wanted to burn the memory of burying his cock inside her this first time on his brain.

"Lucas." She breathed his name in the curve of his neck a second before she sank her teeth into the corded muscle.

He shuddered, his cock flexing inside her, dragging a moan from Cassie and a groan from him. "Don't move." He panted. "Give me a minute."

She didn't hear him or chose to ignore his request, because she bowed her back, arched up and pressed him deeper before rolling her hips and sliding his cock through the gloved grip of her pussy until only the head remained inside. *Fuck!* His body jerked, his hips rocking forward until he was buried to his balls once more.

"Yes. Again." She raked her nails along his ass cheeks. "Faster."

Luc tried to hold back. He tried to keep the pace slow—steady. But he was helpless against the onslaught of Cassie's need. She rocked beneath him. Took control and drove them both to the brink. He gripped her hips in the hope of keeping her still, but she was mindless with lust and continued to fuck him from the bottom. She wrapped her legs tighter around him, squeezed his waist as she used him as leverage to get what she wanted.

Lost in the slick slide of her soft flesh against his hard length, Luc moved with her. Together they found a rhythm that pushed them closer and closer to the razor edge. He powered into her, drove in and out with hard, sharp thrusts.

Sweat coated his skin, dripped from his forehead and down his spine. Her pussy spasmed around his cock and he knew she was close. His own orgasm rode his back, but he couldn't let go before she did. Not before he felt her walls contracting around him would he give in and take his own pleasure.

He gripped her hips tight and rolled until he reversed their positions. Her gasp blew hot air over his ear and he shivered. Letting go of her hips, he spanned her waist and pushed her up.

Fuck.

She looked amazing straddling him, his cock buried deep, her hair tangled around her face and her breasts rosy, her nipples taut peaks of need and her bra twisted around her arms. Luc surged up, latched his mouth on one breast and sought her clit with one hand. The other, he pressed to the middle of her back and held her to him.

Cassie bucked when he found her clit. The hard nub was slick with her cream and he easily established a rhythm that had her hips rocking. He sucked her nipple, pressed it to the roof of his mouth and scraped it with his teeth. She thrashed as a spasm gripped her.

One long second of taut, stiff muscles and then she broke like glass, shattering around him in a rush of wet heat. Luc groaned, thrust in and out as she rode her orgasm. It was too much, not enough, and he flipped their positions and pinned her beneath him once more.

He plunged into her. Again and again. His muscles straining, his nerves flayed raw. Hard and fast, he drove himself to the finish line while Cassie continued to buck against him. In a blinding flash, his release slammed into him. Her hips cradled his as he plunged to the hilt one final time and let everything go.

"Cass!" He name tore from his throat, raw and desperate.

And as he spilled himself inside her he came crashing down to earth.

He wasn't wearing a condom.

assie felt Lucas come inside her and froze. Oh God. They hadn't used protection. They'd totally forgotten. She tried to catch her breath. Tried to think, remember where in her cycle she was. Oh God. This couldn't be happening. After being so careful earlier they'd screwed up completely.

"Cass." Lucas cuddled her close. "Shit, Cass, I'm sorry."

She knew he wasn't apologizing for the sex but for a split second doubt entered.

"You drive me so fucking insane I totally forgot to protect you." He brushed the hair from her face and she was forced to open her eyes and look at him. "What do you want to do?"

"Um…" She had no idea what to think, never mind what to say.

He took a deep breath. "Look there's no point stressing over it now. What's done is done. We'll be more careful from now on."

Cassie could only nod.

"And whatever happens, we're in this together." Lucas bent forward, pressed his mouth to hers in a soft kiss. "No matter what."

She didn't want to think about what could be happening inside her right now. The idea of possibly being pregnant scared the crap out of her. Actually being pregnant would probably send her into cardiac arrest. Pushing it aside, she smiled. "I'm sure it'll be fine. I don't think it's the right time." Cassie prayed she was right.

Lucas stroked a finger down her cheek. "I'm sure you're right."

From your lips to God's ear.

Her smile wobbled, but she refused to fall apart. She'd never folded under pressure before and she wouldn't start now. And there was no point borrowing trouble. When and *if* the time came she'd deal with it. She stared into Lucas's concerned eyes. No. They'd deal with it. Together.

11

Cassie woke to warm sunshine and the delicious aroma of fresh coffee. Opening her eyes, she found Lucas sitting on the bed beside her, mug in hand. She smiled and sat up. The sheet fell away, revealing her naked torso, and she grabbed at it to cover her breasts.

He chuckled. "Bit late for modesty, don't ya think?"

Heat flooded her face and she ducked her head. "Probably."

"Here. I made you coffee." Lucas passed her the warm mug. "Slug that down and then throw this on and join me in the kitchen for breakfast." He held out a shirt.

She shouldn't be self-conscious. After all they'd done last night and into the wee hours of the morning, embarrassment should be the last thing she felt. "Thanks."

Lucas stood. "I'll be in the kitchen."

Cassie watched him go. His ass was showcased in a pair of board shorts this morning, his torso bare, and she shivered. Heat flashed through her as the video reel of last night played in her head.

They'd used three condoms after that first time, and the twinge between her legs reminded her if the empty foil packets on the bedside table didn't. He'd driven her just about out of her mind. Though she had to admit she'd done an equal job on him.

Neither of them seemed to be able to keep their hands to themselves until complete exhaustion took them under.

She smiled. Her body might have had a serious workout, but even the soreness couldn't take away from the pleasure she'd received from Lucas's hands and mouth—his cock.

Crossing her legs, she squeezed her thighs together in an attempt to ease the ache working its way to a full-on throb. If she didn't detour her train of thought, she'd be jumping him in the kitchen. Cassie put the cup on the side table and then grabbed the T-shirt he'd given her and threw it over her head. The sleeves came past her elbows, and when she stood the hem hit below her knees. Definitely not a fashion statement, but the thrill of wearing something that belong to him far outweighed the hobo look.

Besides, the soft fabric smelled of Lucas. She bent her head, rubbed her nose against her shoulder and breathed deep. Her belly fluttered, her sex clenched. Damn. She'd better pull it together or they'd be spending the day in bed.

Not that that would be a bad thing. Oh no, that would be a very, very good thing. But they'd made a deal and she needed to keep her end of it like he had yesterday. Today she'd make him an apple pie and do anything else he asked of her. Cassie grinned. Hopefully he'd ask for more of what they'd done last night.

With a smile on her face, coffee in hand and his borrowed shirt brushing against her skin, she made her way to the kitchen and the man who'd turned her world inside out and upside down in a few hours of tangled sheets and mutual satisfaction.

Luc turned the bacon over and glanced out the window. He needed to think about today's plan. Cassie would expect to work. Would assume he would boss her around, and she'd be correct, only he intended his orders to make her have fun. From what he could gather she didn't switch off very often. Someone needed to help her remember there was more to life than work. And he was just the man to do it.

"Mmm...something smells good."

He glanced over his shoulder and watched her climb onto a stool at the breakfast counter. The shirt he'd loaned her slipped down one arm, revealing creamy skin and reminding him of kissing the delicate line of her collarbone last night. Luc gulped, had to clear his throat before he could speak.

"Bacon and eggs. Do you want your eggs scrambled or fried?"

"Whatever you're having." She took a sip of coffee.

"Scrambled it is." He turned back to the stove and finished off their breakfast.

When he put her full plate in front of her, she leaned over and took a big sniff. "God, I'm starving." She picked up her fork and dug in.

For long moments, he forgot about his food and watched Cassie devour hers. He loved that she wasn't one of those females who ate nothing and complained about being fat. She'd eaten a few mouthfuls when she noticed he wasn't eating and looked up.

"What's wrong?" she asked around a forkful of eggs. "Do I have something on my face?"

He smiled. "No. I just like looking at you." Luc dug into his breakfast.

"Oh."

Luc grinned wider. "Finish up, we've got a lot on today."

"We do?"

"Yep." He didn't elaborate. Let her wonder. It would do her good to have a day where she wasn't thinking about what she needed to do next.

They were silent for a few minutes, Luc eating his food and Cassie eyeing him across the counter.

"You aren't going to tell me?" she asked as she picked up her coffee mug.

"Nope. It's a surprise." He scooped up his last bite of eggs.

She scowled. "I'm not overly fond of surprises."

"I'm sure you aren't, but I can guarantee all of today's surprises will be good." He picked up his empty plate and headed for the sink. "When you're done come join me in the bedroom."

Luc left the kitchen and an open-mouthed Cassie behind him as he made his way to his room and the first part of the spoil-Cassie day he had planned. He entered the master bathroom and dropped the plug in the big Jacuzzi tub. Flipping on the water tap, he waited for the hot water to come through before adjusting the cold.

She'd winced as she taken a seat in the kitchen, and he figured she'd be sore after they'd spent the night all but swinging from the ceiling. Hell, he was sore and he prided himself on his physical fitness.

He grabbed a couple of fresh towels and laid them on the counter within easy reach of the bath. He'd like to join her in the tub, but if she'd prefer to enjoy the spa jets on her own he'd let her. Today was about what Cassie wanted to do, not what Luc wanted to do to her. The water was halfway when she came in.

"What are you doing?"

"Running a bath."

"Why?"

Luc pulled her into him for a hug. "Because I'm sure you're sore and the jets will help ease your aches." Her face flushed pink and he tucked her head under his chin. "You can either hop in on your own or I can join you and help scrub your back."

She took a deep breath, her breasts pressing against his bare chest. The thin cotton of his shirt did nothing to disguise the hard tips of her breasts. "Join me."

He sucked in a breath. Although he'd wanted her to ask, the idea of spending the next thirty minutes with a naked, wet Cassie had every cell primed and ready. How he'd survive without taking her was anyone's guess. Luc certainly didn't have a clue how he was going to keep this bath from turning into more than a wash-your-back-you-wash-mine event. Drawing on every ounce of control he had, he let her go and stepped over to switch off the taps.

Without looking at her, Luc shucked his shorts and climbed into the tub, his back against the side, he held out his hand for Cassie to join him. His pulse picked up speed as she stripped her shirt over her head.

Her breasts, stomach and thighs were marked red from where his beard stubble had rubbed against her smooth skin and his groin throbbed with renewed need. Not that the desire for Cassie ever went away. Even the second after he emptied inside her he wanted her. She was a drug and he was addicted.

His system had taken one taste, one sip of her essence and craved more. He'd known the second he'd laid his lips on hers in the pantry Friday night. That one kiss had sealed both their fates.

The only question now was whether Cassie would let them have more than one weekend. Luc wasn't about to settle for only two days with this incredible woman. No matter what it took, he'd convince her there was more than a flash of undeniable chemistry between them.

She took his hand and he spread his legs so she could sit down, her back to him. He wrapped his arm around her waist and tugged her backward until her ass nestled snugly against his semi-hard cock. Ignoring his body's reaction to her closeness, Luc picked up the soap.

Lathering his hands, he slid them across her stomach. No inch went untouched as he concentrated on washing her soft skin. His strokes weren't designed to work her up, but her nipples pebbled, her tummy quivered and her backside squirmed against him as he continued to wash her.

He trailed his hands down her hips and over her thighs as far as he could reach before dragging them back up and across her stomach once more. Skimming her ribs, he skirted around her breasts, along her collarbones and up her neck.

She leaned her head against him and a small moan slipped from between her lips. His cock hardened at the little sound, and he ground his teeth and bit the inside of his cheek to take his mind off his own need. She shivered beneath his fingers as he scraped his hands over her shoulders and down her arms.

Luc stroked the curve of her elbows, traced the delicate bones of her wrists and threaded his fingers through hers. She was soft and warm, like molten wax against him, and he couldn't help smiling.

Her skin flushed pink and every muscle in her body was lax. He didn't know if it was the result of the warm water or his gentle care. Either would make him happy. He'd set out to relax her, to give her a few minutes of peace and pleasure and he'd accomplished that with a simple bath. If the rest of the day went this well he'd have Cassie seduced and agreeable to anything he wanted.

And he wanted her.

More than a weekend. More than a few days snatched from the real world. He wanted her in his life and he wanted in hers. It scared the shit out of him, these deep emotions for a woman he hardly knew.

But he'd never backed down from his fears before, and he knew gut deep that he and Cassie had stumbled across something remark-able. Something not many people found. His heart thundered and his stomach clenched as he thought about where this connection could go.

The water was starting to cool and he hadn't washed her back yet. He needed to move things along. There were other things he wanted to do with Cassie today, and while this leisurely soak was satisfying, it was also torture.

His nerves were strung taut, his body tense with desire for the woman in his arms, and it was taking all his effort to keep things on this side of the line. One too many strokes of his hands over her lush curves and Luc's control would snap. With that in mind, he shifted behind her and, curling his fingers over her shoulders, pushed her forward.

"Sit up. I'll wash your back before we get out."

She bent her legs and, wrapping her arms around them, rested her forehead on her knees. Her spine was a smooth curve in front of him and he grabbed the soap to lather his hands once more.

With slow, gentle strokes, Luc worked his way from her shoulders to the sweet little dip above her ass and back again. Moans of plea-sure and sighs of breath filled the moist air surrounding them and his cock throbbed with each one. He'd need a cold shower or a quick hand job if he didn't plan to jump Cassie.

Luc didn't linger, although the urge to was great. He smoothed his hands down her spine one last time before gripping her waist and helping her to her feet. "Hop in the shower to rinse off." He stood behind her, keeping his eyes away from the tempting slope of her bottom.

She turned and slid her hands up his chest and around his neck. Their bodies drew flush and she couldn't miss his arousal with it pressing into her belly. "Thank you." Using her arms to pull him down, she rose up on her toes and kissed him.

It didn't last long. And while the brush of her mouth on his was almost platonic, there was no way she could hide the desire in her eyes. But he understood what she was doing. She was keeping things light, not stepping over the invisible line he'd drawn with his actions. Luc smiled and dropped his forehead to rest on hers. "You're welcome."

They remained standing in the bath, breathing each other in for several heartbeats. Luc finally found the willpower to let her go. Stepping over the tub, he held out his hand and waited for Cassie to follow. No words were spoken, and though he wanted to say so many, he couldn't find the right ones. Not when all he could think of were words that would no doubt send her running for the hills. He wasn't ready to be thinking them, never mind say them. Giving himself a mental shake, he reached into the shower recess and turned on the water.

"Hop in." Luc nudged Cassie's hip with his hand. "Rinse off and then I'll grab a quick shower."

She turned to look at him. "You're not getting in with me?" Her gaze drifted down his body to stop at his erect cock.

He swallowed. "Ah, no, I'll get in after you're done."

Cassie frowned. Little creases formed between her eyebrows. Luc used his thumb to smooth them out.

"Just rinse off, Cass." He pushed her until she stepped beneath the warm spray.

Luc might not have wanted to tempt either of them by getting in with her, but he couldn't bring himself to leave the bathroom either. He watched as she closed her eyes and dipped her face under the water and let it flow down her chest. Turning, she ran her fingers through her hair and soaked the dark strands. She opened her eyes and reached for his shampoo.

"Mind if I use this?"

The idea of her smelling like him all day made his throat go dry. "No," he croaked.

She smiled and got to work on lathering her hair. He couldn't take his eyes off her. With each flex of her fingers his cock pulsed, and he hadn't even thought about moving when he found himself standing beside her, tangling his own fingers in her sudsy hair.

"Oh, yeah," Cassie murmured when he dug his fingertips into the back of her neck.

He massaged her scalp. From neck to temple, Luc turned a simple hair wash into an erotic delight. They were both panting and breathing hard by the time he was done. Tilting her head back, he said, "Keep your eyes shut."

"You're good at this." She rested her hands on his chest. "Do it often?"

Luc could hear the smile in her voice, but he glanced down to make sure she wasn't thinking he spent his time in the shower washing a woman's hair. "No. You'd be the first."

Her eyes popped open and the honey-brown churned with myriad emotions he couldn't name. "I'm glad." A smile turned up one corner of her mouth and he leaned down to kiss the spot.

The kiss quickly turned liquid. Heat and passion that had slowly built over the last half hour exploded between them. Luc sucked her tongue into his mouth. He nipped with his teeth, nibbled with his lips. All the while Cassie fought to do the same.

He slid his hand down her back to grip her ass and he lifted her off her feet and pressed her into the wall next to them. She growled into his mouth as his cock lined up with her clit. Her legs slid around him and she yanked their bodies closer.

His cock throbbed, his balls ached and all his good intentions went out the window. He flexed his hips, pulling back until he probed her opening. With one thrust, he drove himself home.

A ragged moan filled the air and Luc didn't know if it was his or hers. Didn't care. The only thing he cared about was slamming in and out of her body. Plunging hard and fast, he took them both up in record time. She bit into his shoulder as the first shudder racked her. As her orgasm tore through her, it ricocheted into him and shoved him over the edge.

The first spurt of come had his brain engaging. "Fuck!" He pulled out of her clasping pussy and spilt the rest of his seed on her thighs. It was pointless, the damage was done. He'd put them both at risk a second time, and even if Cassie could forgive him he wasn't sure he could forgive himself.

Cassie shuddered on the final waves of her release. Her chest heaved as she dragged in each breath. Lucas held her pinned to the tiles with his body but his cock now lay pressed against her leg. She swallowed around the lump in her throat.

Shit!

They'd forgotten protection. Again. It couldn't happen again. But something about Lucas was proving irresistible. She'd never been so out of her mind with anyone else. And she'd never come so hard or so many times with any other guy either.

She laid her head back against the wall and dragged her heavy eyelids up. He was staring at her, his expression one of self-recrimination, and she couldn't let him take the fall for something they were both responsible for. "It's not all your fault."

The skin around his eyes creased as his mouth kicked up in smile. "Yeah, it is. I shouldn't have climbed in here with you."

Cassie couldn't let him take the blame, especially when she'd purposely tempted him with her nakedness when he'd said he wasn't joining her. "You can't help it if I'm too tempting to resist." She wiggled her eyebrow suggestively and rocked her hips against him in an attempt to lighten the mood.

Except Lucas's expression turned serious again. "You have no idea."

With the cryptic remark, he lowered her to her feet and once she was steady, stepped back under the shower. He rinsed himself quickly then grabbed her wrist and tugged her beneath the spray.

"Rinse off. I'll get your towel." He slipped out of the glass enclosure and wrapped a towel around his waist. Picking up another one, he held it out and waited for her to finish.

He studied her. Numerous emotions flashed across his face and Cassie tried to decipher them. She couldn't tell if he was upset about their latest mindless coupling or not, but she sought to reassure him anyway. "I'll check my calendar as soon as I'm dressed. I'm pretty sure we're safe, but I think both of us could use something a little more concrete than my memory."

Lucas nodded as she turned the water off and stepped onto the bathmat in front of him. He didn't comment and remained silent as he used the towel he held to rub her dry. She wanted to take it off him and do it herself. Give them both a breather to collect their thoughts, but she couldn't deny herself the pleasure of Lucas's touch.

One more piece of evidence that pointed to her inability to resist this man. Whether their unprotected sex resulted in an unplanned pregnancy or not, Cassie knew she was still in trouble. Lucas Wilhelm was someone she could fall for. Hard. She had to guard her heart for the rest of their time together. No matter what, she couldn't expect to see him again after their challenge was over.

12

Cassie growled in frustration. Lucas had twisted away from her again. He'd been doing it all day. Ever since they'd gotten carried away in the shower he'd kept his distance, and she couldn't help wondering if he was pulling back because of their carelessness.

Concerned about their second bout of reckless abandon, she'd checked her calendar. What she discovered put her mind at ease and she'd let Lucas know it was unlikely she'd get pregnant. Of course, they still had to wait to be sure.

It wasn't only his physical withdrawal that had her confused. Their day had been nothing like she'd expected. After their shower he'd loaned her a shirt and drawstring shorts and they'd headed into his front yard to wash his car.

What should have been a simple process turned into a water fight. By the time they were finished they'd been drenched from head to toe and Cassie had needed another shower to get the suds out of her hair. Dressed in her own clothes, Lucas had led her back to his car and driven them into Darling Harbour where they'd had a delicious lunch in a harbor-side cafe while watching the parade of people passing by.

The only time they'd touched was when they accidently brushed up against each other. He hadn't even held her hand when they walked from his car to the restaurant. And now, as they strolled along the water's edge, there was at least two feet of space between them.

She missed his touch—the closeness that had developed between them—and she couldn't ignore the twinge of regret that pinched her chest. If she hadn't caught him looking at her with hungry eyes, Cassie might think he'd had his fill of her and was simply waiting for their time together to be over.

They were slowly making their way back to the car. Lucas hadn't told her what was on the agenda next, and even with her emotions in a jumble, she was looking forward to finding out what he had planned. So far, even with the mixed signals he was sending her as well as her own seesawing feelings toward Lucas, the day had been great.

Cassie couldn't remember the last time she'd smiled so much. She'd overused her facial muscles to the point that her cheeks hurt. And she'd learned a lot about Lucas and his life. He might have pulled back from her physically, but he'd been an open book otherwise.

She'd never had more fun with a guy she liked. And even though she always had a good time with Dan and West, they didn't count. She didn't feel anything for them beyond friendship. With Lucas she felt friendship, lust and a connection she couldn't quite put a label on.

Something deep and absolutely scary.

If any other man had given her the hot-cold treatment she'd have walked away. Cassie couldn't walk away from Lucas no matter how much she told herself she should. Her inability to resist him sent a shiver down her spine.

"Cold?" Lucas moved closer and slipped his arm around her shoulder.

Not willing to admit the truth or give up the contact with him, Cassie lied. "A little. The breeze is always cool coming off the water."

"We'll be at the car park and out of this wind soon." He tugged her in tight against his side.

To her relief, Lucas didn't pull away when they entered the parking garage. Instead, he steered them toward his car with her tucked under his arm. Their height difference meant she fit snugly against him, he didn't need to lean down and Cassie didn't feel as though she should walk on her toes. In spite of him being almost a foot taller, he was the most physically compatible man she'd ever been out with. Not that they were dating. Or that they would.

She sighed. All this mental to and fro was making her tired. Reaching his car, she reluctantly slipped from Lucas's embrace and sank into the soft leather of the passenger seat. Once she was settled, he closed the door and walked around the hood to the driver's side. With the push of a button, the car purred to life and they were soon on their way. Lucas drove for ten minutes before Cassie couldn't contain her curiosity any longer.

"Where are we going now?"

"Back to my place." He took his eyes off the road for a second and grinned at her. "It's time for you to make my pie."

Cassie had forgotten all about his request for a fresh-baked apple pie. A thrill shot through her. If she was making him a pie then he wouldn't be shoving her out the door the second they got back. She knew more time in his company would only make her fall deeper for this compelling man, but she couldn't bring herself to be unhappy their weekend wasn't over. In fact, the butterflies currently swooping in her stomach were a testament to how pleased she was Monday hadn't arrived yet.

Luc knew Cassie was confused by his withdrawal. He owed her an explanation, but he couldn't bring himself to give her one. It was bad enough admitting his lack of control to himself. There was no way he would tell her he couldn't restrain his lust.

Ravaging her in public wouldn't endear him to her, and there was a good chance of that happening if he touched her. He'd seen the sideways glances, the frown marring her pretty face, and he hadn't missed any of her attempts to initiate contact. If they made it home without him pulling over and swooping in for a kiss it would be a miracle.

Mid-Sunday afternoon traffic was light, but the drive to his house took over thirty minutes. Silence hung between them like a thundercloud—heavy, dark and filled with electric tension that had the hairs on his arms standing on end. He'd done that to them. Turned their easy, friendly rapport into a strained acquaintance. He needed to get them back to where they'd been before they'd left his house this morning. Luc could only hope it was possible.

"Is there anything you need at the shops?" he asked, trying to break the unease between them.

"No. We picked up everything I need yesterday."

"Only a few more minutes and we'll be home."

Their conversation stopped and Luc racked his brain for something to say. He came up empty. Cursing himself a fool, he pushed the accelerator down harder and nudged the car over the speed limit to reach their destination quicker. Not wanting to get into a discussion about his behavior in the car, he kept quiet for the last few minutes of the trip. As he pulled into his driveway his phone rang, the handsfree system blasting the sound through the car's speakers.

Luc didn't want to take the call where Cassie could listen. No one rang him except work, and while it was unlikely the conversation would hold any confidential information, he couldn't risk it, so he reached over and diverted the call to voicemail.

Let whoever it was leave a message. He'd get back to them once they were inside and Cassie was busy making his pie. He pulled up in front of his garage and Cassie had her seatbelt off and was opening her door before the engine stopped ticking. It seemed as though she couldn't get out of the car and away from him fast enough.

Slipping from the car, he took a deep breath before he followed her along the path. He fished his keys from his pocket and unlocked the door. The alarm beeped, letting him know he had sixty seconds to punch in his pin code or have the security company notifying the police of a break-in. Stabbing at the keypad with more pressure than necessary, he disengaged the system. Cassie closed the door behind her and Luc activated the at-home mode.

They made their way into the kitchen and Cassie went straight to the fridge to pull out ingredients. He watched as she efficiently set out the food then began opening cupboards looking for bowls. Taking pity on her, Luc walked over and pulled out what she needed.

"Do you want a mixer?" he asked.

"No, I like to do the pastry by hand. I need a saucepan though, for the apples." She patted the bag of fruit on the counter.

"I would have been fine with tinned ones."

"Nope. Fresh means fresh." She took the apples to the sink. "What drawer is the peeler in?"

"Second down." Luc peered into the cupboard with his saucepans. "How big do you want the pan?"

"Medium."

He pulled out the one he thought would work and placed it on the stove. "Do you mind if I go and check my voicemail while you get started?"

"No, go ahead. I'll be fine here. If I need something I'll just open every door and drawer in the place 'til I find what I'm after." She smiled at him.

"Okay. I shouldn't be long." Luc went to his office with the sound of Cassie puttering around his kitchen echoing behind him. His lips curved up in a grin. He could definitely get used to hearing her in his house.

His phone call turned out to be an update on the fallout from Friday night's party, and Luc found himself back in the kitchen watching Cassie roll the pastry while the apples gently bubbled away on the stove. She hadn't noticed him, so he stayed where he was and leaned on the wall. Her hands drew his gaze, or more precisely her long, slender fingers working the mound of dough.

He remembered what it was like to have those hands and fingers on his skin. A shudder stole through him and he had to shift his stance to make room for his growing cock.

The movement caught her eye and she glanced up with a smile.

"Are you going to stand there all day or are you planning to make yourself useful?"

Luc grinned. She had asked him almost the exact same question Friday night. He pushed off the wall and closed the distance in a few easy strides. "What do you want me to do?"

"I could do with a drink."

"What would you like? I've got juice, soft drink, water or wine?" He opened the fridge and pulled out juice for himself.

"A glass of wine would be nice." She glanced over her shoulder at him. "Oh, but don't open a bottle just for me."

"It's fine. You can have a glass now and we'll have the rest with dinner."

Her eyes widened and then her lips spread into a smile that lit up her whole face. "In that case, yes, please. I'll have wine."

He selected a wine from the fridge, a sweet, refreshing one perfect for a summer afternoon drink. She'd seemed surprised when he'd mentioned dinner, and Luc figured she'd thought after today he would send her packing once she'd made him the apple pie. She was in for a bigger surprise, because not only did he plan to keep her here through dinner, but if he had his way she'd be spending another night in his bed.

Cassie sat back with her wine glass cradled in her hands. Across the table from her, Lucas dug into his third piece of apple pie. She smiled. He certainly wasn't worried about eating a whole pie. The first slice she'd cut for him had been rejected.

Too small.

He'd taken the knife and cut himself a quarter instead. There was less than a quarter of the pie left. Her tiny piece had been more than enough to satisfy her, but Lucas seemed to be eating each mouthful like it was his first.

He forked up the final bite from his bowl and eyed the pie dish. Glancing at her, he asked, "You want any more?"

She shook her head. "No, I'm good."

A grin spread across his face as he reached for the remaining pie. He didn't bother serving it up, just ate it from the plate. When he was done he leaned back and closed his eyes, his hand splayed over his washboard abs. "Damn, that was good."

The compliment sent warmth rushing through her. She was pleased he'd enjoyed the dessert. More pleased than she should be probably, but there was no stopping the thrill of delight that buzzed in her veins, or the smile that stretched her lips as she watched Lucas devour every last crumb. "Glad you liked it."

"Mmm..." He rubbed his hand in circles, drawing her gaze to the perfect ridges of his stomach. "That's the best pie I've ever had."

"Flattery won't get you anywhere." Cassie went for humor in the hope of squashing the over-inflated bubble of elation filling her heart. "I bet you say that to all the pie makers."

His eyes popped open and that dark gaze lasered hers. She swallowed over the lump in her throat. "I'm not known for flattery," he murmured. "If I tell you the pie is the best, it's the best."

"Oh." Cassie's hands twisted in her lap.

"I've noticed you don't take compliments very well." He leaned forward and snagged a lock of her hair. Tugging, he pulled her closer. "You make great pie, Cass."

Heat flamed in her cheeks. His praise brought equal embarrassment and delight.

He gave her hair a sharp yank. "Say thank you, Luc."

"T-thank you, Luc."

His eyes widened, his nostrils flaring as he sucked in a breath. "Say it again."

Puzzled, Cassie complied. "Thank you."

"No, no." He let go of her hair and cupped her jaw. "Say my name, Cass."

"Lucas?"

"No." His thumb brushed over her lower lip sending a shiver down her neck, goose bumps in its wake. "Not my full name. Luc. Say Luc again."

"Luc."

He closed his eyes and sighed. "That's the first time you've called me Luc." His eyelids rose halfway and he licked his lips. "I want to hear you say it when I make you come."

Cassie's breath stalled, her heart raced and goose bumps broke out from head to toe. Heat pooled between her legs and her pussy clenched. A few words and she was primed and ready. It took so little work on his part to have her panting for breath and begging to be taken. She'd never experienced arousal this intense—this immediate —with anyone but Lucas.

"Let's get all this cleaned up." He stroked her jaw as he pulled away. "Don't want to wake up tomorrow to a mess like I did this morning."

Lucas pushed back his chair and stood as he piled the dirty plates. Cassie's pulse sprinted and she couldn't seem to catch her breath. How could he say what he did and not be affected? She had trouble breathing never mind thinking about dirty dishes. Her hands trembled and she gripped the table edge to steady herself. He had her so off-balance. He'd been almost chaste in his behavior today, and now he was talking about making her come.

She'd barely gotten to her feet when he disappeared into the house. She closed her eyes, took a deep breath and pressed her hands to her fluttering stomach. Aroused as much as she was confused, Cassie forced her chaotic thoughts to the back of her mind and concentrated on helping clean up.

They'd abandoned last night's dinner for Lucas's bed, and she was mortified to realize he'd cleared up their mess before she'd woken this morning. Even more shameful was the fact she'd completely forgotten about it until he'd mentioned it just now.

Lecturing herself on her shoddy manners, she collected the rest of their dishes and followed Lucas into the kitchen. He was already stacking the dishwasher and he took her handful and pointed toward the breakfast counter.

"Take a seat. I'll have these dealt with in no time then we can decide what movie to watch." He turned away and got busy.

"Movie?" He hadn't mentioned anything about going out. "Are we going out?"

"Nah, I've got a good selection of movies. There's bound to be something you want to see." Luc glanced over his shoulder. "Your job is to choose one."

"Is that an order?" she asked.

"Yes." He grabbed the tea towel from the bench and flicked it at her. "Now get going."

She laughed. "I'm sure our movie tastes run in different directions. I doubt you'd have anything I'd like."

He grinned. "You'd be surprised. But it doesn't matter. I'm the boss and I say you have to pick a movie to watch."

"The boss, huh?" She arched one eyebrow.

"Yep." He tapped his watch. "It's still my twenty-four hours."

Cassie waited for him to continue but he only turned back to the dirty dishes and finished loading the washer. She wandered over to the family room. A large TV mounted on the wall dominated the left side of the room and a big sectional lounge filled the opposite one. The wall across from the entry was covered in bookshelves filled with books and movies. Walking over she began to scan Lucas's selection.

"Find anything yet?" She hadn't heard him come up behind her.

"Yeah, but I doubt you'll agree with my choice."

"I told you, it's your choice." He cupped his hands on her shoulders and she leaned back into him. "Which one did you want?"

"*An American President*."

"Excellent movie." Lucas stepped around her and grabbed the DVD from the shelf. "Do you want another glass of wine? Popcorn?"

Cassie groaned. "I couldn't eat another bite of food if you held me down and shoved it in my mouth, and I think I've had my quota of wine today already. I've had three glasses to your two."

He waggled his eyebrows. "All part of my plan to take advantage of you."

Laughing, she walked over to the couch. "I think you've proved you don't need to get me drunk to do that."

Lucas grinned at her before turning to the complicated looking system beside the TV. It took him only seconds to load the disc and join her on the most comfortable couch she'd ever sat on.

"Ready?" He held the remote in his hand.

"Yep."

He pressed a few buttons and not only did the movie start playing but the lights dimmed as well. "Wow. That's cool."

Shrugging he said, "What can I say? I'm into gadgets."

Cassie smiled. What guy wasn't? She snuggled down next to Lucas and waited for the movie to start. She'd watched *An American President* at least a dozen times, but it never failed to pull her in and make her all gooey and romantic. Unfortunately, tonight wasn't like every other time she'd seen it. Tonight all she could think about—concentrate on—was the man next to her and the heat radiating off his body.

He wrapped his arm around her and she sank into his cozy warmth. Relaxed, Cassie let the anxiety of earlier go and soon found her eyelids drooping. Cuddled up next to Lucas, she slowly slipped off to sleep.

13

Luc skimmed a finger down Cassie's cheek. She twitched but didn't wake. She'd fallen asleep halfway through the movie and he'd decided not to wake her in favor of sitting through the rest of the film with her curled up next to him.

He was selfish enough to not want to give up the pleasure of having her asleep beside him, not to mention the trust she showed by doing so. After last night and today he'd wondered if perhaps she didn't feel the same deep connection he did, or had he destroyed it with his mixed signals?

He'd confused her today. Hell, he'd confused himself too.

He couldn't explain the reasoning behind his behavior because what had seemed the right thing earlier in hindsight appeared completely wrong. He'd complicated the situation by trying to manage it. From now on he'd think less and act more. Speaking of acting.

"Cass," he whispered in her ear. "Time for bed, baby."

"Hmm..." She turned her face into his chest.

"C'mon, sleepyhead." Luc scooped her up in his arms and stood. "Let's go to bed."

She wrapped her arms around his neck and nuzzled his throat, her lips warm against his skin. He tried to concentrate on making it to his room and not on the hot woman in his arms. Once they hit the bed though, all bets were off and he'd be all over her. She'd soon be wide-awake.

"Lucas?" Her words were rough with sleep.

"Yeah."

"I should go home. We both have work tomorrow."

His grip tightened. "Not on your life, sweetheart. You still owe me a few hours."

"Oh."

She didn't attempt to get out of his hold and Luc took that as a good sign. And right now he would take whatever he could get because he had a horrible feeling Cassie was going to use every argument she could think of to end their time together for good the minute their challenge was over.

Luc lowered her to his bed and stepped back. "Hop under the covers while I go lock up the house."

He left the room without looking back. The sight of Cassie in his bed would stop him from walking away, even if it was only to shut the house down for the night, he didn't think he could pull himself away from her all sleep-tousled on his sheets.

Luc made quick work of closing the deck doors and then switching off lights. Lastly, he set the alarm to sleep mode and was back in his room as Cassie climbed beneath the covers. A flash of bare thigh had his cock aching and his fists clenching.

Luc would love nothing more than making Cassie more than a little rumpled, but if all she wanted was to go back to sleep he'd grit his teeth and bite his cheek for the duration. Of course, he'd wrap his arms around her and try to convince her it was worth staying awake for a few hours yet.

With a grin, he whipped his shirt up over his head and shucked his pants. Cassie stared at him with wide eyes, her gaze glued to his rapidly filling erection. Naked, he walked to the bed and slid in beside her.

The big king-size bed meant that she was too far away, so he reached over and dragged her close. She didn't protest and he took advantage. Slipping his arms around her, he turned her so her back was to his front. Spooned together, he took a moment to savor the sensation of having her in his arms.

It didn't take long for desire to take over. He started slow, running his hands over her stomach and along her ribs in sweeping caresses that were designed to inflame. When her ass began to wiggle against his groin, he knew his attention was accomplishing its purpose.

He moved his hand up and palmed her breast. The nipple puckered tight and pressed into his palm. He trailed his other hand down her side, over her hip and into the dip between thigh and body.

A sweet little moan slipped from her throat and egged him on. Moving lower, he found her slit, wet with need, and wiggled a finger between her folds. She was slick and hot to the touch, and he was helpless to stop his hips from rocking into her ass.

She thrust back and he lost all thought of going slow. Gripping her thigh, Luc raised her leg and slid his cock along her pussy from behind. Her head arched back, and another sultry moan broke free. His sac tightened, drawing his balls up into his body in preparation for release.

He flexed his pelvis in several fast pumps that drove his shaft through her silken folds and spread her juices over both of them. Heat scorched his skin, spread through him like wildfire, and he knew in seconds his control would be a thing of the past.

Withdrawing, he leaned back and reached for one of the condoms he'd dumped on the bedside table earlier. He tore open the packet and sheathed himself in record time. Ready, he spooned behind Cassie and pulled her leg over his once more.

Angling his hips, he lined his head up with her drenched opening and drove forward in one hard thrust. She cried out, the sound ripping from her as her walls clamped around him.

He held still, buried to the hilt as he searched out the hard knot of nerves between her legs with his fingers. She pushed back against him and Luc moved with slow, steady strokes. Circling his fingertips on her clit and thrusting his cock into her soon had them both breathing hard and wanting more.

Cassie bucked, her hips thrashing back and forth as she worked herself up on his hand and cock in turn. Her gaspy breaths and sexy cries of pleasure drove him closer to the edge, but he held back, wanting her to reach the peak before him—waiting for her pussy to milk him of his orgasm.

"Luc," she cried out as she went over.

Her climax hit her hard and fast, slamming into her with such force that she almost dislodged his cock as her body undulated with each spasm. Heat—wet and slick—flowed over his shaft, easing the glide of his length as he drove it in and out of her body.

He gripped her hips and rolled until he pinned her beneath him. He dug his fingers into her soft flesh as he rammed himself in and out of her clenching pussy. Five quick thrusts and he was coming undone, filling the condom with spurt after spurt of come.

Spent, he collapsed forward. At the last second, he dropped his elbows to the bed and held his weight off her. Breathing hard, he tried to clear his mind and instruct his muscles to move. He forced himself into action and pulled from Cassie's still-quivering body, both of them making a cry of distress as their bodies separated.

He'd love to remain inside her until they drifted off to sleep but he needed to dispose of the used condom or wearing it would be pointless.

Luc headed to his en suite and dropped the rubber in the bin. He cleaned up and then grabbed a washcloth and dampened it with warm water. When he returned to Cassie he found her exactly where he'd left her. Face down with her beautiful rear end on full display. Smoothing his hand over the sleek curve of one cheek, he tapped her hip to get her to turn over.

"Let me get you cleaned up."

She mumbled something he didn't catch but rolled over. Luc parted her legs and wiped the cloth over her well-loved folds before tossing it aside and climbing back into bed with her. He pulled Cassie into his arms and tugged the covers over them. Her breasts were pressed into his side, her head rested on his shoulder and one leg lay draped over his.

A smile curled his mouth. This was exactly where he wanted to be. *She* was exactly where he wanted her to be. Now he just had to convince her it was what she wanted—where she belonged.

———

Cassie woke in the pre-dawn light and attempted to roll over, except something held her pinned to the bed. Lucas. He had one arm thrown over her waist, his chest plastered against her spine and his morning erection pressed between her ass cheeks. Aroused and embarrassed by their intimate position, she felt heat flood her face.

She tried to wiggle out of his grasp but the man wasn't budging, not without considerable effort, and after all they'd done she wasn't ready to face him yet.

So she lay there contemplating their weekend. Their challenge hadn't really been a challenge. They'd simply hung out together.

There was no bossing each other around and certainly no toes had been stepped on like she'd imaged when they'd shaken on the deal. She was forced to admit spending time with Lucas had been more than fun.

It had felt natural—right.

She'd never expected them to hit it off the way they had. Never expected this deep connection with someone who before Friday night had been a stranger.

She wasn't looking for a relationship, didn't have time with everything going on at work. Only Cassie couldn't bring herself to think about leaving him and never seeing him again. The thought alone produced a twinge in her chest and a heaviness that felt distinctly like sadness—regret. He'd made it clear he wanted more than one night, but did that mean he wanted more than the weekend?

"Stop thinking so hard." Lucas's deep voice rumbled in her ear, his warm breath bathing her neck. "It's too early to be awake."

Cassie smiled. "It's not that early. And I need to get home before going to work so I can't lie about in bed all morning."

"Ha, it's not even morning. Go back to sleep." He pulled her tighter against him.

She sighed. "I really do need to go soon."

"Not yet." He nuzzled the slope of skin beneath her ear. "Let me enjoy this pleasure a little while longer."

With no desire to leave his embrace, Cassie settled more fully against him. "Fine, but if I don't get out of here on time you're in trouble."

"Trouble? What kind of trouble?" He dragged his teeth over her ear and sent a shiver down her spine. "I can think of *all* kinds of trouble we could get into."

In spite of his deliberate twist to the subject, Cassie smiled. She could think of all kinds of trouble too. Starting with the hot rod of flesh poking her in the ass. Not wanting their time to end without one more taste of Lucas, she spun around and pushed him to his back.

Catching him by surprise, she was straddling his hips before he knew what hit him. Giving him no time to protest or take control, she took his mouth with hers and rocked her pussy on his cock.

He groaned into her mouth as he thrust his tongue deep. She tangled her tongue with his while she mapped his sculpted chest and abs with her hands. The man was to die for yummy and Cassie wanted to lick every inch of him.

Her pulse sped up and her blood heated, rushing through her body at lightning speed. It happened every time they came together. Each joining only increased the craving instead of satisfying it. She'd already had all of him and yet she yearned for more.

Cassie traced his bottom lip with her tongue, scraped it with her teeth and pulled it into her mouth to suckle. He let her have her way.

For long moments, she controlled their kiss until her thirst for more of him drove her to take her lips on a journey over his stubbled chin, down the strong column of his throat to the broad expanse of his chest. She breathed in his scent as she made her way to the flat brown nipple nestled within the smattering of dark hair. Flicking with the tip of her tongue, she soon had the small disc puckering tight.

Lucas moaned and drove his fingers through her hair when she moved over to his other nipple and lavished it with the same attention. His cock grew harder where it rested against her stomach and Cassie pressed into him to add to his pleasure. He groaned and rocked his hips up, thrusting his length back and forth over her skin. She wanted to taste him. Wanted to wrap her lips around the head and suck him deep until he was lodged in her throat.

She raised her head and caught his gaze. With their eyes locked, she crawled down his body until her mouth hovered over his engorged cock. Breathing deep, she inhaled his masculine scent. It was stronger here—more potent. Her insides quivered at the tempting aroma and her mouth watered with anticipation of his taste.

Lucas's gaze clung to hers as Cassie lowered her head and pressed a closed-mouth kiss on the swollen crown. Liquid beaded in the slit and, never taking her eyes off his, she lapped it up with the flat of her tongue.

He tightened his fingers in her hair, tugging the strands and sending a zap of pain shooting over her scalp. The sting shuddered through her and settled in her belly, curling deep and contracting muscles as desire burned hotter. She slipped her lips around the head and closed her eyes at the taste and feel of him on her tongue.

Sucking hard, Cassie took him to the back of her throat in a quick slide before instantly reversing until her lips once again surrounded the mushroom tip. Fast lashes of her tongue along the sensitive rim drew a staggered breath and bucking hips.

She repeated the action. Again and again. With each stroke, she pulled him closer to release and Cassie's own arousal climbed. Her cheeks hollowed when she sucked him deep, her teeth grazed as she let him out and all the while her tongue caressed every inch of his shaft.

Cassie brought her hand up to cup his balls. Squeezing gently, she tugged and fondled until Lucas's breath was no more than ragged pants and his hand tangled in her hair. His cock pulsed against her tongue and he yanked on her hair. Hard.

"Stop," he gasped. "Shit. Stop. I want to be inside you when I come."

Cassie's lips barely cleared his flesh when he grabbed her arms and flipped her over onto her back. He came down on top of her, his hips settling between hers, his hot length pressed into the folds of her drenched pussy, and she widened her legs farther. She arched, rubbed her needy pussy against his erection and, with her hands on his head, dragged his mouth down to hers.

She wasn't in control this time. Lucas took with wicked greed. He left nothing untouched, allowed nothing but surrender to his demands, and Cassie reveled in his need for her. Basked in the pure hunger he refused to hide. He gripped her hips, tilted them to his liking as he rocked his pelvis into hers. Her pussy wept as he thrust his cock along her slick folds. Lucas pulled his mouth from hers.

"Condom." He indicated the bedside table with his head. "Now."

Cassie reached over and grabbed a foil packet. She tore it open and Lucas snatched the protection from her hand. He pushed to his knees between her legs and sheathed himself quickly. She'd barely taken a breath—blinked—when he was back on top of her, thrusting his cock deep in one smooth stroke. Buried to the hilt, Lucas gazed down at her, emotions she didn't want to acknowledge burning in his eyes.

She closed her eyes and tucked her face into his neck. Flexing her hips, she urged him to move and tried to pretend this was nothing more than great sex, a physical connection that didn't go beneath the surface. But as Lucas drove in and out of her clutching body, Cassie knew she was lying.

"Look at me, Cass." Lucas stopped moving and brushed his fingers over her cheek.

He kept up the gentle caress on her face and Cassie had no choice but to do as he asked. Taking a deep breath, she leaned her head back and raised her eyes to his.

"Don't." He dropped a kiss on her forehead. "Don't overthink this, just enjoy it for what it is, Cass, no strings, no pressure."

No matter what he said, his gaze told her there were strings and they were tangled around the blazing desire consuming them. She licked her lips and Lucas's eyes followed the action, dilating until they appeared jet-black.

"But—"

He placed his finger over her mouth. "No buts, not now."

Cassie wanted to argue. Wanted to clear the air. Make sure they both knew where this was going. Where it wasn't. Except she didn't know where this was headed. She had no clue what all these conflicting emotions churning inside her were.

She nodded and pulled his hand away, leaned up and pressed her mouth to his. It was all he needed to take them out of the emotionally charged moment and back to the mind-blowing pleasure.

His lips ate at hers, his hips rocking in a slow rhythm that built in small increments that had her clawing at his back and digging her heels into his thighs in an attempt to make him move faster. He chuckled into her mouth and kept up his torturous pace.

Cassie groaned. Her pussy convulsed with the desperate need for more and she pulled her mouth free of his to trail her lips over his shoulder. She scraped his skin with her teeth, pulled him closer with her arms and legs and drove her hips up to meet his every thrust.

"Move, dammit." Cassie dug her nails into him.

"You want faster?" he spoke into her hair.

"Yes." There was no hiding the raw edge of need in her voice.

He slowed down further. "You don't like slow?"

"No."

He angled his hips and the base of his shaft hit her swollen clit.

"Yes."

"Make up your mind." She could hear the smile in his voice.

"Fast," Cassie panted. "Faster. Harder."

"Harder?" Lucas drove his length into her in a bone-jarring slam that had her pussy clenching and her vision blurring. "Is that what you mean?"

"God. Yes." Her nails stabbed into him as she clung to his back. "Yes."

She was so close. Her muscles were coiled tight and ready to let go in what would no doubt be a blinding orgasm. He picked up the pace. Advance and retreat, over and over, as they raced for the top together.

"C'mon, Cass." Lucas pushed up on his elbows until his torso was suspended above hers, the part of their bodies slamming together visible to both of them when they looked down. "Fuck, that's hot."

Cassie had to agree. His condom-covered cock glistened with her juices and her nether lips flared out around his shaft as he withdrew. She'd never seen anything as sexy or done anything this raunchy. He'd shown her a new kind of sex—a new side of herself. And as she gazed down at his cock impaling her time after time, she let go. Shattered into a thousand million pieces.

"Luc."

Lucas followed her, his body ramming into hers one final time before he held still, shuddering with release. "Cass."

He collapsed to the side, half-on and half-off her, their bodies still joined intimately, and Cassie wondered how she was ever going to walk away from this man and all he made her feel.

14

"Oy, Cassie, wait up!"

Cassie turned to find West jogging across the car park. "Hey, West, what's up?" She waited for him to catch up.

"I need to run the weekend's comings and goings by you."

"Why? You have a key. You come and go as you need. Just label everything clearly for my staff." West walked beside her.

"Don't I always?" He grabbed the door and pulled it open, ushering her through before him. "Actually, I wanted to check it was okay to use the kitchen for personal use."

She glanced his way. "Personal? Sure, you paid for the thing, use it however you want."

"Thanks."

"So, what's the personal thing or is it a secret?"

"Not a secret, but..." West ducked his head, but not before Cassie saw his cheeks flush red.

"Oh my God! Are you blushing?"

He grabbed her in a headlock before she could rib him anymore. "Knock it off, squirt."

Cassie laughed. "Big bad Weston Mann has a crush," she sing-songed.

"I'm warning you." West rubbed his knuckles on the top of her head while tightening his grip and bringing her head closer to his chest. He smelled like the yummy curry puffs that were one of his company's specialties.

"You don't sca—"

Cassie was ripped from West's arms as Luc's voice boomed through the warehouse. "Get your hands off her!"

"Whoa!"

Cassie peeked around Lucas to see West with his hands up as though a gun was pointed at him. She had to check there wasn't one in Luc's hand. Just in case. Although with the way Lucas vibrated with tension he probably didn't need a gun to kill West. If she didn't step in quickly this could turn into a bloodbath she wasn't in the mood to deal with. Not today.

"Lucas, we were just mucking around." Cassie tried to step between them but Luc put his arm out and stopped her.

"He had you in a headlock," he growled.

"Yes, but he wasn't hurting me, and it's not the first time he's done it. Probably won't be the last either." Cassie rolled her eyes behind his back.

"Yes. It will." Luc's tone brokered no argument, and with West still standing there with his hands in the air he obviously wasn't going to give one.

"Seriously?" Cassie shoved at Luc's back. "Who the fuck do you think you are?" She thumped his back with her fists.

"What?" He spun around and grabbed her wrists to stop her from hitting him again. "Why are you beating me up?"

She glared at him. "Because you're acting like a Neanderthal idiot, that's why!" Cassie yelled.

"I wasn't the one with my arm around your neck!" Luc yelled back.

"He wasn't trying to hurt me, you moron." Cassie couldn't believe anyone could think West would actually hurt her. She turned to West, but before she could say anything West took a step back.

"I'll go get started on those pastries you need done today." West turned, but Cassie reached out and grabbed his shirt.

"No, you don't. You're not getting away that easily." She yanked on his shirt. "Turn around so I can introduce you two so next time Luc doesn't rip your damn head off."

West reluctantly turned around. "Fine." He crossed his arms over his chest.

"Lucas Wilhelm, meet Weston Mann, better known as West. West, Luc." She waved her hand between the two of them. "Now, if we're finished playing damsel in distress, bodyguard and villain, I have work to do."

Cassie didn't wait for either of them to say a word. She spun on her heel and headed for the stairs. Taking them two at a time, she mumbled about idiot men until she reached her office where she took great pleasure in slamming her door.

The air slid from her lungs when she saw the neatly wrapped present sitting in the center of her desk. Cautiously, she made her way across the room and picked up the small box. A tiny card attached read:

Cassie,

These remind me of your eyes.

Luc

With shaking fingers, Cassie tore open the pretty paper to find a silver box. Lifting the lid, she stared at the glass bead bracelet inside. The beads were a selection of browns and golds. Her breath stalled. Luc must have made it at the birthday party on the weekend.

It was such an unexpected gesture. One that pulled at every conviction she had that she shouldn't see him anymore. She fell into her chair, the leather creaking beneath her, and contemplated what it meant. He'd let her walk out the door this morning without a word about seeing her again. And now he was leaving her a gift.

Cassie closed her eyes and dropped her head back. Just when she thought she was okay with her decision to cool things with Luc, he went and did something that threw up a host of unwanted emotions.

The biggest being longing. How could she want a man so deeply when she'd only known him three days?

Her phone rang, snapping her out of her thoughts. She didn't have time to dwell on her personal life, she had a business to run, and that was exactly why she shouldn't see him. Lucas was too much of a distraction and Cassie couldn't afford that any more than she could a Ferrari.

L uc watched Cassie until she disappeared from sight. He guessed he owed her and this guy, West, an apology. He'd fucked up. She couldn't blame him though. Seeing her caught in a headlock just about exploded *his* head.

Every instinct in him had gone on red alert at the scene he'd found when he'd come down the stairs five minutes ago. Having never laid eyes on West before, Luc's first impulse was to think threat, especially when the guy had Cassie in such a menacing hold.

"Cassie hasn't mentioned you, so I assume you're someone she just met."

He turned to find West had stepped closer. The guy had puffed out his chest and stood ramrod straight too. Probably in an attempt to intimidate him, but Luc didn't scare easily, so the guy was shit out of luck. "Yeah." Luc wasn't about to reveal anything about him and Cassie.

West grinned. "The strong, silent type, are you?"

The mockery in the guy's voice set Luc's nerves on edge, not that they weren't already there. "If Cassie wants to tell you anything that's up to her, but I'm not about to share my business with you." Luc turned to leave but West's next words stopped him.

"Want to know how to win her over?"

He turned back to face a smirking West.

"Yeah, thought you might, but let me give you some info first." West crossed his arms and squared his shoulders. "I've known Cassie since I was a kid. Her brother is my best friend and I've been to as many family events at the Moreland house as she has, so I know a little more about the woman than most."

Luc's gut churned. He didn't like that West had so much history with Cassie. Didn't like the implied intimacy of it. He opened his mouth but stopped when West held up a hand.

"No. I've never gone there. Never thought of going there, so don't insult us both by asking. She's always been a kid sister to me regardless of our lack of blood ties." West stepped forward and got in Luc's face. He had to give the guy credit. He had balls. Luc topped him by a good three inches. "You fuck her over and it's not just me you'll deal with. She's got five older brothers who would gladly take you apart with me."

Luc laughed. He couldn't help it. And when West scowled at him, he laughed harder.

"Listen—"

"Sorry, not laughing at you." Luc sucked in a breath and got his mirth under control. "I just find it hilarious that you even think there'd be anything left if I fucked her over. She doesn't need you or her brothers to fight her battles. She'd have me castrated, drawn and quartered and hung from the nearest lamppost before I ever *fucked her over*."

West smiled. "Ah, so you have met the real Cassie then."

"Oh, yeah. We spent most of Friday night butting heads."

"Obviously something changed between now and then, though."

Ah, they were back to fishing for info. "Something changes every second."

"You know, I think I like you." West stuck out his hand. "West Mann."

Luc gripped his hand and shook. "Luc Wilhelm."

"So, about winning her over."

"At this point." He turned his head to look over at the stairs Cassie had disappeared up. "I'll take any advice you have."

"Don't push her. Let her come to you, but don't let her think you're not hanging around. Small things will get her over the big ones, so don't go ordering flowers or some such shit. Stick with simple things like making sure she's got lunch on a busy day. She's always forgetting to eat and then she'll gorge on chocolate bars or those horrible TV dinners she has in her freezer." West shuddered as he said the last part.

Luc could see how that might work. And he wanted to look after her, wanted to be sure she took care of herself. She'd already admitted to eating crap most of the time. "Thanks. I'll keep that in mind."

"No worries. Just don't go overboard. Something simple will get her every time. She's a sucker for thoughtful gestures, not so much the extravagant ones like jewelry."

Jewelry. *Shit.* He hoped she wouldn't think the bracelet was over the top. It was only a kids' party trinket not a diamond ring. He looked toward the stairs again. She hadn't come back down and thrown it at him. And surely she'd found and opened it by now.

Then again, maybe she'd tossed it in the bin. Luc hoped not, but he didn't really have a say now that he'd given it to her. She'd do with it whatever she wanted. He'd just have to accept any choice she made.

West's hand clapped him on the shoulder. "Good luck, man."

Luc turned back to him. "Thanks." He smiled but he wasn't really feeling it. For the first time since Cassie had walked out his door this morning, he had real concern about the outcome of their relationship.

———

Cassie looked up from her paperwork at Dan. "Thanks, but I don't recall you asking me if I wanted anything for lunch."

"You didn't." He put the paper bag on her desk. "And I didn't order it."

Before she could get a word out, he'd turned to leave.

"Wait. What do you mean you didn't order it?" she called to his retreating back.

"The deli down the street delivered it," he said over his shoulder.

Cassie stared at the bag. He hadn't. Not again. It was the same yesterday. And the day before. And both nights. Lunch and dinner, Monday, Tuesday and now Wednesday. She didn't see him during the day, but he was always either waiting—with food—in his car, or on her doorstep within seconds of her getting home. He'd not stayed. Instead, he'd delivered her meals and left. That confused her more than anything.

Why would he not want to stick around and eat with her?

Confused and frustrated, she reached for the bag and ripped it open. A BLT. Her mouth watered.

Damn, he'd ordered her favourite sandwich.

She sighed. It was even toasted.

How was she supposed to keep her distance when he kept doing nice things for her? The man was making it hard to stand by her decision not to continue their all-consuming relationship. Plus he was making her arguments about distractions useless when he wasn't around during the day to interrupt her work and barely said ten words to her at night.

She peeled back the wrapper and sank her teeth into the sandwich, closing her eyes as salty bacon flavor flooded her mouth. She polished off half before putting it down. Cassie grabbed her phone and she flicked through her address book until she came to Luc's number.

She'd programmed it in after asking Jody for it. It'd felt strange to have to ask her new employee for a number she should already have, but Jody hadn't seemed fazed by the request and rattled it off without a second thought.

Thumb hovering over the screen, she debated calling him or texting. She wasn't sure how she'd react to hearing his voice, so she pulled up a new message and fired off a quick thank you. Within seconds her phone beeped with a reply.

You're welcome.

Cassie tapped out a reply. *You can't keep doing this.*

Again his reply fired back. *Why not?*

Yes, why not? It was a good question and Cassie couldn't think of a good answer. It took her a few minutes to think of a reason, but even then she knew it wasn't a strong argument. *Because you can't keep paying for my food.*

You can pay next week.

Cassie laughed. The man was insane.

And not going away.

But she had to be honest.

As much as she didn't want to see him again, she did. If she found him on her doorstep tonight she'd invite him in before he could run off. She'd been too shocked to think the last two nights so he'd gotten away with little more than a nod hello from her.

That changed today. She fingered the beads around her wrist. He hadn't said anything to her about the bracelet. Not yet, but she knew he'd seen her wearing it Monday night.

She wasn't sure why she'd put it on. With everything she'd told herself about not getting attached to him, even she couldn't understand why she wanted to wear it. Okay, that was a lie. If she was going to start lying to herself she was in trouble.

She'd put it on and kept it on because Luc had made it. For her. It was a way to keep him close without keeping him close, and wasn't that just fucked-up reasoning. Cassie let out a deep breath and slouched back in her chair. Her phone beeped, bouncing on the desk as it vibrated with an incoming message.

Is it yummy? Mine is.

A smile curved her mouth. They were having lunch together. *Yes.*

How does pizza for dinner sound?

Will you join me?

Can't.

Cassie frowned and sent a text with a frowny face in reply.

Have to work but I'll order the pizza for 7. Sound good?

She didn't want to eat alone again and really she should just organize her own dinner. *Don't worry, I'll take care of myself tonight.*

Too late. Ordered already.

Damn him. *Fine. But I'm cooking tomorrow night.*

Aren't you working tomorrow night?

Shit. She was. Wait. How did he know that? *How do you know?*

Jody mentioned it.

Plausible. He'd obviously been speaking to his sister, and Cassie knew he was worried about Jody, so she fired off a quick message to alleviate some of his concern.

She's doing great. She'll be running her own events in no time. Thanks for sending her my way.

You're both welcome. Gotta go. Meeting. See you later.

Cassie read his last message over and over. Did he mean he'd see her tonight? He'd said he'd ordered her a pizza but he wouldn't be there, so was he planning on stopping by after he finished work? A pang of disappointment and a bubble of hope vied for space in her chest. She'd see-sawed back and forth about what she wanted so often over the last few days that she was beginning to get motion sickness.

She leaned forward and thunked her head on the desk. There was no getting around it. Lucas Wilhelm wasn't just a distraction. He was a roadblock.

15

Cassie stared at the man on her doorstep. It was Thursday evening and the fourth day in a row she'd seen or heard from him. Monday morning, when she'd left his house determined not to think about him and all he'd made her feel in one weekend, she'd thought that was the end of it.

She'd been wrong. Lucas had been in her face but not.

He'd found an excuse every day since then to see her. She wanted to be pissed off about it, only the thrill of excitement that swept through her with each sighting wouldn't let her get a good mad up. Besides, he never stayed for long and *that* was beginning to piss her off. He was teasing her with his presence only to disappear before she could give in to her body's desire for his.

She sighed. Damn the man. She got out of her car and then took her time shutting the door to gather her thoughts before she walked toward him. He pushed off the wall and picked up the plastic bags at his feet.

The closer she got, the more obvious it became that he'd brought dinner. Again. He'd fed her lunch and dinner every day this week. Cassie suspected he was getting her work schedule from his sister, Jody, because he seemed to know exactly where she'd be at all times.

It was Jody who'd insisted she head home now. Insisted she and Dan had tonight's cocktail party under control. And Luc had even mentioned she was working tonight, so he had to have known she was heading home early somehow.

The mouthwatering aroma of curry wafted toward her and all turbulent thoughts stopped. "Oh my God, is that Indian?" She stepped onto her small porch.

"Yep. Complete with naan." Lucas raised the bags and shook them slightly.

Shit. She couldn't turn him away now even if she wanted to. Not when he'd brought her favourite food and her stomach was rumbling with hunger. Slipping her key in the lock, she twisted and glanced over at him. "Is that for one or two?"

"Two?" He arched one thick brow.

Well, this was a first. He was planning to eat with her this time. Cassie shoved the door open.

"Come in. If you want to put all that in the kitchen I'm just going to get out of these work clothes first, then I'll dish it up." She headed down the hall to her room, the sound of Lucas shutting the door and moving toward the kitchen behind her.

A smile curled her lips and Cassie had to admit, if only to herself, that she was pleased he was here. With each quick visit she'd missed him more. She couldn't count the number of times her mind had wandered to thoughts of Lucas over the last few days.

He'd found his way deeper than just under her skin, and as much as she'd told herself she didn't have time for a relationship, she couldn't fight the needs rising inside her. And it wasn't only about the sex either. As good as it was between them physically, there was an emotional connection too.

It was time she faced facts and accepted the feelings he provoked and dealt with them. And him. She stripped out of her work clothes and grabbed a T-shirt and shorts. Stepping into the pants, she thought about how the next few hours might go.

If his constant appearance in her life was a clue, then she could only conclude that he wanted to move past their weekend together into a possible future. The very idea of spending more time with Luc heated her blood and sent a shiver down her spine.

She'd been fooling herself. She couldn't deny their connection, and her arguments against seeing him held no real substance when he'd not once interfered with her work schedule.

Her last venture into relationship territory had blown up in her face when her ex had turned up to a job she was overseeing one Saturday afternoon. He'd caused a huge scene, and she'd been forced to refund the client's money. Not to mention word had gotten around and she'd lost three more bookings because of his angry outburst.

Cassie had to admit that she'd been gun shy with men since, and she'd been unfair to Lucas by assuming he'd behave the same as her ex and using it as an excuse to keep her distance. Shame washed through her.

She owed Luc an apology and an explanation. He deserved both whether he wanted to continue seeing her or not. She'd take his frequent visits as a good sign and hope her fear of getting involved hadn't ruined any possible future for them.

With what had to be a goofy smile on her face, Cassie tugged her top on and headed out of her room to find Lucas. She found him in her dining room, table set with two places and the food spread out in front of them. Watching him as he poured them both a glass of water, she felt warm and soft.

It would be easy to get used to seeing him there. Too easy perhaps, but she wasn't going to dwell on that. Instead, she'd make the most of enjoying a meal with a great guy and see where things went.

Luc leaned back in his chair and rubbed his stomach. Dan had been right. The little Indian place in Balgowlah made *the* best Indian food outside of India. It also happened to be Cassie's favourite take-away dinner. He'd eaten more than he should, but the flavors had been too mouthwatering to give up.

Cassie was still going. She'd probably eaten as much as if not more than him already, but that didn't stop her from scooping up another spoonful of Baltic curry.

"Good?" he asked even though he knew the answer already.

"Mmm…" She swallowed. "Delicious."

She slipped her tongue out and licked across her bottom lip. Luc's groin tightened. Dinner had been a study in restraint and he was beginning to think he might not be able to stick to his plan of hands off for much longer. Dragging in a deep breath, he reined in his libido and tried to distract himself with mundane chatter.

"So Jody's working out?" Discussing his sister was bound to dampen his arousal.

"Yes." Cassie wiped her mouth with a napkin. "Like I said yesterday, she's great. She and Dan have had a few hiccups, but I think that's because he's still against bringing in another supervisor."

"Really?" Luc had been speaking with Dan all week. The guy didn't seem the type to hold a grudge against someone who wasn't at fault, and Jody definitely had nothing to do with Cassie expanding her management base.

Cassie's forehead wrinkled. "Actually, I'm not sure if it is that. There's some crazy sparks flying off those two."

Sparks? As in sexual sparks? *Shit.* Luc needed to call his sister. The last thing she needed was another man fucking up her life.

"Whatever it is, they don't let it interfere with the job and that's all that matters." She waved her hand in the air. "But enough about work. I'm home early for the first time in months. I want to enjoy it while I can."

"Okay, how about we watch some TV?"

She glanced at her watch. "You know I wouldn't have a clue what's on at this time anymore. I can't remember the last time I sat in front of a TV and vegged out."

Luc laughed. "That would be last weekend when we watched *An American President.*"

Cassie's cheeks turned a pretty shade of pink. "Yeah, well, I didn't exactly watch it."

"No, but you certainly vegged out." He pushed his chair back and stood. "I'll clear this away, you go see if there's anything on."

"Don't be silly. You made dinner, I'll clean up."

"I didn't make it."

"Still, you organized it, so I'm on cleanup duty." She stacked the empty containers on top of their plates and carried them to the kitchen. "Do you want a coffee or something?" she called out.

"No. I'm good." Luc wandered into her living room and picked up the remote from the side table. He flicked through channels before he found an episode of *The Big Bang Theory*. "You okay with a comedy?"

"Sure." She came into the room carrying a tray with a plate of Tim Tams and two glasses of water. "Snacks." She grinned.

"Snacks? We just finished dinner. I couldn't possibly eat another thing." Luc dropped to the couch behind him.

"There's always room for Tim Tams." Cassie set the tray down on the coffee table and sat beside him. "But I'll happily eat your share."

He smiled. "I just bet you will."

Relaxing back, Luc pretended to focus on the TV when every cell in his body was tuned to the woman next to him. He didn't want to push her, but damn, he really, really wanted to get his hands on her again.

The no-pressure, take-their-time course was wearing thin, and he couldn't tell if his slow wooing of Cassie had gotten him any closer to the goal. He'd give anything to be able to read her mind, and while he'd wanted to pump his sister and Dan for information, he hadn't. Now he wished he'd given in and asked either of them if she'd at least mentioned him.

"You're thinking too hard." Her words jolted him out of his thoughts.

"What?"

"You accused me of overthinking last weekend." She turned on the seat next to him, her knee pressing into his thigh. "And you were right. I was worrying this thing between us to death. Now you're doing it."

One side of his mouth kicked up. "Yeah, I am."

"I need to explain something."

Luc sat up straighter, her tone sending a shaft of dread through him. "Go ahead."

"I had a bad experience with my last boyfriend. We dated for a few months and when all my time was taken up by establishing Are You Game?, he made it clear he wasn't happy. He wanted me to spend more time with him, and when I wouldn't cut back my hours, he turned up at a child's birthday party and made such a scene that I not only had to refund the client's money, I lost bookings too."

"Asshole." Luc wanted to find the guy and punch him.

Cassie laughed. "Yeah, turned out he was."

A thought occurred to him. "How long ago was this?"

"Two years."

"And you haven't dated since then?" Luc wasn't sure if he was pleased by her lack of dating or upset that some jerk had hurt her so badly that she'd erected walls around herself.

"No, you're the first guy I've even looked at, never mind spent time with."

He grinned, pleased to have been the one to break through her shell. "Do you think I'm going to do what that asshole did? Demand more time than you have?"

"No. Yes. No." She sighed. "It was a knee-jerk reaction. I'd have been the same with anyone."

"But I'm not just anyone, Cass."

Luc watched her throat work as she swallowed. Watched her tongue slip out to slide across her lip before she spoke. "No. You're not."

"Who am I?" He waited to see if she remembered what he'd said nearly a week ago.

"You're the guy who's going to bring me to my knees."

He smiled. "Yeah, but want to know something?"

"What?"

"I'm going to be right there beside you. On my knees, holding your hand."

Her eyes widened, her lips parting a fraction as she sucked in a breath. "Y-you are?"

"I'm already there, Cass, just waiting for you to join me."

"Oh."

Luc waited for her to say more, but she didn't. His stomach dropped like a lead ball. He couldn't take back what he'd said or the depth of his feelings the words revealed, but he could make it easier for her. "Wanna catch a movie with me sometime this weekend?"

She smiled. "I'd like that."

"Good. Let me know what time suits you. I'm free all weekend." He didn't want to push her and send her running for the hills, so he'd take whatever he could get when he could get it. That might make him desperate, but he didn't care. When it came to Cassie, he felt desperate.

Cassie reached over and smoothed the skin between his eyebrows. "You're doing it again."

"What?"

"Overthinking."

He shrugged. "Maybe."

"Want to know what I think?" She didn't give him time to answer. "I think we should just go with it. See each other when we can. Let's not label it or stress about where it's going. We'll enjoy it while it lasts. No strings."

"I've got one string." He leaned toward her.

"Oh yeah, what?" Her breath fanned over his face.

"We're exclusive."

Cassie reared back. "Of course. Jeez, I barely have time to see you. How the hell would I fit in anyone else?"

He stuck out his hand. "So we have a deal?"

She looked at his hand then brought her gaze back to his. "Oh, I think we can seal the deal better than that."

Before he could register the words, Cassie was in his arms and her mouth was on his. Once his brain unfroze, he took what he'd been craving all week. He thrust his tongue between her teeth and coaxed hers out.

Slipping his hands under her T-shirt, Luc found her breasts and made quick work of flicking the front closure of her bra undone. Her soft mounds fell into his hands, her nipples growing hard against his palms. With thumb and forefinger, he tweaked the tips until they were puckered tight.

"God, yes. Do that again," she breathed into his mouth, and Luc obliged.

He played with her breasts while taking her mouth in a soul-deep kiss. It wasn't long before neither of them was satisfied with just kissing. She pulled free and grabbed the hem of her top. Whipping it up and over her head, her voice was muffled but the demand was clear.

"Clothes. Off. Now."

Luc didn't want to take Cassie on her couch this first time. He wanted to lay her out and reacquaint himself with every inch of her. "Bedroom."

He scooped her up as he stood. She slipped her arms around his neck and her legs wrapped around his waist. His blood pounded in his ears as he made his way down the hall to her room. Using his foot, Luc pushed the door open and strode to the bed where he fell forward. Bracing his elbows, he took his weight on his arms while pinning her beneath him.

"I want you naked and spread out before me," he growled in her ear, his arousal already at a fever pitch.

She wiggled against him. "Then you better let me up so I can get naked."

Luc didn't need to be told twice. He sprang to his feet and began tugging off his clothes as he watched Cassie do the same. Damn, she was sexy. She wasn't even trying to turn him on and she had him panting and drooling.

This wasn't going to last long. Not the first time at least. He'd beaten her by a pair of undies, but they were the sexiest strip of pink lace he'd ever seen so he didn't care that she wasn't naked yet. Grinning, he launched himself back on top of her as she kicked her undies off.

He swallowed her gasp as he took her mouth with his. They

rubbed against each other, both seeking the friction necessary to find release. Luc shoved his knee between hers and spread her legs wide. Her hips cradled his, her pussy the perfect resting place for his throbbing cock. She was hot and wet and he couldn't wait another second to be inside her.

"I need to be inside. Now."

"Condoms are in the drawer." She tilted her head to the left.

Scrambling over her, Luc retrieved the unopened box of condoms. He tore the plastic off and grabbed a foil packet, ripping it open in record time.

"Here. Let me." Cassie took the protection from him and began to sheath his length.

Luc clenched his jaw, gritted his teeth and tried to think of something other than Cassie's hands on his cock. It was such a close thing that the second the protection was in place he pushed her to her back and jumped on top. All finesse deserted him in his driving need to be buried within her tight depths. She spread her legs and welcomed him with outstretched arms. Taking her invitation, he thrust into her.

A cry tore from her throat. The sound, one of shocked pleasure, sent a bolt of lust through his veins. He couldn't hold back. She was like a drug he'd been withdrawing from all week, and now that he'd had a dose he couldn't stop. Hard and fast, he surged in and out. Her back bowed, her hips rising to meet his with each plunge. They rocked together in a rapid tempo that pushed them both over the edge in minutes.

Cassie cried out, "Luc."

Her pussy walls clenched around his cock in a red-hot grip that bathed his entire length in fire and lit the fuse in his balls. His orgasm slammed into him. Come bursting free like a bullet from a gun. And the recoil was just as bad. He shuddered and trembled as he continued to empty himself. Air sawed in and out of his heaving chest and he collapsed forward, unable to do more than bend his elbows and hope he wasn't crushing her.

"Jesus, I think you killed me."

He smiled against her throat. "My sentiments exactly."

She laughed, her breasts vibrating where they were pressed into his chest. "But what a way to go, right?"

Luc couldn't find the energy to speak again, so he nodded. He needed a second to catch his breath and then he'd move. For now he was more than happy to stay spread over Cassie with his still-hard cock buried in her sweet pussy.

"I think we should do that again. Make sure it wasn't a fluke."

"No fluke. Just Cassie."

"Oh no, I'm not taking all the credit for that." She ran her hand up his spine and into the hair at his nape. "If it was just me, I'd have been this blissed out before now. It's the two of us together."

"Then we better stay together. Besides, after that you've ruined me for all other women. You better take pity on me and let me stick around."

Cassie laughed. "Ditto, buddy." She slapped his ass. "Now get off me. The fact I can't breathe is beginning to annoy me."

Luc levered himself up and to the side. His cock slid from her body and both of them shuddered in reaction. He slid his hand under his belly and removed the used condom. He still hadn't gone down, but there was nothing he could do about it until he regained some of his strength. Cassie had wiped him out. A glance to the side showed her sprawled on her back, one arm thrown over her head. She looked as done in as he felt.

At least his quick draw and fire hadn't left her wanting.

A smile curled his mouth and he closed his eyes. He couldn't help thinking about what he and Cassie had. They had chemistry in spades, but it was the friendship and admiration that was growing between them that had him thinking of the future she told him not to worry about.

No matter how much he argued against it being too soon, he knew Cassie was in his life to stay. She was everything he'd ever wanted without knowing it.

"Cass?" He opened his eyes to look at her.

"Hmm."

"This is going to get complicated, you know that, right?"

She sighed and turned her head toward him. "Yeah, I know."

"And you're okay with that?" Luc didn't want to pressure her but he needed her to know where he was in this.

"Surprisingly, yes." She reached over and brushed her fingertips down his cheek. "Last week I would have said no. Four days ago I would have said no, but I can't argue with this. Nor do I want to."

"We'll go as slow as you need."

Cassie smiled. "Thank you. Although I'm a little offended that you think I'm the one who'll need time."

Luc grabbed her wrist and brought her hand to his mouth, placing a kiss in the center of her palm. "You don't want to know how fast I want to take this."

"Tell me." She grinned. "Not that I'll agree to your pace."

"Move in with me."

"Shit! Yeah, not happening anytime soon."

"Let me have a drawer in your dresser, clothes hanging in your wardrobe, a toothbrush in your bathroom."

"We can probably work our way up to those in the next few weeks."

Luc sat up quickly. "Really? You're okay with sleepovers? With personal space being encroached?"

Her forehead wrinkled. "I think so."

"Promise you'll tell me if I push too fast or something I do freaks you out." He leaned over her and brought his mouth within a breath of hers. "Promise me."

"I promise."

"We need to seal the deal." Luc smiled as he took Cassie's mouth with his. Long moments later, he pulled his mouth from hers and stared at her.

"What?" She licked her lips and Luc's gaze immediately returned to her kiss-swollen mouth.

"You."

"What about me?"

"You're here."

She shoved at his chest. "Don't get all mushy on me, Lucas."

"Sorry. I can't help it. You fill me with something I've never had before."

"What?"

"I can't explain it, but I can show you." He rocked his hips against her, his erection trapped between them.

"I think you have it backward. It's not me filling you." She laughed.

Luc chuckled. "Then let me fill you."

EPILOGUE

Cassie scanned the room and found nothing out of place. Jody had done a great job on her first event. She really did need to thank Luc for suggesting his sister for the new supervisor's position. The party was well into the second hour and was already a success.

Music thumped through the house's sound system, food made the rounds on silver trays held by black-tuxedo-wearing wait staff and glasses were turned bottoms up quicker than they could be filled. Sydney's social elite were letting their hair—and pants—down. Heading in the direction of the pants-dropper, Cassie was beaten there by Dan.

He'd insisted on attending tonight's event along with her even though it was Jody's job. There was tension between her new and old employees that she needed to keep an eye on. Cassie had known Dan was against hiring new staff, but she didn't think he would carry his anger this far.

Fortunately, Jody either didn't notice Dan's open hostility, or she was choosing to ignore it—and him. Smiling, she watched Jody enter the room and quickly extricate the unclothed guest from Dan and remove him from the room. She chuckled at the consternation on Dan's face.

"What's so funny?" Warm breath fanned over her ear and neck, and the unmistakable scent of Luc surrounded her.

Smiling, she turned around and looked up. "Luc. What are you doing here?"

He leaned down and placed a hard peck on her lips. "Can't seem to stay away from my woman."

She frowned. "We've talked about that."

"Aw, c'mon, Cass." Luc scowled at her. "We've been seeing each other exclusively for four months, don't you think it's about time you accepted that you're mine and I'm yours?"

Her stomach flipped. He'd been so patient with her, letting her dictate how much they saw each other and where. She knew he was getting frustrated with her inability to commit to more than casual dating and hot sex. And it was super-hot sex.

They couldn't keep their hands off each other. Which was why she wasn't ready to take their relationship to the next level. Only a few people knew they were an item. Someone bumped into her back and she was abruptly reminded of their surroundings.

"We can't have this discussion here," she said.

"Fine." Luc grabbed her hand and wove his fingers through hers. He all but yanked her off her feet as he spun around and began pushing his way through the crowd.

She stumbled in her attempt to keep up and he slid his arm around her waist and clamped her to his side. They hit the hallway where the crowd thinned out, but she needn't have worried about someone overhearing the rest of their conversation.

Before she could gasp a breath, Luc opened a door, shoved her inside a closet and followed. Darkness enveloped her and she threw her hands out to protect herself from crashing into the wall.

"Jesus, Luc, what the fuck?"

He spun her around, and with his hands on her ribs, lifted her off the floor. "Put your legs around me," he demanded.

His mouth found hers before she moved. For a split second, she froze. Then everything moved at once. Her blood rushed, her heart slammed against her sternum and her arms and legs wrapped around him. He drove his tongue between her lips and stroked hers with wicked intent.

Like all their kisses, it shot to carnal desperation in a heartbeat. This was why she couldn't hand herself over to him completely. This desperate, clawing need that took her under within a breath had her careening out of control faster than a speeding car and wiped her mind clear of all except Luc.

She dug her fingers into his scalp and pulled him closer. He nipped at her lips, trailed his mouth over her cheek to her ear where he set about driving her insane. Licking and nibbling at the delicate flesh, he had her panting for breath and begging for more.

"Oh, God, Luc. Please."

"You can't deny me, Cass," he growled against her skin.

She couldn't. As much as she wanted to, wanted to protect her heart from the pain he could inflict, she accepted that it was already too late. He'd stormed her defenses and left her bare.

He buried his face in her neck and breathed deep. "Dammit. Cass." Her name was a plea and she tightened her body around him in reflex—in comfort.

"Luc." She kissed his head and held on while he continued to crush her against him.

"I need you." He rocked his hips and pressed his hard cock into her sex.

"Yes."

Luc did it again and Cassie all but purred as sensation fired through her pussy.

They wasted no time in ridding themselves of their clothes. In the months since they first had sex, they'd perfected the art of removing the minimum necessary to get what they needed.

He set her down and her nimble fingers quickly worked the button and zip on his pants before shoving them down his thighs. She sucked in a breath. Commando. The knowledge that he'd been naked beneath his jeans speared through her. She reached out to wrap her hand around his thick shaft.

Luc pushed her skirt up over her hips. He curled his fingers into the sides of her panties and yanked them down her legs as he dropped to his knees before her. He buried his face in her pussy, thrusting his tongue out to probe between her folds.

The first flick on her clit made her gasp. The second made her tremble. The third had her collapsing to the floor. With his help, she slid onto his lap.

"Take me inside," he murmured against her mouth.

Reaching between them, Cassie raised her hips and, hand around his length, guided him home. She sank down and took him in. The angle drove him deep and they moaned in unison when her body sat flush to his.

"Fuck, I'm glad you went on the pill." Luc wrapped his hand in her ponytail and tugged her head back so he could meet her gaze. "This is the best damn place in the world. You're the best damn thing in the world."

She smiled at his words. He always took their coupling, no matter how raw and dirty, to an emotional level. Without fail, he took more than her body every time. A lump formed in her throat, her mouth dry as she struggled to see his eyes and all they could reveal in the darkness.

"Ride me, Cass. Show me heaven, baby."

He gripped her hips and helped her find a rhythm. Up and down, she took him in, let him out. Long glides of slick swollen flesh over rigid steel. He bucked up as she plunged down, driving them quickly to the edge. They picked up the pace as they moved closer to release.

Her clit slammed into the base of his cock each time he hit bottom and she found his mouth with hers, wanting to taste him as she went over.

Luc growled into her mouth as the first spasm gripped her. The walls of her pussy convulsed around him, sucking him deeper as he took control and drove himself up into her with savage thrusts.

Light exploded behind her eyelids as she came apart completely. Seconds later, Luc followed, setting off another set of rolling contractions in her core. Their mouths separated as they gasped for air.

She curled into him, sought the closeness she only ever found with Luc. He held her, rubbed his hands up and down her back as they came down from another mind-blowing encounter. "How can it keep getting better?" she mumbled into his shoulder.

"You know why." He kissed her temple. "I can't hold it in any longer, Cass. I know you're not ready to hear what I have to say, but I'm not expecting anything more than you're willing to give. Shit. I'll take any scrap you'll throw my way."

Cassie leaned back to look at him. The darkness was no longer blinding, her eyes having adjusted to the lack of light, but she still couldn't quite make out the expression on his face. She didn't want to believe what she thought she saw for fear it was a trick her heart was playing on her.

Luc trailed a finger along her lips. "I love you, Cass."

She jerked, fear and longing warring inside her. "I...I..."

He placed his finger over her mouth. "Shh. Don't say anything. I don't need to hear it back, Cass, but I need you to hear it. Need you to let me love you."

"Oh, Luc." Cassie threw her arms around him and hugged him close. "I love you too."

Luc's whole body sighed in relief. He'd been holding back for weeks—months—and he'd finally decided that hell would probably freeze over before Cassie declared her love first. He understood her reluctance. They were so out of control when it came to being together. Neither of them could keep their hands to themselves for long.

Tonight was a classic example. His intention had been to find her and help out before taking her home to bed where he'd reveal his love for her in a romantic setting. Instead, he'd taken her in a closet.

He rolled his eyes and held her tighter. She'd been a breath of fresh air in his life these last few months, and he knew to his marrow that he couldn't live without her. He'd hoped she'd come around, but as the days ticked by with her still keeping him at a distance, he'd realized he'd have to push her, nudge her in the right direction.

It was probably underhanded, and some of what he had planned to convince her a trip down the aisle was required was definitely sneaky, but the end was worth it. Everything about Cassie was worth it.

They'd taken the first step. Now he just had to keep them moving in the right direction. She squirmed against him and Luc's softened cock pulsed with renewed lust. It never failed to amaze him that he could want her so badly after just having had her. But there was no denying the driving need that consumed him where Cassie was concerned.

He dropped a kiss on her cheek and then gripped her waist and lifted her off his lap. Her cry broke the silence and a matching moan rumbled in his chest. His balls throbbed and blood filled his length once more.

On wobbly legs, Cassie stood in front of him. Luc climbed to his feet and reached behind to feel the wall for a light switch. There was no way he was searching for their clothes in the dark. Both of them blinked when the room lit up.

Squinting, Luc looked down and found Cassie's underwear. He helped her step into them before scooping up his jeans and thrusting one leg into them. Hopping on one foot, he slid the second leg in while she straightened her skirt. They didn't say a word.

Worried, he tipped up her chin so she'd look at him. "You okay?"

The smile she gifted him warmed his heart. "Are you kidding? Not only did the man I love just declare his love for me, but I got to play seven minutes in heaven with him."

Luc laughed. "Seven minutes in heaven with you is nowhere near enough." He leaned down and kissed her.

"Mmm...you're right. We should get out of here." She spoke against his lips. "I think Jody has it under control, so how 'bout we head home for another slice of heaven?"

"Lead the way." He stepped aside and swept his arm out to let her go first.

Cassie opened the door and strode into the hall like it was perfectly normal to be leaving the hall closet with a guy you'd just fucked senseless. He'd barely shut the door after them when a blonde with silicone breasts, trowelled on make-up and an outfit no bigger than a hand towel bounced next to them.

"Oh, is this where we're playing 7 minutes in heaven?"

Luc couldn't help it. He burst out laughing. Grabbing Cassie's hand, he ignored the blonde and headed out of the house with a giggling Cassie right beside him.

CATCH'N'KISS

ARE YOU GAME? BOOK 2

DEDICATION

Mr. C. you can catch'n'kiss me whenever you want.

1

—

Dan O'Conner reached for the warehouse door only for it to fly open and almost take his hand off. He took a half step back when a curvy behind appeared first through the doorway. Jody. She was bent at the waist, her lust inspiring curves on perfect display as she attempted to drag a huge box outside.

He stepped forward. "Here, let me help you."

"No, thanks. I've got it." She might not have snapped at him as usual, but there was a steel edge to Jody's voice that told him to back off.

"Whoa." Dan raised his hands and stepped out of the way as she cleared the doorway, tugging the box with her. Or trying to at least, but the thing was as wide as the door, and if she wasn't careful it would be wedged good and tight. "I was just offering to help."

Jody turned her head, flicking her blonde ponytail out, and lasered him with stormy-blue eyes. "And *I* said I've got it."

Dan took another step back. He had no clue why this woman didn't like him. It went beyond their initial introduction where he'd been pissed off at his boss, Cassie, for bringing in someone to share his workload. He'd been an ass about it all, and after that first day,

Jody had avoided him or cut him off at the knees. The animosity hadn't improved one iota when he'd swallowed his pride and apologized for his behavior either. For some reason, Jody was still determined to dislike him. Which was a definite shame, because once he'd pulled his head out of his ass he'd realized she was one woman he wouldn't mind getting to know better.

Not that he'd take it beyond friendship even if she did like him. They worked together, and he'd been burned by a workplace relationship before. He wasn't about to tread in that territory again no matter how much his libido stood up and took notice whenever she was near. She wiggled her ass as she attempted to pull the huge box clear of the doorway, and Dan's pants got a little tighter. If she didn't want his help he'd be quite happy to stand here enjoying the view until he could sneak past and go inside.

A car pulled up behind him and Dan turned to see Cassie's boyfriend—and Jody's brother—climb out of the driver's seat. "Hey, Luc."

Luc raised an eyebrow and tipped his chin in Jody's direction. "How's it going?"

"Good. You helping out tonight?" Dan asked.

"Nah, just a quick stop to see Cass before I have to get back to work." Luc stood beside Dan and eyed his sister. "Ah, Jody, do you want—"

"No!" Jody snapped as she yanked hard on the box. It sprang free of the frame and sent her stumbling back a couple of steps.

Dan and Luc both jumped out of the way to avoid a collision. Jeez, she really was in a mood. Good to see it wasn't just him she was lashing out at though. If she was that short with her brother, maybe it was her natural disposition and not anything to do with him. Except she was all smiles and laughs with everyone else at work most days. Stepping around the box, he grabbed the door. Jody huffed out a breath and stared at him. He could see her struggling to hold her tongue, so he smiled and pushed the door wider so it wasn't resting on the box and restricting its movement at all.

She narrowed her eyes and pulled her normally plush lips into a thin, straight line. "Don't you have things to do before we head out to the venue?"

Dan grinned. "Yeah, guess I do. See ya later, Luc." He wasn't stupid. He knew when he wasn't wanted, and if Jody was going to treat him like crap even the draw of checking out her hot bod couldn't convince him to hang around.

Jody took a deep breath and grabbed the box again. She knew Luc was still standing behind her, could feel his eyes boring holes in the back of her head. She'd been a bitch with a capital B. Damn. What was it about Dan that rubbed her the wrong way? He'd apologized for his initial hostile treatment weeks ago, and yet she couldn't seem to let go of her animosity toward him.

"Wanna talk about it?" Luc asked.

She let go of the box and turned to face him. "Not really."

"Are you pissed off in general or just at Dan?"

"Neither."

Luc's eyebrows hiked up to his hairline.

Jody sighed. "You know he was an ass when I first started working here."

"And?"

She shrugged.

"C'mon, Jody, it isn't like you to be nasty when it's not warranted, and I know Dan apologized for being a prick ages ago."

"I know." She dug her nails into her palms. "He just rubs me the wrong way."

"By offering to help?"

Dammit. Why did Luc always have to be logical? "By breathing," she mumbled.

"What?"

"Nothing." She looked at the ground and tried to clear her

thoughts. Something that proved difficult whenever Dan was around. She brought her gaze up to meet Luc's. "I don't want to be a bitch to him, honest, it's just...argh. I don't know why I'm like that with him. It's not like I treat anyone else that way."

Luc shook his head. "You don't even treat Colin that badly, and God knows if anyone deserves to be treated like shit it's your ex."

He had a point. But she'd always kept things civil for the girls' sake. "That's for Leigh and Amy's benefit not his."

"Want to know what I think?"

She laughed. "If I say no, is it going to stop you from sharing?"

"Probably not." He grinned. "I think the animosity between you is hiding some serious sexual sparks."

Jody closed her eyes and drew in a deep breath. God, not only was her brother logical, he was smart. She opened her eyes and her gaze met Luc's knowing one. What could she say? She certainly couldn't argue. Dan did get her sexual juices flowing. Something that hadn't happened in so long she'd begun to think that part of her had died a slow, agonizing death along with her marriage.

"Look, I understand if you don't want to acknowledge or do anything about it, but you can't keep acting the way you are. It's not fair to Dan—or you—and you've got Cass worried. She said the two of you had a shouting match yesterday, and while I know you'd never do that at a party, you can see how it might be a concern for her."

"Shit. I thought Dan and I were the only ones here." She squeezed her eyes shut.

"Hey." Luc pulled her into a hug. "It wasn't Cass that heard you. West was here."

"Oh God." Jody buried her face in Luc's chest. "That's even worse."

He laughed.

She pulled back and thumped his arm. "It's not funny."

"Yes, it is." He gripped her forearms and set her away from him. "You need to sort it out."

"I know. I will."

"All right then. Want some help with that?" Luc pointed to the box.

Jody laughed. "Yeah. Help me get it into my car."

Luc bent his knees, wrapped his arms around the sides and picked it up as if it weighed no more than a box of tissues. She rolled her eyes and led the way to her car. She pressed the button on her alarm and opened the tailgate of her SUV. "Shove it in there."

"What's in here anyway?"

"Decorations for a kid's party next week. I'm going to get the girls to help me put them together on Sunday."

"Isn't there a law against child labor?"

"Probably." She grinned. "But don't tell them."

"My lips are sealed." He mimed zipping his lips.

Tears stung her eyes, and for the life of her she couldn't work out why she was on the verge of crying. As Luc straightened from the back of the car, Jody stepped next to him and threw her arms around his waist. She clung to him and swallowed the emotion clogging her throat.

"Hey, hey. What's wrong?" He held her close and patted her back.

"I just wanted a hug."

Luc squeezed her tighter. "Anytime, you know that."

"Yeah, I know." He'd always been there. For as long as she could remember, her big brother had been watching over her—supporting her. But it was time to stand on her own two feet.

Jody allowed herself a few more seconds of leaning on Luc before she pulled free. He watched her with that all-seeing gaze of his and she fought against the need to wrap herself around him again. It wasn't often that she let her doubts and fears creep in, but since she'd gone back to work fulltime, she'd found her emotions in a complete jumble. She flipped from confidence in her ability to support her and the girls to absolute terror that she'd default the mortgage and not be able to put food on the table. It was irrational and stupid, and she'd had enough of her seesawing state of mind.

"I'm good." It was a verbal assurance for both of them. Luc would take over if she let him, and that was the last thing she or the girls needed. "I gotta go. We're heading out in an hour."

"I'll walk you in. I want to spend a few minutes with Cass before I have to head back to work," Luc said.

They walked back to the building. "You don't normally work nights."

"I've got a couple of new guys on tonight's detail, so I want to be on hand." Luc held open the warehouse door for her to step through. "Plus, Lachlan is worried about Cameron. This is her first official public appearance since she disappeared from the spotlight years ago."

"Not to mention she's now the future Mrs. McDermott. That's got to garner a boatload of attention." Jody had met Lachlan a few times, and while the dark, brooding man wasn't her type, she could see his appeal and understand why a woman who'd shunned the limelight would step back into it for him. She glanced at Luc. "Are you expecting a late one?"

"I don't think so. As soon as I'm happy with the way my men are working, I'll probably cut out." He stopped at the stairs. "I might even see you later if I get off early enough."

"If not, I'll talk to you next week. We have to sort out Mum's birthday present soon."

"Why don't you just get whatever and bill me," he suggested.

"Ha. You're not getting out of it that easy. Besides, we should decide whether or not to go out for dinner or just have it at my place."

"Why don't you have it at Luc's?" Cassie asked from halfway up the stairs.

"Hey, gorgeous." Luc spun around and took the stairs two at a time. He wrapped an arm around Cassie's waist and yanked her against his chest. "Ah...just the person I was looking for."

Jody watched as her brother planted a kiss on her boss. It wasn't a quick peck on the lips either. No, this was a carnal assault that made Jody's stomach knot with envy. She turned away.

She didn't begrudge her brother happiness, but she'd been married and had two kids and not once had her husband given her the kind of contentment that glowed on Luc and Cassie's faces. Of course, it had a lot to do with the no-good scumbag she'd married and the huge bubble of denial she'd lived in for years. Well, no more. She might not have someone to share the rest of her life with, but she was determined to find happiness and satisfaction in every other aspect of her life. Starting with her job and the friendships she'd begun to form.

And that included Daniel O'Conner.

D an stood off to the side and watched Jody shut down the party. He was supposed to be here only as backup, but he'd been helping out all night much to her disgust. She'd finally told him to quit interfering in her event, find a spot and stay in it. And he had to admit, she knew what she was doing. He'd underestimated her abilities and owed her another apology. Of course, he'd wait until after everyone had gone home before he gave it to her.

The host and hostess had disappeared behind their bedroom door hours ago and Jody was currently seeing the last of their guests out the door. Clean up was well underway, and he figured they'd be heading out and locking up within an hour, possibly less. There'd been only one glitch to the evening, and while he'd been prepared to deal with it, Jody had taken the situation—a half-naked partier—out of his hands and dealt with it with speed and efficiency. He really did owe her that apology.

She must have felt his eyes on her, because she turned his way and raised one finely sculptured eyebrow. The question was clear. The answer not so much. He couldn't say why he had the urge to follow her with his gaze. Sure, she was easy on the eyes, more than easy, she was a knockout. Especially when you considered she was the mother of two teenagers. Definitely one for the MILF column. A smile tugged the corner of his mouth and she narrowed her eyes.

He straightened off the wall as she headed his way. Her stride was determined and he noticed her hands were clenched at her sides.

This could go either way. She'd either rip him a new one or...actually, he wasn't sure how else it could turn out. Dan waited.

"Is there a problem?" she demanded.

"Nope."

"Then what are you doing?"

"Um, staying out of your way like you asked?" He arched one eyebrow.

"Oh, *now* you back off. Typical." Jody spun on her heel and headed for the kitchen.

"Hey, what the hell does that mean?" he called after her but she ignored him and kept going.

Damn woman. There was no way he was leaving it there. He followed her into the laundry off the kitchen where they'd stored supplies. Dan didn't think about it, he just moved up behind her, grabbed her shoulders and turned her around to face him. Her gasp had warm minty breath fanning over his chin and neck. A shudder rolled down his spine. His fingers flexed and dug into the flesh at the top of her arms as he pulled her closer until her breasts pressed against his chest.

"W-what are you doing?" She tried to push him away but he held tight.

"Something I should have done weeks ago."

Dan crushed his mouth to hers. He slid his hands over her shoulders and up her neck until he gripped her head. He tilted his head to the left, moved hers to the right and sealed their mouths completely. Her lips parted on a puff of air and he took advantage. Diving deep, he thrust his tongue past her teeth and stroked hers. A hot, wet slide that stole his breath and shot molten blood through his veins. She tasted of peppermint. The Tic Tacs she popped like an addict. Speaking of addicts. He could *so* get addicted to this.

To her.

He pressed closer. Pressed his suddenly rock-hard cock against her soft belly. Her curves cradled him and he lost a little more of his sanity. He'd been in denial. Had ignored the rush of desire that coursed through him whenever she was near. There was no denying it now. With one kiss, he'd smashed every wall blocking the way. He couldn't go back to pretending he didn't want this woman.

She tore her mouth from his. Her breath rasping in and out as she dragged oxygen into her heaving chest. He was pleased to see he wasn't the only one blown away by a simple kiss. Not that what they'd just done was simple. Kissing Jody was the least simple thing he could ever do. His gaze locked on hers and he wanted to yell in triumph when he saw her dazed, lust-filled eyes.

"Jesus." The word whispered over her lips a second before she slipped out her tongue and licked across her red kiss-swollen mouth.

A growl rumbled in his chest and he leaned in to take her mouth again. This time, he took it slower. He still plunged deep, tangled his tongue with hers and explored every dark recess. But he did it with a little finesse, a little less desperation. His chest screamed for air but he wasn't done tasting her. Wasn't done sinking into the most sublime kiss of his life. Easing back, Dan turned it down a notch until he caught his breath again. He'd planned to dive back in. Planned to submerge himself in the carnal pleasure that was Jody's mouth, but it was the wrong time, wrong place.

"Jody!"

They sprang apart just as one of the servers rounded the corner. Dan sucked in air, his chest lurching with the effort. Jody's eyes widened. He couldn't read the myriad of emotions flashing through her eyes except the last one. That was anger. Her cheeks were a delicate pink, whether from their kiss or her escalating outrage, he wasn't sure, but he could guarantee she'd be lashing out at him in three, two—

She shoved past him, almost knocking him off his feet. "What's up, Kerry?"

Her voice was a little raspy and he took satisfaction in knowing he'd affected her even if it meant she'd avoid him even more now that he'd laid one on her. Dan almost rubbed his hands together. He might not have wanted to tempt fate and pursue her due to their working relationship, but he wasn't an idiot. That kiss did not fall in the bracket of normal by a long shot. If she wanted to bury her head in the sand and run from their explosive chemistry so be it. He'd let her run for now.

He had to think it through anyway. Come up with a plan. Because there was no way he was living his life without a repeat performance. And if he had his way, they wouldn't stop at a kiss. So he'd let her run, but she wouldn't get far. It was a good thing he wasn't afraid of a little chase. In fact, back in school he'd excelled at catch 'n' kiss, and he couldn't wait to start the game.

2

Jody splashed cold water on her face and wrists. She couldn't believe Dan had kissed her. Kissed the ever-loving life out of her. Dear God, that had been a toe-curling, panty-melting lip lock of epic proportions, and she wasn't sure she'd ever breathe normally again. The man had serious skills. They'd been seconds away from tearing each other's clothes off. She'd never experienced such mindless lust before. Not even in the heady first days of her relationship with Colin.

She sighed. It couldn't happen again. The last thing she needed was a man complicating her life. Her stomach cramped at the thought of never kissing Dan again. He'd had her on edge for weeks. She'd told herself she was still pissed by his obnoxious behavior when they were first introduced but she couldn't lie to herself any more. Dan O'Conner made her want things. Sex. God, yes! He made her want sex. Jody couldn't remember the last time she'd even had sex. Five years? Six?

Could it really be that long? The more she mulled it over the more she had the sinking feeling that six years was an understatement. She hung her head and let out a deep sigh. She'd buried her needs along with her marriage. Neither had ever been that satisfying, but at least she'd had them. Sort of. Okay, who was she kidding? Both her marriage and sex life had sucked. And not in a good way. Jody smiled. At least she'd kept her sense of humor. Then again, she'd probably curl up in a little ball crying her eyes out if she hadn't.

She grabbed a towel and used it to pat her face dry before checking herself in the mirror. She needed to get back out there, but she'd needed a few minutes to regain her composure. Never let it be said that Jody Walsh couldn't hold it together no matter what life threw at her. Spine straight, shoulders back, she flung the door open and got on with it. The crew had everything packed up and all that was left was one final walk through. She pulled her phone from her pocket and opened her picture gallery to compare each room to the photos she'd taken before they'd set up for the party. It was cheating, but she had no intention of screwing this job—any job—up.

Each room appeared as it had hours earlier. Looking at the house now, you wouldn't know it had been crowded with people partaking in a risqué adults-only party for the last couple of hours. She glanced at her watch. Three fifteen. It had run longer than expected, but instead of being dead on her feet, she was strangely wired. Her system buzzed, every nerve alive and ready for action. Hopefully, she'd be able to sleep. The girls were due home at seven in the morning and she still had to head to the warehouse and unload the night's equipment.

Rounding the corner, Jody ran into a solid wall of warm muscle. Dan. Why was he still here? "Sorry."

"No worries." He steadied her with his hands on her waist. "All done?"

"Yes. I just need to lock up on the way out."

"Let's go then." He cupped her elbow and steered her to the front door.

"What are you doing?"

"Leaving?"

"So go already." She really didn't want to spend any more time with him tonight.

"I came with you in the van, remember?"

Oh shit. He had. Jody closed her eyes and prayed for strength. They'd spend at least another thirty minutes together. "Right. Sorry." She fished the keys from her pocket and picked up her pace. The faster she got him back to his car, the quicker she could take a breath and clear her head.

"Where's the fire?"

"Huh?" She opened the door and climbed in the driver's side.

"Never mind." Dan buckled his belt and stared straight ahead.

She couldn't be sure, but she thought he was looking at her from the corner of his eye. A shiver skipped down her spine and goose bumps broke out on her skin. Her mind replayed their kiss and she licked her lips as the memory of his taste flooded her senses. No doubt about it, the man was lethal to her equilibrium. She stuck the key in the ignition, turned it and fired up the engine. Hot, stale air blasted through the vents and she quickly wound the window down to let in some of the fresh autumn breeze.

The drive back was quiet. Only the soft sounds of the radio and the early morning filtered through the cabin. She couldn't think of anything to say and had no intention of discussing their encounter, so Jody concentrated on getting them to the warehouse safely. A tall order when her mind wanted to circle back to those few minutes with his mouth on hers.

Jody pulled into the driveway and hit the remote for the loading door. The doublewide metal panel slid up in a smooth, noiseless motion before grinding to a halt. She glanced up as she drove under.

"That reminds me. I need to get the installer back out to check the roller door," Dan said.

"But it's brand new."

"Oh, I don't think it's broken. But the guy did say sometimes they need an adjustment after the first so many uses. Better to be safe than sorry." He opened his door when she brought the van to a stop. "I'll start unloading. You go file the paperwork."

"You're hanging around?" Too late. The door closed behind him before she even got one word out. By the time Jody swung out of her seat, Dan had the cargo doors open and was carrying the first of the equipment boxes to the racks. She might not be rid of him as quickly as she liked, but at least she'd get distance—and possibly some sense —when she went upstairs. Perhaps then she'd manage to catch her breath.

She picked up her backpack and headed to her office. A thrill of delight ran through her. *Her* office. After years of working any part-time job she could get, not only did she have a fulltime job she loved, but she had an office. There was no stopping the grin. Even sharing the workspace with Dan couldn't dampen her excitement. The room appeared a little cramped with two desks, but at least they could share the filing cabinets. In the beginning, she'd worried about the combined work zone, but so far it had worked seamlessly. Not that they'd found themselves in the room at the same time very often since she started working at Are You Game?

Jody thought he'd been avoiding her in the beginning, and with her own turbulent emotions about the man, she hadn't worried about it. But now... Now she figured that her initial assumption the tension between them would cause problems had been correct, and couldn't imagine how they'd work in such close proximity after their latest encounter. Not that the conflict between them had headed in the direction she originally expected it to. She swallowed through a constricted throat when she thought about just how close they'd been a little while ago.

Her body still hummed with arousal. She'd done well to mask her reactions to his kiss up until now, but there was a very real possi-bility she wouldn't be able to hide them any longer. Definitely time to get out of here. Unzipping her bag, Jody pulled out her clipboard and began flicking through the pages. She grabbed a pen and flopped into her chair. Marking off each task, jotting notes about the evening and signing off on staff timecards took her about fifteen minutes, and it wasn't until Dan cleared his throat that she looked up.

"Done?" he asked as he pushed off the doorjamb.

"Almost. You?"

"Yep." He perched his hip on the corner of her desk and her eyes were drawn to the way his pants pulled tight across his muscular thighs.

Jody coughed and jerked her gaze back to the paperwork in her hand. "I'll see you next week then."

Dan laughed.

"What?" She risked a glance up and regretted it the second his gaze snagged and held hers.

"Trying to get rid of me?" One corner of his mouth tipped up.

"Ah, no, but there's no need for you to hang around waiting for me."

"Good manners dictate that I do." He picked up the picture frame she kept on her desk. The one with her and the girls at SeaWorld last year. "They look just like you."

"Really?" She'd never seen the resemblance, but he wasn't the first to make the observation.

"Yeah. How old are they?"

Crap. She didn't want to have this conversation with him. It brought them closer, this whole sharing of personal lives. But she couldn't ignore him. "Fifteen and thirteen."

"Shit. What were you when you had them? Twelve?"

She smiled. The compliment was nice, but she knew she looked every one of her thirty-four years. "You should know better than to ask a woman how old she is."

"I peg you at thirty." He arched one eyebrow.

"Ah, you sweet talker you."

"Hey, if all it takes is sweet talk I'll lay on the sugar until the cows come home."

She'd have to be stupid to miss the undertone of his remark.

"Seriously, how old are you?"

Jody had the sudden thought that her age would be a good deterrent to his obvious pursuit. "Thirty-five in two months."

"June? What date?"

She nodded. "Fourteenth. Why?"

"Well, how about that. We share a birthday. I'll be twenty-eight. We'll have to celebrate together."

"Ah…" What the hell was she supposed to say to that? "The girls and I usually do something fun—go bowling, see a movie."

"Great. Count me in." Dan leaned over and flicked the pages on her calendar. "Okay, the fourteenth is a Saturday so we can do both. Oh, unless they'll be with their father on the weekend?"

He was fishing for information, and Jody couldn't decide if it was a good or bad thing that he didn't balk at their seven-year-age gap or spending time with her daughters. "No, they're with me most weekends, but the last thing you want to do is hang out with a couple of teenagers on your birthday—"

"Stop." He held up his hand. "Here's the thing, Jody. They're part of you. I want to spend time with you so that means I want to spend time with them."

Her stomach clenched. Their father didn't want to see them half the time, so she couldn't imagine Dan really wanted to spend the day in their company. "Look. I don't know what you're trying to do, but pretending to like my kids won't get you in my bed." Jody's face flushed. Where the hell had that come from? She hadn't even been thinking of sex with him. *Liar.*

Dan laughed. A rich deep rumble that shook his shoulders. He leaned over her desk and got right in her face. "Make no mistake here, Jody. Wanting in your bed has nothing to do with wanting to spend the day with you and your kids. I want both. I'll get both."

Dan watched Jody closely. No doubt about it, he'd put it out there. He hadn't even thought before the words were flying across his tongue. Her assumption about his motives pissed him off. She was the only woman he'd ever met who made him want to shake her and kiss her at the same time. It wasn't the first time she'd questioned his intentions, and he wasn't going to let her get away with it from now on. She'd know where he stood every step of the way.

He wasn't sure when he'd made the decision to pursue her. Probably in that first nano-second his lips had touched hers. Her silent, wide-eyed stare almost made him laugh, but he didn't think she'd find his humor acceptable at the moment. Then again, she hadn't exactly found his statement to her liking either. With a sigh, he pulled out of her personal space and grabbed a pen out of the ceramic mug that reminded him of something he'd made back in high school. One of her daughters must have given it to her.

Marking the fourteenth of June with a big star, he scribbled *birthday celebration with girls and Dan* in red. He underscored the whole thing with two lines. "There. It's on your calendar." Dan pulled his phone from his pocket and he added it to his own planner where he discovered the reminder for dinner with his family. "Oh, and keep the night free too. We'll have dinner as well."

She hadn't said a word, and he glanced at her to check she was still there. Her eyes were comically wide and her mouth hung open, so he reached over and nudged her jaw up.

Jerking back, she pulled away from his touch. "What are you doing?"

He smiled at her. "I think I've made it pretty clear."

"Well, yes, but..."

Finding her inability to voice her thoughts shouldn't be gratifying, but Dan loved that he could knock her off her feet this way. "Here, let's make it simple. I like you. You like me. Uh, uh, don't argue, you can't deny we have chemistry. Not after that kiss." He waited to see if she'd remain quiet and let him finish. "Good. So I like you and you like me."

Her mouth moved, and for a second he thought she'd offer an argument, but in the end she rolled her lips inward and stayed silent.

"As I was saying, we like each other and I think it's worth seeing where that goes. Actually, I know it's worth it."

"How can you know that after just a kiss?"

"Just a kiss? Jody, that wasn't *just* a kiss. That was a life-altering moment that neither of us saw coming or should walk away from." He had to get her to agree with him. The more he thought about it the more he wanted to know every little thing about her. Wanted to spend hours and hours getting to know her.

"But we work together. When this goes pear-shaped we'll be stuck here, in this tiny room, when we won't want to lay eyes on each other."

Dan could see her point, but he didn't think they'd have that problem. "We'll cross that bridge if we come to it."

"No!" She pushed her chair back and stood. "I won't risk my job. Not for you. Not for anyone."

"It won't come to that."

"You can't guarantee that." She opened the drawer in her desk and pulled out a handbag.

"What? You're running?" He stood up and faced her across her desk.

"No. I'm going home," she said as she slipped the strap of her bag over her shoulder. "I'll finish the paperwork there."

"You are running." He wanted to grab her. Shake her. Stop her.

"There's nothing to run from." Jody rounded the desk and headed for the door. "Lock up on your way out."

She was gone before he could get his legs to move, but once his brain got the signals right, he chased after her. "Jody!"

"No!" She spun around and threw her arm up, palm out, to stop him. "We're not talking about this anymore. There's nothing to talk about."

"Bullshit!"

Her eyes narrowed. "Bullshit? *Bullshit?* Bullshit is the fact you think you can kiss me and then proceed to tell me what we're going to do about it. We might have chemistry. It might be off the charts, but I'm not a slave to my hormones, and I'm certainly not some meek little woman you can order around to your liking."

With that, she turned and continued down the stairs. Her ponytail swung from side to side and he had the urge to grab it and pull her back. *Fuck.* He was turning into a caveman. He'd never felt this razor-sharp need for a woman. Never wanted on a bone-deep-can't-breathe-without-her level. And why the hell was he suddenly so desperate for her? She was the same woman she'd been this morning. The same snapping didn't-want-to-look-at-him Jody he'd been butting heads with for months. Only she wasn't the same. *He* wasn't the same. Not after that kiss.

"We're not done," he yelled at her retreating back.

"Yes, we are," she screamed back, followed by the slamming of the warehouse's outer door.

"*Fuck.*" He speared his fingers through his hair, dug his nails into his scalp and growled. She'd as good as told him to fuck off. If she'd been anyone else he would have taken her at her word. But he wasn't backing down. Wasn't walking away from something he knew could be special—unique—life altering. "Fuck!"

Dan dropped his chin to his chest and drew in a deep breath. The light scent of vanilla teased his nose. Dammit, he could smell her. He pulled the front of his shirt up and sniffed. It smelled exactly like Jody. Some of her perfume must have rubbed off when they'd been locked together. Like an addict, he sucked in another big breath and let her fill him. His body tightened, his cock going from semi-hard to rock hard in a heartbeat.

It didn't matter what had happened before their kiss or after. He wasn't about to let either of them pass up the possibilities their chemistry offered. Jody might be right. Hormones may be the driving force behind their sparks, but Dan knew lust. He'd spent his whole adult life letting it lead him from one woman to the next, and what he felt when he held Jody—kissed her—was a billion times more potent. She could run as far and fast as her sexy long legs would take her. It wouldn't matter, because he'd catch her in the end. And when he did, he'd kiss her and prove their first lip lock wasn't a fluke.

3

Jody jumped as the door of her office burst open.

"Oh, good, you're still here." Cassie marched over to Jody's desk and slapped down a folder. "I need you to handle this for me."

"Sure." She leaned forward to pull the file closer.

"Wait. Before you agree you should know what it entails."

Jody eyed her boss, the woman who'd become her friend, the woman who was dating her brother. And if she was reading the signs correctly, Cassie would eventually be her sister-in-law. "What could possibly stop me from saying yes to a job?"

"It's a full weekend." Cassie chewed her lip. "Away."

"What?" Jody grabbed the folder and flipped it around.

"Not yet." Cassie slammed her palm on the cover. "I wouldn't ask if I wasn't desperate. I know I promised you the weekend off, but I need to replace Jeremy. He just rang and said his mother has been rushed to hospital with a suspected heart attack, and you're the only one without an event this weekend so you can fill the two-day gap. I'd have to cover a shift for anyone else."

"I already said I'd do it." She tugged the file from Cassie's hold and opened it. Air zapped from her lungs and her stomach cramped so tight she swore her belly button hit her backbone.

"What? What's wrong?" Cassie leaned over to see the page Jody was looking at.

"Nothing." *Oh God.* There was no way she could say no now. "Just a cramp from too much lunch." They'd visited a new sushi place down the road together and she'd definitely eaten too much, but that wasn't what had her insides contracting. Jody took a deep breath and smiled up at Cassie. "Leave it with me. Don't worry. I'll get everything sorted out."

"Luc said we can have the girls. He'll watch them while I work Friday night and Saturday afternoon."

"You sure?" Jody's brother had been having the girls more since he'd begun dating Cassie, but having them for the whole weekend might be a stretch, especially when her big brother had always been uncomfortable around their little girly ways. Although now they were both older, he was finding it easier to deal with them.

"Yes. We love having them. Plus, I want to go see that new Pixar movie and it'll look a lot better if I actually take some kids with me." Cassie grinned. "Not to mention we can hit the arcade afterward."

"Okay, I'll get them to head home after school tomorrow, and Luc can pick them up from there whenever he finishes work." A whole two days without the girls would normally bring a thrill, but not this time. This time she'd be spending those two days with the one person she'd been avoiding like the plague.

"Great. I owe you. I'll let Luc know the plan." Cassie headed out with a wave.

Jody slumped in her chair. It'd been two weeks and six days since the moment. She refused to think of it as a kiss. That just bought back memories and sensations she didn't want to deal with, so it was *the moment.* Either he'd given up, was avoiding her or was biding his time. None of those scenarios made her happy. He'd been so adamant the other night, and then when she'd brushed him off—okay, it had been more than a brush-off—he'd all but disappeared. Well, there'd be no escaping each other this weekend.

Dan was the lead coordinator and she was the assistant. But that wasn't the kicker. No, the huge problem was they were sharing a hotel room. She leaned her head back, closed her eyes and tried to put a lid on the panic bubbling in her chest.

"Sleeping on the job?"

She catapulted forward, her eyes opening wide and her breath rushing from her lungs. "Shit. You scared the crap out of me." Her heart beat against her ribs like a drummer on speed.

It had been like this for days. She'd lived on tenterhooks waiting for the other shoe to drop. Of course, he'd been all smiles and friendly workplace-acceptable talk. All the while, she'd been worrying about touching him—stressing about him touching her. The hairs on her arms and neck stood at attention just being in the same room as Dan. She could only imagine her body's reaction if they actually touched.

"What's got those creases in your forehead?" He sat behind his desk and Jody breathed a sigh of relief. He wasn't coming closer.

"Oh, I was running through my mental to-do list." She held up the folder Cassie had given her. "Lots to get organized before the weekend."

"You agreed to fill in for Jeremy?" He raised his eyebrows.

"Yes." She clamped her mouth shut. As soon as she was alone again, she'd ring the hotel and see about getting another room. She'd pay for it out of her own pocket so Cassie would never find out there'd been a problem.

"It's fully booked." Dan leaned back in his chair and crossed his muscular arms over his chest, the sleeves of his polo shirt stretching tight.

"What is?" She forced her gaze away from his bulging biceps and up to meet his.

"The hotel." A smile curled his mouth. The same mouth that had turned her into a puddle of need two weeks ago.

Oh my God. Was he a mind reader? She wanted to wipe the silly grin off his face.

"But don't worry, the room has two beds. As long as you don't snore, we'll survive."

"Snore? That's all you're worried about?"

"Well, there's also the small issue of me sleeping naked..."

Naked? Heat pooled in her belly, dripped lower and moistened flesh that had been barren only a few weeks ago. With one kiss, he'd brought her body back to life. And now she'd have to share a room with him. A naked him. This couldn't get any worse.

"It's about a three-hour drive from here, so we'll leave at lunch time tomorrow. Make sure we get there with plenty of time to check in and set up for the evening." He scanned a sheet of paper in front of him. "Oh, and don't forget to pack your swimmers. There's a hot tub on our patio."

Jody gulped. Images of a wet, naked Dan flashed through her mind. Her palms grew damp, her skin stretched tight and the crotch of her undies grew wetter by the minute. She had to get out of here. Had to get some fresh air before she did something stupid like throw herself over his desk and beg him to kiss her and take away the ache expanding in her sex. Leaping out of her chair, she all but ran from the room.

Dan watched Jody dash from the room and smiled. She might want to pretend there was nothing between them, but she couldn't hide from her feelings any more than he could. He'd seen the telltale reactions her body had presented on more than one occasion over the last few weeks. He wanted to thank his lucky stars that they'd ended up thrown together this weekend, but that seemed horrible when he considered the reason she'd had to come along on this job. Then again, fate was a fickle bitch and he wouldn't look a gift horse in the mouth.

He rolled his chair back and swung his feet up on the desk. He'd wait her out. She had to come back, and he'd been laying low long enough. Time to push her a little. Dan knew he was being arrogant in his approach. Figured she'd call him on it too, but he was enjoying the game. His usual MO when it came to women was simple. Get in, get out. The two long-term relationships—if a few months could be considered long—had been more a convenience than any real need. He wasn't all that sure he liked the man he was.

With Jody, he wanted to savor the chase. His mother had taught him nothing worth having should come easy, and he should always strive to make something better than it was. That probably explained why he'd never stuck when it came to relationships. The women he'd dated *had* come easily, and those that hadn't weren't even a blip on his radar. But this woman. Jody. She was different. Everything about her made him stand up and take notice. From the moment they'd been introduced, he'd felt the buzz.

At first, he'd been so set on disliking her—or the idea of her—that he hadn't registered what was really going on. And if he were honest, he'd admit he'd still been blind right up until the instant he'd laid his lips on hers. He shook his head. Damn, he was an idiot. Blind. Stupid. Ignorant. Each word described him perfectly. Right up until the kiss. In that second, the fog had cleared from his mind and he'd seen with HD-Technicolor clarity. Jody Walsh had rocked his world to its foundations. But if he was lucky—and God help him, he wanted to be—she'd help him build them back up again.

Oh, he knew it was too soon to be thinking so seriously, but he'd had days to think about their chemistry, weeks to ponder the absolute rarity of such a connection, and there was no way around it. What he felt for Jody wasn't just simple lust. He knew lust. Christ, he'd spent his whole adult life letting it lead him around by the dick. This was bone deep and raw edged. For the first time in his life, he felt as though he'd be missing out on something amazing if he didn't *get the girl.*

Jody walked back in, her steps faltering when she saw him leaning back in his chair. "Oh, I thought you would be gone."

Hoped more like it. "Nope." He smiled. "Still here."

She headed for her desk. Without looking his way again, she

scooped up the file for the weekend job, pulled her bag from a drawer and turned to leave. "Bye."

He could have predicted her snub. She'd made an art of ignoring him for the last three weeks, except he wasn't about to let her get away with it any longer. He pushed out of his chair and met her near the door. "I'm heading out too."

The scowl on her face said it all, and it took considerable effort and a bitten cheek to keep from grinning. Dan let her precede him through the door, let her lead the way downstairs, but once they made it to the bottom of the stairwell, he crowded close behind her. She picked up her pace, and this time there was no stopping the smirk from stretching his lips. When they neared the door, he scooted around her and opened it before she could. He waited for the I'm-capable speech. Women these days couldn't seem to accept a kind gesture no matter how small.

"Thank you," she murmured as she walked past.

His shock was so great it took him a second to follow. He'd expected her to lash out. God knows she never accepted his help when he offered. Suddenly she was thanking him for giving her a hand without asking? Dan wasn't sure what to make of this latest shift in attitude, but he didn't have time to dwell on it. He had something else he wanted to do before they parted ways. Hurrying, he caught her just as she reached her car.

"Hey." As he'd hoped, she spun around, putting her back to her car, and he moved right in.

"Wha—?"

Dan lowered his head and slanted his mouth across hers.

Her lips parted as she sucked in a breath—his breath—and he took the opportunity to slide his tongue inside her mouth. The moan that issued from her throat had his blood racing and his balls tightening. Minty fresh, her taste exploded—saturated his mouth with memory and need. He'd wanted this for weeks. Days. Hours.

Forever.

He tangled their tongues and pressed in closer. They touched from chest to thigh, and Dan wanted the barriers between them gone.

Wanted to rip the clothes from their bodies and really feel her against him. Except that wasn't going to happen here. There were enough brain cells still functioning for him to know that. Instead, he angled his hips, pushed his leg between hers and rubbed against her pussy. She moaned into his mouth and he increased the pressure. She rocked her hips, the motion growing quicker with each stroke of his tongue—thrust of his leg.

Dan worked his hand from her waist to her breast. He cupped the mound, tested the weight in his palm before pinching the taut nipple between thumb and fingers. Jody murmured, half-demand, half-plea, and the sound egged him on. His cock screamed for action and he twisted a little to the right, pressed his straining length into her hip in an attempt to find the friction he desperately needed. She bucked against him, her spine arching like a bow, and he pulled back, separated their mouths, to see her face.

Her skin was coated in a fine sheen of sweat, her cheeks flushed pink and her pulse hammered at the base of her throat. She was the picture of a woman on the edge, and it blindsided him to think just a kiss and a few well-placed touches could get her there. The swollen flesh of her bottom lip lay wet and inviting, and Dan couldn't resist sliding his tongue over the curved length. He barely registered the traffic meters away, rushing along the road as people made their way home.

He saw the second she realized what they were doing—where they were doing it—and before she could protest, he planted his mouth on hers once more. This time he savored. Licking and stroking in wet glides that stole his breath and gave him hers. She made that sound again—the one between a demand and a plea, and Dan's good intentions fell at their feet. He squeezed her breast, pressing his thigh into her pussy until she rose to her toes. Off-balance, she leaned in, rocked her hips and ground her sex against him.

Something snapped. In him—in her—he didn't know, but all of a sudden they were moving together in a frenzy of need that left Jody panting in his mouth and Dan clenching every muscle in an effort to hold off the orgasm burning in his balls. She arched, her muscles stretched tight, and her breath stalled. Then it happened. She shattered. The climax tore through her. Her body thrashed between him and her car, and he pulled them away so she didn't hurt herself on the hard metal surface. He held her close, his mouth still devouring hers, soaking in the sounds she made, while she rode out the final waves.

Dan enjoyed the moment. Took it all in and engraved it on his mind, because he knew the second she came down, the moment reality returned, she'd be all over his ass about what he'd done. Sure she'd let him, she'd definitely been willing, but he'd pushed himself on her, taken her by surprise and left her no recourse but to surrender. And surrender she did. Beautifully. Completely. He wanted her to do it again. And again.

Jody dragged air into her straining lungs. Every part of her felt replete—relaxed in a way she hadn't in so long it took her a moment to get her head around what had happened. She'd come all over Dan's leg. Gotten off in the damn parking lot. On his *leg*. She wanted to hate herself for allowing it to go that far, but the pleasure still zipping through her veins, pleasure she hadn't experienced in years, wouldn't let her. He held her close and she buried her face in the curve of his neck to avoid facing him a few minutes more. Not that she could ignore him. Not with the huge erection pressing into her hip.

She couldn't evade the inevitable forever, so she took a deep breath to brace herself. Big mistake. His scent filled her. Soaked into her pores and surrounded her with renewed desire. He smelled like sex. *They* smelled like sex. Her insides quivered. A trembling of nerves and cells brought to life by the man holding her close. She'd never done anything like this before. Never dreamed she'd climax without stripping naked and spending long minutes building toward an orgasm that often proved elusive.

"You okay?"

The quietly uttered question brought her out of her thoughts. She was more than okay, but she wasn't about to stroke Dan's ego by telling him. Managing a nod, she tried to pull from his grasp.

"No. Not yet." He roamed his hands up and down her back, soothing and arousing, the motion keeping her in place. "There's no one around and nobody can see us from the street."

She sighed. At least Dan was the only witness to her embarrassingly wanton behavior. As the seconds ticked past, Jody began to realize the full extent of her mistake. She'd been so easy. So ready to ride his leg and take what he offered. Embarrassment didn't begin to cover it.

"Stop beating yourself up," he murmured in her ear, his warm breath flowing over her neck.

She shivered and a groan slipped up her throat. How did he read her so well?

"I know what you're thinking, but don't. Take it for what it is. Mutual pleasure."

Jody laughed. "Not so mutual."

"Oh, you're wrong there." He gripped her ass cheeks and pulled her hard against him. "Feeling you get off is one of the most pleasurable things I've ever experienced."

She highly doubted it. His hard cock still pressed against her. He had to be in some sort of discomfort if not outright pain. "I..." Words failed her.

"Here's what we're going to do. When you're ready, I'm going to let you go and you're going to get in your car and drive home." He gave her ass a gentle squeeze.

"But—"

"Nope. The only butt is the one I've got my hands on. The same one that will be in that driver's seat in a few minutes."

"Dan."

He kissed the top of her head. "'Night, Jody. I'll see you tomorrow morning." With care, he let her go.

No argument came to mind. No words or thoughts or anything that might make this moment easier. Thank you was on the tip of her tongue, but the words seemed out of place and inadequate at best, so she turned around and opened her door. She slid into her seat and felt the stickiness of her come-soaked undies between her legs. Sliding the key into the ignition, she reached for the door only to have Dan close it for her. They stared at each other through the window and she pressed the button to lower it.

"Please, don't say anything." He brushed a finger down her cheek, over the swollen flesh of her lips. "I'll see you tomorrow."

"O-okay."

He grinned and stepped back. "Don't forget to pack your swimsuit."

The reminder of what lay ahead had Jody's insides springing back to life. Thinking about sharing a hot tub with Dan sent a shiver down her spine and a host of sexually charged images through her mind. She needed to leave. Distance would help her think clearly. Turning the key, she started the car then put it in reverse. With one last look at Dan, she lowered the handbrake and reversed out of her spot. It took everything she had not to glance in the rear view mirror to see if he watched as she drove away.

She had no idea what to think or how to feel about the last few minutes in his arms. There was no denying she'd enjoyed herself, the evidence was in her drenched underwear and making the drive home extremely uncomfortable. Stripping out of her clothes and jumping in the shower was the first order of business when she got home. Hopefully, the girls would be busy with homework and she could sneak to her room without having to stop.

Jody flipped the visor down and slid open the mirror. Her face was flushed and her hair was a mess with numerous strands escaping her ponytail and hanging in her face. Any adult would know exactly what she'd been doing, but at fifteen and thirteen, she hoped the girls would be oblivious and assume she'd just had a hectic day at work. A car cut her off and she shook herself free of her thoughts and concentrated on the madness of peak-hour traffic.

It was a bitch. Everyone seemed to be in a big hurry to get where they were going and nobody wanted to let someone else get in front of them. She barely missed being part of a three-car smash, braking hard to miss the vehicle in front and spewing some choice words she'd never utter with her daughters around. Then again, it had been an afternoon of doing things she'd never do with the girls present.

With fingers curled tightly around the steering wheel, Jody negotiated the roads until she hit the quieter suburban streets near her house and she could relax her grip. She lived in an area where the median house price was considered low, but it was a beautiful older area of Sydney that she loved and one that she could afford on her own with two kids to support. As she pulled into her driveway, she wondered what Dan would think of her small clapboard house. Would he see the fading, chipped paint? Would he notice the lawn needed mowing and the garden weeding?

Giving herself a mental slap, she switched off the car and got out. It shouldn't matter what he thought. She didn't need his approval of where she lived. Besides, she owned it. Well, she owned three quarters of it, the bank owned the rest. Perhaps the peeling paint and messy yard were the bank's quarter. Jody glanced down the street then back at her house and tried to forget about the man she'd just driven away from. What mattered was what lay before her. Her house and the girls tucked safely inside its walls.

She didn't need a man to give her a home. She'd done that herself without the help of the man she'd married. Nothing Dan offered could compare with what she had. But even as she thought the words, she knew she was a liar. The dampness of her undies and hum of pleasure still vibrating in her blood proved that.

4

Dan glanced over at a silent Jody. The woman had barely spoken two words to him all morning at the office, and that was a feat in itself considering they'd had to pack equipment for this weekend's job. They'd loaded the van in silence, climbed in and driven for over an hour and still she'd said nothing. It was starting to get on his nerves, but he didn't know what the right words to disperse the awkward tension humming between them were.

He couldn't tell if she was embarrassed by what had happened yesterday or pissed off at him for taking advantage of her. Again. He'd been angry with himself for ambushing her a second time until he'd accepted the fact that, right or wrong, he'd made a move and he had to live with the fallout. Of course, that was easier said than done, especially when he sat beside a stone-faced Jody. Dan figured he had two choices. Ignore it—which appeared to be how Jody wanted to handle it—or bring it up and discuss it. Right now, neither option appealed.

They had roughly another two hours on the road, so she was effectively a captive audience until they reached the hotel. Once they got to their destination, they'd be caught up in the prep for tonight's welcome dinner, so if he was going to clear the air between them, now would be the perfect time. As much as he didn't want to, Dan couldn't take any more of this strained silence.

"About yesterday—"

"Stop." She turned in her seat to face him. "I don't want to talk about it."

Dan took his eyes off the road for a second to look at her. "What?"

"I don't mix my personal and professional lives and we're working right now."

Was she for real? "Considering we were on the job both times I've kissed you, I'm not sure your argument holds."

"We weren't yesterday. We'd left for the day."

He could see her squirming in her seat from the corner of his eye.

"Look. Can we just stick with work?"

"Why? So you can continue to ignore the sparks between us?" He couldn't believe Jody thought that was even possible. Any idiot could see there was something going on. The air between them vibrated with the tension.

Dan kept his eyes on the road, but he could see her moving in his peripheral vision so he knew she'd turned away to look out the passenger window. Half of him wanted to leave it alone, not upset her, but the other half wanted to drag it out in the open and deal with it. Hopefully in a positive way—like Jody agreeing they should explore what had them drawing closer together with every breath.

"Jody." He swiveled his gaze from the road to her and back again. "I can't pretend it never happened."

She sighed. "I know. I'm not asking you to forget, exactly. It's just... I can't deal with this right now."

"When then?" He didn't mean to push her, but he couldn't help it.

"Can we just stick to work for now?"

Dan glanced over again to find her still facing the side window. Her shoulders were hunched and she was twisting her fingers together in her lap. As much as he didn't want to drop it, he knew it was pointless to keep pushing. He wouldn't get anywhere at the moment. He let out a breath. "If that's what you want, but the second this job is over we're dealing with us."

"Thank you," she murmured.

Manners had him almost saying you're welcome, but he stopped himself because he didn't want her thanks. Dropping the subject wasn't what he wanted to do, except the only way he'd get his way was to back off and try again later. He leaned forward and hit the switch for the radio. Music filled the cab as they sped down the freeway at a hundred and ten kilometers an hour. Traffic was minimal this time of day so he was able to stick to the speed limit for most of it. If they'd left the office any later, they would have been caught in not only the evening rush home but the weekend travellers as well.

The next two hours were accompanied by the radio, a quiet Jody and Dan's brooding silence, making for a less-than-comfortable trip. By the time he pulled into the driveway of the hotel, he was more than ready to get out of the tomb the van had become. As he hopped out and made his way to the rear of the van, a valet came over. "You'll need a couple of trolleys for what we've got, mate," Dan said.

The valet's eyes bugged out when he peered through the back doors. "Right, two trolleys," he said before scurrying back the way he'd come.

Jody stepped beside him. "I'll check in while you get the equipment unloaded."

"Okay. Make sure you ask for Keith Mooney, he's our hotel contact for the weekend."

"Will do." She turned toward the hotel but glanced over her shoulder before she took a step. "Anything else?"

"No. We just need to get all our gear inside." Jody nodded and Dan watched her walk away. Staring at her, he had to wonder if he'd ever get what he wanted. He always seemed to be staring at her back as she left him in her wake. He'd give anything to be walking beside her. She disappeared into the hotel as the valet came out pulling two trolleys. Dan frowned. It didn't matter what he wanted right now. He had a job to do, and as much as he wanted to blow it off and deal with Jody and the pull between them, he couldn't. Focusing on the van, he began stacking boxes on one trolley while the valet put their bags on the other.

Jody took a deep breath of air-conditioned air and slowed her pace as she walked to the registration desk. Being trapped in the car with Dan for the last three hours had just about broken her. So many times, she'd been a breath away from asking him why he'd kissed her. She wouldn't ask about what had followed, it seemed to be a natural progression whenever their lips met. If they hadn't been interrupted the first time they'd kissed, she had no doubt they would have ended up without clothes and in a similar state of passion as yesterday. Possibly more so. They were combustible.

She couldn't ignore the chemistry any more than she could ignore the man himself when he sat a few feet away. Ten minutes tops. That's all she had before he'd be with her again and all her intelligence went south along with every rational thought. Reaching the counter, she smiled at the woman behind it. "Hi, is Keith Mooney around? I'm Jody Walsh from Are You Game?. He's expecting us."

"Oh, yes, he told me to keep my eye out for you. I'll let him know you're here." The woman, Keisha if her nametag was correct, picked up the phone and punched a button. "Mr. Mooney, the people from Are You Game? have arrived."

Jody opened her bag and pulled out the credit card Cassie had given her for work use. She also retrieved the run sheet she'd printed off for herself before leaving the office this morning.

"Mr. Mooney will be right out. I can check you in while you're waiting."

Jody stopped reading and returned her attention to the young woman. "Great." Rattling metal had her turning to see Dan pushing a trolley laden with their equipment through the front doors, a valet right behind him with their luggage on another. "Could someone take our luggage to our room while we get set up for tonight?"

"Certainly," Keisha said.

"Checked in?" Dan asked as he joined her at the desk.

"Doing that now, and Mr. Mooney is on his way."

"Good. I want to take a look at the rooms we'll be utilizing before we set anything up."

"Why? I think what you had drawn up was good."

"Yeah, I was lucky the hotel sent me the room sizes and layouts, but I still want to take a look before we unpack."

He had a point. Sometimes something as little as the placement of a power point could throw out an entire layout. "Just let me know what you want me to do and when." As soon as the words left her mouth, Jody realized their unintended double meaning.

Dan grinned and leaned closer, whispering in her ear, "I like the sound of you doing what I want, when I want."

A shiver raced over her skin and her stomach flip-flopped before dropping low and sinking heavy and hot into her pelvis. She took a sharp breath and pulled in his unmistakable scent—a mix of coffee and leather and something uniquely Dan. Without conscious thought, she tipped toward him and would have leaned against him if they hadn't been interrupted.

"Mr. O'Conner. Ms. Walsh. Lovely to have you both with us. I'm Keith Mooney."

A striking blond man in black trousers and light-blue business shirt with the hotel logo on the left breast pocket came toward them. He was almost too good looking, and Jody had to look away or risk getting caught staring at his surprising beauty. She focused on Dan and found herself comparing the two. While Dan wasn't quite as handsome, he wasn't anything to sneeze at either. And while Keith was blindingly attractive, it was Dan who set her pulse racing and her breath hitching.

Dan extended his hand to shake the other man's. "Pleasure is ours. We're looking forward to working with your employees."

"They're all quite excited about the weekend seminar. I hope the trip up wasn't too long." He turned and offered Jody his hand.

It was the longest drive she'd ever endured, but not in the way Keith implied, so she shook his hand and lied. "It was very pleasant. It's a while since I've driven through this part of the state."

"You're here at a good time too. We haven't hit the freezing temps of winter yet and with the autumn rain all the plants have recovered from the brutal heat of summer." Keith turned to Keisha. "Are they checked in, Keisha?"

"Yes, Mr. Mooney." Keisha placed two key cards on the counter. "Ms. Walsh asked that their luggage be taken to their room while you show them around, so I'll get Dave on that right away."

"Good, good." Keith grabbed both keys and held one out to each of them. "Right, if we're ready, we'll tour the conference rooms. Would either of you like something to eat or drink while we're wandering around?"

"I'm fine, how about you, Jody?" Dan asked as he took his key.

"I'd like a bottle of water if I may." She'd finished the small bottle she'd brought with her over thirty minutes ago, and with her body temperature spiking whenever Dan was around, her mouth had become as dry as the Nullarbor Plains. She took the key from Keith and slid it into the back pocket of her slacks.

"Give me two secs to grab your water and we'll get started." He walked behind the counter and entered a door. Gone less than a minute, he was back with her drink and leading them across the hotel lobby. "This is the original part of the hotel, the section we're about to enter and the one your room is in are the additions. You'll notice the architects and builders did everything they could to marry the old with the new. I think you'll agree they did an excellent job."

Jody cracked the bottle and took a sip while she listened to Keith explain how the hotel had gone from being a small forty-room boutique hotel to a four-hundred room one with conference facilities and five-star-resort amenities. She had to admit it was lovely, in particular the way gardens and seating had been incorporated throughout the public indoor areas to give the place a relaxed atmosphere. She would love to sit in one of the many nooks with a book in her hand. Shame she was here to work really. It would have been lovely to enjoy some down time.

They toured the two rooms set aside for their workshop sessions and neither of them found a problem with the layout and what Dan had drawn up from the specs the hotel had sent him. The larger room they were using for the night events met their demands as well, and with the wall of windows looking out over the gardens that would be lit up after dark, Jody thought it would have a magical feel once the lights were turned down low and the evening's festivities began.

"Jody?"

She spun to face Dan. "Sorry. What?" Looking around, she realized they were alone in the big room. Where had Keith gone? When had he gone?

"Did you hear anything I just said?"

Embarrassed to admit she'd completely zoned out, she tried to bluff her way through. "Sure. Tonight's function is in here."

Dan laughed. "Nice try. But, no. I asked if you wanted to go to the room for anything before we get started with set up."

Her face heated. He'd caught her out. "Um. No, I don't need anything."

"Are you feeling all right?" He stepped closer. "You're looking a little flushed."

She definitely felt warm, but it wasn't illness that made her that way. "It's a little hot in here, that's all. Plus, we've been rushing around for the last few minutes." Okay, so they hadn't been running or even walking fast. As excuses went, it wasn't a very good one.

He stepped closer and pressed the back of his fingers to her cheek. "Are you sure? You feel a little hot to me."

Jody swallowed. It wasn't his words that had her stomach clenching and her blood racing. Dan didn't bother to mask the desire burning in his eyes. His hand might be gentle and innocuous, but those eyes...they were dark with arousal and dangerous to her self-control. She fought the urge to lean into him and instead pulled away. "I'm fine."

Putting some distance between them, she headed toward the door to see if the trolley with their gear had found its way to this area of the hotel. She needed to get busy—distract herself—with work. Not that anything could divert her wayward hormones or her body's reaction to being close to Dan. Jody knew she was in trouble. Pushing him away was becoming more and more difficult, and it was only a matter of time before she succumbed to the volatile chemistry arcing between them.

D an wiped the sweat from his brow. They'd been working for three hours and the room was finally the way he'd imagined it. He'd wanted the tables set like the house tables in Harry Potter. Each group would have a long table and a house flag, in this case a department logo. Food and beverage, meet and greet, and housekeeping. Management would be working alongside their staff—on equal footing—for the duration of the weekend.

Cassie had a marvelous program for her corporate sessions, and this one was tailor-made for the hotel industry. Over the course of two days, the participants would be working together in games designed to teach them problem solving and interacting as a team. He'd run these workshops before so he knew them well, but Jody had had limited exposure to the corporate side of the business. Until now, she'd been dealing with the adult and children's party lines. He wanted her to be comfortable with the seminars she'd be running on her own.

"Okay, we're done." He headed over to where Jody was laying out the house flags on the end of the long tables. "Let's go up to the room and run through the program for each of the sessions you're doing. I want to be sure you're familiar with all aspects of them."

"Oh, I already went over them. I didn't see anything that caused me concern."

"Well, we're done down here anyway. Plus, we have to get ready at some point." Dan placed his hand on her lower back and urged her toward the door. "And I'm feeling a little hungry, so I'm planning to order some room service and sit out on the patio for a few minutes of downtime before the chaos begins."

"I'm not hungry." Was she trying to dodge him? Probably.

"It's been hours since lunch, and it'll be another few before dinner."

"I don't snack between meals," she argued.

"I'll order you a coffee." He wasn't about to let her weasel out of spending some time with him, which is exactly what she was attempting to do.

Dan thought he was home free when they reached the door only to run into Mooney. Who, Dan noticed, couldn't take his eyes off Jody. A growl rumbled in his chest and he had to fake a cough to cover it.

"Hey, you're done." Mooney peered past them into the room. "Good, I thought you might like a guided tour through the gardens." His gaze was focused on Jody once more.

"Actual—"

"That would be lovely." Jody stepped away from Dan's hand and he curled his fingers with the need to grab her shirt and yank her back. "Dan was just heading—"

"I think a walk through the gardens would be great." Dan tried not to grit his teeth. He wasn't about to let this guy sneak off with his woman. *Ah, shit.* She wasn't his. He knew that. But he couldn't let her go off with Mooney on her own. Not when they still hadn't reached an understanding. "Lead the way."

"Oh." The look on Mooney's face almost made Dan laugh. Obviously, the guy had expected only Jody to accept his invitation. Dan smiled and held out his arm to indicate Mooney should lead. "Right. This way then," Mooney mumbled as he turned.

Mooney led them out through a side door and into a lush garden with weaving paths and stone benches for those who wished to sit a while. Dan wasn't into plants or gardening, but he could easily appreciate the beauty of the place. He listened with half an ear to the names Mooney rattled off as they passed each new bed of color. Jody appeared to be soaking up every word the guy said, and Dan's insides churned. Why couldn't she pay *him* that much attention?

They made their way around the building to the rear where the hillside dropped away to reveal rows and rows of grapes. With the area being one of Australia's premier wine producers, he wasn't surprised to find the fruit vines, but until Mooney explained about the hotel's own line of select wines served only to guests, Dan hadn't realized the place was more than a hotel.

"We'll be offering our wines to a few of Sydney's bigger restaurants in the near future, but until then you're only able to sample them here," Mooney said.

"I'd love to try some. Are you serving them tonight?" Jody asked.

"Yes." Mooney grinned. "Are you a wine connoisseur?"

Jody's laughter echoed around them. "Hardly. I just like the occasional sip."

"That's more than you're allowed." Dan couldn't fight his need to squash Mooney's delight. "We're working."

"Oh, surely you're able to have a glass or two?" Mooney asked.

"Nope. The boss has a very strict rule about drinking on the job." Dan smiled smugly when Mooney frowned.

"Dan's right. Even having a sip could get me fired." Jody gave Dan a narrow-eyed look before turning to aim a smile at Mooney. "Perhaps I'll be lucky enough to try it some other time."

He wasn't overly concerned by Jody's supposed anger at him. She knew as well as he did neither of them would be drinking alcohol this weekend. Although, if she did have a couple of glasses she might soften toward him...

"Oh, look at the time." Mooney held up his arm, displaying his watch in an exaggerated fashion. "I have something I have to do before I finish for the day. I'll see you both tonight."

Before either of them could say a word, the man was striding away and out of sight.

"Ouch!" Dan rubbed his upper arm where Jody had just landed a punch. She was surprisingly strong. "What the hell was that for?" Surely if she was going to hit him it would have been one of the two times he'd planted a kiss on her without permission or warning.

"For being an ass." She turned on her heel and headed in the opposite direction to Mooney.

"When?" Dammit. She was running away from him again. Chasing after Jody was becoming an annoying habit. It didn't stop him from following though.

5

Jody slipped into the elevator and pressed the close-door button. Unfortunately, she wasn't quick enough and Dan threw his arm between the doors just before they sealed shut. Of course, that meant the damn things opened again and he stepped right in and kept on coming. The look on his face was a good reason to move back out of his way. When he continued to come at her, she kept reversing until she came up against the rear wall just as the doors closed with a soft thump.

She swallowed over the throbbing lump in her throat. It could only be her heart because the stupid thing was racing so hard there was no way it had remained in her chest. He glared at her with green eyes turbulent with emotion. Anger then arousal flashed before his eyes lowered, his gaze following the sweep of her tongue as she slipped it out to wet dry lips. His pupils dilated and her breath stalled as he bent toward her.

He gave her time. Closed the distance in long, drawn-out seconds that allowed her to escape if she chose to. She knew what was coming. Could read it in his hooded eyes, the angle of his head and the smile kicking up one corner of his mouth. But she didn't pull away. Didn't turn her head. Not at all. Instead, she held her breath, tipped her chin up and waited for him to kiss her.

Their lips touched in a whisper-soft caress that did little to alleviate the need curling low in her belly. Jody couldn't wait for Dan to take them deeper. Rising to her toes, she tilted her face and sealed their mouths fully. He groaned, the sound vibrating across her lips and sending shivers through her jaw. He flicked out his tongue, licked from corner to corner before probing the seam of her lips and seeking entry. Opening for him, she tangled her tongue with his.

Lost in the pleasure of kissing Dan, she moved closer, slid her arms around his neck and tugged him to her, pressed her body along the length of his so every part of her front touched every part of his. It was her turn to groan when he nipped her bottom lip while wrapping his hands around her ass and yanking her sex against his. He was long and thick, rubbing against her intimately as he rocked them together.

Jody moaned and moved even closer. She threaded her fingers through his hair, the soft strands sliding over her skin in a sensual caress as she held him to her. Dan's hands weren't idle either. One still gripped her bottom, the other swept over her hip, up her side and between them to cup her breast. He stroked his thumb across her taut nipple and sent a jolt of desire arrowing straight to her core. She couldn't help the whimper of need or the bucking of her hips.

A rush of air blew past and she had a split second to wonder where it came from before she heard a woman gasp. Abruptly brought out of her lust stupor, Jody pulled away from Dan. But he wouldn't let her go. He held her close, cradled her against his chest when he leaned over and hit the button for their floor. Just before the doors slid closed again, she saw the stunned look on the elderly woman's face. Heat filled her face and she buried her stinging cheeks in the curve of Dan's neck.

"Shit. We really have to stop doing this in public places." He smoothed his hands up and down her back in long, sweeping strokes. "One of these days we're going to get carried away and end up getting arrested for indecent exposure."

Jody could hear the humor in his voice, but she didn't smile. She appreciated his attempt to lighten the mood, though she couldn't find the funny side of once again being so caught up in Dan she'd forgotten where she was. The man was lethal to her common sense. He turned up and good judgment went right out the door along with every other reason she needed to ignore the way her body wanted his.

With a sigh, she slipped from his arms and moved to the front of the elevator. She didn't say a word and, thankfully, neither did he. The bell dinged and the car eased to a stop. Breath held, she waited what felt like hours but was probably no more than a second, for the doors to open. Exiting, she scanned the plaque in front of her to determine which direction to go. They were on the executive level of the east wing, and according to Keith, their room would have a view of the valley they'd seen earlier as well as a terrace hot tub.

She turned right and moved down the hall at a clipped pace. Why she thought she could leave Dan behind when they were sharing a room was beyond her and, again, she could only blame the fact he seemed to disconnect her from her brain whenever he was near. She slowed her steps, allowed him to catch up halfway to the room so they could continue the rest of the way side-by-side. He produced his key before she could and slid it into the sensor to deactivate the lock.

The mechanism clicked, the light turned green and he pushed the door open. "After you."

"Thanks." She walked in and was immediately taken by the large window that did indeed give them a view of the valley. But even the spectacular scenery couldn't hide the fact the room was barely big enough for the two double beds. Two beds no more than a foot apart. Beds they'd be sleeping in tonight. Dan slept naked. Naked. *Oh God.* She couldn't do this. Spinning around, she smacked right into Dan's hard chest, jarring her so hard her teeth clacked together.

"Hey." He curled his hands around her shoulders to hold her still. "What's wrong?"

She couldn't tell him, not without appearing as though she were a halfwit. Then again, if the shoe fit... Taking a deep breath, she searched for something believable to say. Spying their bags beside the door, she came up with the perfect out. "Our bags. I was checking to see they'd arrived safely." All right, not so perfect, but it would do if he stopped looking at her like she'd grown a second head or perhaps a third eye.

"They're by the door." He let her go and moved back. "I almost tripped over them when I walked in. Not sure how you missed them."

"Um, well, I…" Why was it she turned into a stammering idiot around him? Oh that's right, her brain disconnected whenever he got within sight.

"Hey, let's see what this hot-tub-terrace thing looks like." Dan walked past her and through a door she hadn't noticed beside the window. He stuck his head back inside. "Wow, you *have* to come see this thing."

With no other option, she followed him outside and found herself in little piece of paradise. Lush green vines covered the side walls designed to give the small space privacy from prying eyes. The tub was positioned against a half wall that allowed for an uninterrupted view of the sweeping hills below. Jody guessed you could fit four people in the hot tub if you squeezed in, but the area was definitely intended for one or two. Dan opened a cupboard that ran along the wall next to the door.

"Hey, there's even a bar fridge out here." He pulled out a Coke. "Want a drink?"

"No. Thanks."

He bent over to replace the drink and Jody couldn't stop her eyes from zeroing in on the way his pants stretched tight across his butt and thighs. Before she could get lost in the whole Dan intoxication again, she turned away and headed back inside. Perhaps a little space was needed, and not the kind found out on the balcony. Space as in miles and miles between them. She'd have to settle for a room and locked door for now. She grabbed her bag and flipped it over before unzipping it. By the time Dan came back in, she had her toiletries and tonight's clothes out.

"I'm going to shower and get ready now." Jody didn't wait for him to comment. She gathered her things and entered the bathroom, making sure to lock the door behind her.

———

Dan sighed as he flopped back on the bed. She'd run away again. Sure, she'd only gone as far as the bathroom, but a wall and locked door were the equivalent as far as he was concerned. He stared at the ceiling and replayed their kiss in the elevator. He'd never touched a woman who instantly drew need so deep he thought he might drown in it. She wasn't like anyone he'd ever been with in more ways than that though. Jody was mature for a start. As much as it shamed him, he had to admit his usual preference was for women younger than himself. Women less likely to be looking for something more than a few hours of fun.

Call him shallow, God knows his mother had on numerous occasions in the past, and until now it hadn't worried him. Now he wanted to go back and erase history so Jody wouldn't see what kind of man he was. Dan knew he'd never treat Jody in the sometimes callous way he'd treated other women, but she couldn't know that. And if she looked at his behavior before now, she'd be forced to make the conclusion that he was only after one thing. And he couldn't deny it no matter how much he wanted to.

He dragged his hands through his hair, scraping it away from his face and tugging on the ends until pain lanced his scalp. He'd have to prove to her she was different. Whether she knew about his insensitive—though unintentional—actions before or not, he wanted her to see he could care—*did* care. With every fiber of his being, he wanted to prove he was worthy of her time.

Rolling onto his side, he gazed out the huge picture window at the sun-soaked fields of grapes. The afternoon light left dark shadows and bright spotlights scattered over the vines as the sun slowly slipped beyond the horizon. He wasn't one for appreciating nature, but he had to admit the countryside surrounding the hotel was breathtaking. Almost as much as the woman currently showering a few plasterboards, timber and tiles away.

Just the thought of Jody naked behind that closed door had every muscle in Dan's body stretched tight. The throbbing in his groin hadn't quit since the first time he'd kissed her and had only intensified with each one since. She was like a drug in his system. He'd had a hit and the high had made him crave more. He wanted her worse than he'd wanted his first car. And that had been a six-year yearning that he'd finally managed to quench the day he'd turned seventeen and plunked down the three and half grand he'd scrimped and saved his entire teenage life.

Needing a distraction, he reached over to the bedside table and picked up the room-service menu. Scanning the pages, he didn't see anything that appealed, but then the one thing he did want wasn't on the menu. He'd have to come up with a substitute until he could get his hands on his first craving. Unable to decide, he went with a standard feel-good food. Fries. He snatched up the phone and hit the room-service button. When the woman answered, he ordered two plates of fries and hung up. By the time Jody came out of the bathroom there'd be a snack waiting for her, and hopefully he'd have gotten his libido in check by then too.

Dan sat up and rolled off the bed. He'd unpack while he waited for Jody and food. The hot tub beckoned, but he didn't have time to luxuriate in it like it should be enjoyed. They had a little over two hours before they had to be back downstairs ready to meet this weekend's participants. If he remembered right, they had a four-hour gap between the last session tomorrow and the evening function. He rubbed his hands together. A four-hour window was plenty of time to not only enjoy the tub but to convince Jody to join him.

The door opened behind him and he turned to find Jody wrapped only in a towel. He swallowed. Hard. His throat was dry, his mouth more so, and the erection he'd managed to subdue came roaring back to life. Before he could think, he'd taken a step, causing her to back up. Her reaction was enough to stop him in his tracks.

"I forgot my..." She darted over to where her suitcase lay open on the floor and whipped out a black lace bra.

He groaned and clenched his fists tight enough to cut the circulation to his fingers. His balls retracted into his body as more blood filled his cock. How he stayed in place and didn't rush over and ravish her he couldn't say. All he knew was one wrong move and she'd run farther than the bathroom, and he couldn't live with that. Not when everything he never dreamed he wanted was in front of him all pink and wet from her shower wrapped in a fluffy white towel. If it was the last thing he did, he wouldn't blow it with her.

"I ordered some food." His voice sounded tight, but it was a wonder he could get any words out through his constricted throat.

She paused on her dash back to the bathroom. "Oh."

"Yeah." Dan rubbed his jaw. "Just some fries to see us through until dinner."

"Ah...okay. I won't be much longer." She disappeared behind the door, the soft click of the lock echoing through the room as she shut herself away once more.

He felt like an idiot. He was an idiot. She'd been naked and he'd frozen like a randy teenager getting his first look at a set of boobs. The woman did a number on him, plain and simple. Only nothing he experienced—no emotion, no physical reaction—when he was around Jody was simple. Everything about her—about them—was complicated and confusing and downright scary when he let himself think about what he wanted for longer than a few minutes.

She'd blown into his life and turned it upside down without trying. In fact, she'd tried everything she could to avoid him, but the second they were in close quarters and she quit running, they went up in flames. They just had to find a way for neither of them to get burned. Considering they wanted different things, one of them was at least going to be disappointed. Whether that was him or her remained to be seen, but Dan hadn't given up on something he wanted before now, and he didn't see himself backing away from Jody and all being with her offered.

He'd have to convince her they were a good bet. He knew she was divorced, knew she had two teenage girls, and from what little he'd gleamed from Cassie and Luc, he also knew she hadn't had an easy life up until now. Dan didn't expect things to be smooth sailing between them. He fully expected to fight her every step of the way. She'd already proven her opposition to his intentions. It was a shame her body told a different story whenever he got close. She might have had a chance of keeping him at arm's length if her mouth and body spoke the same language.

Dan would have to make sure her mouth fell in line with her body. And soon. His own body couldn't take much more of this constant state of arousal. Besides, it was getting to be embarrassing walking around with a hard-on all day. He could take matters into his own hands—literally—except he felt no urge to satisfy his needs that way. When he finally found relief it would be with Jody. Inside Jody.

Jody took a deep breath to gather her courage and opened the door. Unlike before, she was dressed. Not that her clothes were a barrier against Dan's probing gaze. Starting at her toes, his gaze slowly slid up her body until those piercing green eyes met hers. He had a way of stripping her bare with just a look—of touching her without laying a hand on her.

A shiver skipped down her spine and goose bumps broke out on her arms and neck. "Bathroom's all yours." She sounded breathless so cleared her throat.

"Excellent. I'll be quick. Keep an ear out for room service."

"Oh, I was going to go down—"

"Plenty of time to be working later. Take a few minutes to relax."

Dan disappeared into the bathroom, leaving her to wonder why she had the urge to run at every turn. She knew their overwhelming attraction played into it, but she'd never shied away from the tough things before. Not like she was doing with Dan. She'd stuck out her shitty marriage in the hope of things improving for more years than were sensible, and while she couldn't compare that with her attraction to Dan, she couldn't help think she'd stayed married because it had been easier than facing the fear of what would happen when she walked. It hadn't even been her decision.

She closed her eyes and pushed the horrible thoughts aside. Colin may have been the one to make the break, but once he had, Jody had moved forward with steely determination to prove to everyone that she and the girls would be fine. And they were. *She* was. Except now she had a thing for a younger man and she didn't have the first clue what to do about it other than run for the hills. If she couldn't do that then she'd ignore it until it went away. Only he wasn't going away. He was getting closer, and with each step he took she wanted to take her own toward him *and* away from him.

Could she be any more screwed up?

A knock on the door made her jump and her eyes popped open. She strode over and squinted through the peephole to see a uniformed staff member. This would be a good opportunity to observe the food and beverage service. Jody opened the door and held it wide. "Come in."

The young man headed for the small table jammed into the far corner. It shouldn't be there, not when there was so little space in the room that the beds were almost touching. He placed the small tray down and turned with a small folder and pen. "Sign here please."

After a quick check of the bill, Jody signed and handed the folder back. "Thank you."

"You're welcome. Enjoy." He let himself out with a quiet click of the door.

Grabbing a pen and paper, she made some notes about lack of interaction with guests. While the young man was professionally presentable and polite, he didn't engage in any conversation that wasn't necessary, and she wanted to be sure to bring it up during the sessions tomorrow. She wandered back to the table and lifted the lid on one of the plates. A steaming-hot pile of crispy fries filled the plate. The smell alone had her mouth watering and her tummy rumbling. Maybe she was a little peckish. Lifting the second lid, she saw that Dan had ordered a meal for each of them.

"Hey, no pinching mine. You've got your own."

Spinning around, she found Dan out of the bathroom, towel slung precariously low on his hips, standing not two feet away. He was barely covered. His thighs, thick with muscle and sprinkled with a smattering of dark hair, were on display. Glancing up, she saw his ripped abdomen with a tantalizing trail of dark hair running down from his belly button to disappear under the towel. Jody tilted her head to the side in her effort to figure out what was wrong.

Oh my God! It wasn't a bath towel wrapped around his hips. It was *hand* towel! Good Lord, if he moved too fast the thing would be on the floor in a flash and she'd be getting flashed. Turning back around, Jody stared at the plate of fries and tried to catch her breath. Having a nearly naked Dan in front of her did a number on her libido, but the thought of a completely naked Dan had her pulse racing, her breasts tingling and her sex swelling. She felt his heat behind her and knew he stood close enough to touch. If she turned back around...

He reached around her and grabbed a handful of fries. She heard the crunch as he sank his teeth into them. Heard the moan of delight as he devoured them and reached for more. His arm brushed hers and she could smell the soap on his skin, the damp heat still clinging to him from the shower. Taking a step to the side, she avoided contact and grabbed some much-needed breathing room.

"These are great. Aren't you going to eat any?" he asked as he picked up another handful.

"Um, yes, but I want to get a drink first." Scooting past him, being careful not to brush up against him at all, Jody exited the room to the terrace where she got a drink from the mini fridge. She pressed the cool can against her hot cheek.

"Jody, can you grab me one while you're there?" Dan called through the door.

She closed her eyes and breathed deep. As much as she wanted to hide out here, she couldn't. She'd just have to suck it up and deal as

Leigh was fond of saying. The thought of her girls made her smile. They were the two most important people in her world and for them she'd make it through this job—the weekend—without doing anything stupid like jumping the man who insisted on tempting her with every breath he took.

6

———

Dan reached over and flicked off the bedside lamp. The red glow of the alarm clock mocked him. One thirty and Jody still hadn't returned to the room. Dinner had been a success and he couldn't fault her in any way when it came to the job. She'd done exactly what she was supposed to. She'd mingled well and spent time getting to know each of the men and women participating in the weekend's workshops with the skill of a seasoned professional. There wasn't a single thing he could be angry about when it came to work.

It was her after-hour's behavior that had his nerves raw and irritated. She'd been talking with Mooney and two of the other men at the end of the evening. Dan had wanted to interrupt, remind her they had an early start, but playing the demanding boss or worse, a jealous jerk, wasn't something he was comfortable doing. So he'd walked away, leaving her downstairs while he came up to the room. Alone. That had been over an hour ago.

He couldn't help the jealous thoughts rolling around his head. Couldn't stop the images of Jody and Mooney tangled together from flooding his mind and tormenting him. Dan knew his jealousy was unfounded. Other than Mooney's obvious interest in her, Dan had no reason to suspect they were hooking up. And as much as he wanted to, he wouldn't go hunt her down and drag her back to their room. Turning over, he punched his pillow. Again.

Dan took a deep breath and held it before letting it out in a rush. He needed to calm the fuck down or he'd be pinning her against the wall, peppering her with questions of where she'd been the second she set foot in the room. He'd thought sharing a room would be torture, but not this kind. Keeping his hands—and mouth—off her had been his biggest concern. Not once did he think she'd find a way to drive him crazier than worrying about being in close quarters.

A full moon hung low in the sky across the valley. He'd left the curtains open so the room was bathed in a soft glow. He snorted. His brilliant idea of letting in the moonlight to give the room a romantic intimacy had certainly blown up in his face. Hard to get romantic when the object of your desire wasn't even here. Throwing back the covers, Dan jumped out of bed and strode over to stand in front of the window.

The landscape, even in the shadows of night, was breathtaking, but he didn't really see it. He only saw the possibility of Jody being with another man. A man who wasn't him. Why he thought this way when he knew in his gut she wouldn't be with anyone else pissed him off the most when it came to the out of control emotions he experienced when it came to Jody. She'd made it clear she wanted nothing to do with him by avoiding him at every opportunity. Had he listened to her not-so-subtle rebuff? No. He'd taken every chance to get closer to her and he'd continue to do so.

He was a masochist. There was no other explanation for his continued pursuit. Rejected at every turn, he kept coming back for more. He'd never done that before. No meant no, and with the abundance of women available, Dan had always moved on to the next one with ease. Until Jody. She pulled him back, made him more determined to win her over with every rebuff.

Dan ran a hand down his bare chest. True to his word, he was naked. He didn't even own pajamas, so unless he slept in his underwear and a T-shirt, which he had no intention of doing, she'd just have to put up with the possibility of seeing him naked. The door rattled behind him and he glanced over his shoulder to see Jody, head down and shoes off, sneaking into the room. She didn't look his way, kept her gaze on the floor as she tiptoed across to her bag.

He thought about clearing his throat or moving to get her attention. Instead, he stood perfectly still and watched as she pulled clothes out of her suitcase. She tossed them on the bed behind her. The one he'd crawled out of not ten minutes ago. For someone who'd had a jumble of thoughts in his head, he suddenly found himself with a clean slate. Nothing except the sight of Jody lowering the zipper on her dress filled his mind.

She let the simple sheath slip from her shoulders and drop to the floor, leaving her in only a skimpy pair of bikini pants and bra. Her back was to him and he clenched his hands as the urge to walk over and run his fingers down her spine stole through him. He didn't breathe, didn't make a sound as he watched her turn and scoop up the top she'd thrown on the bed. For a split second, Dan had the glorious view of Jody from the front. One second of sheer bliss before she went perfectly still then screamed loud enough to wake the whole damn hotel.

"Fuck." Dan slammed his palms over his ears and ducked when she threw what was in her hand at him. "It's me. Dan!"

Jody froze on her way to the bedside table and he could only assume she'd planned to toss the lamp at him next. "Dan?"

"Who the fuck else would be in our room?" He bent to pick up the shirt she'd lobed at his head. "Surely you hadn't forgotten I was here?"

"Um, no, but…" She looked at the bed behind her, the one in front of her. "I thought you were asleep."

Thought? More like hoped. "Obviously I'm not."

He stepped up to the bed and dropped the shirt. It was at that moment he remembered how unclothed they both were. Her gaze lowered to his groin and bounced away quickly. Dan thought about covering up but dismissed the idea. He had nothing to hide, whether physically or emotionally, he wanted her to know where he stood. And some parts of him were standing very tall right now. She fidgeted, bare feet shuffling on the carpet, and looked everywhere apart from his direction. Figuring he had nothing to lose, he threw out the question burning in his throat.

"Were you with Mooney all this time?"

Her gaze snapped to his. "What? No."

Everything he was wanted to believe her. "Then where were you?" He had no right to interrogate her, but for the life of him he couldn't stop himself.

She sighed, her shoulders drooping with the release of air. "In the garden."

In the garden? "With who?" he demanded.

"No one." She reached over and grabbed her shirt, quickly tugging it over her head before continuing. "I was hoping to avoid this."

"What?" Him?

"You. Naked."

Ah. He'd always been comfortable without clothes on, so he couldn't understand why others were embarrassed when it was he who was on display, but he accepted most people couldn't handle nudity when they weren't intimately involved. "Does my nakedness offend you? Surely you've seen a naked man before." God, he hoped so. She'd been married for Christ sake.

Jody laughed and headed for the bathroom. "Yes, I've seen a few in my time."

A few? *What the fuck?* The bathroom door banged shut. "Who other than your ex have you seen naked?" he yelled at the closed door.

Jody leaned against the door and took a deep breath. My God, the man was breathtaking. Every sculptured inch of him. She'd seen him earlier with just a towel, but that was nothing compared to the sight of a completely naked Dan. Her mouth watered along with other areas of her anatomy. He hadn't shown one single shred of self-consciousness about his nudity either. If anything, he'd been more commanding—more compelling—than he appeared when clothed. She had to face it. The man did it for her.

Trouble with a capital T. That's where she was. Sighing, she shoved off the door and got ready for bed. She'd left her sleeping shorts in the room but the T-shirt she wore came past her thighs so the essentials were covered. Her bra was digging into her sides and she popped the catch through her shirt then slipped the straps off her shoulders and out through the sleeves in one of those contortionist tricks most women knew. More comfortable, she cleaned her teeth then used the loo before taking a brush to her hair.

Instead of her normal ponytail, she'd worn her hair out, and as usual when she did, it was a tangled mass of knots. She really should think about getting it cut except she liked the ease of long hair. Liked being able to gather it up into a tail out of her way and forget about it. She'd never been the type to bother with fussy hairstyles even in her younger years, and once the girls had arrived she'd barely had time to shower, never mind spend hours blow-drying. Jody yanked the last snag free then gathered it all together and wrapped an elastic band around it.

With nothing else to do, she had no excuse to hideout in the bathroom any longer. Determined to show Dan he didn't get to her even though he did on so many levels she refused to examine them, Jody opened the door and entered the room. The moonlight filtering in lit the area enough for her to see he was lying on the bed closest to the window. He had the sheet drawn up to his waist but the effort was too little too late. She knew what lay beneath the covers and wanted to crawl under there with him. But she wouldn't give in to the urge.

Using the skills she'd learn through years of self-denial, she crawled into the other bed. He didn't say anything and she was grateful. The last thing she wanted to do was rehash the evening. She was dog-tired and just wanted to go to sleep. She'd stupidly stayed away from the room in the hope of finding him asleep when she returned so they wouldn't have to face each other. Fat lot of good that idea had done her. Not only had he been awake, he'd been standing there in all his naked—aroused—mouth-watering glory waiting for her.

"Sorry." Dan's voice broke the quiet.

"For?" Jody didn't think he was apologizing for being naked. Or aroused.

"For hounding you about where you've been and with whom." His sigh echoed through the room. "I have no right to question you."

She smiled. She totally understood why he'd asked so she couldn't let him think she'd been offended by his questioning. "It's okay. I should have just come to the room straight away."

"Why didn't you?"

The darkness made it easier to reveal her true feelings and she found herself disclosing more than she should. "I was trying to avoid being alone with you. Especially seeing how I knew you'd be stripping out of your clothes at some point."

"The chance of seeing me naked repulses you that much?" he asked.

Jody laughed. "No. Not repulsed."

"What then?"

"Honestly?"

"Yes." His answer was muffled by the rustling of the bedcovers and she imagined him rolling over. "I wouldn't expect you to be anything but honest with me, Jody."

He sounded closer and she turned her head to find him stretched out on the very edge of his bed closest to her.

"I was more concerned with keeping my distance from you. Naked or otherwise."

"I scare you?"

"No, not exactly." She sighed and returned her gaze to the darkened ceiling. "I can't explain it really, and even if I could I'm not sure you'd understand."

"Tell me about your marriage."

The abrupt change of subject threw her. "My marriage?"

"Yes. How old were you? How'd you meet him? How long were you together? Did you love him?"

"Eighteen. High school. Years past when we should have been and I thought I did. Now I'm not so sure."

"You don't know if you loved him?" Shock laced his words.

Jody turned her head to look at Dan. He lay on his side, elbow bent, head resting on his palm while he watched her. "I loved him with everything I was, but I'm not sure it was ever the kind of love that lasts a lifetime. Or perhaps it was the fact he didn't love me the same way in return."

"You don't think he loved you?"

"I think he did as much as he's capable of." How did she explain her ex without sounding bitter or mean? Because she wasn't either of those. They'd both made mistakes in the relationship and Jody fully owned her side of their failure. "Colin is a very selfish, thoughtless person. I'm not sure he's able to love anyone deeply. He definitely isn't willing to make the effort necessary to sustain a relationship. My error was in thinking I could love enough for both of us."

"He didn't deserve you or the girls."

Dan's quiet words brought the sting of tears. He was right. Colin had never deserved the devotion she'd shown him and he certainly didn't deserve to have two beautiful daughters. Her only consolation was that he didn't really have the girls. They'd never bonded even when she'd been married to their father, and he hadn't made any attempt to maintain the fragile connection they'd had once he'd left. "Thank you."

"I think I should be thanking him."

"Why?" What could Dan possible thank Colin for?

"Because if the guy wasn't such a douche bag, I wouldn't have the opportunity to get to know you. Not the way I want to."

"Oh." Jody didn't know what to say to that. She and Dan had hardly been on good terms after they'd first met and now they seemed to have stepped right past getting to know each other straight into being physically intimate.

"I know what you're thinking." She went to speak but he talked right over her. "You don't want to get to know me. I get that you've erected barriers after your marriage and I accept that getting to know you is going to be an uphill battle, but I think you're worth it. I think what we have between us, and don't deny there's something there, is worth the effort it's going to take for me to climb those barriers."

"Jeez, you don't pull any punches."

"I'm not going to trick you into this, Jody. I'll be honest every step of the way. I'm also going to push you when you won't want me to. But if you really want me to back off. Really want me to leave you alone and only be a workmate, I will."

Stunned speechless, Jody mulled over what Dan had said. On one hand, she wanted him to back off and leave her alone, but on the other, she liked that he was pursuing her. She'd never had that. Never had the rush of excitement that came with a man wanting her above all others.

"Here's what I suggest we do. We take this weekend to think about it. Ask me anything. Tell me anything. I'll do the same, and for just these two days we'll be nothing but honest and open. And when Sunday rolls around, we can decide where we're going from there. How does that sound?"

"Like you're backing off."

"Oh, no, definitely not." He got out of bed and came over to hers. Planting his hands on the pillow either side of her head, he leaned over and put his face right in hers. "I'll be in your face, stealing kisses and touching you every chance I get. I'm planning to stack the deck in my favor and I'll use every trick I have to do it."

She didn't get the opportunity to respond before he followed through on his words. He slanted his mouth over hers, but unlike the hurried, frantic kisses of before, he took his time. He swept his tongue across her lips, probed the seam until she opened and slipped her tongue out to tangle with his. A moan echoed between them and Jody wasn't sure if it was his or hers. The kiss was slow and lush, a gentle exploration of new territory that stole her breath and sped up her heart rate.

Her pulse beat a rapid cadence that reverberated through every nerve—every cell. Just when she thought he'd go deeper, he eased back, took them to soft nips and tender licks until he pulled away completely, leaving her panting for breath and wondering what was wrong. Before she could ask, he placed his lips on her forehead in a quick peck.

"Good night, Jody. Sweet dreams."

And then he was gone. Disappearing into the darkness as the moon slid behind a cloud. The lack of light left her feeling cold and bereft, or was that from the sudden lack of Dan's heat?

Dan lay beneath the covers listening to Jody breathe. She'd fallen asleep not long ago. Before that she'd tossed and turned. He'd been on the verge of going over there and pulling her into his arms when she'd stopped fidgeting and her breathing had evened out as she drifted off. He wished he could find sleep now she'd settled. Unfortunately, his mind wouldn't quit. The discussion about her marriage and ex had been enlightening. She hadn't revealed all that much, but what she had—coupled with what little he'd gleaned from Luc and Cassie—was enough for him to draw some very sad conclusions about her life up until now.

He was relieved to know she had the girls even though they tied her to the man who'd obviously taken her for granted. She'd at least had their unconditional love and affection. There was nothing he could do to improve her past, but he'd do everything in his power to make her future a happy one. If she'd let him.

Turning over, he stared out the window and watched the sky light up as a storm rolled through the valley. The weather matched his mood—dark and brooding—and he couldn't help the gloomy thoughts he had about her ex. Dan hoped Luc had given the man what he deserved at some point, except what he knew of Jody told him his wish had probably gone unfulfilled. She wasn't the type to take revenge or even want it. Her lack of hostility toward the man who hadn't given her any of what she deserved spoke volumes. He figured he'd have to learn to hold his tongue about her ex if he wanted to be a part of her future.

It wouldn't stop him from thinking bad thoughts though. He smiled. He'd definitely make her ex pay in his mind. Over and over again.

7

Jody let out a deep breath as she slipped into her room. Damn, it had been a long, long day. Six hours had seemed like sixty, and she was looking forward to the next four hours off to recharge. This was her first corporate event and she had to admit they were more strenuous than the usual adult's and kid's parties she dealt with. She'd coped with the program fine. There was never a point where she'd thought otherwise. It was being the center of attention that she found draining. Usually she stayed behind the scenes and let the parties unfold. Today required constant input from her. Not to mention a couple of the men had been a little too friendly and attentive.

She'd soon nipped that in the bud, and Dan's scowl at morning tea had proven a major deterrent that had them backing right off. Unfortunately, she'd still had to deal with Keith Mooney's unrelenting interest. His pursuit had been anything but flattering toward the end, and she'd had to pull him aside and lie about being involved with someone so that he'd leave her alone. The fact he'd immediately jumped to the conclusion that it was Dan she was seeing had her troubled. Jody had no idea what would happen if word got back to Cassie.

She slipped off her shoes and kicked them aside before making her way to the mini-bar and a cold drink. She'd popped the top and had just collapsed into one of the chairs on the terrace when she heard Dan come through the door. Twisting around, she leaned over and peered through the doorway back into the room. He walked toward her, his stride purposeful as he stalked over and yanked her out of her seat. Barely a protest left her throat when his mouth slammed down on hers.

There was nothing gentle in his kiss. He took. Conquered every inch of her mouth without remorse. She couldn't catch her breath. Couldn't think beyond the man holding her so close the name badge on his shirt dug into her chest. Just when she thought she had a handle on it, when she sought to meet his demands, he pulled away. Ripping their mouths apart, he pushed her to arm's length. His chest heaved with each ragged breath and his eyes—greener than she'd ever seen them—studied her with such intensity her heart skipped.

"Do you have any idea how badly I want to smash Mooney's face in?" Dan's words were spoken through clenched teeth and razor sharp.

Jody shook her head. She wasn't following the conversation. Not when her mind was still lost in the darkness of that carnal kiss.

"I saw him put his hands on you and I wanted to break every one of his fingers. Slowly. One. By. One."

She swallowed. The violence vibrating in his words sent a quiver through her belly. She should be appalled by his confession—should be disgusted with the brutality of it. Instead, a thrill of excitement shot straight to her core. She'd never inspired such intense emotions in anyone.

He loosened his grip then slid his hands up and down her arms. "Sorry."

Jody shook her head, confused by his apology. "For what?"

Dan smiled, although it wasn't a happy one, more a twist of his lips. "I was rough with you."

Funny. She hadn't thought so. "Were you? I didn't notice." Jody stepped closer and brushed the backs of her fingers along his jaw. "Want to talk about it?"

"That depends."

"On what?"

"Whether you're into the whole alpha man thing." He let her go and moved away to retrieve a can of drink from the fridge. "Basically, some guy put his hands on the woman I think of as mine."

She nodded. "I get that."

His gaze met hers. "You get that you're my woman?"

Laughing, she said, "No, I get that you *think* of me as yours."

"Ah, I can think it but it doesn't mean it's true, is that it?" He popped the top on the can and liquid sprayed the front of his shirt as the drink fizzed and bubbled out. "Shit!"

He brought the can to his mouth and sucked the overflowing soda. Her gaze was drawn to the splash of brown covering the front of his white shirt and she immediately thought about the stain that would be impossible to remove if he didn't do something about it now. "You've got it all over your shirt. Take it off and I'll soak it in cold water so the stain doesn't set."

Dan arched one eyebrow. "You're telling me to take my clothes off now?"

She smiled. "Just your shirt, smartass, and only so you don't ruin it."

Dan hadn't waited for her to finish speaking. He'd put the can down and whipped the shirt over his head before the last word left her mouth. Muscles rippled in his arms and torso, and she ogled his chest with barely concealed desire. The trail of dark hair bisecting his abdomen and disappearing into his pants drew her gaze. Jody swallowed, her throat constricting with the burst of lust zipping through her system. Holding out her hand, she waited for him to pass her his top.

Once he did, she just about ran inside to avoid the temptation of touching his smooth skin. Heading straight to the bathroom, she ignored the man following her and concentrated on taking care of his shirt. She removed his name badge then turned the cold water on in the sink and shoved the stained area beneath the flow. When she was satisfied she'd removed all she could, she stuck the plug in the drain and let the basin fill up until it covered all the material.

"There. We'll leave it 'til later then rinse it again to make sure it's all out."

"You know I could just send it to be laundered by the hotel."

"Nonsense. No point wasting money when I can fix it for you."

She was drying her hands when he moved in behind her and slid his arms around her waist. "You know a guy could get used to being looked after." He nuzzled her nape, his lips warm and soft against her skin.

"D-don't get too used to it." A shiver rippled down her neck. "I'm not your mother."

Dan laughed as he let her go and stepped away. "You most certainly are not. She'd have boxed my ears for spilling the drink and told me to wash my own shirt."

Jody turned to see him reach into the shower recess and flick on the water. "W-what are you doing?"

He glanced over his shoulder. "Jumping in the shower to rinse the sticky Coke off my chest, then I'm going to make use of the hot tub."

Before Jody could blink, he popped the button on his pants and slid the zipper down. She quickly turned away and started out of the room only to catch sight of Dan's naked ass in the mirror as she did. The view stopped her in her tracks. He had the best ass. She'd always been a butt girl. Something about a taut male behind did it for her in a big way, and Dan had a world-class rear end.

"Wanna join me?"

Her gaze darted up to meet his in the mirror. "What?" she squeaked. God, she'd actually squeaked.

He grinned at her. "In the hot tub. Although if you want to join me in the shower…"

Before she could be tempted to answer yes to either, she made her escape, closing the door behind her. The timber barrier did nothing to silence Dan's laughter.

Dan sighed as he sank into the warm bubbling water. Jody refused to join him and had found some busy work to do in their room. He wouldn't force her to take a break, but he planned to tempt her until she did. He'd start by letting her know how great it was.

"God. This feels amazing. You really should try this," he called out.

"I didn't bring my swimmers." He turned to find her standing in the doorway, her fingers twisting together in front of her and her teeth biting into her plush bottom lip.

"Well, I'd be more than happy for you to jump in naked, but I doubt you're up for that, so why don't you just wear your undies and bra. They couldn't be any more revealing than a bikini." He slipped lower in the water and leaned his head back on the side of the tub, his eyes closing on a moan. Damn, it really did feel good.

He could hear her moving around but he stayed where he was—head back, eyes closed—as his body relaxed by slow degrees. The day hadn't been particularly taxing. Watching the men fawn all over Jody had though. How he'd managed to get through the last few hours without punching anyone Dan would never know. To her credit, she hadn't encouraged any of them, and the fact she'd lied to Mooney about the extent of their relationship showed him just how much she'd disliked the other man's advances.

Mooney had pulled Dan aside to apologize for poaching on his territory. At first Dan had been confused, clueless as to what the other man was talking about. It didn't take Mooney long to impart the necessary words to enlighten him. Dan wasn't sure what surprised him more—Mooney's apology or Jody's outright lie.

Lost in thought, Dan was surprised when the water surged up over his chin. Opening his eyes, his gaze connected with Jody's. She'd slipped in on the opposite side of the tub. The churning water came all the way to her neck so there was no way to tell if she was in her underwear as he'd suggested or if she'd been brave enough to climb in naked. Either way, his cock stirred at the thought of her lush body all slippery wet and within touching distance.

He smiled. "Feels good, doesn't it?"

She nodded as she watched him warily.

His smile grew. "So are you naked over there?"

Her eyes rounded and her lips parting on a gasp as she dipped lower in the water.

Dan laughed. He loved teasing her. "Don't answer. I might not be able to control myself if you do."

"Are you always so direct?" she asked.

"Yeah, don't see any point playing games—especially when it comes to getting what I want."

"And that's me?"

He stretched his arms out along the edge of the tub. "Yep."

"Why?"

"Why do I want you?" For someone who didn't want to play games, he couldn't seem to come up with a straight answer to that question. He shrugged. "Who knows why we're attracted to each other. All I know is it's there and I plan to act on it. With your consent of course."

"Good to know I have some say in it." Her smile softened the seriousness of her words.

Dan forgot all about keeping his distance—forgot about not crowding her—and reduced the space between them to zero. He put his hands flat on the bench seat beside her thighs and brought his face a breath from hers. "You will always have a say in this." Then he slanted his lips over hers.

He captured her gasp on his tongue as he dove into her mouth. Within a heartbeat, she caught up and tangled her tongue with his. Dan didn't touch her with anything except his mouth, but that didn't deter Jody. Her hands landed on his shoulders, her fingers digging in for a moment before she trailed them down his chest. She dragged her nails over his nipples and the flat discs instantly pebbled rock hard beneath her rough touch.

She splayed her hands and swept them lower. His stomach

clenched, every muscle going taut with the anticipation of where she was headed next. He didn't have to wait long to find out. With feather-like caresses, Jody stroked the area between his hips, the stretch of skin where the waistband of his pants would normally be. Yeah, he'd chosen to climb into the tub naked, and right now he was thankful for his penchant for nudity.

She pulled her mouth from his when the back of her hand brushed the head of his cock. "You're not wearing any pants?"

It was a question except they both knew there was no real need to ask or answer. Dan replied by sliding his lips over the soft skin of her cheek up to her ear where he blew a stream of air over the damp shell. She shivered. Then a shudder rolled over her as he latched onto her lobe and sucked it into his mouth. Toying with his teeth, he nipped the delicate flesh before soothing the slight sting with the flat of his tongue.

A moan slipped up her throat, the sexy little sound ramping up his arousal and urging him to take more. An answering groan rolled off his tongue when her hands found his cock, her fingers circling the shaft in a loose grip that made him dizzy with want. God. He wanted to fuck her.

"Jody." Her name was a plea and a demand. He wanted her to grip him harder, to stroke those talented fingers from root to tip and back again. "Please," he breathed in her ear.

"You're so big."

Nothing could have brought him to his knees faster than those breathless words. Every guy wanted to hear that tone of awe from the woman he planned to bed. He leaned back until their gazes connected. Her hands stayed with him, caressed his straining flesh with a mixture of tentative brushes and firm squeezes.

"If you don't want this to go any further you have to stop." His voice was ragged with need. "Now."

Her eyes studied his. She must have found what she was looking for because she gripped him harder and pulled his cock in several quick strokes. "I don't want to stop."

Dan closed his eyes for a split second before meeting her gaze once more. "Are you sure?" *God, please let her be sure.*

She nodded once then pressed her mouth to his as she continued the incredible hand job designed to drive him mad. Closing his eyes once more, he sank into the kiss and let her take them where she wanted. He wasn't sure how, but he knew Jody needed to lead this first time. If he wanted this to be more than a one-time deal, she had to meet him more than halfway. Had to be the one to take them that next step.

He slid his hands along the seat until they brushed against the outside of her thighs. Letting the water help support his weight, he moved his hands to her hips as he knelt on the bottom of the tub. The thin layer of cloth separating his fingers from her skin had to go. "Undies off," he spoke against her lips.

Their mouths separated, both of them panting for breath as their gazes locked. He thought she might back out. Thought now that he was this close to getting her naked she'd pull back and leave him hanging. But he should have known Jody wouldn't chicken out. With the confidence he'd seen from her at work, she pushed him back and stood. She brought her hand to the front of her bra and flicked the clasp that held the cups together. In an instant, her breasts were free. The lush globes drew his hands and he reached up to cup them—weigh them—while stroking his thumbs over the taut peaks.

"Beautiful."

Her skin flushed a deeper red. "I'm old. They're saggy." She covered his hands with hers as though trying to hide herself from him.

Dan stood, pulling his hands away from her body and capturing her fingers in his before she could conceal those sweet curves from him again. "Don't." He held their arms out so he had an unobstructed view. "The only thing I see is a gorgeous woman who sets my blood on fire."

Leaning forward, Dan buried his face in Jody's cleavage. He groaned at the silky feel of her skin against his face. Moaned when he slid his tongue over one curving slope until he reached a puckered nipple and sucked it into his mouth. With a shake of her hands, she broke his hold and tangled her fingers in his hair and tugged him closer—holding him to her. Dan growled and drew harder on her rigid flesh. The tight bud fit between his tongue and palate as though it were made specifically for that spot.

Jody moaned and arched her back, pressing her breast deeper into his mouth. Her grip on his hair tightened—pulled—and sent a sharp sting across his scalp, drawing a rumbling groan from deep in his chest. Dan increased the suction on her nipple then scraped his teeth over the ribbed tip. She jerked, her body jack-knifing in his arms and popping the tasty nub free of his lips.

He nuzzled her silky skin as he made his way up her chest. Her pulse fluttered beneath his tongue when he licked her neck. The sexy little noises she made drove him mad and he had to taste them. Nibbling his way to her mouth, he sampled every inch of her delicate throat before finding her lips and joining their mouths in a breath-stealing kiss that threatened to turn his bones to liquid and shatter his control.

Dan slid his hands down her ribs to her waist then over her hips where he hooked his fingers in the sides of her undies as he continued to feed on her mouth. Her hands joined his and together they pushed her underwear off. He let go of her mouth and lowered his gaze, but he couldn't see beyond her hipbones where the bubbling water swirled between them. Stepping back, he bent forward and shoved her pants to her knees. His mouth was inches from her waist and he couldn't resist leaning in and placing a trail of tiny kisses from her belly button to her hip.

Her stomach trembled beneath his lips and he took great pleasure in making her shudder further. Memorizing the more sensitive areas for later use, he continued his journey south. But when his chin dipped into the water he straightened, put his hands on her waist and urged her to sit on the side of the hot tub. Jody kicked her undies free under the water before sitting up on the edge. Pressing his hands on the inside of her thighs, he nudged them apart so he could step between them. He didn't look down. If he did, he'd never be able to resist sampling her sweet pussy, and he wanted—needed —to slow things down, to savor every second of this moment with her.

He moved closer until his cock fit snug against her sex. The heat of her surrounding him drove him a little further into the fierce need and want being with her delivered. Dan shuddered when she dragged her fingers through his hair and tugged his mouth to hers. They slid into the kiss as though they'd done it a million times. Each stroke of tongue, brush of lips, nip of teeth was a perfect caress in a sensual slide deeper. In seconds, they went from lazy to frenzied. Neither of them satisfied with a leisurely ride any longer.

Jody skimmed her hands over his shoulders and down his back, making his groin throb with want. Dan gripped her ass and yanked her closer as a bolt of lust speared him. He tore his mouth from hers and nibbled his way along her jaw. She arched her neck, offering him free rein, and he took all she gave. Her breath panted in his ear, the sexy sounds floating on those small puffs of air firing his blood and filling his cock with white-hot need until he couldn't wait to have her.

Pulling back, he cradled her face in his hands and waited for her gaze to meet his. "I want you."

"Yes."

"Now."

She moaned. The cry cut short when he sealed his mouth to hers once more. The kiss was quick, barely long enough for their lips to touch, before he pulled away. Dan flexed his hips, rubbing his length on the slick folds of her pussy, drawing a whimper from her, a groan from him. Wet heat coated his shaft and he couldn't wait another second to sink his cock inside her. He rocked against her, sliding his engorged flesh through the welcoming clasp of hers, coating them both in her creamy essence.

"Please," Jody pleaded.

Protection. He needed to suit-up.

He froze. He didn't have any condoms. He'd never expected to get here with her so soon. Stupidity on his part, because whenever they touched it was like match to flint. Instant flame.

Dan laid his forehead on hers. "I don't have any protection. I didn't expect..."

"What?" Jody murmured, her breathing labored.

Dan pulled back to meet her desire-filled gaze. "Condoms. I don't have any."

"Oh." She chewed the corner of her lip. "I-I'm on the pill. And I'm clean. I haven't—"

"Me too. Clean that is. I've never had sex without a condom."

Jody stared at him and he realized she was waiting for him to say more.

"We don't have to." He made the offer but prayed she wouldn't take him up on it.

"You want to stop?"

"Hell no, but I'm not expecting you to take me at my word on something like this."

"I trust you. I wouldn't be here—naked—if I didn't."

What was she saying? Did she mean they could continue? That they could have sex without a condom? "Are you saying we don't need a condom to have sex?"

She nodded.

"You're sure?" Dan sucked in a breath and held it.

8

Jody couldn't think—didn't want to think—if she did she'd put a stop to this madness. Instead, she agreed to have sex with Dan. Without a condom. They might have only known each other a few months, but those months were sufficient time for her to know she could trust him with her safety. And she did. Her marriage had taught her all about mistrust, and Dan didn't evoke any of those all too familiar suspicions.

"Jody, are you sure?" His gaze searched hers "I don't want to do anything you're not comfortable with."

Even now Dan was showing her she could trust him. He'd never force her, and he hadn't been the one to suggest continuing regardless of their lack of protection. She'd told him she was on the pill, safe from disease and willing to have sex without a condom. She refused to second-guess herself now.

"Yes. I'm sure."

"Not here." He placed his hand on the edge of the tub and vaulted over the side onto the terrace. "C'mon. I want you on a bed."

Before she could think about moving, he slid his hands under her arms and lifted her out of the tub. Her toes barely touched the floor when he spun her around and picked her up, holding her against his chest. With quick, long strides, he walked them into the room.

"I can walk." Her protest was weak. She was enjoying this macho side of him far too much.

"Yep."

He didn't put her down. He just continued until he reached the closest bed and fell forward, turning at the last second so his back hit the mattress and she came down on top of him. Her legs bracketed his, her sex lined up with his erection, and she couldn't help the little roll of her hips that dragged her clit across his length. She moaned as sensation shot through her core. Bracing her knees on the bed, Jody rocked against him in a slow rhythm. Each pass sent heat and moisture flooding her pussy.

Dan tangled his fingers in her hair, holding her still so he could devour her mouth. With each rock of her hips, he thrust his tongue between her lips. The duel assault drove her higher, pushed her closer to that jagged edge she craved like air. She'd been there before. He'd shown her how good he could make it, and Jody wanted to experience it again with blinding intensity. Breaking free of his kiss, she pushed herself up to her knees and hovered her sex above his.

"Now." She panted. "I want you in me now."

She reached between them and grabbed his cock. Dan gasped and shuddered beneath her. Lowering an inch, Jody lined his body up with hers and slowly began to sink down. The bulbous head breached her opening, stretching her drenched hole with a delicious combination of pleasure and pain. It had been far too long. Her muscles fought against the invasion and she bit her lip, concentrated on relaxing her pelvis until she'd taken more of him.

"Fuck. You're so tight." Dan bared his teeth. "Don't want to hurt you."

"You're not." She took a little more of him. "Just need a second."

Jody took a deep breath and willed her body to accept his. She'd never dealt with this level of discomfort. Not even when she'd lost her virginity had it been this difficult to take a man inside her.

"You're not ready." He gripped her waist and raised her up.

"No." Her hands surround his. "I just need a second. I'm more ready than I've ever been, but it's been so long." Jody couldn't believe they were discussing this.

"I'm not going to hurt you."

Before she could argue, Dan lifted her off him completely and reversed their positions. From one breath to the next, she went from being upright to flat on her back with Dan looming over her.

"We'll do this my way."

"But—"

His mouth came down on hers. He stroked his tongue across her lips, pressed between them and swept inside. She moaned into his mouth when he slipped his hand over her hip and along her thigh. Shifting to the side, he dragged that questing hand toward her center. Her breath stalled, her muscles tensing as she waited for the moment he'd touch her.

He didn't disappoint. With skill, he played her. Slid his fingers along her slit, back and forth, never venturing between her folds to where she wanted him most. She rocked her hips, tried to force his fingers deeper only to have him pull away from her completely. His mouth. His hand. He took them both away and she cried out in protest.

"Easy." He chuckled against her neck. "I'm not going far. Just moving down here."

Jody whimpered when he moved his mouth over her collarbone. He licked across her breast until he reached her nipple and sucked it between his lips. Using his teeth to hold the bud still, he lashed it with his tongue, making it pucker tighter. The other breast didn't go unattended. With finger and thumb, Dan pinched her other nipple while increasing the suction on the one in his mouth. Streamers of sensation unfurled, rolling out into her abdomen to tickle her core. Her pussy clenched. Her walls weeping with want.

Letting go of her breasts, he wiggled lower on the bed. He slipped his legs between hers and moved lower still. His intent was clear. She held her breath and looked down her body to watch him settle his face over her sex.

"Damn, I can't wait to taste you." He ran his fingers through the short hair covering her mound. "I can smell you."

To Jody's embarrassment, Dan bent forward and took a deep breath. Her face heated and her thighs tensed against his shoulders as she tried to close her legs.

"Oh, yeah," he breathed against her wet center.

There was no more time for discomfort. Not when he was swiping his tongue through her folds and sending her to the moon. He lapped at her. Licked up one side and down the other. And when he latched onto her clit, sucked it between his lips and flicked it with his tongue, her world splintered into millions of tiny sparkles. But he wasn't finished. As she came down off that surprising peak, he drove two fingers into her pussy and pressed the flat of his tongue against the now super-sensitive bundle of nerves.

"Oh, God." The whimper whispered over her lips as he found a tender spot deep inside her core.

He worked his fingers in time with his tongue until she was panting for breath and begging for him to stop. To never stop. None of the words leaving her throat made sense. Nothing but the devastating pleasure rocketing through her registered in her overwhelmed mind. And then he did it again. Took her up and over and into that burst of blind relief that left her spent with satisfaction so great Jody doubted she'd ever move again.

Dan crawled up her body, dropping kisses every few inches until he reached her mouth and nibbled on her bottom lip. He licked the slight sting before joining their lips in a scorching kiss. Her mind still reeling, Jody barely managed to keep up. Her body still tingled, her limbs like lead weights that her muscles refused to move. Her chest rose and fell in rapid succession as her lungs worked overtime to keep up with her galloping heartbeat. She opened her eyes to find Dan staring at her, a silly, smug grin on his face.

"Do you have any idea how gorgeous you look all flushed with release?" he asked.

She shook her head, words still beyond her.

"Gorgeous and hot, and I'm so close to losing my load that if I don't get inside you in the next few seconds you'll be wearing it all over your leg." He thrust his cock against her thigh to prove his point.

Jody found the strength to move and spread her legs until he slipped between them, her hips cradling his. "We can't let that happen." She arched her back, angled her hips so his crown nudged at her opening.

"No, we can't." He drove forward, his cock sliding in with little resistance as he sank his entire length into her. "Fuck, that feels amazing."

She had to agree. She'd never felt so full and yet so empty. The two opposing emotions warred inside her and drove her to move. Wrapping her legs around his thighs, Jody used him to propel herself back and forth. Her movements were limited but she managed to slide up and down his shaft a few inches with each squeeze of her legs. It wasn't enough.

"Move." When he didn't respond, she dug her fingers into his ass. "Move, dammit."

"This is going to be over way too quick," he growled in her ear just before he exploded into action.

Jody cried out as he withdrew and slammed back in repeatedly. Over and over, he impaled her on his length. Her back bowed, her feet dropping to the bed, her hips rising to meet his thrusts. He was breathing hard, panting in her ear as he pushed himself deeper and deeper. His pace increased, his cock tunneling in and out in a pounding beat that left her breathless.

"Are you close?"

The question startled her.

"I can't hold off any longer."

She didn't want him to wait for her, didn't think she'd be able to come again anyway, so she rolled her hips, clenched her vaginal muscles and sent him soaring.

Dan came with a roar. Blood rushed in his ears and pounded in his groin. Fire shot up his spine and out his dick as Jody's pussy milked him of every last drop of come. She did something with her muscles. Something that felt as though she was squeezing him in a rolling touch from root to tip. And the heat. Jesus, he'd never experienced anything like it. Her body surrounded him in a blistering grip he'd give anything to feel over and over again. His arms shook—hell, his whole body shook—his muscles on the verge of giving out as the last of his seed spilled inside her.

With a groan, he fell forward. Half on, half off, he braced his arms and tried to keep from crushing her. His cock remained hard and buried deep in her rippling pussy, totally oblivious to the fact he'd just come hard enough to lose brain cells. He wasn't sure if he could find the words to express how he felt right now. Or if he had the wherewithal to get his vocal cords to form them. She squirmed beneath him and he forced himself to pull free of her body—the action drew a shudder and a groan from each of them. Dan rolled to the side and took her with him, not willing to let her go just yet.

"That was…"

"Uh-huh." He couldn't manage more than a murmured sound.

Jody sighed, the puff of air rushing over his neck and shoulder where her face was tucked against him, and goose bumps rose in a shivery wave down his back. He couldn't recall his body ever being so sensitive. Then again, he couldn't remember the last time he'd held a woman in his arms after sex either. His usual mad dash out the door held no appeal. Not this time. For once, he wanted to hold his bed partner close, and it wasn't with the hope of a second round. Although he wouldn't knock that back.

For now, all he wanted was to lie here and cuddle Jody—feel her softness pressed against him. She satisfied him on so many levels, and yet he couldn't seem to get enough of her. Wanted so much more from her—with her.

"What are you thinking?"

Her question surprised him, though it shouldn't have. As much as she'd avoided him she'd never held back. Her genuine honesty appealed more than he cared to acknowledge. *She* appealed. The thought of possibly screwing this thing with her up terrified him.

She poked him in the ribs. "Did you do the typical guy thing and go to sleep on me?"

Dan laughed. "No."

"Good, because my arm has gone to sleep." She wiggled the arm pinned beneath him.

"Shit. Sorry." He rose up so she could slip her arm free. "You should have said something."

"I just did."

"I meant before it went to sleep." Dan cuddled her close once more.

"Well, I didn't know it wasn't fine until it went numb."

"Oh, right." He scooted over, rolling to his back and pulling her with him. She laid her head on his shoulder, her body plastered to his side. "Better?"

"Mmm."

Dan held her close, his mind replaying everything that had happened from the minute he entered the room. He wasn't sure at what point she'd changed her mind about them or even if she had. It was quite possible she'd back away after today. Dan was prepared for her to do that. He just had to have a plan to keep her from running too far. If he could work out what had convinced her to let him closer, he'd be able to use the same tactic in the future.

Jody moved her leg over his and the residual heat in her pussy pressed against his outer thigh. His cock stirred, pulsing as his body responded to her nearness—to the memory of the pleasure he'd found between her legs. He'd roll over and pin her beneath him if he had the strength, but he still couldn't get his muscles to work properly.

She rocked her hips, that hot center rubbing on his leg and driving his arousal higher. He groaned when she pushed herself up. Thinking she was going to pull away, he was surprised when she crawled over the top of him and stretched her body out along his.

From breast to ankles, skin touched skin, and she wiggled her sex on his as she settled herself against him. Her mouth was an inch from his and he wrapped his hand around the back of her neck and tugged her down until he could fit her mouth to his.

He took his time. Explored every inch of her mouth while he used his hands to map her curves. She wasn't skinny like the fashion mags dictated women should be. Her body was rounded like a woman should be, and he took great pleasure in running his hands all over her. But his arms could only reach so far and he wanted to touch all of her. Trail his fingers across each valley, every slope, and follow with his lips.

Pulling back, he separated their mouths and searched out her gaze. Her eyes were hooded, her lashes shielding her expression, but there was no missing her flushed cheeks or her shallow pants for breath. She was climbing toward that peak again, and this time he wanted them to go over together. He gripped her hips and urged her up. "I want to be inside you again."

Her eyelids fluttered, her searing blue gaze meeting his. She didn't speak. She didn't have to when she sat up, rose to her knees and reached between them to grab his cock and hold it still while she lined up their bodies and slowly sank back down. The moan that left her lips matched the one caught in his throat. Heat surrounded him, engulfed him as Jody took him all the way to the root in one long slide of carnal delight.

They held perfectly still when her pelvis sat snug against his. One heartbeat. Two. Neither of them breathed. Moved. Then Dan's fingers tightened. Dug into the flesh of her ass where he held her. That was all it took to bring them out of the daze their physical contact put them in. She rolled her hips, rocked back and forth, making his cock slide in and out in minuscule increments. His gut clenched, his thigh muscles tightening as pleasure seared him.

"Faster. Deeper," he growled as he used his hands to guide her. But she wouldn't be led. Instead, she kept her slow, shallow pace and just about drove him out of his mind. "Fuck!"

Left with either the option of letting her have control or flipping them over, he took a breath, ready to move when she kicked things up a notch. Using her legs, she rose and fell at an ever-increasing speed and distance until she was riding him like a cowgirl rides a bucking bull. Root to glans, Jody slid up and down in a mind-blowing rhythm. He gripped her hips, holding on for all he was worth as she drove them both toward that ultimate prize.

Dan bucked his hips, thrusting up on each of her down strokes. She braced her hands on his chest, digging her nails in to his flesh as she upped the tempo once more. Her breathing came in ragged bursts, her breasts bouncing in an erotic tease that keep his gaze firmly trained on her jiggling tits. He wanted to wrap his tongue around her nipples, except he wasn't ready to give up the view of Jody riding him as though her life depended on it.

He stayed with her, arching up as she plunged down, slamming their bodies together time after time until he had to grit his teeth to stop from coming apart to soon. Letting go of one hip, he trailed his fingers over her skin to her pussy. Her folds were slick, the wet heat coating his fingertips and making the slide across her flesh slippery smooth. Dan searched out the knot of nerves guaranteed to have her joining him on the edge.

Jody jerked, her rhythm stuttering as he circled her clit. Stroked. Pressed. Pinched. Then he did it again. And again. And watched while she ground against him and finally let go. Her pussy squeezed him in a breath-stealing vice that pulled his release from him in a bone-jarring punch to his groin. Fire lanced his cock as spurt after spurt erupted from his balls.

His body throbbed. His ears rang. And his chest ached as his lungs struggled to function. Jody collapsed forward, draping her body over him in a damp blanket of satisfaction. Dan's eyes had shut at some point, and when he opened them he was seeing double. Lowering his lids, he sucked in a deep breath and wrapped his arms around the woman sprawled on top of him.

Her breathing came in jagged puffs and her body vibrated against his as the last of her orgasm ebbed away. He could feel the final ripples of her release along his softening length. His body seemed to have been satisfied this time. Stroking his hands up and down her back, he held her for as long as she'd let him. Dan figured they'd both sated the hunger between them for now and wouldn't be at all shocked if Jody retreated. What they'd shared—twice—wasn't just sex, and he had no doubt she wasn't ready to accept anything more.

With a sigh, he pushed the troubled thoughts from his head. He turned to the side and glanced at the clock. They had two hours before they had to be anywhere, so he closed his eyes and savored holding Jody in his arms. He'd give anything to make this a regular occurrence, but with the way they'd come together he didn't see that happening any time soon. Dan just hoped having sex hadn't taken them back a step.

He wanted to move their relationship forward, and he didn't think Jody would see sex as a step in that direction. If anything, she'd see it as a reason to avoid him. There was no way he'd stand for that. Not now that he'd had her beneath him—above him. Around him. He'd need to make a connection outside of the bedroom, and the only way to do that would be to insinuate himself into her life.

Dan smiled. He'd make it his mission to woo her. To slowly seduce her into not just letting him between her legs. Because even though he wanted to be there, he knew it wasn't all he was after. He could only hope he had the skills and patience required to win her over. Now that he'd been inside her, there was no chance he'd settle for anything less than possessing all of her. Body, heart and soul.

9

Jody woke wrapped around a warm body. Startled, she jerked back and came face-to-face with Dan. "Oh."

"Hey." He smiled, but the corners of his mouth wobbled and the uncertainty in his eyes troubled her.

"I fell asleep." Stupid conversation considering they'd just had sex. Twice.

"Yeah." He reached up and brushed the hair off her face with his fingertips. "You weren't out long. Ten minutes tops."

"Oh." She glanced away, his penetrating gaze made her nervous.

The phone on the bedside table rang, making her jump. Who would be calling their room? She scrambled over Dan, snatched up the receiver and brought it to her ear. "Hello?"

"Mum?"

Jody bolted upright and dove off the bed. "Leigh? What's wrong? Where's Uncle Luc?"

"Nothing. He's here. Can I go to the movies with some friends tonight? Uncle Luc and Cassie said it was okay if you said yes. They'll be at the same cinema with Amy so I'll be safe."

The movies? With friends? "Why—?"

"I know it's last minute, but we only just organized it and I really, really want to go. Everyone will be there. Please."

"Leigh, put Uncle Luc on for me." If Jody didn't get her brother on the phone Leigh would launch into another stream of babble in order to get a yes. It wasn't the first time her daughter had used the ploy.

"Hey, Jody, how goes it?" Luc's deep voice rumbled across the line.

Jody glanced at Dan. How did she answer that question? "Um, good. Listen. Leigh can go, but make sure you see her with the group before you leave her. I'm going to ask her who's going when you put her back on but I'm pretty sure it'll be the usual crowd."

"No worries. We'll be there. Cassie and Amy are going to watch some cartoon flick that neither Leigh nor I are interested in, so if I don't find something else to see I'll be hanging out in the coffee shop."

"Okay. Let me know what I owe you. I didn't give either of them any money before I left." She wanted to slap herself in the forehead. She'd left her kids with her brother and not only hadn't she given either of the girls cash, she'd neglected to give any to Luc or Cassie for anything the girls might want.

Luc laughed. "I think I can manage to shout a movie or two. But you know popcorn doesn't come cheap…"

Jody smiled as she knew he'd have expected her to. "Fine. I get the hint."

"Good. Now I'll put Leigh back on so you can grill her. Text me if you find out anything I should know. Catch ya tomorrow night."

Leigh squealed in her ear. "I can go? Oh my God. You're the best mum ever!"

She pulled the phone from her ear and waited for Leigh's enthusiasm to calm down.

"Thank you, thank you, thank you." Leigh finally ran out of steam.

Jody brought the phone back to her head with a smile. "Not so fast. Who's going exactly?"

"Oh, Jenny, Michelle, Monica, Erika, Drew, Claudia and Jason.

Oh, and Monica's mum is taking her little brother and sister to the same movie Cassie is taking Amy to so there's plenty of adults going to be there."

Jody loved that her daughter still felt comfortable with parental concern and supervision. She knew there'd be a day when Leigh wouldn't want her to know what she was up to, but until then Jody would make the most of their open, close relationship to build a level of trust between them. "Say hi to Monica's mum for me and make sure you mind your Uncle Luc and Cassie."

"I will. Hey, Amy wants to say hi."

She could hear the phone being passed to an excited Amy and wondered if she should pull the phone away so her other daughter didn't burst her eardrum.

"Hi, Mum. You should see what I helped Cassie make." Amy may have been animated, but unlike her sister, she didn't do it at an ear-splitting decibel.

"What did you make?" Jody lowered herself to the bed behind her.

"These really cool paper-flower bouquets. They're for some party next weekend."

Jody knew the event Amy was talking about. It was a last-minute baby shower booking. "I can't wait to see them."

"Cassie said I could make an extra one for my room so you can see it." Jody could hear the grin in Amy's voice.

"That was nice of Cassie. Make sure you say thank you." Jody jumped when Dan draped the blanket around her shoulders. Glancing over to the side, she saw he sat behind her listening to her conversation. Seeing him reminded her of what she'd done—what they'd done—and she couldn't stop the ripple of fear that flowed through her. Amy's voice jarred her out of her thoughts and a slam of guilt hit her. She should be paying attention to her child, not the naked man next to her. "Sorry, Amy, what was that, the phone cut out a bit." It was a lie and Jody hated telling it.

"I was trying to describe my bouquet, but you can just see it tomorrow when you pick us up from Uncle Luc's house."

Dan's hand landed on her shoulder and she shook it off and stood, putting some distance between them so she could keep her head in gear. "Okay, I'll see you tomorrow, baby girl. Love you. Hug your sister for me."

"Bye, Mum." Amy hung up before Jody could reply.

Jody replaced the receiver and wondered why they'd phoned the hotel and not her mobile. Gathering the edges of the blanket, she wrapped it more tightly around her and headed for her handbag. Rummaging inside, she found the reason her child had found it necessary to ring the hotel to track her down. Her battery was dead. She'd meant to plug it in when she got to the room, but Dan had distracted her. Boy howdy, hadn't he. She looked at the clock and almost choked on her own tongue. They'd been in the room for over two hours and she hadn't thought about anything except Dan and sex.

"I don't think I like that look." Dan moved beside her. Naked.

"Huh?" Jody tried to follow the conversation except her mind couldn't focus on anything other than the very attractive male body in front of her. Her breasts grew heavy and her sex tingled and clenched in remembered sensation.

"You're feeling guilty about something to do with your daughters."

"How do you know that?" Was her face that revealing?

"I've seen the look before. My mother wore it a lot the year my sister slipped on the wet kitchen floor and broke her back." He frowned, sadness pulling at the corners of his eyes.

"Oh my God, is she all right now?"

"Yeah, both of them are. Mum got over her guilt of being the one to drench the floor and Reagan's back healed without major damage. She never played sport again, but her bones healed and she leads a normal life."

Jody couldn't imagine what it must have been like for Dan's mother to go through something like that. Or his sister. "I don't know what to say. My forgetting to charge my phone or leave the girls with money seems like petty issues now."

"Oh, don't go feeling guilty about doing what comes natural to a mother. That wasn't my aim. All I wanted to do was explain why I knew what you were feeling and maybe make you feel a little less that way. Obviously I screwed that up." He shrugged and headed for the bathroom.

Jody wasn't sure what to do or say and found herself following him. "About earlier—"

He spun around, arm up, palm out. "Stop. Before you say anything you don't mean or I don't like."

"Ah..."

"Let's just get ready for tonight and not overanalyze the situation."

"We can't pretend it never happened," she argued.

Dan stepped forward until he was right in front of her, his chest brushing against her hands where she held the blanket bunched in her fists between her breasts.

"I have no intention of forgetting—pretend or otherwise—what happened in this room this afternoon. But I'm not about to let you make me regret what we did, and I'll be fucked if I let you either."

Jody gasped. The firmness of his words, the confidence that radiated off him had her taking a mental step back. "I—"

He placed two fingers over her lips. "No. Don't say anything." Bending forward, Dan replaced his fingers with his mouth. The kiss was quick. Hard. And then he was turning away, leaving her floundering in confusion.

She didn't know which she felt more. Guilt, shame or embarrassment. Or satisfaction. There was no ignoring the hum of contentment infusing every part of her with a lightness she hadn't experienced in years.

For a long twenty-four hours, Dan had tried his hardest not to pressure Jody. The weekend hadn't gone anything like he'd expected. There had been some good and bad, and as he loaded the last of their boxes into the van, he wasn't sure if he dreaded the trip home or not. She'd barely spoken to him since their strained conversation the day before. They'd remained civil and pleasant in public and private, but the intimacy he thought they'd developed in those few stolen hours had proved as elusive as fog.

"We're all checked out and I grabbed us each a bottle of water for the trip home." Jody stepped up beside him and held out a plastic bottle.

He looked at the drink then back at Jody. Her eyes were a little wild—fearful—and he hated that it was him who'd put that anxiety there. "Thanks."

"You're welcome." She turned on her heel and headed for the passenger side.

Scrubbing a hand down his face, Dan wondered if he shouldn't try to smooth things over. The problem was, he didn't have a clue how to do that. He'd fucked up with that whole let's-not-over-analyze-it speech. He'd known it the minute the words left his mouth, but he hadn't backed down. Instead, he'd gotten in her face and spoken without thinking first. It was even worse that his words were said in anger. She'd pissed him off when she'd assumed he wanted to pretend they hadn't shared such an intimate moment.

She could hide or run for as long as she liked, but there was no way she could take back those hours of openness she'd shared with him. She'd let him in. Further than any man in a very long time, and if it was the last thing he did, he'd make sure she knew what that meant to him.

Fishing the keys out of his pocket as he made his way to the driver's door, he decided to ignore the tension between them and carry on as though they hadn't had a few heated words. Climbing in, he said, "What time do you have to pick up the girls, or is Luc dropping them off?"

"Oh, I'm picking them up."

"Well, we better get on the road so you're not too late. They've got school tomorrow, right?" Dan slid the key into the ignition and started the engine.

"Yes."

He glanced at the dashboard clock. "It'll take us three hours to get back to the warehouse, so you should be on your way to Luc's by six." Checking his mirrors, Dan pulled out of the parking spot.

"Six? We'll have barely gotten back then, and we have to unpack."

"I can do that. You need to get home to the girls. Spend some time with them seeing how you've been away all weekend." He wanted her to know he understood and respected her role as a mother.

"I can't let you do that."

"Don't be silly. It'll only take me a few minutes to unload the equipment and then I'll be heading home. We can both do the paperwork tomorrow in the office." Dan wanted to give her space, not too much, but enough to forget the tension of the last two days and perhaps let the good bits float to the top of her memory.

"Are you sure?"

He smiled. The tone of her voice told him she wanted to accept his offer. "Yep. Besides, it'll probably take me less time to unpack on my own than with you."

She sputtered until he turned his grin on her. "Jeez. You had me going for a second there." Her laughter filled the cabin and Dan breathed a sigh of relief.

Reaching over he turned the radio on. "Mind if I play a little music?"

"No, go ahead. I think I'll text Luc and let him know what time to expect me."

"Do you mind sending Cassie a text with the info about the date Mooney wants us to come back and do the second batch of staff?" he asked as he turned onto the expressway.

"Sure. Might be best if I just ring."

"Probably." Dan leaned over and flicked the volume on the radio down while Jody made the call.

She ended up on the phone for twenty minutes. Both girls wanted to talk to her after she'd spoken to Luc and Cassie, and from what he heard of Jody's side of the conversation, her eldest wanted to have a sleepover next weekend. Jody had said no because she had to work Saturday afternoon. Dan could hear the yelling all the way across the cab. He glanced over to see Jody's cheeks were bright red and figured she was embarrassed about her daughter's outburst. With the skill only a mother had, she ended the call and the conversation.

"Teenagers. There's no reasoning with them." He tried to infuse his words with humor but he didn't think he pulled it off.

"Mmm. Normally Leigh is the more reasonable of the two."

"She's the older one, right?"

"Yeah, fifteen. Amy's two years younger."

"I remember Reagan at fifteen. She was a hellion. I think my mother went gray overnight when my sister hit puberty." Dan overtook a slow moving truck.

"We hit that a few years ago. I'm not sure what prompted that shouting match. I just hope she isn't horrible to Luc or Cassie because I've gone from being the best mother in the world to the worst in the space of twenty-four hours."

"If you go by that standard you'll be the best again by tomorrow."

Jody laughed. "Thanks. I needed that levity. You're right, come tomorrow she'll have forgotten all about it and moved on to the next thing she wants me to say yes to."

"You're doing a great job, you know." He bounced his gaze from the road to her and back again. "From what you've said and what I've gleaned from Luc, their father isn't involved in their raising."

She sucked in a breath. "No, he's not."

"That must be hard. Having to do it on your own now."

Her laughter sounded hollow. "Yeah, because I had so much help before."

Dan would have to be stupid to miss the sarcasm in her words. "Sorry, didn't mean to bring up a sore point."

Jody sighed. "You didn't. I'm not bitter or angry, just sad really. The girls don't deserve to be an afterthought, and with their father that's all they'll ever be."

"At the risk of repeating myself...he didn't—doesn't—deserve you or the girls."

"Thank you. I know that in my head, but sometimes it's nice to hear someone else say it."

They were quiet then. Only the sound of the tires rolling over the road and the whoosh of the air-conditioner pumping the cab with cool air to fill the silence.

Jody pulled up in front of Luc's house and took a deep breath as she switched off the engine. She wasn't sure how she felt about Dan sending her home as soon as they got back. The gesture was nice, and she appreciated it, but she couldn't shake the feeling he was being overly nice because of what had happened yesterday. They should clear the air. Needed to clear it. If they didn't, working together and moving past the shift in their relationship, would be impossible.

She didn't want to give him the wrong impression. There was no room in her life for a man, she didn't need the added complication another person would bring. She'd finally gotten to a point where she was happy with her life—content. Okay, if she were honest, she'd admit the sex had been amazing. Better than amazing. And she'd certainly been shown what she was missing, but she wasn't the type to have a no-strings affair, and she didn't have it in her to attempt another serious relationship, not now, possibly not ever.

A tap on the window made her jump, and she looked over to see Luc standing on the curb watching her. Pulling the keys from the ignition, she steeled herself to face her brother and hoped to hell he wouldn't be able to tell she'd had sex with Dan. She'd barely opened the door when he started talking.

"Cassie has the girls distracted."

"Okay." Jody had no idea where he was going with this.

"I thought you might need a moment to talk before you turned back into super mum."

She smiled. His uncanny ability to judge her moods had always bewildered her. "Talk about what?"

Luc shrugged. "Anything you don't want to say in front of the girls."

"Thanks, but I think I'm good."

"Are you sure?" He studied her for a moment. "I can take Cassie's place and send her out here."

Jody loved her brother, but there was no way she'd discuss her sex life or her confused emotions about Dan with him or her boss. She patted Luc's arm. "I'm fine. Let's go in and I'll get those girls out of your hair so you and Cassie can have some peace and quiet."

"Actually, it hasn't been that noisy. I think Cassie makes more noise than the girls put together." He slung his arm around her shoulders and led her along the path. "We've had a great weekend and I'm beginning to see how much I missed when they were little. Why didn't you make me see more of them?"

Jody couldn't help but laugh. "Lucas Wilhelm, you were terrified of them. Neither of them could move without you freaking out."

He had the grace to color up. "Well, they were tiny. Hell, compared to me they still are."

"Here's the thing." They stopped on the front step. "When they were little they didn't need more of your attention than you gave, but now that they're older and their father really isn't around, I'd like you to have a bigger role in their lives. They have Dad, but they need a good male influence as well as a grandfather, and I'd like that to be you."

"You know I'd do anything for you and those two."

She smiled and stood on tiptoes to kiss his cheek. "I know, and I thank you for always having my back."

"Anything for you, Budgie." He grinned as he used the nickname he'd given her as a child because he said she chirped like a bird.

Jody slapped his arm. "C'mon, let's go inside." She followed him in, but she couldn't help wishing he wasn't the only good male role model in the girls' lives, which totally went against her earlier thought of not needing a man in her life. No doubt about it, Dan had her brain going haywire. And if she didn't sort out her emotions soon she'd be in all kinds of trouble.

10

Dan stretched out on his couch, phone in hand. Undecided about calling her, he'd hovered his thumb over Jody's number for the last hour. He wanted to check she'd picked up the girls and returned home safe. Which he really had no right to wonder. Only he did worry and he knew he'd give in to the urge to ring her eventually. Checking the time, he figured if he didn't do it soon he'd wake her up.

Giving in to temptation, he pressed the call button and brought the phone to his ear. It rang four times before she answered.

"Hello?" She sounded out of breath.

"Did I catch you at a bad time?"

"Dan?"

"Yeah." What other guy did she expect to call her? "I wanted to make sure you got home safe."

"Oh, well, we did."

"Good. I'm glad."

Silence filled the line.

"Right, well, I bet you have things to do..." He shouldn't have rung her.

"Actually, you caught me just getting ready for bed."

X-rated images filled his head. He'd seen her in her pajamas. He'd seen her out of them too. His throat and mouth suddenly dry, he swallowed. "Oh, um, I should let you go then."

"No, it's okay." Did she answer a little too quickly? A little breathlessly?

"I don't want to keep you up."

"You're not. I was going to read for a while."

"Anything interesting?" Dan wanted to know what type of book held Jody's attention.

"Not to you I wouldn't think." Her words held a smile.

"How do you know that? We might have the same taste in reading material." He hoped they did. It would give them something in common as well as something to talk about.

"It's a romance novel."

"Is it one of those that are all the fad at the moment?" The genre escaped him, but he knew the books were full of sex. His sister read them. "You know, the ones with explicit sex in them."

"Um…"

He could almost hear her blushing. "It *is*."

"Ah, maybe."

"Read a racy bit to me."

"W-what?"

"Read me something hot."

"No."

"Aw, c'mon, just a paragraph," he coaxed.

"I can't."

"Why not?"

"Because."

"Because why?"

"Jeez, now you sound like the girls when I can't think of a reasonable explanation when I say no to something." She laughed, the sound echoing down the line and tightening Dan's groin.

"C'mon. Just one little bit. Pretty please." He put as much pouty whine into his voice as he could, hoping to convince her to read him something.

"Fine. Give me a second to find a good spot."

He could hear her moving around and imagined she was crawling into bed. The idea alone had his pulse racing and his cock growing thicker. She was silent for so long he began to wonder if she'd changed her mind and was waiting for him to hang up. "Found a good bit yet?"

She cleared her throat. "Yeah."

"Hang on. Let me get comfy." Dan popped the button and lowered the zipper on his jeans. "Okay. Go."

"'Harley leaned back on the bed and spread her legs. The view her position gave Todd had his eyes widening and his pants bulging. She knew what he'd see. She'd made sure there was no hair to hide her cunt.'"

"Fuck. Say that again." Dan shoved his hand in his pants and pulled out his throbbing cock.

"S-say what again?"

"Cunt." He squeezed his eyes shut as he stroked his hard-on. "That sounded so fucking hot coming out of your mouth."

"I'd prefer to just keep reading."

"Does it get hotter?" Dan slowly dragged his hand up and down his length.

"I-I think so."

Jody sounded a little breathless and he closed his eyes and pictured her in the position she'd described. He almost swallowed his tongue when he thought about her pussy stripped of hair. "Keep going," he urged.

"'Todd came toward her, stripping his shirt over his head as he did. The muscles in his chest rippled and her cunt wept with joy. If his chest looked that good she couldn't wait to see his cock. "Lose the pants," she demanded. He stopped beside the bed and did as she asked. He'd gone commando and his magnificent rod sprang free and slapped against his washboard abs. She licked her lips. She'd taste him first, then when he'd blown his load down her throat she'd make him eat her out until she screamed his name, yanked on his hair and came all over his face.'"

Dan groaned. His balls tucked up into his body and pre-come

oozed from the slit in his cock. "Stop. Shit. Jody." He wasn't sure what he was trying to say.

"W-what?" She was breathless and he could only imagine how wet she was from reading that passage.

"Hearing you read that is so fucking hot. I'm close to blowing my load, only there isn't anyone to share it with."

"Oh..." Her breathy little sigh sent a shiver over his skin.

"Talk to me."

"You mean read more?"

"No. Tell me what you want me to do to you. Tell me what you'd make me do if that was you and me in that scene."

She was quiet so long Dan didn't think she was going to grant his request. And when she did finally speak, he had to strain to hear the words at first.

"I'd want to lick you while you licked me."

"Man, I'd love to do that. Sixty-nine is my favourite number."

"I've never done that before." Her words whispered through his ear.

"Never?" What the hell was wrong with the guy she'd married? "Next time I get you in a bed we're doing that first."

"Oh. That won't—"

"I'll lie on my back with you on all fours facing the other direction and I'll lick you from front to back and front again. Over and over until your pretty pussy is dripping all over my face. Put your hand on your pussy, Jody. Are you wet for me right now?" Dan tightened his grip but slowed his strokes so he didn't come before he could convince this amazingly innocent woman to indulge in a little phone sex with him.

"Um..."

"Are you wet?"

"Yes," she hissed, and he visualized her fingers sliding through her slick folds.

Fuck. "Play with you clit, Jody, pretend it's my tongue circling and flicking and driving you crazy with lust." Dan's breathing grew jagged when she panted in his ear. "Are you playing with your cunt, Jody?"

He used the word from her book, prayed it would make her hotter, because this whole thing had him so close to coming his eyes were about to cross.

"Y-yes."

He heard the hitch in her breath, heard the little whimpers he remembered from Saturday and knew she was close. "Use your other hand and slide two fingers inside that clasping cunt for me. I'm not there to do it so I need you to do it for me."

She moaned and gasped, and Dan closed his eyes and stroked his cock harder. Faster. They were nearly there. Just a little more and she'd go over and then he'd follow.

"Do it harder. Faster. Fuck that wet cunt with my fingers, Jody."

A muffled cry tore through the phone line and he could picture her biting her lip to keep the sob of pleasure from breaking free.

"Oh, God." Her voice shook and he could hear her thrashing about. It was all he needed to go over.

With a growl, he came. Hot spurts of come coated his hand as he milked his cock with a punishing grip. When the last pulse left him, he sagged into the leather cushions and listened to Jody's breath settle back into a normal rhythm. Neither of them spoke. It wasn't necessary when they could hear the other breathing. How long they lay there, he couldn't say. It could have been seconds, minutes or hours. Time didn't matter when they'd connected in such an intimate way. And no matter what she said or did, Dan knew she trusted him.

To do what they just had, to be open enough to have phone sex with him, showed him more than anything else that she was letting him in. He still had a long way to go, but he was making progress and that was all he cared about. As long as they kept moving forward they could go as slow as a snail and he'd be happy, because they'd be doing it together.

Jody figured she'd lost her mind. Why else would she have had phone sex with Dan? *Phone sex.* She'd never done anything so bold. Hours later, her body still hummed with the release she'd given herself but couldn't take all the credit for. Reading the scene from the book had her so wound up it hadn't taken much to push her over. And when he'd started to describe what they'd do together, how he'd lick her, well, even if he hadn't suggested she touch herself she would have.

She glanced at the clock and groaned. Four in the morning and she'd barely slept. Disturbingly dirty dreams of her and Dan doing every single one of her secret fantasies kept waking her up in a frenzied state that had her breath harsh and her body aching. Tomorrow was going to be bad if she couldn't manage a few more hours sleep. As it was, the alarm went off at six so she could shower and get ready for work before she dragged the girls out of bed and got them moving.

With a sigh, she threw her arm over her face. Hours ago, on the long drive home, she'd decided the thing with Dan couldn't go anywhere. She had her girls, a job she loved and family and friends who filled her life with as much happiness as she needed. And then Dan had rocked her world—again—with a single phone call. The man was lethal to her sanity. Every time he was around or she thought about him she did something out of character—like having an orgasm in a parking lot for God's sake.

Moaning, Jody rolled over and stared at the wall. The picture that hung there should remind her of all the reasons she should keep her distance. It was one of her favourite pictures of her and the girls. They were all laughing and happy, and it wasn't until now that she could see the sadness of the image. Colin hadn't been able to make the family-portrait sitting. Even back then, barely five years into their marriage, she should have walked away. Instead, she'd stuck it out for another five.

Hindsight was all good and well, but it didn't change the fact that she'd wasted most of her adult life on a man who'd never loved her or the girls. Her biggest shame was she'd picked a man who couldn't—or wouldn't—connect emotionally to be the father of her children. She'd overcompensated for Colin's lack of involvement over the years and she honestly thought she had a stronger bond with her girls because of that. Still, she wished they had an interested dad in their lives.

After another ten minutes of lying in the dark wide awake, Jody gave up on sleep and figured she'd catch up on things around the house that had gone undone over the weekend. She started with her bathroom and moved on to the girls' one in no time. Heading for the kitchen next, she wiped down cupboard doors and counters, finishing with the stove. Opening the fridge, she decided to put a slow cooker on for dinner and quickly found some carrots and sweet potato to toss in with the steak she pulled out of the freezer.

While the steak defrosted in the microwave she chopped the veggies along with a couple of onions and threw them into the crockpot. She pulled the meat out before it was fully thawed and cut it into cubes. A liter of stock and a few herbs and spices and she turned on the power and switched the machine to low. By the time the girls got home from school it would be ready. She'd leave a note to ask them to turn it off and some money so they could walk down to the local bakery and get a crusty loaf of bread to go with it.

Satisfied she'd been productive instead of lying in bed mentally flipping through her messed-up life she smiled. Next she'd tackle the washing. It didn't take her long to realize the washer was broken. Again. Last time it had been a coin caught in a hose. The machine wasn't even a year old. She'd have to ring the repairman first thing tomorrow—no, today—and beg Luc to use his if she couldn't get hers looked at before Wednesday.

Heading back to her room to get her phone, Jody wondered what else she could do to occupy her until it was time to get the girls up. She grabbed her phone and went back to the kitchen where she opened her bag and pulled out the paperwork from the weekend and spread it out on the breakfast counter. Putting a memo in her calendar to ring the repairman, she quickly got to work finalizing the weekend's papers.

It took longer than expected because her mind kept wandering off on a Dan tangent every few minutes. The man had definitely taken over her thoughts in recent weeks. Ever since he'd laid that first kiss on her, she'd been helpless to stop her memory and imagination from bombarding her with real and dreamed-up pleasure to be found with him. He was trouble whether she gave in to him or fought against him.

Disgusted with herself for losing track of what she was meant to be doing yet again, she tossed down her pen and pushed her stool back with a screech. She'd grab a shower now. With any luck, the hot water would wash away all thoughts of a certain man and everything he made her feel.

The day had been tense. Dan hadn't brought up last night's phone call and neither had Jody. But for all the personal apprehension and strain between them, they'd worked together seamlessly and finalized the weekend's job and locked the second date on the calendar. Dan had spoken to Mooney and emailed the questionnaire Cassie wanted the first group of employees to fill out. Those would be returned by the end of the week so now he could put the file away and call it a day.

Jody was on the phone and as he didn't want to leave without talking to her and possibly heading out together, he waited. He couldn't help overhearing her conversation and it didn't take him long to work out her washing machine was broken and the repairman couldn't fit her in until next week. When she hung up the phone with a sigh, he ventured over to her desk and rested his hip on the edge.

"I could take a look at that washer for you."

She glanced up. "What?"

"Your washer. I worked for my dad all through my teens and he ran a repair business, so I'm pretty handy when it comes to fixing anything mechanical." Dan smiled. He tried not to let his need to spend more time with her leak into his voice.

Jody's forehead crinkled, her eyebrows rising almost to her hairline. "Really?"

Her skepticism didn't sit well with him. "Yep, and because you're obviously convinced I can't fix it, I'll add an incentive to take me up on my offer. I'll buy dinner for you and the girls, and if I don't have the machine working by the time you finish eating, I'll buy you a new one."

She rolled her eyes. "Jeez, what is it with men and proving they can fix things?"

"What do you mean?" Had someone else offered to repair her broken washer?

"You and Luc. He's already tried to convince me to let him look at it."

"Does he know anything about the mechanics of a washing machine?"

"Probably not, but that wouldn't stop him from pulling it apart if I said yes. But never mind that, the damn thing is less than a year old, so it's covered under warranty. I'm pretty sure I'd void that by letting you look at it."

"Probably, but what if it's something simple that me fixing wouldn't void the warranty, and you wouldn't have the expense of calling out the service company." Dan was reaching. Unless she'd forgotten to plug the machine in and switch it on, she'd still have to call the repairman or risk voiding the warranty even if he could fix the problem.

"Thanks, but no." Jody bent over and retrieved her handbag. "Now if I don't head home and get organized I won't get to Luc's before midnight, and if I don't have a washer for the rest of the week I need to wash tonight."

"Isn't Luc a thirty-minute drive from where you are?"

"Yes, why?"

"Well, my place is only about ten and my washer works. Drier too." Dan held his breath.

"You're offering to let me use your machines? What's the catch?" She eyed him suspiciously.

"No catch. Well, other than you actually have to spend time with me outside of work." He grinned.

"Why?"

"Why not?" He wasn't sure why Jody needed a reason, but he'd give her one. "It's just one friend loaning their washer to another. No strings."

"In my experience there's always a string or two."

Dan held up his hands. "Nope, no strings." He grabbed a pen and her sticky note pad, and scribbled down his address. "Here. If you want to take me up on my offer I'll be home all night. If not, no worries."

Jody eyed the note then met his gaze again. "You really do only live ten minutes from me."

"Yeah, a lot closer than your brother's place." Dan pushed to his feet. "Anyway, come or don't, doesn't matter to me, but with the girls having to get up for school tomorrow, I would think cutting some time off your evening might guarantee them getting into bed at a reasonable hour."

Dan got all the way to the door before she stopped him.

"Wait." She hustled to catch up with him. "If you're serious I'd love to use your washer, but there's one condition."

He didn't think it was the kind of condition his body craved. "Shoot."

"I'll bring dinner."

"I don't—"

She grabbed his arm. "Please. It's already made anyway. I put a hotpot together before I left for work this morning. I'll just bring it with me. Oh, and the girls. I don't like leaving them home alone at night." She smiled.

"What time should I expect you?" Dan wasn't about to argue. If she felt comfortable enough to introduce him to her kids he wasn't about to say anything to make her change her mind.

"Seven? That gives me time to get home, gather the dirty washing, dinner and the girls."

"Great. See you then."

11

———————

Jody wasn't sure what Leigh's latest outburst was about. She'd been hostile from the moment Jody had gotten home. Amy on the other hand was being the perfect child. She wouldn't have worried if they weren't currently pulling up to Dan's house. There was nothing worse than a child misbehaving in front of others, and Jody turned in her seat to look at both girls.

"Please be on your best behavior. Dan has been kind enough to let us use his washer and drier, so I don't want to thank him by bringing a couple of naughty kids into his house."

"Then why'd you bring us?" Leigh sat in the front seat, arms crossed and a frown on her face.

"Why wouldn't I bring you?" Jody asked.

"Because we might cramp your style."

"What? Why would you say something like that, Leigh?" Jody was flabbergasted. Who was this child and where had her pleasant daughter gone? One weekend away for work and she'd turned into a monster.

"Never mind. You don't get it." Leigh grabbed the door handle and yanked it open.

Before Jody could reply, Leigh slammed her way out of the car and stomped toward Dan's front door. What the hell was going on?

Amy sighed dramatically from the backseat. "Sometimes she's so selfish."

Jody turned to look at her youngest daughter. "Why do you say that?"

"Because Leigh wants to be home so that *Benji* can ring her."

"Benji?"

"He's some stupid boy at school that's going to ask her out or something." Amy's cheeks flushed with color. "I overheard her talking to Monica on the way home."

Ah, so Leigh had finally discovered boys. Jody took a deep breath and let it out slowly. She'd been dreading the whole boys talk and she had hoped for another year of ignoring that particular subject, but obviously she couldn't put it off any longer. The girls both knew the basics, they'd had those talks often enough. But Jody had avoided talking about dating, what was okay, what wasn't, and what to expect from any boy interested in them.

Jody found it mildly amusing that both she and Leigh were dealing with interest from the opposite sex. Then again, she hoped Leigh wasn't dealing with the same level of interest. She didn't want to even think about the possibility of her daughter having sex yet. Christ, she was only fifteen. Except she'd heard kids were becoming sexually active a lot younger now days, and the thought of her child being one of them terrified her.

"Mum, are we going to sit here all night?" Amy asked.

"Oh, no." Jody pulled the keys from the ignition and put them in her pocket as she climbed out of the car. By the time she'd opened the tailgate on her SUV, Dan was beside her.

"Here, let me carry that for you." He reached in and picked up the basket of dirty clothes. "Is that dinner I smell?"

"Yes. It's just a basic beef stew." Jody didn't want him to think she'd gone to any trouble on his account.

"Nothing basic about that smell. My taste buds are already

watering with anticipation." He grinned at her then walked toward the house. "C'mon, I'm starving."

Jody followed Dan into a nicely decorated house. Most of what she saw had a woman's touch and it suddenly struck her that he might have a woman in his life. Her gaze darted over to him to find he was watching her carefully.

"Do you like it?" He indicated the living room with the lift of his chin. "My mum and sister helped me decorate when I first bought the place."

Relief swamped her. She wasn't sure what surprised her more. The fact she'd never thought to ask if he was involved or the spike of jealousy that had stabbed her in the belly when she thought of him with someone else. "It's great. Very homey."

"That was what my mum said they were going for. C'mon, let's get a load in the washer and then we can have some of that yummy smelling food." He turned and headed down a ceramic-tiled hallway. "Girls, there's a Play Station and computer down this way in the family room," he called over his shoulder.

"Oh, no. I didn't even introduce you to the girls. Dan, this is Amy and Leigh." Jody felt her cheeks heat with embarrassment as she pointed to each of her daughters in turn.

Dan paused and spun around to face them. "It's nice to finally meet you both. I've heard so much about you from your mum, Luc and Cassie that it feels like we've already met." He smiled. "C'mon, I'm sure I've got a game or two you'll like."

Jody had to prompt both girls to say hi before they followed Dan deeper into the house.

Amy walked ahead of her, bouncing along right behind Dan and asking a million questions while Leigh dragged her feet about ten paces behind Jody. The two couldn't be more polar-opposite in mood if they tried. Resigned to spending the evening with grumpy and happy, she hoped Dan didn't mind sharing his time on the teenage emotional roller coaster with her.

"Wow. Leigh, you have to come see this." Amy disappeared into a room at the end of the hall.

"Jeez, could she be any more juvenile?" Leigh muttered as she brushed past Jody and followed her sister through the doorway.

Jody raised one eyebrow at Dan. "What?"

His smile seemed shy and totally un-Dan like. "She's found my electronic game collection."

"Game collection?"

"Yeah, I have every one ever produced." He shrugged. "I've been collecting them for years."

She popped her head in the door to see the girls both had devices in their hands. "Hey, don't touch—"

"No. It's okay. They all work and they're supposed to be played with," Dan said.

"But what if they break them?"

He laughed. "If they've survived this long, I'm sure they'll come out unscathed today. And if not I'll just fix them."

"You can do that?"

"Yep, washers aren't the only things I know how to repair." Dan turned and walked into the kitchen. "The laundry is this way."

Jody followed him through a gorgeous kitchen. Stainless-steel appliances, gloss-white cupboards and black-marble countertops made the space a cook's dream. She'd love to have a kitchen like this, but on her budget that wasn't going to happen anytime soon. "This is amazing. You must cook up a storm in here."

"Ah, yeah, no. I'm not much of a cook. My mum uses it when I host the family dinners though," he called out from the room on the far side.

She joined him in an area far too fancy for a laundry. "My God, even the dirty clothes get a great room to hang out in."

Dan looked around them then shrugged. "The people who remodeled the kitchen did the laundry and bathrooms as well. I got a cheaper deal getting them all done together."

"Well, if these two rooms are anything to go by the bathrooms must be gorgeous."

"Let's get a load on and I'll take you on a tour."

Jody looked for somewhere to put the crock-pot in her arms.

"Here, I'll take that into the kitchen while you sort your wash. Do I need to plug it in?" He took the heavy pot from her.

"No. It was just easier to grab the whole thing than pull out the inner pot and worry about burning something on it."

"Okay, I'll set the table while you get a load on."

She watched him walk away and wondered what the hell she was doing in his house. She'd managed to sabotage her decision to keep her distance at every turn. Rolling her eyes at herself, she crouched down and began sorting the washing into lights and darks. By the time she'd thrown the lights in the machine, Dan was back, leaning against the doorjamb. His close scrutiny made her nervous, but that was nothing compared to the look in his eyes. They smoldered, the desire he felt for her going unchecked as he watched her.

"Um, I'm not sure how this works…"

Dan pushed off the wall and stalked toward her. Her pulse spiked and her breathing turned choppy—jagged. "Here, let me show you." He crowded in close and leaned over her to press the buttons on the control panel. His breath fanned out over her neck, sending a shiver down her spine and goose bumps racing to catch up.

"Mum! Leigh won't let me play with the Game Boy!" Amy yelled from out in the kitchen.

Jody jumped and Dan immediately moved away. When Amy came charging into the room they were no longer in a compromising position, and Jody turned her attention to her daughter.

"Please don't yell, Amy."

"But Leigh's hogging the Game Boy and I want a turn."

"You can have a turn when she dies or whatever it is that happens when a game is over."

Dan laughed. "You obviously aren't a game fan."

"Well, no, not really." Jody smoothed a hand over Amy's hair. "We'll be eating in a moment, so go tell you sister to put the game away and wash her hands."

"There's a bathroom across the hall from the games room, Amy," Dan added.

"Sorry about that. They've been at each other's throats since I walked in the door this afternoon." She headed in the direction of the kitchen. "I better make sure there's no blood spilled in your bathroom."

Walking quickly, Jody made her way to find the girls and make sure they weren't embarrassing her further by fighting over the soap.

Dan sat on his sofa in a death match with Amy. Leigh was sulking on the other side of the room with the Game Boy she hadn't let out of her hands since she'd arrived. Momentarily distracted by the brooding teenager, the younger one took him out.

"Yes!" Amy pumped her fist in the air. "Die, sucker, die."

"Language!" Jody called from the kitchen where she'd insisted on cleaning up after dinner.

"Fun police strikes again," Leigh murmured.

Dan arched an eyebrow and looked at Amy who shrugged and said, "She's pissed at Mum for making us come here tonight. Some guy from school was supposed to call and ask her out, but she's not home to answer."

"Amy! Shut up!" Leigh looked ready to launch across the room and strangle her sister.

"You two aren't fighting again are you?" Jody asked from the doorway.

He glanced over and saw the frown on Jody's face, the concern in her eyes, and tried to pacify her a little. "Amy beat me again. She's a tough one."

Jody smiled. "She always thrashes me at Wii bowling."

Ah, so they did have a game console at home. "I didn't know you played. I can hook up the Wii and challenge you to a game if you want."

"No, it's okay. I'm going to fold that first load of washing while the other takes its turn in the dryer."

When Jody left the room, he glanced back at Leigh who was still shooting daggers at Amy. "You think this guy won't call back if you're not there to pick up?"

She shrugged. "I don't know. I'm not even sure he'll call. He told his best friend who told my best friend, so it might not even be true."

Dan could tell she wanted it to be, and while he wasn't sure where Jody stood on the whole dating thing, he felt he should at least try to make Leigh feel better. "You know, if he likes you, really likes you, he'll keep trying until he talks to you."

Her face brightened. "You think so?"

"Definitely. But if he doesn't, he's not the guy for you."

"Why not?" She'd gone on the defensive again, her brow wrinkling up in the same way Jody's did when she was about to go to battle over something.

"Because if he's not prepared to put in some effort to be with you, then he doesn't deserve to spend time with you."

"Oh, so I should play hard to get? That's what Monica's older sister said."

"No, I just mean if he gives up after ringing you once then he obviously wasn't that interested. But I'm betting he either talks to you at school tomorrow or rings tomorrow night." He'd probably stepped over the line by giving Jody's daughter dating advice. He'd have to tell her what they'd talked about before Leigh or Amy mentioned it to their mother. "Who wants some ice cream?"

"Me. Me. Me," Amy chanted.

"Chocolate or vanilla?"

"Both." She grinned at him and he couldn't resist tweaking her pert nose.

"Hey." She rubbed the tip with her hand.

"Leigh?"

"No, thanks. I don't need the extra fat."

Uh-oh, he wasn't touching that comment with a ten-foot barge pole. "Right. One bowl of chocolate *and* vanilla ice cream coming up."

Dan quickly made up a bowl for Amy and took it back to the games room. Certain they were both occupied for the moment, he went in search of Jody to confess he'd blundered into a parent-type conversation with her eldest daughter. He might not be a father, but he was pretty sure he'd handled the discussion correctly. Hopefully, Jody thought the same.

He found her on the floor in the laundry. She had three piles of folded clothes around her. Hunkering down beside her, he picked up a shirt from the basket and attempted to fold it. Jody laughed and took it out of his hands.

"Give me that. Watch." She grabbed the shirt under the armpits and shook it out. Then she folded the thing in half, bringing her hands together. After that, she tucked in the sleeves and folded it twice lengthways until it was a neat little square of fabric. "See. Easy."

"Yeah, right," he grumbled as he picked up another shirt to give it a try.

"How do you fold yours then?" she asked as she quickly made another neat square with a pair of shorts.

"I don't. I hang them all up." He dipped his chin close to his chest. "It's easier."

Smiling, she turned her head to look at him. "Why do men always take the easy way?"

"I can't speak for all men, but I'm all for cutting corners where I can."

"Yeah, cutting corners." She snatched up a pair of shorts and snapped them out, making them crack like a whip.

"Hey, just because I cut corners with my laundry doesn't mean I cut them everywhere."

She let out a burst of air. "Sorry. I shouldn't have implied you do."

"Speaking of the easy way, I, um, may have overstepped the lines of our friendship just now with Leigh."

Her gaze snapped up to his. "What?"

"Oh, wait, that didn't sound right. Let me explain."

She glared at him with narrowed eyes. "Go on."

"Amy let it slip why Leigh has been sulking all night and we got into a conversation about some guy she thinks is going to ask her out."

"Oh, that." Jody's shoulders drooped. "I'm not sure what to think about that."

"Well, anyway, I asked what the problem was and then offered some advice."

"What did you say?"

Dan wasn't sure what was going through Jody's head. For all he knew, she was about to thump him for interfering. "I told her that if this guy couldn't get her tonight, if he was really interested he'd talk to her tomorrow at school or try ringing her again tomorrow night. I also tried to tell her that if he didn't try again after missing her tonight then he wasn't worth her time."

She remained quiet and Dan couldn't take the suspense for longer than a few seconds.

"Well? Did I fuck up?"

A smile tilted the corner of her mouth. "No. In fact, what you told her was good advice and probably more acceptable coming from you than me."

"Really?"

"Yeah, ever since the weekend we've been butting heads. I'm not sure she'd have listened to me if I'd said the same thing word for word. I seem to have been relegated to the enemy camp."

"I'm sure it won't last long. I remember my teenage years being like a pendulum swinging between love and hate when it came to my mum and dad." He picked up another shirt and this time managed to fold it in a semi-neat square.

Jody took the top off him and put it on one of the piles. "You're right. I know that. It's just frustrating not knowing what tips the scale in either direction."

The dryer beeped and he leaned over and popped the door open. Together, they pulled the second load of clothes out and dumped them in the basket. "Oh, I forgot, I gave Amy some ice cream. I didn't even think to ask if she could have it." Damn, he was an idiot. The kid could be allergic or something.

"That's fine. She's the ice-cream ho in our house."

"Yeah, Leigh said she didn't need the extra fat." He still couldn't believe a fifteen-year-old was worried about fat intake.

"Jesus. Another confusing, worrying aspect of raising a teenager in this era of thin is beautiful." Jody shook her head. "Lucky for me, she's fairly sensible and loves food." She laughed. "She'd never starve herself."

"I think West's sister had an eating disorder. She does a whole heap of seminars at high schools about food and nutrition. West helps put her menus together. You could ask him for some advice if you're really concerned."

"That's not a bad idea. I know their school has sent home a few notes about healthier options in lunch boxes. Maybe they've seen or heard something to be alarmed about."

"Maybe." Dan continued to help her fold. Unfortunately, he wasn't getting any better at it and Jody had to refold half of what he did. "Sorry. I should stop trying to help. I think I'm making more work."

"I'll have to remember to ask West in the morning." She grabbed the last piece of clothing before he could.

"I can remind you. I think he's in to make a cake for that kid's party Cassie is doing in the afternoon." Dan got to his feet and offered Jody his hand.

"Thanks." She got to her feet and they stood there just staring at each other for long moments. "I should get going. It's late and the girls have school."

"Yeah, you probably should." But neither of them moved.

Jody licked her lips and Dan couldn't resist leaning in for a taste. He pressed his mouth to hers and nibbled the sweet curves before sweeping over them with his tongue. She trembled against him before parting her lips and inviting him inside with the hesitant touch of her tongue. That was all it took for him to lose it and go deep. Thrusting his tongue between her teeth, he stroked and teased until they were caught up in a frenzied give and take.

Dan skimmed his hands over her hips and up her ribcage to her breasts. He cupped them, squeezed with his fingers and flicked her hard nipples with his thumbs. It wasn't enough—he wanted to feel her skin on skin, so he slid his hands back down until he could tuck them up under her T-shirt. Her flesh was warm and rippled beneath his fingers as he trailed them up her bare torso. She moaned into his mouth when he pushed her bra aside and palmed her bare breasts.

He wanted more. Pulling his lips from hers, he breathed her in as he nipped his way along her jaw to her ear. Scraping his teeth over the delicate flap of her lobe, he toyed with it until she whimpered. Then he sucked the whole thing into his mouth and tongued it with rapid flicks. She gasped and shuddered against him.

"I want you," he growled in her ear.

"Yes." The word left her lips in a rush of air.

"Mum?"

And just like that Dan's body went stone cold.

12

———

Jody still hadn't gotten over almost being caught making out with Dan by Leigh. The thought still made her shiver with fear. He'd been so accepting and even a little relieved when she'd hustled the girls out of there. And the text he'd sent her late last night had only made her soften toward him more. He was so understanding of her lightning-quick changes of mind. She really didn't deserve his patience or persistence, but she was more than willing to take it.

"Hey, wanna get some lunch?" Cassie strode into Jody's office.

"Sure. What did you have in mind?" Jody glanced at Dan who was busy on the phone with a client.

"I thought we could go to the sushi place again."

"Sounds good." Jody shuffled some papers back into their folder. "Give me five minutes?"

"I'll meet you downstairs." Cassie left with a small wave in Dan's direction.

Jody busied herself with putting the few files on her desk away while she waited for Dan to get off the phone. She wasn't sure why she was waiting to talk to him, but she couldn't leave before she did. When he finally said goodbye and put the phone back on its cradle, she took a deep breath. But he spoke before she could get a word out.

"Can you bring me back something?"

"Ah, sure. What do you want?"

"Just get me an assortment. There isn't anything I don't eat, so whatever looks good." He stood up and pulled his wallet out of his pocket.

She waved him off. "No, I've got it. It's the least I can do after you let me use your washer."

"I thought dinner was payment for that?" He smiled.

"Well, yeah, but then the girls did the whole war of the teenagers thing, so I figure I owe you for that too." She'd tried to apologize this morning when she'd first arrived at work, but he wouldn't let her. At least now she could assuage some of her guilt over subjecting him to her warring teens.

"I told you that wasn't a problem." He came around his desk. "They were perfectly well-behaved, and I'd be more than happy to spend time with them again."

"You would?" She couldn't imagine why. He was single and none of his siblings had children, so it wasn't as though he was used to being around kids.

"Yep. In fact, what about doing something together this weekend? You can come over early Saturday and use the washer again. Then we can head out for lunch somewhere. What do the girls like to eat?" He held up a hand. "Wait, let me guess. MacDonald's."

"I don't think that's a good idea..."

Dan frowned. The corners of his mouth creased and his brows scrunched together above his nose. "Why?"

"Look I know we've kind of moved beyond workmates but—"

"Don't say it." He leaned in close. "Can you for one second forget about everything except whether or not you want to hang out with me? Don't think about work. Don't think about anything but spending the day doing something fun with me. And the girls."

Jody opened her mouth, except Dan put two fingers over her lips before she could say a word.

"Think about it over lunch. Give me your answer when you

deliver my food." He bent forward and planted a quick, hard kiss on her mouth.

Shocked by his bold action, she stood frozen in place until the sound of Cassie yelling her name up the stairwell registered. Shaking herself, she glanced around to see Dan had left the room and she hadn't even realized he'd gone. He really did short-circuit her brain. She grabbed her bag and hightailed it downstairs to a waiting Cassie.

"About time. I was thinking of sending out a search party. What kept you so long?" Cassie asked as they headed across the warehouse.

Jody's cheeks heated and she knew they'd be flaming red. She wasn't about to tell Cassie Dan had kissed her in the office. "Sorry, filing took longer than I thought it would."

"You could have left it until we got back."

"I know, but I sort of lost track of time." Boy had she ever. Only it wasn't the filing that had kept her spellbound.

"Never mind. It's still early so we shouldn't have trouble getting a seat next to the train."

Jody laughed when she remembered her boss's fascination with the sushi train. Cassie seemed more excited about the moving plates than what was on them. "You just want to watch the food go round."

"Oh, c'mon. It is kinda cool." Cassie bumped her shoulder into Jody's. "So wanna talk about Dan?"

"What?" Jody choked.

Cassie wrapped her arm around Jody's waist and gave her a quick squeeze. "You don't have to, but I thought you might want to. I'm not listening as your boss, so chuck that notion right out. I'm your friend. The woman dating your brother. Hell, I'm all but living with him now days."

"I'm not sure what you expect me to say."

"Look, let's lay the cards on the table. From the minute you started working for me, I've seen the sparks between you two. You were both so intent on disliking each other to begin with that neither of you worked out those sparks weren't hatred." Cassie glanced at her as they walked down the sidewalk. "Am I right?"

Jody sighed. "Yeah."

"So something happen last weekend?"

She laughed. "You could say that."

"Good or bad?"

"Oh, good. Very, very good." Jody's body flushed hot with the memory of just how *good* Dan was.

"Judging by your flushed face and breathless voice, I'm going to assume you got laid but good." Cassie grinned. "And can I just say about damn time. High five for you, honey."

Cassie held up her hand and Jody slapped her palm with hers. She couldn't stop the giggle that bubbled up her throat. "Jesus. I feel like a sixteen-year-old talking boys and high fiving."

"Hey, guys regress all the time, I figure we should too." They reached the end of the street and stopped to wait for the light to change. "So, are you seeing Dan now or are you going to do the whole I'm-a-single mum, he's-a-younger-man thing?"

"What makes you think I'd use that argument not to see him?"

"I noticed you didn't deny the not-seeing-him part."

Jody grimaced. "I don't know what to do."

"Why not?"

"I don't need any more complications. The girls and I are doing great. I love my new job and don't want to jeopardize it by having an affair with a workmate—"

"Too late for that." Cassie turned to face her. "Look, I can't say what will happen, but I can say that you would not lose your job if things between you and Dan didn't work out. There are plenty of options to keep the two of you from working together. The only reason you're sharing the office and quite a few of your early jobs was so you could learn the ropes. I can easily move either of you out into another space and make sure you're rostered on different events."

"I'm scared to get involved." There. She'd said it. She was scared. Colin had been her one true relationship and look how she'd fucked that up.

"Not scared to get involved with Dan but involved in general?" Cassie asked as the walk light turned green and they stepped off the curb. "Because I can tell you now, I don't think he'd ever do anything to hurt you or the girls. If he's pursuing you, he's serious. I've never known him to go after any woman. They all usually fall at his feet."

"So I'm a challenge then?" That idea didn't make Jody feel any better. In fact, it made the whole situation worse.

"No. No, I don't think it's that. He's not the type to go after something just because it's a challenge. More the type to only work for those things he really wants. What he's serious about."

Jody mulled that over for a minute. They entered the sushi restaurant and were directed to two seats in the back near where the chefs loaded the fresh food on the train.

"Yes. First pick." Cassie slipped onto her stool and nabbed a plate straight away.

"Good Lord, woman, at least put your ass on the seat before you start eating."

Cassie grinned at her around a mouthful of prawn and rice. "I'm starving. I skipped breakfast. Actually, Luc made me skip breakfast."

Jody put up a hand. "Do not start talking about you and my brother and before breakfast. I don't need to know what you two get up to in the hours between sunset and sunrise."

"Oh, we don't restrict our activities to the cover of darkness."

"Shit." She stuck her fingers in her ears and hummed.

Cassie laughed hysterically, drawing the gazes of a number of surrounding customers and penetrating Jody's makeshift earplugs.

Jody pulled her fingers free and searched her handbag for the little bottle of sanitizer she kept in there. It was a shame she couldn't use it to clean her mind of the thought of her brother and Cassie doing something that made them so late they had to skip breakfast.

The last thing Dan wanted to be doing on a Friday night was stock take. But he'd drawn the short straw this month, so here he was, going from one tub to the next, counting every damn thing in the place. Thank God, he didn't have to count all those beads, just the little boxes of them, although that was bad enough. And if anyone else interrupted him while he was counting, he was throwing the clipboard at their head. He was on the final row. Luckily, West was taking care of the kitchen supplies. He'd definitely go insane if he had to do those as well.

One thing about this job was he had plenty of time to think. Something he'd been doing a lot of since Jody had agreed to see him again. He wasn't sure what had changed her mind, but he knew she wouldn't back out because the girls knew they were going ice-skating. He'd tried to come up with something different and fun to do. When he'd asked Jody if they skated and she'd told him none of them had ever been, he knew he had to take them the first time.

He better get a move on with the rest of the count or he'd still be here when they arrived on his doorstep to do their washing in the morning. Glancing at his watch, he saw it was ten minutes until midnight. He'd hoped to be home by now. The house could do with a bit of a tidy up before the girls arrived. Especially the one who'd cleaned his kitchen so well on Monday night that he'd discovered the section of counter behind the cook top wasn't black. It was silver.

His mother would have his head if she knew he'd let a woman deal with his neglect. Then again, if she knew about Jody and the girls she'd be in his ear about bringing them round. That was something he wasn't ready for. Yet.

"Hey, you're still here." Cassie walked toward him.

"Yep, almost done though. Party over already?"

"Just about. I let Kerry take over. I wanted to get home before midnight because I've got the Winter's birthday tomorrow morning." She indicated the clipboard in his hand. "How much left?"

He nodded to the rack beside her. "Last few boxes."

"Good. Want me to help out so you get out of here faster?" she asked.

"No. You go on. I'm sure Luc is waiting up for you."

"Actually, he's at Jody's."

Dan's head snapped around. "What? Why?"

Cassie chewed her lip and diverted her gaze. "I'm not sure I should say anything."

"Cassie. Tell me."

"Fine. But if Jody wanted you to know, I'm pretty sure she would have told you herself."

"Just spill it." If she didn't tell him in the next few seconds he was out the door.

"Colin turned up at her house earlier tonight drunk. Apparently, he took a bat to Jody's car after she wouldn't let him in the house."

He'd dropped the clipboard and was at the end of the row before Cassie had finished speaking. He pulled his phone out of his pocket and checked for missed calls. Messages. Nothing. She hadn't rung him. Dan wasn't sure how he felt about that. He only knew he had to go to her now and make sure she was all right.

"I'll finish the stock take," Cassie yelled behind him.

Dan didn't bother to acknowledge her. He sprinted across the warehouse and slammed out the door. He'd ridden his bike this morning and was thankful because he could dodge through traffic a hell of a lot faster on the Ducati than in his Jeep. Throwing his leg over the seat, he snagged his helmet off the handlebar and strapped it on. In seconds, he had the motor thrumming between his legs as he sped out of the parking lot.

Traffic was light, and with him sitting ten or so kilometers above the speed limit, he was pulling into Jody's driveway in record time. Luc's car remained at the curb and Jody's SUV sat in the driveway next to where Dan had stopped, every window was smashed and most of the panels had taken a beating too. Dan switched off the bike and kicked the stand down. Jody's front door opened as he pulled his helmet off and Dan's heart stuttered until he realized it was Luc standing there and not Jody.

"Hey." Luc nodded at him. "Cassie rang."

"Is Jody okay? The girls?" Dan's long strides ate up the distance to Luc.

"They're all asleep. The girls are in with Jody. None of them would tell me what went on before I got here, but they all have to go to the police station in the morning to make statements. I was planning on going with them."

"I'll be there." Dan waited for Luc to step aside, but he didn't. "Are you going to make me sit out here all night?"

Luc sighed. "I guess not, but considering she asked me not to call you when Cassie suggested it, I'm not sure if it's good for my health. She's pissed, man. I've never seen her so angry before."

"Good. Maybe she'll finally give Colin what he deserves instead of treating him like a respected friend."

Luc arched an eyebrow. "She told you about him?"

"Enough for me to know he doesn't deserve her loyalty even if he is the girls' father."

"C'mon, let me get you a beer and we'll talk. There are a few things I'd like to do besides let the police take care of the situation."

Dan knew in Luc's line of business he could probably have a man disappear, and while he would love for Jody to be free of her ex-husband, he didn't think getting rid of the man completely was the right move. "As long as you're not going to ask me to help you hide the body, I'm in."

Luc laughed as he led Dan into the kitchen. "Nothing as dramatic. But we are going to make him wish we'd chosen that avenue."

The sinister grin that spread across Luc's face made Dan's blood run cold. If he wasn't serious about this man's sister, now would be the time to back out. Even with that threat hanging over his head, Dan didn't plan on going anywhere. He wasn't sure how this thing with Jody would play out, or whether they were meant to be together, but he was more than ready to find out. And definitely ready to put in the effort necessary to make a relationship between them work. He'd even grown fond of the girls, and they'd only spent one evening together so far.

"Dan?"

Jody's voice had both him and Luc spinning around. "Hey. You okay?" Dan asked.

She stood in the doorway, her hair all messed up, half in, half out of her ponytail. "What are you doing here?"

"Checking up on you and the girls." He walked toward her in

slow, measured steps. She seemed fragile somehow. "Do you need something?"

"No. I heard voices."

"Sorry, we didn't mean to wake you." Dan got within touching distance and couldn't help but put his hands on her. He cupped her shoulders then ran his hands up and down her arms. "Are you cold?"

"Stop." She stepped away. "I don't need coddling."

"Okay." He moved back a step. "But maybe I do."

"What?" Her sleepy gaze met his.

"I need to know you're okay. I saw what he did outside..." Dan shuddered. "I need to know he didn't hurt you, Jody."

Jody's mouth kicked up on one end. "Physically? No, I'm fine and so are the girls. Emotionally, he may as well have taken that bat to my heart and soul because of what he said in front of the girls." She closed her eyes and a single tear slid down her cheek.

He couldn't do it. Couldn't stand back and watch her struggle to hold it together. Stepping close, he wrapped his arms around her and pulled her in. This time she came. It was like a dam bursting. Her whole body shook with the sobs racking her chest. Dan glanced over at Luc to see the other man clenching his fists, a jaw muscle ticking, and wondered if they were having the same murderous thoughts right now.

Dan indicated the living room with his head then scooped Jody into his arms and carried her into the darkness. He sat on the couch and held her in his lap. She cried and cried, her tears soaking the front of his shirt, but he didn't care. If he could, he'd take away every one of those drops, every bit of her pain. Except the only thing he could do was hold her tight and let her fall apart somewhere safe. Luc moved in front of him and placed a box of tissue on the coffee table. Nodding thanks, Dan went back to soothing Jody until her sobs turned to the occasional hiccup and she slipped off to sleep.

Sitting in the dark, Dan held her while she slept and came to a startling realization. He'd fallen for this woman. Hook, line and sinker, he was done. She'd found her way under his skin and he'd never seen it coming. He wanted to laugh. To shout it from the rooftops, but he figured she'd think he was insane for admitting to such deep emotions when they'd barely moved into being friends. Sure, they'd had sex. But if anyone knew sex wasn't love it was him. He'd spent half his life having sex, and not once had he loved any of those women.

Instead, it had taken someone not looking for love, or a relationship, to snag his heart. And didn't that just fuck with his head. He could have professed his love to any other woman and she'd have been glad to hear it. Except, like his mother always said, nothing worth having comes easy, and Jody would have to be the least easy woman he'd ever dealt with. Now he had to figure out how to convince her he was serious. And how to make her fall in love with him in return.

13

___

Jody wasn't sure why she was annoyed. She should be more than happy to have everyone's support. And she was. Kind of. Cassie had taken the girls to Luc's house a little while ago, but she was still stuck at the police station going over and over her statement. The officers had been wonderful with the girls. She'd been worried about letting them talk about what had happened with their father, but there had been a police psychologist waiting when they'd arrived and then Luc had pulled some strings somewhere and had a private counselor come in to help them deal with the trauma.

The counselor had gone with Cassie to spend the rest of the day with Leigh and Amy. Jody couldn't believe any of this was even necessary. Colin had really gone off the deep end this time. Mind you, in all the years she'd known him, last night was the most emotion she'd ever seen from him. Shame he'd chosen to put that level of intensity into a negative sentiment. She took a deep breath and tried to shake off the black cloud hanging over her. She'd be more than happy for this ordeal to be over. Now.

Unfortunately, she now had to file papers with the courts restricting Colin's access to the girls. The idea made her sick, but the two lawyers either side of her—and the police—had insisted it was the best option. Luc had pulled more strings to get her the best representation in Sydney. Mackenzie Harris wasn't even in family law, but here he was on her right, taking charge of all the legal proceedings. On her left was Mackenzie's family-law expert. Jody was pretty sure this guy was smart enough to convince the court Colin wasn't the girls' father even with DNA proof.

"Can we take a break?" Dan asked from his position leaning on the wall.

She'd almost forgotten he was here. Almost. The low hum vibrating over her nerves didn't allow her to eradicate him completely from her mind. Her eyes met his and the sudden sting of tears blinded her.

"Never mind. We're taking one." He strode over and pulled her from the chair. "We'll be back in five." Dan didn't wait for anyone to agree or disagree, he slipped his arm around her shoulders and ushered her from the room.

They walked a short way down the hall then entered the men's restroom where he locked the door after checking they were alone. He yanked a bunch of paper from one of the cubicles and handed it to her.

"Let it go." He pulled her back into his arms and held her. "I've got you."

She leaned on him. Let him take her weight—and not just the physical kind. Her tears were muffled against his chest, but the wretched sound of her sobs echoed off the walls. He held her close, ran his hands up and down her back and let her cry herself out. For the second time in twelve hours, she took advantage of Dan's generosity, of his compassion, and gave in to the need to be weak—to allow someone else to hold her up.

Jody knew she couldn't keep doing this. It wasn't his problem to deal with, and it was less than fair to expect him to put up with her messy life. God, she'd give anything to go back to being just a single mum dealing with a couple of emotional teenagers. Now she was the woman with the psycho ex as well. Not something she'd ever thought to be. Or something Dan had signed on for. With strength she didn't think she had, she pulled out of his arms and moved over to the sink.

She turned on the cold water and ran some clean paper towel under the flow then pressed it against her closed eyes. The cool pads brought a little relief to her stinging eyes, but nothing would help the red puffiness that greeted her when she looked in the cracked mirror. Even the chipped and peeling glass couldn't hide the ravages of hours of crying. She'd tried to conceal some of the damage this morning, except she'd washed that away with her latest jag. Her purse was back in the room so there'd be no emergency repairs.

"Better?"

She met Dan's gaze in their reflection. "I'm sorry."

"For what?" He stepped closer behind her. "You've got nothing to be sorry about."

He cupped his hands on her shoulders and she was so tempted to lean back into his solid strength, but she didn't. She couldn't afford to rely on him, not when it was her battle to fight. "I'm sorry you got dragged into this. I told Luc not to call you."

Dan spun her around to face him and brought his face down to within an inch of hers. "I didn't get dragged into this, and we'll talk about why you think I didn't deserve to know about this later. For now, let's get you ready to finish what you have to do to make sure you ex-asshole doesn't do this again."

"But—"

His hand covered her mouth. "Nope. Not listening to anything except 'thanks, Dan, I really needed a few minutes out of the room to regroup'."

God, he was so right. That nagging sense of annoyance had gone, and she felt ready to face the last of the necessary actions to deal with the fallout of Colin's behavior. "Thank you," she mumbled against his palm.

He smiled. "Much better." Dan removed his hand and replaced it with his lips. But just when she thought he might really kiss her, he pulled away and reached for the wet towel. With gentle pats, he wiped her face.

Her bottom lip trembled and Jody knew she was on the verge of crying again. Only this time it wasn't sad tears that clogged her throat. Instead, it was his simple act of caring that had her on the brink of another meltdown. This man who'd been in her life less than a year had given her more of himself than her husband had in over a decade. How did she keep her heart from getting involved when Dan was doing everything her heart wanted?

He'd not once pushed her for more than she was willing to give. Sure, he'd made it perfectly clear what his intentions were, but he'd not forced her to become involved with him at any stage. Not really. He may have ambushed her with the occasional kiss, but she'd willingly surrendered when he had. And she wouldn't have done that if her heart wasn't already involved on some level.

"Ready?"

Was she? Jody wasn't sure she was ready for anything right now. Not when she'd just come to a shocking conclusion. She was falling for Dan. She might not be completely in love with the man, but it wasn't far away, probably as close as one kind gesture or simple acceptance of her suddenly crazy life. He studied her with a probing gaze and she had to turn away to gather some composure—to bolster her walls.

"Jody?"

She turned back to him and nodded. "I'm ready."

"Are you sure? 'Cause we can take as long as you need. They aren't going anywhere."

"No, they're not, but they're busy men who need to get back to their lives, and I really need to move on with mine. Can't do that until I've sorted out this mess, and I need Luc's friends to do that."

"I know you'd do it without them if you could or had to. Don't for one minute think it says you're weak for accepting their help." Dan rubbed his hands up and down her arms.

One more thing in the Dan-is-a-great-guy column. He got her. Totally understood that she needed to prove she was capable of taking care of herself and her girls. But he was right. Accepting help didn't make her helpless, it made her smart.

Nodding, she said, "I know. I'm just not used to anyone except Lucas and my parents helping out or needing help with something this big. Colin has never gone off the rails like this before. Not even when I filed the divorce papers."

"So what set him off now?"

Jody sighed. She knew. Colin had made sure it was perfectly clear what had pissed him off enough to come after her and the girls this late in the game. As usual though, it was too little too late. "He was served the divorce papers yesterday. We've been officially divorced in the eyes of the law for a few months, but he's been MIA so he hadn't gotten the final paperwork before now. And for some reason that is beyond my comprehension, he didn't take it too well."

Dan's eyebrows shot up his forehead. "But he knew the papers were filed and would be processed in due course."

"Again, beyond my comprehension." Jody took a deep breath and let it go slowly. "Okay, let's get this over with. I want to get home to Leigh and Amy."

"After you." He swept his hand out to indicate she lead the way.

She smiled but didn't quite feel it. The sadness that settled over her wouldn't shift. It was extremely depressing to think her marriage had come to this. She'd had such high hopes and dreams for so many years. And for a while, she thought she'd found them only to have the rug pulled out from underneath her when she'd discovered Colin's cheating. Even then she'd stuck it out, listened to his apologies and promises. Until she'd been confronted by the blonde. There was no way to ignore the fiasco that was her marriage then.

Of course, she hadn't walked or even insisted Colin leave even after that confrontation. No. He'd walked. And for that she would always hate a part of herself. But that was in the past and she wasn't going to let him ruin any more of her self-esteem or her life—or the girls'. With that in mind, Jody made her way back to the interview room and the papers that would sever all ties she had with her ex and keep him away from Leigh and Amy until they reached the age of eighteen.

. . .

Dan stood behind Jody as she signed her name to legal papers that would remove her asshole of an ex from her life. He should be thrilled with this development, and part of him was, but there was also the complete sadness radiating off her that ate at his gut. She'd been forced into this by her ex's actions, and no matter how right it was, she didn't like doing it.

He'd understood the basics of what Mackenzie was advising even with all the legal jargon the man had used. And Luc trusted the guy, so Dan was inclined to do whatever he suggested. Except it wasn't up to him to make the decision. Jody hadn't agreed immediately. She'd been full of questions, and only after thirty minutes of asking did she agree to lodge the documents to prevent her ex from seeing her or the girls. She made sure there was a provision for the girls to change their mind before they were adults but their father had no say in it and couldn't contact them until they reached eighteen.

Dan thought it was a good compromise considering both lawyers wanted her to block all contact between now and when Leigh and Amy were older. She signed the last paper and the officer who'd been in charge of the domestic-violence case added his reports and the two suited lawyers left them to file the paperwork with the court.

"Please, take my card, and if you need anything further from me, don't hesitate to get in contact." The officer handed over a business card before he left the room.

"I guess that's it then." Jody glanced around. "I thought I'd feel more relieved than I do."

"Give yourself some time. It's been a crazy twenty-four hours." Dan helped her from her seat. "Let's get you home to the girls."

"Thanks." She grabbed her purse from the table. "Where did Luc go?"

Dan didn't want to lie to her, but he also didn't want to reveal where her brother had gone. "He said he had something to do."

She eyed him wearily. "He better not be doing anything that will jeopardize the papers I just signed."

He smiled. She knew her brother well. "Haven't a clue." With a hand to her lower back, he ushered her out of the police station and down the street to where they'd parked hours ago.

Luc was there, leaning against the hood of his black Explorer, arms crossed, dark shades covering his eyes, in a tough-guy stance that had people veering right to the edge of the sidewalk near the building to avoid him. As they got closer, Jody tensed until she all by vibrated beside Dan.

"Do not tell me you did something I'm not going to like," she said when they were a few feet away.

Luc straightened to his full height. "Okay, I won't tell you."

"Lucas!"

"Relax. All I did was make sure he saw me when that weasel of a lawyer got him released on bail." Luc walked to the passenger side and opened the door. "Hop in, the girls have decided we're having barbeque for dinner at my house. Cassie has taken them to the shops to pick up some food, so you have time to go home for a change of clothes."

"Why do I need a change of clothes?" Jody asked as Dan helped her up into Luc's SUV.

"Oh, did I not mention they want to have a sleepover at Uncle Luc's house?" Luc grinned, but Dan didn't miss the worry lines creasing his forehead.

"I don't think that's a good idea. I'd rather just pick up the girls and go home." Dan could hear the strain—the exhaustion—in Jody's voice.

"At least have dinner at Luc's. Besides, you won't have to worry about cooking and Leigh and Amy will be occupied by the three of us and not constantly thinking back to last night." Dan wasn't sure his arguments were enough to sway her. "It'll be good for all of you to have a number of distractions."

Dan saw the moment she gave in. And while he was happy she agreed to Luc's suggestion, he didn't like watching the fight drain out of her. He hoped it was just the results of the long stressful day. He'd never seen her look so vulnerable before. She buckled up and he closed the door and turned to Luc.

"I'm worried," Dan murmured.

"You and me both, which is why I'm not letting her stay at the house alone tonight," Luc said.

"They can stay at my place." The offer was out before Dan thought better of it.

"Yeah, well, I don't like that idea any more than I like the one of her going home." Luc seemed to grow two inches as he leaned over Dan.

Stifling a smile, Dan stood his ground. "Look, I get the whole big-brother-protection thing. I'm guilty of the actions myself, but I can guarantee you I'm not going to hurt Jody or the girls."

"Big talk for a guy she didn't want me to call last night."

"Did she call you?" Dan already knew the answer to his question but felt the need to point it out.

"Shit. No." Luc rubbed his jaw. "How'd you know that?"

"I overheard a couple of the officers talking earlier. Do you think she would have called you?"

Luc looked away for a few seconds before meeting Dan's gaze again. "No. Leigh freaked out when her father started yelling and rang me. I was on the phone when he started killing her car. The hardest thing I've ever done was tell that kid to hang up and call the police. For those few minutes, I was scared out of my mind I'd get there and find them all dead."

Fuck. Dan hadn't known the details, and hearing it from Luc sent a chill down his spine. "We need to thank Leigh for keeping it together enough to ring you and then do what you told her to."

"Agreed." Luc took a step away and stopped. "Oh, and for the record, I don't ever want to feel that way again."

Dan nodded. He didn't want Luc to feel that way again either. "Do you think he'll leave them alone when the court order is granted?"

Luc shrugged. "Hard to say. Before last night I'd have said he was a harmless loser. Now he's a dangerous loser."

Tapping on glass grabbed their attention. Jody sat in the car scowling at them. "We better get going," Dan said.

"Are you ready for the third degree when we get in?" Luc asked.

Dan laughed. "Yeah."

Luc grinned. "She's going to be relentless."

"I hope so. I'm a little worried this whole thing has taken the wind out of her sails."

"Nah, it'll take more than this to keep Jody down." Luc clapped Dan on the back as he walked past and headed for the driver's side. Taking a deep breath, Dan steeled himself for the coming questions and opened the rear passenger door.

"What were you two plotting?" Jody twisted around to peer between her seat and the door.

"Nothing. We were just talking about today." He didn't meet her gaze, which he knew would have given the half-lie away.

"Ha. Bullshit."

"Oh, she's swearing. Always a good sign," Luc said as he climbed in behind the wheel.

"You." Jody spun around and leveled a finger at her brother. "Don't you do your zipped-lip security-man impersonation on me."

Luc laughed. "Jody, Jody, Jody. Would I do that to you?"

"*Argh.* Yes, you would. Now I want to know what is going on. Don't feed me a line, Lucas Wilhelm. I might not be able to stop you from going all macho-protective big brother on me, but you can at least do me the courtesy of treating me like the adult I am and tell me what the hell you're doing."

Luc sighed as he started the car and then moved them out into the flow of traffic. "I'm not planning anything other than making sure he sticks by the court order when the judge puts his stamp on it."

"How?"

"I'll have someone keep an eye on him for a while."

"You're not going to have me or the girls followed are you? I won't stand for that, Luc."

Dan sat quietly listening to the two of them interact. They were close, and he wondered if they'd always been that way or just since Jody had separated from her ex.

"I promise not to have either you or the girls under watch. Just the loser ex who suddenly went from harmless to dangerous with the swing of a bat. What the fuck set him off anyway?" Luc asked.

"He was raving about getting the divorce papers before he started remodeling my car."

"But that's been in the works for well over a year and final for months."

"I know." Jody sighed and slumped down in her seat. "I don't get why he had a sudden objection to it."

"Did you see him before he showed up with the bat?" Dan asked. He wasn't convinced the guy had gone off the deep end over the finalization of their divorce.

"No." She bolted upright. "Wait. Leigh said he'd come around before I got home but she hadn't answered the door."

Dan caught Luc's eye in the rear view mirror. "Do you think she said something to set him off?"

"What could she possibly say? And why would she even talk to him? Leigh said she didn't answer the door and I believe her. She has no reason to lie about it."

"Maybe not, then again, maybe she doesn't want to tell you what happened," Luc offered.

"I still don't see why she wouldn't, but I'll ask her when we get to your place." Jody settled back in her seat and Dan put his hands over the top of her seat and gave her neck and shoulders a rub.

"Don't worry about it. I'm sure you're right and Leigh didn't answer the door."

14

———

"You told him what?" Jody couldn't catch her breath. "Why would you do that, Leigh?"

"Well." Leigh's gaze darted over to Dan before coming back to her. "I thought—"

"You thought wrong, young lady, and that may have been the trigger that set your father off." Jody paced between the couch and the television.

"Jody—"

She quieted her brother with a look and continued to pace. Leigh's confession explained a lot. Colin's behavior had been so out of character. Even when they were together he'd never gotten violent when drunk. Then again, his daughter hadn't told him he was being replaced in their lives by another man before. Dan stepped in front of her and grabbed her arms.

"Stop." He gave her a slight shake. "Leigh didn't do it out of spite."

Jody was appalled that he would even suggest that. "Of course not."

"Then take a breath and calm down before you scare Leigh to death," Dan whispered as he turned her around to face her daughter.

Oh God. Jody rushed over to where Leigh sat curled up on the couch beside Luc. The poor thing was crying her eyes out and all because Jody hadn't thought Leigh might misinterpret her reaction to Leigh's admission.

Jody pulled Leigh into her arms and rocked her like she had when she was a baby. "Oh, sweetie, I'm not mad at you. I'm mad at your father for even thinking he has the right to care about who's in our lives."

"I hate him!" Leigh sobbed against Jody's shoulder.

"Leigh, don't say that. Hate is such a strong word. Things are okay to hate, but not people."

"But he's horrible. And he said he didn't want us to be happy."

Jody's gaze darted up to meet Luc's as she ran a hand over her daughter's head. "Baby, what he wants doesn't matter."

"But, but, he trashed our car so we couldn't spend the day with Dan. Because I told him that's what we were supposed to do today." Leigh sobbed so hard she choked and all Jody could do was hold her and let her cry. She wasn't sure what else to do or say to soothe her daughter's fears.

Cassie came over and held out a box of tissues. Jody tugged a couple from the box and waited for Leigh to calm down a little. Luc indicated he was getting up and she glanced over to see Amy standing in the doorway, thumbnail caught between her front teeth. She hadn't chewed her nails in years, and Jody prayed this incident hadn't set her back on that bad habit.

She was grateful when Luc and Cassie ushered Amy out with the incentive of helping make the hamburger patties for dinner. Jody smiled. Amy loved to get her hands into food. And unlike Jody, her youngest daughter showed a real aptitude for cooking. Dan slid into the space vacated by Luc but remained quiet. She'd love to know what was going on inside his head right now. The poor man had been thrown into the middle of her family's drama without consent, and she was surprised he wasn't running for the hills by now.

When Leigh quieted and her sobs had turned to sniffles, Jody eased her away and handed her some tissues. "Feel better?"

Leigh shook her head. "Why does he hate us?"

The million-dollar question. No mother wants to have to answer that. Not when the *he* in question is the child's father. "I don't think he hates you, Leigh."

"But he doesn't love us either."

Jody closed her eyes and prayed for strength. She wouldn't lie, but at fifteen Jody didn't think Leigh was old enough to process the truth either. "He loves you the best he can." Jody wasn't about to include herself in that notion.

"Well, it's a seriously shitty way." Leigh pouted and Jody breathed a little easier. If she was resorting to childish pouting then she wasn't as upset by the lack of fatherly love Colin possessed as Jody feared.

"Life is shitty sometimes. But we can't let those bad things destroy the good," Jody said.

"I know." Leigh sniffed into her handful of tissues. "But it still fucking sucks."

"Leigh, language." It didn't matter how crappy the situation, Jody wouldn't let her rule about swearing slide.

"Aw, Mum, c'mon. It's not like Amy's in the room," she whined.

Dan chuckled and Jody gave him the evil eye, prompting him to cover up with a fake cough.

Leigh's head swiveled back and forth, her gaze bouncing between the adults like spectators at a tennis match. Before her daughter could say anything, Jody said, "Why don't you go wash your face and I'll see if Uncle Luc has any of that ice cream you love."

"Ice cream before dinner?" Leigh's voice rose with hope.

"Yep. I think today calls for dessert first, don't you?"

"Yes." Leigh bounded off the couch and ran from the room.

"So is that a treat, a reward, bribery or distraction?" Dan asked.

"I have no idea, but I figure we could all do with something frivolous and pleasurable right now." Her gaze caught his just as she said the word pleasurable and all sorts of adult pleasures flitted through her mind. She'd love to lose herself in his arms right now. Sink into the oblivion of pure ecstasy Dan delivered. Except that wasn't happening any time soon. After last night and today, Jody wasn't ready to add another complication to her life.

And Dan O'Conner was one huge complication.

———

Dan had no idea what was going on. Jody had gone completely cold on him. It was like a switch had been flicked. Dinner had been interesting. She'd avoided looking at him, and if she'd said more than two words directly to him he'd hand over his beloved Ducati. Luc had given him a questioning look across the table that Dan couldn't even begin to answer. Luckily, the girls and Cassie had carried the conversation enough to cover up any lag in talk.

Jody was currently in Luc's living room with the girls. They were watching a movie from Luc's collection. A chick flick. Which meant he and Luc were more than happy to be stuck in the kitchen cleaning up after dinner.

"Wanna tell me what happened?" Luc asked as he took a stack of dirty dishes from Dan.

He shrugged. "If I had a clue I would."

Luc straightened. "You two didn't have a fight or something?"

"Hell, no. I can't even pin-point when exactly she started giving me the cold shoulder."

"What happened with Leigh after we took Amy out of there?"

"Nothing. There were no more big revelations. Although it does appear as though Leigh mentioning me set off the ex."

"I wouldn't have thought he'd care. There has to be something else driving the sudden shift in behavior." Luc began loading the dishwasher. "I've got someone looking into his recent activity."

"Does Jody know?" Dan could only imagine her reaction if she didn't.

"Not specifics, but she knows I'm not staying out of it this time. I did that when she caught him cheating on her and look where that got her, years of crappy treatment."

"He cheated on her? Is he an idiot?" Dan didn't expect an answer really. As far as he was concerned, the guy had to be stupid to let Jody go.

Luc chuckled. "Among other things."

"Look." Dan tried to collect his thoughts. "I'm not sure where this thing between me and Jody is going, but I can tell you where I want it to end up. I like her. A lot. I like spending time with the girls already, and we've barely managed a few hours. She intrigues me, not to mention gets my engine revved with just a look."

"Whoa." Luc put up a hand. "I don't need to know any of that. And I'm not just talking about you two getting it on. All I need to know is that you're serious, and I think you've proven that in the last twenty-four hours."

Dan nodded.

"But you've just been given a front row seat to her less-than-pleasant past, and I'm not all that sure that all the emotions and drama associated with it aren't still weighing on her mind. She swore she'd never get involved with a guy again when Colin walked, and I believe she meant it, which is why you and her raises more than my eyebrows."

Dan pretty much figured the specter of her past stood between them. He just had to work out how big of an obstacle it was. "Neither of us expected to connect the way we do."

"Maybe that's a good thing, because if she's got time to think about something she'll worry it to death before she ever gets started."

"So what are you saying?" Dan asked. If anyone could give him some insight it would be Jody's brother.

"It'll be an uphill battle."

"But it's winnable, right? You're not suggesting I give up?"

"What? No. I'm making sure you understand how difficult and stubborn she can be. Shit, she stayed married to that idiot out of stubbornness. She'd probably still be married to him if he hadn't been the one to walk."

"He walked? She didn't tell him to go?"

"Put it this way, I think he got to the punch line first. She was ready to leave, had made the decision, but the girls made it harder to just up and go." Luc ran his hand over his head. "Look. I shouldn't be telling you any of this. It should come from her. I just think you need to really be sure you want to continue seeing her. Those girls, all of them, have been through enough, and if you're not in it for the long haul then back out now."

"I'm in it as deep as a man can get." It wasn't a confession of love. He'd save that for Jody, but he figured Luc would understand what he was saying.

"Good. Good then."

Neither of them had a chance to say anything further because the bundle of energy that was Amy came barreling into the kitchen. "Uncle Luc, Uncle Luc. Cassie said you could make us popcorn. Can you?"

At thirteen she hadn't quite given up some of her childishness, but Dan could see the woman starting to unfold inside her. "Aren't you still full from those two hamburgers you ate at dinner?" he asked.

"No. In fact my tummy is so empty it's aching."

Luc laughed. "Yeah, right, your eyes have always been bigger than your belly. Give me five minutes and I'll bring a bowl of salt and vinegar popcorn in."

"Yes!" She fist-pumped the air and disappeared back the way she'd come.

Luc shook his head. "Her energy levels always amaze me. I wish I could bottle it. I'd make a fortune."

"She'll lose some of that when she gets older. My sister was the same. Then she hit puberty and turned into a slug that we had to drag out of bed every morning." Dan leaned against the kitchen counter. "Do you have a popcorn machine or do you use the trusty old saucepan?"

Rubbing his hands together, Luc opened the pantry. "Neither. I'm a microwave man all the way." He pulled out a box of microwave popcorn and tossed it at Dan. "You pop, I'll get the toping ready."

Jody could not believe she'd agreed to this. After she'd made the decision—again—to distance herself from Dan, she'd done the complete opposite. Again. Okay, so the girls—or more pointedly, Amy—were the reason she'd said yes, but she still had to take responsibility for her own actions. If it were anyone but her, she'd conclude the woman chopping and changing her mind was bipolar. Instead, she had to admit she was totally smitten and not willing to do what her brain kept telling her she should.

"C'mon, Mum." Amy grabbed her hand and tugged her toward the ice. "Quick."

"What's the rush?" Jody stumbled as she tried to walk on the thin blade of metal on the bottom of the very uncomfortable boots she'd spent the last ten minutes lacing up.

"I want to beat Leigh." Amy let go and raced for the opening in the barrier that surrounded the ice rink.

"Be careful," Jody called out. She shouldn't have wasted her breath. Amy was off and running. Literally. Her long, colt-like legs took her across the icy surface so fast Jody's head spun. "Jesus."

Dan chuckled behind her. "I doubt *he* can even help you with that one."

She sighed and glanced over her shoulder at him. "You're right. Nothing short of Valium can help with that one once she gets going."

"I don't think you need to worry." He indicated the ice rink with his chin. "She's already got the hang of it."

Jody turned back to see Amy skating past as though she'd been doing it all her life. "Oh my God, look at her."

"She's a natural." Dan moved beside her and took her elbow. "C'mon, your turn."

She allowed him to guide her onto the ice. Her knees shook, which didn't help, but she did manage to stay upright. At least she did the first time around. The second saw her getting a little too confident and paying the price. One slightly bruised backside. And while the fall had hurt, it wasn't enough to have her leaving the ice. Both the girls were whizzing past with the speed and skill only the young possessed.

And Dan. Well, he'd obviously done this more than once. He spun circles around her, tugged her along when she was steady and picked her up off the ground when she wasn't. In spite of all her doubts and fears where this man was concerned, she couldn't deny she always had a good time with him. The girls did too. They laughed and joked and played like they'd been doing it together forever, and Jody couldn't remember the last truly carefree day they'd had.

She made her way off the ice and sat on a bench to watch the three of them play tag around the rink. She was pretty sure Dan could catch either of the girls without any trouble, but he made it a game by stumbling and slipping whenever he got close to one of them. After Friday night and Saturday, she was eternally grateful for the happy smiles on the girls' faces—the rippling joy of their laughter as they chased each other around. Tears stung the backs of her eyes and throat. They owed Dan for today.

Jody quickly wiped at her eyes as the three of them headed her way. The girls giggled as they both tried to barge through the exit together. Dan scooped his arm around Amy's waist and pulled her off her feet to break the standoff. He swung her around and plunked her back on her blades as Leigh bounced in front of her.

"Dan said we could get an ice cream. I want a strawberry one."

"I want chocolate and vanilla," Amy yelled.

"Okay, keep it down. I'm right here, Amy." Jody laughed as both of them shouted yes and raced off in the direction of the kiosk.

"You want one?" Dan asked.

She turned back to face him. "Are you kidding? It's freezing in here already. I'm not making it worse by eating ice cream."

"Yeah, I'm not sure I'm up for a cone, but what about a hot chocolate? We can sit over by the kiosk where it's a little warmer."

Jody glanced over to where Leigh and Amy waited impatiently for someone to come and order their ice creams. "Okay. A hot chocolate sounds good."

"If you're not up for more skating we can take your boots back now. I'm happy to supervise the girls for the rest of our allotted time." He offered her his hand.

She slipped her cold fingers inside his warmer ones and let him pull her to her feet. "I think I'll take you up on that. These things are killing me. I think I've got blisters on my heels."

"I'll get the first aid kit from the counter. They should have some cream and Band-Aids."

They made their way over to the girls and it wasn't until they reached the counter that Jody realized they still held hands. Dan didn't make a big deal out of it, he just casually slipped his hand from hers to retrieve his wallet out of his pocket.

"Why don't you go grab that table?" He pointed to the table farthest from the rink. "The girls and I will carry everything over."

"Okay." She limped away, her feet suddenly hurting beyond a mild ache.

"And get those boots off so I can take a look at your feet," Dan called out behind her.

Jody waved her hand and kept going. She was afraid she'd never make it if she stopped to answer. Sliding into a cushioned seat, she immediately began unlacing the hundreds of hooks. Hundreds was an exaggeration, but it certainly felt that many by the time she had both boots unhooked and her wet-socked feet out.

"Mum, you're bleeding!" Leigh cried as she rushed over.

"What?" Looking down, Jody saw a patch of blood on the back of one heel. Okay, blisters were a tame definition. Gingerly, she peeled her sock down and off. Sure enough, she'd rubbed her heel raw.

"Damn, Jody, you should have said the boots were too small." Dan put two steaming mugs on the table and dropped to his knees in front of her. "Amy, hand me that kit you've got."

Amy handed over the small plastic container she carried while licking the side of her ice cream cone. "Does it hurt?" she asked.

"Just a little," Jody said.

"It looks like it hurts a lot. Do we have to go home now?" Amy asked.

"No, sweetie, you can finish your ice cream and skate some more.

I'll just put some cream and a Band-Aid on and it'll be fine." Trying to reassure both her daughters, she smiled. "Who's going to give me a taste of their ice cream?"

As distractions went, it worked. While Dan doctored both her feet, she shared Leigh and Amy's cones. She ended up eating most of Amy's as she'd ordered a double scoop and couldn't finish. Sitting back, she sipped at her no-longer-hot hot chocolate. It managed to remove some of the chill a belly full of ice cream delivered.

"Will you be all right while we go skate some more?" Dan asked.

"Yes. Please. Go have fun." She shooed them off with her hand. "I'll stay right here where it's warmer."

"You want another drink?"

"Actually, yes, a refill would be good."

"Coming right up. Girls, why don't you go ahead and I'll be there as soon as I've gotten your mother another hot chocolate."

Without a word, Leigh and Amy raced back to the rink. Concern for their mother's bleeding foot was forgotten in the face of more fun on the ice. Jody waited for Dan to order another drink before saying what needed to be said.

"Thank you."

"You're welcome. Just wave if you want another one, but I'll come check on you in a few minutes anyway."

"That's not what I'm thanking you for."

"It's not?"

"Well, yes, thank you for the drink, but I want to thank you for today. You've given us all something we desperately needed, and I was a little ungrateful when you used the girls to convince me to accept your invitation. I'm sorry."

"Jody, never be sorry for a genuine feeling no matter how misplaced it is. And I'll accept your thank you if you agree to have dinner with me."

15

D inner hadn't been in the plan, but he couldn't resist taking any opportunity to spend more time with Jody. She'd wanted the girls home at a reasonable hour as they had school tomorrow, so they'd picked up Chinese on the way to her place after their ice skating adventure. Things were a little tense between them again and Dan wasn't sure how to get around this latest setback. Hell, he didn't even know what had made her pull back this time.

"Sorry, the girls won't be a minute. We can start dishing up the food if you like." Jody entered her kitchen. She'd changed into a pair of comfy looking sweat pants and a hoodie. Both looked a size too big but neither did anything to curb his libido. She looked hot.

"I'm happy to wait."

"Oh, but you must want to get home soon." She started opening containers and adding serving spoons. "Dish up what you want."

Dan wanted something other than food. He wanted an explanation, but as he went to open his mouth the girls came rushing in.

"I'm starving," Amy said as she sank into a chair.

"Me too. Did you get that spicy chicken that I like, Mum?"

Jody pushed the container of Szechuan chicken across the table. "Yes. And there's salt 'n' pepper calamari if you want some."

"Oh, yes, please." Leigh was already dishing up a mound of the chicken.

Dan passed the container of calamari over and picked up the fried rice. He dished up a couple of spoonfuls and waited until everyone else had taken what they wanted before filling his plate. Conversation was non-existent for a few minutes while they ate, but then Dan decided the quiet should end.

"When does the repairman come to look at your washer?" he asked.

"Oh, I forgot all about that. Tomorrow afternoon. Why?"

"I just wondered if you needed me to take any dirty clothes home with me to wash and dry. I can bring them to work in the morning."

"No, no, I can't ask you to do that. We've got enough to get us through until the machine is fixed."

"There's no point piling it all up until then. And what if it's not a simple fix? Give me a small-essentials load and I'll get them back to you first thing." Her objections to his help were really starting to grate on his nerves, and Dan was determined to get her to agree. "It's no trouble. I have to do laundry when I get home anyway."

She chewed her lip and he knew she was trying to come up with another protest.

"Honestly, it's just a few clothes, Jody, one load. It's not like I'm asking to do it for the rest of your life." Although he would. In a heartbeat.

"Fine. I'll get a basket together after dinner."

Leigh kept her gaze glued to her mother as though she were waiting for the other shoe to drop. She might only be fifteen, but she was extremely aware of her mother's moods and Dan had to agree with the wary look. He was waiting too.

They finished dinner in silence, a squirm-in-your-seat quiet that left the hairs on Dan's neck standing on end and his teeth on edge. The girls got up and cleared the table, which left him and Jody alone again. She fiddled with the cord on her jacket and looked everywhere except at him. Something snapped inside him. He'd had enough of this back and forth between them, and he planned to have it out with her before he left tonight.

"Well, I better get the girls organized for school tomorrow." She pushed back her chair. "I'll get a basket of stuff together for you too."

Before Dan could say or do anything, Jody bolted from the room like her pants were on fire. With a sigh, he leaned back in his chair and pulled out his phone. He shot a quick text to Cassie to let her and Luc know Jody and the girls were home and that he'd be leaving soon. Jody might not be happy about it, but Luc had arranged for someone to watch the house last night and tonight. It was the only reason Dan hadn't slept in his car outside overnight and why he was okay with her shoving him out the door in the next few minutes.

Which was exactly what she did about five minutes later. He found himself on her doorstep with a basket of clothes in his arms and not so much as a goodnight peck on the cheek. It was not the way he wanted to end their fun day together but he didn't seem to have a choice. Once again, she was in the driver's seat and was driving off without him. He was getting really tired of chasing after her. Except he didn't have any other option. If he wanted to get anywhere, he had to play the game her way.

Or at least he had to keep her within his sights, and to do that he had to follow where she lead even if that was round and round the mulberry bush. Carrying his load, he headed for the Jeep. Stashing the basket on the backseat, he took one last look at Jody's house before climbing in the driver's seat. He thought he saw movement in one of the windows but dismissed it when he didn't see anything else. Dan cranked the engine with a rev before shifting into reverse and backing out of the driveway.

His hands were tied for now. He'd give her some space and then he'd be sure she knew he wasn't going anywhere. Unlike her ex, Dan had no intention of letting the best woman he'd ever met get away. Come tomorrow morning, he'd have his next step ready to go. And as much as he hated using the girls, he figured they were the way to get to her. Luckily for him, he thought they were great fun and wanted to hang out with them as much as he did their mother.

As he made the ten-minute journey to his house, he tried to come up with another outing that would grab their interest. Jody had mentioned they went bowling, so perhaps he should suggest disco bowling next weekend. He'd have to check the roster, but he was pretty sure both he and Jody had Saturday night off.

He pulled into his driveway with a smile on his face. Cassie had already volunteered to pick Jody up for work and drop her off until her car was repaired, but it made more sense for Dan to do it seeing how they lived so close. He'd work it out with Cassie tomorrow. One way or another, he was going to get more time with Jody.

Jody couldn't get away from him. And other than her irrational need to run, she really had no reason to avoid him. He was everywhere she went, and if he wasn't then her stupid traitorous mind conjured him up in Technicolor splendor to remind her of what she was trying to walk away from. She tossed her handbag on her bed on the way to her wardrobe. He'd used the girls to get her to agree to go out again, and while she was glad Leigh and Amy were being kept busy and therefore distracted from the mess that was last weekend, she didn't like Dan's manipulative ways.

She'd heard from Mackenzie Harris that Colin was fighting the restraining order and the no-contact request. She should have known he wouldn't go for it. Not because he wanted to have contact with his own children, but because she didn't want him to have it. Colin's lawyer was arguing that the girls were old enough to have their say and wanted them in court to do so when the paperwork went before the judge next week. Jody felt sick to the stomach just thinking about it. Then again, she'd been queasy the last two days, so it might just be a bug she'd picked up and not the anxiety of the coming court visit.

She glanced at her bedside clock. Dan would be here in an hour and her mum had said she'd drop the girls off in about fifteen minutes, so if she was going to shower she needed to do it now. Today's party had been an easy one, but an excited father-to-be had spilt champagne all down Jody's back and she really did need to shower off the smell of alcohol as well as the stickiness. Pulling jeans and a sweater out of the cupboard, she then grabbed undies and a bra from her top drawer and headed for the bathroom.

A wave of dizziness struck her as she bent over to turn on the shower. Jody grabbed the edge of the bath and held on until the flashes of light before her eyes cleared and she didn't feel like she was going to fall over anymore. Her breathing was a little shallow and her pulse raced, so she sat on the closed toilet seat to give herself a minute. She needed to eat something, her sugar levels were obviously down seeing how she hadn't consumed any food since the toast she'd rushed down before heading out to work.

The front door slammed a second before Amy yelled at the top of her lungs. "We're home!"

Pushing up, Jody stuck her head out the bathroom door. "I'm just about to jump in the shower."

"Hey, honey, I'll hang around until you're done if you like," her mother said.

"Hi, Mum, were they good?"

"Always." Her mother waved her arm. "Now go shower and I'll get these two sorted."

Jody did as her mother suggested but she made it quick. She didn't want Dan to arrive before her mother had gone home. That would just invite questions she wasn't ready to answer. Dressed and feeling a lot better, she headed to the kitchen where her mum had a cup of tea and a slice of chocolate cake waiting for her.

"Oh my God, I love you." Jody lunged for the cake. Her mother made the best chocolate cake in the world. "Mmm..." she moaned around her first mouthful.

"Did I not teach you manners, Jody Maree?" Her mother clucked her tongue.

Jody smiled and swallowed. "Sorry. But you have no idea how much I needed that."

"Good thing I brought the whole cake over then." Frances

Wilhelm smiled as she brought her mug to her lips. "So I hear you girls are all going on a date with some man named Dan."

Jody sprayed tea across the counter as she choked. She coughed a couple of times before catching her breath. "What?" she asked from behind her hand.

"Leigh and Amy have been telling me all about him. He sounds lovely."

"Lovely?" Dan? Lovely wasn't the word that came to mind when Jody thought of him. More like yummy. "He's a guy I work with."

"And you're seeing him?"

The mother inquisition had begun. "No, not really. We've just hung out a few times." She shrugged. No point giving her mother the wrong idea. It was bad enough that her brother knew about her seesawing relationship with Dan, the last thing she needed was for her mother to get involved.

"Dan's here!" Amy screamed from the direction of the front door.

Too late.

Jody dropped her head and prayed for strength.

"Do you want some chocolate cake? My gran makes the best cake." Amy chatted behind her and Jody knew she had to do the introductions before her mother slapped her upside the head.

She turned on her stool. "Hey, Dan, this is my mum, Fran. Mum, this is Dan."

A genuine smile covered Dan's mouth and Jody wondered why he was so happy to meet her mother. "Hello, Fran. It's nice to meet you. I hear you make the best chocolate cake." He held out his hand.

Her mother sat taller and smiled while taking his hand in hers. "I do. And it's lovely to meet you. The girls talked about you non-stop today. Sit down and I'll cut you a slice of cake. Do you want coffee with that?"

One thing that could be said for Jody's mother was that she was the ultimate hostess. Even when not in her own home. Jody popped up off her stool. "I can get it."

Fran waved her away. "Nonsense. You've been working all day. Let me get it."

Jody sank back onto her seat and let her mother go. She knew from experience she'd not be swayed, and really, she was too tired to bother.

"You all right, Jody? You look a little pale." Dan ran the back of his fingers down her cheek.

She jerked away, frightened her mother would see the gesture for more than it was. "I'm fine. A little tired, that's all."

"We don't have to take the girls bowling if you're not feeling up to it," he said.

"What? No! Can't we go without Mum?" Amy wailed.

"Stop that right now Amy Catherine. If your mother isn't up to going out then you won't be going." Jody's mother rushed around the counter and put her hand to Jody's forehead. "Dan's right, you do look at bit pale. Are you sure you're okay?"

Jody pushed her mother's hand away. "Yes, I'm fine. It's been a long week, and to be honest, I'd rather be out than at home where I'll just brood over what's going to happen in court next week."

"Ah, yes, that's probably it. I dare say you aren't sleeping properly, are you?"

"No, Mum, not really." She shrugged and quickly changed the subject to get everyone focused on something else. "Amy, are you and Leigh ready to go?"

"Yes. Leigh's in the other room talking to that boy on the phone again." Amy's dramatic rolling of her eyes made everyone laugh.

"Well, go tell her to get off because as soon as we finish our cake we're out of here." Jody took a sip of her tea and hoped the conversation about her health was over. "If you don't mind, Dan, can we cut the evening short and perhaps get a pizza to bring back here instead of eating out?"

"Sure. But we don't have to go at all if you're not up to it." He took a big bite of her mother's cake. "Oh my God, this is amazing." He covered his mouth with his hand so he could speak with his mouthful.

Jody's mum frowned at him. "I see you have as little manners as Jody does."

Dan turned to her with one eyebrow raised.

"She scolded me earlier for talking with my mouth full too."

He grinned while he chewed, but he wisely waited until he'd swallowed before speaking again. "Ah, yes, well, it's a good thing my mother isn't here or she'd be giving me a slap on the head and taking away my cake." As if it just occurred to him Jody's mother could do the same, he picked up his plate and held it close to his chest.

Jody laughed and her mother frowned so heavily her eyebrows joined above her nose, making Jody laugh harder. In the meantime Dan scoffed down the last of his cake.

Dan didn't like the look of Jody. She was pale and the dark circles under her eyes worried him. He knew she had a lot going on. It was hard to miss her conversations with her lawyer when they shared an office. With a restraint he had no idea he possessed, he'd refrained from asking what was going on, but tonight, while he had her complete attention and the girls were busy bowling, he wanted answers to some questions.

"Are you allowing the girls to appear in front of the judge?"

She sighed. "I don't have a choice."

"Really? But they're just kids."

"According to the law, they're old enough to have a say, and Colin is within his rights to insist that they do." Jody watched Leigh as she took her turn.

"Have you told them?"

"No. I don't want to color their opinion or coach them at all." She turned to face him. "Mackenzie assures me that they'll be asked questions by the judge in the privacy of his chambers. There will also be a court-appointed counselor and of course Mackenzie and his partner. I'm trying not to worry, but I can't help thinking it might be best to just drop the whole thing."

Dan straightened. "Don't you dare. Don't let him force you into something you know isn't the right thing. Leigh and Amy are strong.

Neither of them wants anything to do with their father, and after the other weekend he doesn't deserve to have any contact with them. It's for their safety. You know that."

"I know." She buried her head in her hands. "It's just so hard to let them do this without being with them."

"You trust Mackenzie, right?"

She glanced up at him through her fingers. "Yes."

"Then you know he's going to do his best to protect them and make sure they're heard." Dan turned to be sure both girls were still occupied. "Do you think maybe you should talk to them about it before it happens?"

"I've gone back and forth on that so many times I'm sick to my stomach, but I think I'm just avoiding the inevitable. Do you mind if we head home early? Tonight is probably a good night to talk to them about it."

"No worries. I'll go order us a couple of pizzas to take away while the girls finish their game. One supreme and a pepperoni, right?"

"Yeah. Thanks."

Dan went to order. He could only imagine what Jody was going through, and he wanted to do anything he could to support her during this ordeal. If she'd let him. So far she had to a point, but he knew if he suggested going to court with her—like he wanted to— she'd shoot him down. Meeting her mother this evening had been a pleasant surprise that he had the feeling Jody would have loved to avoid. And the fact the girls had been talking about him to their grandmother could only be good.

He grabbed a couple of cans of soft drink and made his way back to the lanes where Leigh was bowling the final ball in their game. She was pretty good and knocked down the two remaining pins to get a spare, which of course meant she got another bowl. Amy sat pouting next to her mother, and when he glanced at the scoreboard he saw why. Amy hadn't managed to get the extra shot at the pins in her last frame. A distraction might help brighten that gloomy face.

"Hey, Amy, wanna come pick out some dessert for after pizza?"

"Yes." Her face lit up and he wondered how many more years

before the simple things like dessert couldn't cheer her up. Leigh wasn't as easy to impress, and Dan figured Amy was headed that way with the teenage years spread out in front of her.

"C'mon then." He held out his hand and she didn't hesitate to put hers in it. Dan smiled at Jody and led her daughter over to the shop where a selection of take-home ice-cream tubs awaited.

As they made their selections, Dan kept thinking about what lay ahead for all of them. He hoped Jody would let him stay while she talked to the girls, but he'd respect her wishes if she asked him to leave. As hard as it was to accept, he knew he wasn't a part of this small family unit, and what they were going through really wasn't his concern. Except he felt part of it, and he was concerned so much that he hadn't slept more than a few hours at a stretch.

No matter what happened this coming week, he was not walking away from this woman and her two daughters. He'd had lots of time to think, to ponder, to contemplate life with and without these three females, and he'd come to the conclusion that it wasn't acceptable to live out his days without them. No matter what it took he had to convince Jody they had a future. But first they had to deal with her past.

16

———

O n Monday, Jody woke to a rolling stomach and the urge to vomit. Bounding out of bed, she made it to the bathroom just in time to empty everything in her belly. Hot from head to toe, she broke out in sweat as she continued to dry heave. She leaned her forehead against the cool toilet seat and waited out the spasms. When she was convinced it was safe to leave the bathroom, she washed her face then wobbled on shaky legs to the kitchen where she braved a glass of water.

When that stayed down, Jody breathed a sigh of relief. She had too much to do today to be sick. Tomorrow was the big court appearance so she had to do two days' worth of work in one to have the time off. Of course, Cassie insisted she not worry, but the last thing Jody wanted was to feel guilty about not pulling her weight, especially when it would fall to Dan to pick up the slack.

He'd been more than generous to her over the last few weeks. Since the weekend they'd gone away, he'd found a way to help her out at every turn and while she more than appreciated it, she didn't want to get used to it. At some point he'd no longer be interested in her and find something else to do with his time. If she let herself—or the girls—become dependent on him, they'd be in all sorts of strife when he finally walked away.

The sound of shuffling feet had her turning to see Amy, hair sticking up every which way, dragging herself into the kitchen. "Morning, sweetie. You're up early."

"Bad dream," she murmured as she came over and wrapped her arms around Jody.

"Want to talk about it?" They hadn't had to discuss nightmares for years, and she hoped this wasn't due to their conversation on Saturday night. That hope was soon squashed.

"The court man said we had to go live with Daddy," she sobbed into Jody's side.

She wrapped her arms around Amy tightly and rubbed her back. "Sweetheart, the judge isn't going to do that. He can't make that decision. All he's going to do is say whether or not your father can contact you. It has nothing to do with who you live with."

How did she explain that their father had already given her full custody in the divorce without making him sound unloving? As much as Jody wanted to tell both her daughters what an ass their father was, she wouldn't. Easing onto one of the breakfast stools, she pulled Amy between her legs and cuddled her close.

Leigh came wandering in and stopped short when she saw the two of them. "What's wrong?"

"Amy had a nightmare." Jody held out her hand to Leigh, who walked over and took it. "You know this court thing tomorrow is just for you to talk to the judge about your dad, right? It has nothing to do with who you're going to live with. That decision was made already. The court awarded me full custody and your dad visitation. Tomorrow is not about that."

"Yeah, I know. The judge is going to ask questions about us and Dad," Leigh said. "Why does Amy think it's about going to live with Dad?"

"No, she knows it's not, but she had a bad dream about it anyway. I just wanted to make it perfectly clear that where you live isn't in question."

Leigh wrapped her arms around both of them and Jody enjoyed the quiet moments with both her babies close. Now that the girls were older, cuddles were few and far between. Regardless of the circumstances, she'd take these minutes and soak them up.

She thought Amy might have fallen back to sleep, but when she angled her head for a look, Jody discovered her staring off into space and chewing on her thumbnail. "Hey, none of that." She pulled Amy's thumb away.

"Sorry. I forget I don't do that anymore." She pulled out of Jody's arms. "Can we have pancakes for breakfast?"

Jody glanced at the time and calculated they could manage pancakes. "Yeah, why not. Grab the packet out of the pantry while I get the fry pan ready."

They worked together and soon had the first one cooking. Of course, it was easy when you had a jug of pancake mix on hand. Amy poured, Jody flipped and Leigh ferried them to the table when they were done. A stack of twelve pancakes later, they were sitting down to breakfast. Unfortunately Jody's stomach rebelled at the idea of food and she just picked at hers until the girls were finished and heading to their rooms to get ready for school. She packed up the leftovers and cleared away the dirty dishes before making her way to her room to get ready for work.

D an jumped when Jody doubled over and threw up into her waste bin. There was no warning. Only a little stifled, "Oh God," and then she was head down, stomach contents up. He rushed over and held her ponytail out of the way. After a few more heaves, she was done and Dan helped her sit back in her chair.

"Wait right there. I'll go get a damp cloth and some water."

Jody laughed, well, as much as she could manage under the circumstances. "Yeah, like I'm going anywhere right now."

He raced to the bathroom and grabbed a wad of paper towel. He turned on the tap and held the bundle under the water until it was wet through. Next, he detoured past the small staffroom and the water cooler Cassie kept there. With cup in one hand and wet towel in the other, he headed back to Jody. She hadn't moved and his step stuttered until he saw her chest rising with a shallow breath.

"Here. Try a sip of this." Dan handed her the cup of cold water.

"Thanks." She sipped cautiously, and while she did he had a good long look at her.

She was paler than Saturday, and those circles were so deep her eyes looked like they were going to pop out. "I think you need to see a doctor."

Her gaze snapped to his. "Why?"

"You're paler than you were the other day and you don't look like you've slept a wink in months. Your cheeks are sunken too. Are you eating properly? I know you're worried about tomorrow, but making yourself sick over it isn't going to help."

"I think it's a little worry and something I ate yesterday. I'll be fine." She pushed him away and stood on shaky legs. Picking up the wastebasket, she said, "I'm going to the bathroom to wash my face and get rid of this."

Dan watched her go. Her explanation sounded plausible, but something nagged at him and yet he couldn't put his finger on what. He'd give her ten minutes and then he was following to make sure she was okay.

He didn't even make it to five. She was back, and if he hadn't seen it with his own eyes he would not believe she'd just been sick. The dark smudges under her eyes were still there but her color had returned and her eyes no longer had that spaced-out, glassy look to them.

"Better?"

"Yes, much, thanks." She sat behind her desk and began to work.

"Aren't you going to head home?"

"No." Jody looked up with one eyebrow raised. "Why would I?"

"Because you're not well and tomorrow is a big day. Go home and get some rest." He checked his watch. "If you leave now you can be home before the girls and spend some time with them before you all have to deal with tomorrow."

"Thanks for the suggestion, but I still have things to sort out before I take the day off." She returned her gaze to the file in front of her.

He could not believe she thought work was more important than time with the girls, especially with everything that was going on. Snatching the file out from under her, he leaned in until their noses almost touched. "Go home."

"Dan—"

"No. I don't want to hear it. Go home. Everything is under control. There's absolutely nothing that can't wait until you get back if I can't sort it out." Dan grabbed her arm and helped her out of the chair. "Please, for me, go home and spend time relaxing with the girls. Rent a movie or take them to a movie, whatever, just go be with them."

"Okay, fine. But don't get shitty when something comes up that I should have dealt with." She bent over and grabbed her purse from the bottom drawer of her desk. "If things go quickly in the morning, I'll come in afterward. Mum and Dad are going to be there so they can take the girls out or something so I can come in."

"Don't even think it. If you're out of there early you can all go spend time with your parents."

"But—"

"No buts. Take the time, Jody." Dan was on the verge of begging her to take it when he felt her soften next to him. It was like every muscle she had took a breath and relaxed.

"Okay, but I owe you for this."

"Sure. Dinner."

"What?" She went a little pale.

"Have dinner with me."

The color drained right out of her face and she slammed a hand over her mouth before dashing to the bathroom. Dan didn't care what she said, it was more than worrying about tomorrow, and if something she ate yesterday messed her up this bad then it was food poisoning and that could be deadly.

He walked down the corridor and knocked on Cassie's door.

"Come in," she called out.

"Hey, mind if I shoot through for a few hours?"

"Everything okay?"

"Yeah, Jody's sick and I want to be sure she gets home all right."

"Sure. No worries, but isn't tomorrow the court thing?"

"Yeah, which is why I want to be sure she's okay." He paused to check no one was in the hallway. "I think I'll take tomorrow too. There's nothing that either of us needs to do, and this week is a quiet one, thank God. So if you're cool with it I think I'll take the day and help Jody out."

"Definitely. You've got Luc's number, right? He'll be there tomorrow anyway, but if you need him at all today, ring him."

"Thanks, Cassie, but I'm pretty sure having me hovering around is going to piss her off, we don't need to aggravate the situation by adding Luc." He grinned.

Cassie laughed. "You're right. He can be a little over the top when he worries."

"I'll text you later." Dan heard the bathroom door open. "Gotta go. See you on Wednesday."

"Catch you then."

Dan quickly caught up to Jody. "Here give me that."

"What the hell are you doing?" She pulled away from him.

"Trying to carry your bag for you." He was worried she might still be a little shaky, and the last thing he wanted was for her to topple down the stairs.

"I can carry my handbag. I'm not an invalid."

Whoa. He hadn't heard that tone from her in weeks. "Sorry. Didn't mean to offend."

"No. I'm sorry. I was snapping at you for no reason."

"You've got a lot going on. Add in feeling sick and I imagine just breathing is making you snappy." He grinned to soften his words. Heaven forbid she take offense and snap at him again.

"Probably." They were almost to the bottom of the stairs when it twigged he was walking out with her. "What are you doing?"

"Going out with you."

"What?"

"Coming with you." Dan cupped her elbow and kept her moving when she stopped. "I'm going to make sure you take it easy. I'll organize dinner and occupy the girls if you want to rest or think of something we can all do to pass the time."

"You can't do that."

"Why not?"

"Because...well...because...argh! I have no idea why not exactly, but you can't."

Dan laughed. As arguments went it was a complete wash, but he'd give her credit for trying. He ushered her through the door and out into the sunlight before he turned her to face him. "Here's the thing. I either follow you home and come in and do all I just suggested. Or I follow you home and sit outside your house in my car. Your choice."

"That's not a choice." She was right. There was no way she'd let him sit outside and he was counting on it. "Fine. But when the girls get home you can explain why we're not at work. Oh, and you get to help with homework."

Homework was the least he'd do to spend the afternoon with Jody and the girls. He smiled. "Deal. Unless it's English. I suck at English."

Jody laughed. "Too bad. You already made the deal. No changing the rules now."

Dan followed her over to her car and made sure she was okay to drive before racing over to his Jeep and starting the engine. He knew where she lived so didn't need to tail her, but he was worried she'd have another bout of vomiting, and if she did he wanted to be there to take care of her.

Jody was stretched out on the couch wondering when it was that Dan had taken over her life. He was currently at the dining table with the girls doing their homework. She could hear them giggling and generally having fun, which she couldn't remember them doing whenever she helped them. He'd ordered dinner, which would be delivered around seven. And he ordered her to take a nap. Ha. Fat chance that would happen when all she could hear was her girls and how happy they sounded.

She hadn't been sick again but the nausea was still hanging around. The thought of food made it worse, so she tried to not think about it. But she was thinking about something that made her feel even sicker. It had been a while, a good long while, but she had a sinking feeling she knew exactly what was wrong with her. If she was right, her world—and Dan's—was about to be turned on its head.

She'd put it off long enough. Forcing herself to move, she got to her feet and headed to her bathroom. She found the packet of pills she was looking for and studied it carefully. The sugar pills had kicked in five days ago and she still hadn't got her period. This wasn't good. She checked to see she'd taken all the other pills before she suddenly remembered something that not only confirmed her suspicions but dropped the bomb on her world.

During the first week of this packet of contraceptives, she'd had a throat infection and had to take antibiotics for fourteen days. How could she have been so stupid? She knew the drill. Knew the meds would affect the pill and put her at risk, but she hadn't thought about that when she'd assured Dan that she was safe. Sinking to the edge of the bath, she stared at the empty pouches and wondered what to do. Telling him was out of the question. Not until she knew for sure. There was no point stressing out both of them until she'd either peed on a stick or in a jar.

"Hey, you all right?" Dan asked from the doorway. He noticed the packet in her hand and came into the room, closing the door behind him. "What's wrong?"

"I, um, I'm not sure..." Did she just blurt it out? Oh God. She'd been here before. Pregnant, unmarried and facing an uncertain future. Except this time she was older—wiser—and she had no intention of being forced into something she didn't want. "I was just taking some medicine."

"Do you have a headache, fever?" he asked as he placed the back of his hand on her forehead.

"A slight one," Jody lied.

"Why don't you have a shower and get in your pajamas. If you want to skip dinner and go straight to bed, I'll take care of the girls."

Tears stung her eyes. He was being so nice and she was keeping a huge secret from him. But until she knew for sure, she wasn't about to reveal what she'd discovered. Instead, she'd play the sick card and keep out of his way as much as possible. "If you don't mind, I'd really like that. I can always ring Mum though."

"Nonsense. I'm already here and dinner is taken care of, so there isn't any point dragging her out when I'm more than capable." He grinned at her, which made her want to cry more. Why did he have to be so nice when she was feeling so crappy?

"Thanks."

He backed away. "Yell if you need anything."

"Okay."

"I mean it. Anything."

"I will."

"Good. I'll get you a glass of water for beside your bed. Do you want anything else, food?"

"No. I don't think I could stomach anything right now."

"All right. I'll check on you in a bit."

He was out the door and gone before Jody breathed easy. She had some major decisions to make. Having a baby was not in her plans. She'd been there and done that. The idea of more children had never entered her head after she'd had Amy. Her hand slid over her belly. If she was pregnant, did she want to keep it? Could she even get rid of it? No. There was no way she could abort a child. It just wasn't in her to take that step.

Pushing to her feet, she turned and twisted the hot-water tap in the shower. Steam rose almost instantly, and she adjusted the cold until the water was the right temperature. She stripped out of her clothes and stepped under the warm spray. The heat and massage showerhead did wonders for her tight muscles and she stayed under longer than she should have.

When her fingers began to wrinkle, she decided it was time to get out. The end of her ponytail had gotten wet so she grabbed a hand towel to squeeze the water out before picking up her large bath towel and rubbing the soft cotton over her skin. With the towel wrapped around her, Jody made her way out into the bedroom to find Dan had done exactly what he said he would. On her bedside drawers sat a glass of water.

She fought off the onslaught of tears that suddenly pressed against her eyes and quickly got into some pajamas. Turning back the covers, she climbed beneath and snuggled into the thick quilt. First thing tomorrow, she'd sneak off and buy a home-pregnancy kit. The sooner she knew for sure, the sooner she could make some decisions and plans.

17

Jody stared at the stick in her hand and couldn't believe it when a tiny pink plus sign appeared in the clear window. That couldn't be right. She shook the damn thing in case it was stuck. No change. She grabbed the box and re-read the instructions. Had she peed on the stupid thing right? Maybe she was supposed to pee in a cup and soak the end for a minute or something. She scanned the words as they blurred before her eyes. *Oh God!* She'd done everything exactly as instructed.

Full-blown panic took over. She trembled from head to toe and sweat broke out, slicking her palms so much that the reason for her sudden terror slipped from her grip. It dropped to the bathroom floor and she scrambled to pick it up before someone in another cubical saw.

"Oh God." *This can't be happening again.* "Oh God, oh God, oh God."

She couldn't breathe. Couldn't think. Couldn't get past the terrifying reality that at thirty-four she was a divorced mother of two teenagers and pregnant from what had essentially been a one-night stand.

"Oh God."

It had to be wrong. She couldn't be pregnant. Did these things have used-by dates? Surely it was broken or something—anything other than finding herself in the same position as sixteen years ago. A wave of nausea swamped her and she spun around, flipping up the toilet seat before emptying her stomach into the bowl. Again. She'd never been this sick with either of the girls. That had to be a sign the stick lied. Didn't it? When the last of the spasms passed, Jody got to her feet and almost toppled headfirst into the toilet when someone knocked on the door.

"Are you all right in there, love?" The voice was shaky with age and Jody thanked God it wasn't the smartly dressed twenty-something who'd been her constant shadow since arriving at the courthouse.

"Y-yes." Jody licked her dry lips and bile rose in her throat at the foul taste. "I'm fine. Thank you." Her own voice shook, but it had nothing to do with age.

She needed to pull it together. Revealing her secret here was not an option, and if she didn't get control of her emotions the first person to look at her funny would send her into a meltdown. Water ran in one of the sinks and Jody hoped the elderly woman was about to leave. Drawing in a deep breath, she turned the lock on the door and stepped out of the cubicle.

"Here you go, dear." The smallest woman Jody had ever seen held out a handful of wet paper towel. "Put that against your neck. I always found that helpful when I was suffering morning sickness."

Jody's hand froze in mid-air as she reached for the wadded up towel. "How—"

The gray-haired woman chuckled. "My dear, nothing other than a coming baby can empty a woman's stomach quite like that." She patted Jody's arm. "Now take these and a deep breath. I'm sure it'll pass in a few moments."

Jody took the bundle of wet paper and pressed it against her neck. Dumbfounded, she stood there as the kind old woman turned to leave. At the last second, she remembered her manners and muttered, "Thank you."

"You're welcome, dear. And congratulations. It's an exciting time when you're expecting." With a wave, she disappeared through the outer door, leaving Jody alone in the cold marble room with her decidedly unexcited emotions.

She still held the stick in her hand and she brought it up to look at it one more time before tossing it in the bin when she discovered the plus sign hadn't changed. Remembering her bag, Jody turned around and retrieved it from the hook on the back of the toilet door. The test kit sat on the floor where she'd dropped it when she'd thrown up and she picked it up and shoved it back in the brown paper bag in her purse. There were another two test sticks in the box. She'd wait until later, at home, to do the test a second time. Possibly a third. If the results were the same, she'd make an appointment with her doctor as soon as she could get in.

"Ms. Walsh?" Blonde twenty-something stuck her head in the bathroom door. "The girls are finished and the judge is going to make his decision in the next few minutes."

Jody breathed a sigh of relief. Finally, Leigh and Amy were out. They'd been in with the judge for over an hour, and the longer it went on the more she'd worried. Not about what either of them might say, but about how they'd cope being peppered with questions about a man they barely knew.

"I'll be right there." She dumped the wad of towel in the bin and checked her appearance before deciding she was none the worse for wear after her latest vomiting episode. She'd been doing it so regularly this morning that haggard was her permanent look, and she figured she'd get away with it because of the nature of today's proceedings.

Exiting the bathroom, she found her lawyers, her parents, her brother and the girls waiting for her. It was the person between the girls that surprised her. Dan smiled, and even with the emotions currently swirling around inside, she smiled back and felt a heavy weight lift off her, like he'd taken heavy grocery bags from her hands. She took her time, nerves about the decision—about how the girls went and about the man who'd turned her life on its head—collided together to make her cautious even when it was just approaching those who were here to support her and the girls.

Mackenzie stepped forward. "Leigh and Amy did brilliantly. You should be very proud of both of them."

"Thank you. But I don't need them to answer questions in front of a judge to make me proud." Jody held out her arms and both girls rushed into them. She buried her nose in Amy's hair and breathed in the scent of her familiar shampoo. The three of them held on for longer than normal, but today was anything but normal.

"We'll know for sure in the next few minutes, but I'm confident the judge is going to grant the order," Mackenzie added.

Jody looked up and met Mackenzie's gaze. "Thank you. For everything."

"You're welcome."

The girls started talking at once as they pulled away and Jody had to hold up her hand to stop the excited flow. "One at a time, please."

"Gran and Gramps want to take us to the movies. Can we go?" Leigh asked.

Jody glanced at her mother and father. "Are you sure?"

"Of course. We'll bring them home after dinner." He father pulled her into a big hug and she leaned into him, soaking up his warmth and comfort.

"Thanks, Dad."

"You hang in there, kiddo. Everything is going to be fine." He gave her a final squeeze before letting go. "We'll see you later. Me and my favourite girls have a date."

"Hey, I thought I was your favourite girl."

Her dad tweaked her nose. "Always. But if I don't share it around the others will get upset." He winked, making her laugh.

Her mother gave her a quick hug before grabbing the girls' hands and leading them away.

"Bye. Behave, girls," she called out. They were already halfway down the corridor, their mother and this morning's ordeal completely forgotten. Which delivered equal pangs of relief and sadness.

"You okay?" Dan's warm hand spread across her spine. "Still feeling a little queasy?"

"Yes, how can you tell?" She turned to look at him. He couldn't tell anything else could he?

"You're still a little pale and your eyes have that glazed look you get when you've been tossing your cookies." He rubbed his hand in circles and Jody couldn't help but lean into the support he offered.

"You can stop worrying now. In a few minutes, the judge will hand down his decision and everything will go back to normal," Dan said.

Jody covered a snort of laughter with her hand and a fake cough. If only he knew. Nothing was ever going to be normal again.

Dan hadn't meant to snoop. But when he'd dropped Jody's handbag on the counter and everything had tumbled out...the brown paper bag had snagged his attention first. Then the box with words *Early Test Kit* half hanging out had grabbed him by the gut. He wasn't proud of himself for pulling it out the rest of the way, but nothing could compete with the roller coaster of emotions that followed.

He wasn't sure what to think. Okay, he knew exactly what he was thinking, but what to do about it was the question. Jody hadn't said a word, and he couldn't decide if he should wait to see if she did, or bring up the topic himself. She'd obviously taken the test. The box was open and one of the three test sticks was missing. A burst of excitement exploded inside him quickly followed by anger.

Had she lied to him about being on the pill? Reason quickly asserted itself. Why would she? It didn't make sense or fit with the woman Dan had come to know. He shoved everything back in her bag and put it down on the breakfast counter. She'd raced off to the bathroom the minute she'd opened her front door and he had a pretty good idea why. So far he'd counted four dashes to the toilet today, and he'd only been with her for as many hours. He'd honestly thought she was sick due to the stress of going to court, but if he was reading the signs right—and a box of home pregnancy test kits was a pretty big sign—it wasn't the threat her ex represented that had her throwing up her lunch.

"Sorry. Can I get you a coffee?"

She breezed into the room, her face flushed, her eyes glassy, and he couldn't think of a thing to say that didn't start and end with, "Are you pregnant?" He figured blurting it out was the wrong way to deal with it, so he held his tongue and nodded.

He slid onto a barstool and watched her move around. She wasn't as animated as usual, but after the last few weeks and today that was to be expected. And if she was pregnant—his gaze dropped to her belly, but he couldn't see any evidence of a baby bump—then he was surprised she was functioning at all. Other than the dark circles beneath her eyes and the tired, pale look, Dan couldn't see any physical difference. He'd heard the female body went through numerous changes before it became obvious there was a baby on the way, but other than the obvious swollen belly he didn't know what they were.

A thought occurred to him and he pulled his phone from his pocket and opened his calendar app. He counted back to their weekend job. Seventeen days. She wasn't even three weeks. Things were barely getting started inside her.

"Dan!"

He jerked his gaze up to meet Jody's. "Huh?"

"Do you have milk?"

Oh, his coffee. "Yes, please."

"Where were you? You spaced out on me. I don't think you heard anything I said in the last five minutes." She filled two mugs with boiling water and the aroma of coffee filled the air.

He waved his phone. "Just checking email."

"Oh." She leaned across the counter and put his coffee in front of him.

Dan had to admit he could get used to watching her make him coffee every day. And if she was pregnant, he'd get to do exactly that. He wondered if she'd want a big wedding or if they'd have something small and intimate. He'd never thought about how he'd get married or even if he would. But now that he was thinking about it, Dan had to acknowledge a small wedding would be more his style. Of course, he was putting the cart before the horse. She hadn't even mentioned the possibility of a pregnancy.

He decided to lead her in the direction of a confession. "How are you feeling?"

"Better. I'm sure it'll pass now that the drama is over."

"Are you happy the judge granted your order?" Dan had to wonder how much she cared for her ex when she very rarely badmouthed him. Although he was more inclined to think she pitied the man she was once married to.

"Yes. There won't be any real difference day to day, except the girls and I are protected from another incident like the other night." Jody took a sip of her drink before continuing. "Colin's not in the girls lives anyway. Since he moved out five years ago, he's seen them a total of twelve times. He does the obligatory Christmas and birthday visits and that's it—although he's missed both of their last birthdays and Christmas. Other than the child-support money that drops into my account once a month, I don't even think about him most of the time."

"I don't understand how anyone can walk away from their children like that." He wanted his position on any children he might father clear before Jody brought up her possible pregnancy. "I'd never abandon a child of mine even if I was no longer involved with their mother."

He thought she stiffened for a second, but then she turned around and, opening the dishwasher, began emptying it. "Not all fathers feel the same way obviously."

Dan bit his tongue. He wanted to confront her. Wanted to know for sure so they could make plans, except something told him she wasn't ready to face this yet. He'd been chasing after her from the start, and he suddenly had the sinking feeling that he'd always be trying to catch her. In this, he had to let her come to him. And if she didn't by the end of the week, he'd say something.

He got up and walked around the breakfast bar and helped her put away the clean dishes. He was beginning to know where most things were in her kitchen. And while he liked that they'd become close in that way, he wanted to get closer. What he'd really like was for her to move in with him. His place was bigger and the girls could still attend the same school, keep in touch with their existing friends and not disrupt their lives at all.

When she told him about the baby, he'd suggest they combine their households before the wedding, although he wanted a ring on her finger—and his—as soon as possible, he understood she might want to wait. Either way, in the next few months they'd build the foundations of their future together.

***

Jody woke with a start. Her nose was pressed into the hard wall of Dan's chest while one of his arms was wrapped around her back holding her close. They were on the sofa in her living room, the television turned down low and the darkness of dusk shrouding the room in shadows.

"What time is it?" She stretched her arms over her head as she sat up.

"Not quite six. You slept for about two hours."

"Oh God. Why didn't you wake me?" She went to stand up but Dan stopped her with a hand on her arm.

"Because you needed it and there was nothing urgent that you had to do. The girls are with your parents and won't be home for a while yet. For once, just sit and relax, Jody."

He pulled her back against him and she gave in. The warmth of his body, the scent of his skin, the sound of him breathing, it all calmed her in a way she'd never experienced before. It was as though just having him close would make all her problems go away—or at least make them easier to deal with—and Jody couldn't decide if she liked the sensation or not. For now, she'd let him hold her while it was just the two of them. The outside world would intrude soon enough.

She watched the sitcom Dan had on. She wasn't a fan of much on TV, but she had to admit this particular show always made her laugh and tonight was no different. She'd seen the episode before and even that didn't dull the impact of the humor. He'd wrapped his arm back around her and Jody soon found herself dozing off again. When she did it for the third time, she decided she'd better get up or getting to sleep tonight would be impossible.

"I think I need to get up and do something."

"Why?"

"Because I keep nodding off."

"And?" He pulled her up and over his legs until she was draped across his lap. "You've had a big few days. Take the time and rest while you can."

She knew he was right. It was beyond rare for her to have a few moments to herself, never mind hours. Usually when the girls were with her parents it was because she had to work. Settling into Dan's arms, Jody allowed herself this indulgence while she could. Things would be different once he knew about the possible baby. Her decision to keep it from him until she'd had it confirmed by her doctor weighed on her mind.

He deserved to know. And if she were honest, she'd concede the need to have his support. She had no doubt he'd stand up and take responsibility once he knew, and the longer she mulled over it the more she realized waiting until she saw her doctor was her way of putting the inevitable off. And that wasn't fair to either of them.

"Dan."

"Mmm."

Jody couldn't work out how to tell him in a way that wouldn't blindside him. Then again, she doubted that was even possible. "Um, remember the other weekend?"

He turned his gaze her way and muted the television. "Which weekend? We've spent the last few together."

"The one in the Hunter." Her mouth went dry and her tongue stuck to her teeth as she spoke. "When we...you know."

"Had sex?" He waggled his eyebrows.

She smiled. "Yeah, well, I was sick a couple of weeks before that, remember?"

"Didn't you and the girls all have tonsillitis or something?" Dan skimmed his fingers over her waist, sending tingles through her, and she struggled to stay focused.

"Yes. We were on antibiotics."

"Okay. Any reason we're taking this medical history trip?"

"Medicine can make contraceptive pills ineffective." There. She'd said it.

"Meaning?"

Oh God. She was going to have to spell it out—say the words out loud. She'd avoided it until now. The words might have sounded in her head, but they hadn't once passed her lips. Scrunching her eyes closed, she buried her face against his chest and let the words out. "I think I'm pregnant."

"Okay."

Her eyes popped open as she jerked her head backward. "What? Okay? That's all you have to say?" She tried to get off his lap, but he held her down by wrapping both arms around her waist.

"I have to confess I saw the kit in your handbag earlier."

"You looked in my bag?"

"I didn't mean to snoop, but it fell out when I dropped your bag on the counter and well, I added that to the frequent trips to toss your cookies and figured you had something to tell me."

Jody stumbled over what to say next. Until Dan opened his mouth again.

"As soon as we're sure, we'll get married, but we can move you and the girls into my place this weekend."

"Wow. Wait a second." This time she did scramble off his lap. She got to her feet and stood, legs apart, hands on hips. "Who said anything about getting married or moving in together? I'm not uprooting the girls again. They've had enough uncertainty in their short lives."

"Then I'll move in here, but I thought it made sense to move into my place because it's bigger. And the girls will still be in the same area so they won't have to change schools or lose friends."

"No."

"Jody, be reasonable. If we're having a baby we need to combine our lives to give our child the security and stability of a family."

"I did that already and look where it got me. I'm not getting married or moving in with you just because we made a baby together. Jesus, we haven't even slept together since it happened." Couldn't Dan see how stupid it was to get married or move in together at this point?

"Is that what happened? You got pregnant with Leigh and married the guy? And now you're comparing me with him? I'm going to pretend I didn't hear you say that."

Jody opened her mouth to speak when the front door flew open and Amy came rushing in talking a mile a minute. Their conversation was officially over and it hadn't gone anything like she'd expected.

18

Two and a half days. Dan hadn't spoken to Jody in over forty-eight hours, and he was starting to go stir crazy. He'd left her house not long after the girls had arrived home on Tuesday night thinking he'd see her Wednesday, only she hadn't come into work. Cassie had come into his office to tell him Jody had called to say one of the girls was sick, except he was pretty sure it was Jody who was sick. He hoped she'd used the day to visit the doctor and confirm her pregnancy. The sooner she did that the sooner they could move forward.

And then she hadn't shown up on Thursday or today. He'd dialed her number numerous times but only allowed the call to go through a few of them. He didn't want to pester her if she was resting, except now that she hadn't returned any of the five messages he had left in the last three days, he was beginning to worry. Tonight he was turning up on her doorstep whether she wanted him there or not and he'd see for himself she was okay even if he had to peer in through the damn window.

"Hey."

Dan looked up to see Cassie leaning on the doorjamb. "What's up?"

She came into the room and closed the door. "Mind if I sit down?"

"Um, no." He arched one eyebrow. "Is there a problem?"

"No." She chewed her lip as she slid into the seat across from him. "More that I just want to have a chat. Friend to friend."

"Jody. Luc asked you to talk to me about Jody didn't he?"

Cassie laughed. "Actually, no. He told me to stay out of it." She grinned. "As you can see, I'm taking his advice."

"Oh?"

"Look, I don't know what's going on and I don't want details, but I think you need some advice from a woman who might understand the working mind of another woman better than you."

Dan wasn't sure if he followed that correctly or not, but at this point he'd take any and all advice under consideration. "Go on."

"Jody is ready to move on from her disastrous marriage, so don't think she doesn't have feelings for you. Quite the opposite. If she didn't she wouldn't have let you close. Her problem is she's been hurt by someone she trusted before. Badly. You know that, so I don't need to go into details. Unfortunately for you, she's going to tar you with the same brush."

She already had. When she'd insinuated marrying him or moving in with him for the baby's sake would end up the same way her relationship with her ex had, Dan was pretty sure he'd been tarred by that asshole's brush. He nodded for Cassie to continue.

"Straight out, no lies, Dan. Are you serious about Jody?"

"Yes."

"Okay." She stood. "That's good then."

Dan watched puzzled as Cassie got up to leave. Where was the advice in any of what she'd just said? "Is that it?"

She glanced over her shoulder. "Oh, no. See you Monday."

"What? I didn't think you had a job off site today."

"I don't. But you're heading home early. Oh, and I gave your Saturday party to Kerry."

"What?" He pushed his chair back and got to his feet.

"I'm giving you the rest of the day and the weekend off. Go fix whatever the hell needs fixing with Jody."

With that, Cassie disappeared into the hallway, leaving Dan wondering if he'd been dropped into the twilight zone. Cassie's head popped around the door. "The girls are at school and Jody's home resting, but you didn't hear that from me."

He stared at the space his boss's head had just occupied for ages before he shook himself out of his daze and glanced at his watch. It wasn't even eleven o'clock. If he headed to Jody's now, they'd have a few hours of alone time to get things sorted out. With a plan in place, he scooped his keys off the edge of his desk and headed out.

Perhaps he should pick up some lunch? Although he wasn't sure what she'd be able to eat with her tummy upset the way it had been the last time he'd seen her. He'd done some research and he knew morning sickness often lasted months. He hoped she didn't suffer that long or get it as severe as some of the information suggested was possible. Dan hit the outer warehouse door just as West was coming in.

"Hey, man, leaving early? I didn't forget a job, did I?" West asked.

"What? No. I've got some personal stuff to deal with so I'm cutting out early."

"Lucky you. I've got at least another twelve hours before I can call it a day." West held the door for Dan to pass through.

"But busy means you're making money, right?"

"According to my accountant, I'm making too much money and should hire a manager. Hey, you're not looking for a job are you?" West asked.

"You trying to poach me from Cassie?" Dan arched one eyebrow. "Brave. If I take you up on the offer she'll be serving testicles at the next function."

West laughed as he covered his groin and glanced around. "It'll be our secret. But I'm serious. If you ever want out of Are You Game? come knock on my door. Whether I'm looking or not I'd hire you on the spot."

"I'll take that as a compliment."

"Hell no. I'm complimenting Cassie. She's got your ass so ship-shape you'd be a fantastic addition to my team." West slapped him on the back. "Anyway, you go enjoy your time off while I go slave over a hot stove."

"Yeah, right, you love your job. Meanwhile, there's not much enjoyment in what I have to do." Dan hoped there would be, but he had to be realistic. Jody was avoiding him and their last words had been spoken in mild anger.

"Ah, woman troubles." West nodded.

"That obvious?" Dan asked.

"Only because I've seen that look in the mirror a time or two lately."

"Oh? Anyone I know?"

West mimed zipping his lips and throwing away the key.

"So that means I do know her." Dan grinned. "Which means it has to be someone who works for you…"

"You want me to start speculating on what you did to fuck things up with Jody?" West asked.

"Who said anything about Jody?"

"C'mon, you'd have to be deaf, blind and stupid to miss the fireworks shooting between you two."

Dan frowned. He hadn't realized they'd been obvious in their attraction.

"Relax. Nobody's talking if that's what you're worried about."

He wasn't, but Dan was relieved to know it anyway. Except the lack of workplace talk would change once Jody's pregnancy became public knowledge. Everyone would be talking then. "Look, I gotta go."

"Sure thing. Catch you later. Oh, and that job offer stands." West grinned as he ducked inside, the door closing behind him.

Dan wondered what was going on with his friend. He'd been so wrapped up in his own life that he hadn't spent much time with West in recent months. Not that he should be worrying about someone else's problems when he had his own to sort out. Shaking his head, he opened the door on his Jeep and climbed in. In the next hour he'd know if he had any hope of fixing the situation between him and Jody.

Jody dragged herself off the couch and crawled toward the door. She hadn't kept any food down since Monday and her muscles just weren't up to walking. Holding onto the wall, she barely made it into the hallway when the banging started. God, it sounded like someone had snuck into her skull and was hammering away at her brain with an axe.

"I'm coming." Her voice was hoarse and scarcely more than a whisper. Her throat and mouth were so dry her tongue stuck to her teeth, and her lips stung in places where she knew they had to be cracked.

The thumping on the door continued and Jody grabbed her head, cupping her ears to try and lessen the noise. She collapsed against the wall and slid the rest of the way to the floor. Her arms and legs were like lead weights that an Olympic lifter would struggle to get off the ground. Curling in a ball, Jody cried, except she was so dehydrated that no tears formed and her eyelids grated against her eyes as she lowered them and prayed whoever was at the door would stop bashing on it soon.

"Jody?" She had no idea how much time had passed before Dan kneeled on the floor beside her. He shook her shoulder and she moaned.

"Jody? Can you hear me?"

"Yes," she whispered over dry lips.

"C'mon, baby, let's get you off the floor." He scooped her up and stood, sending her head spinning and her stomach flipping.

"Oh God, gonna be sick." She slammed a hand over her mouth as he dashed her to the bathroom where she dry heaved for what felt like an eternity.

He pressed a damp cloth to her forehead when the wave of nausea had gone. "Can you hold that there?"

Jody couldn't manage a shake of her head never mind move her arm. The only thing she could do was groan as Dan picked her up once more. She closed her eyes and fought against the bile rising in her throat as he moved out of the bathroom and into her bedroom. He laid her on the bed and she could hear him moving around but she had no strength to even open her eyes.

The bed dipped and Dan's warmth brushed her side. "C'mon, try a sip of this." He held her head up and pressed a cool glass against her mouth.

She parted her lips on a breath and let him tip a little water inside. He waited for her to swallow before repeating the process.

"How long since you ate anything? Drank anything?"

Jody's head swam, her mind spinning as she tried to remember what day it was. "No."

"No, you don't want to tell me or you don't know? C'mon, Jody, help me out here. Have you kept anything down since Tuesday?"

She knew that answer. "No."

"Damn, Jody, have you been to the doctor?" He wiped the cloth over her face and her eyes fluttered open.

When her eyes focused, she saw his face twisted in deep concern. Tears stung, and her throat constricted, making it difficult to swallow even with the water he'd recently fed her. "Couldn't." She licked her lips. "Get in."

"Where's the number? If they won't see you now I'm taking you to emergency."

"Phone." Her eyes closed as fatigue threatened to take her under again. She seemed to spend all her time sleeping. "In. My bag."

The bed rose as Dan left her to go in search of her bag. She couldn't tell him where it was because she couldn't remember what she'd done with it. Turning on her side, she curled into herself and hoped her stomach didn't repel the fluid churning in her belly.

"Jody?" Dan's hand smoothed over her cheek. "Jody, you have to wake up, baby. I spoke to your doctor. She said to take you straight to casualty. She's ringing ahead so they'll take you right in."

"Girls?"

"I'll take care of them, but let's get you sorted first." He wrapped the quilt around her and picked her up once more. She snuggled close and let his warmth and comfort surround her.

D an was going out of his mind. He'd lied to the nurse so they'd let him behind the security doors, but that hadn't done him any good because they'd whisked Jody away on a bed and hadn't brought her back yet. It had been an hour. He ran his fingers through his hair again. At this rate he'd be bald by the end of the day. Glancing at his watch, he noticed the time and pulled out his phone to call Luc. Someone had to be there for the girls and he didn't want to leave Jody yet. Not until he knew how she was.

He thumbed through his phonebook until he came to Luc's number and hit call. It rang twice when Jody's brother answered.

"Dan? What's up?"

"Someone needs to go to Jody's and get the girls. I'd go but I don't want to leave Jody."

"What do you mean leave her? Where the fuck are you?"

"We're at the hospital." Dan sighed. He'd have to talk fast or Luc would put him six feet under before his next heartbeat. "She's sick. I think it's the baby but the doctor hasn't come back yet and they're still running tests."

"Baby! What baby?" Dan pulled the phone away from his ear but didn't have any trouble hearing Luc yelling at him. "Did you get my sister pregnant? Jesus H. Christ, O'Conner, what the hell were you thinking?"

"Let's not do this now. Can you get the girls or not?"

"Yes. Shit, of course I can. Which hospital are you at?"

"North Shore." Dan turned at the clatter of metal behind him to see two nurses pushing Jody back into the room. "Gotta go, I'll call you back."

Dan hung up to Luc screaming at him not to. He stepped out of the way so they could wheel the bed into the correct position. "Is she okay?"

The nurse who'd greeted him at reception smiled. "She will be. We've started an IV and the doctor is going over her results now. He should be in with you shortly."

He wanted to ask more—know more—but the nurses left before he could get another word out. Dan looked at Jody. She looked so small curled on her side, the IV tube running into the back of one hand. Her hair was matted and the black circles beneath her eyes were so dark—so deep—he wondered how her eyes remained in her head. Gently, he ran his fingertips down her cheek, along her jaw. His phone rang and he quickly hit reject and turned it to silent so it wouldn't disturb her.

She stirred, her eyes fluttering open and the ghost of a smile tipped the corner of her mouth. "Dan."

"Hey, baby." He leaned down and dropped a kiss on her forehead. "You'll feel better soon."

"Girls?"

"Luc is going to pick them up. Do you want them to come here?"

She licked her lips and he looked around for some water. "No. Scare them."

"All right, I'll ring Luc back and tell him to take them home with him or to your mum and dad's."

"Please." Her eyelids lowered and he wanted to let her rest but he wanted answers too.

"Why didn't you ring me, Jody? You're far too sick for this to be normal."

"Too tired." Her mouth went lax as exhaustion took her under again.

A throat cleared behind him and he turned to find an older stout man in a white coat in the doorway. "Daniel O'Conner?"

"Yes?"

The man held out his hand as he came into the room. "Doctor Moore, I'm in charge of Jody's care. I've spoken with her GP, Doctor Simmons, and we believe the best thing is to admit her. She's suffering from hyperemesis gravidarum, or in layman's terms, severe morning sickness. She is very dehydrated so I'd like to administer fluids intravenously for at least twenty-four hours. I've also started her on some medication to counteract the nausea, though it won't stop it altogether. But she should at least begin to eat and drink normally before we send her home tomorrow if she responds to the treatment well."

"Will that affect the baby?"

"No, no, it's fine, and she's not the first woman to experience such extreme morning sickness. Doctor Simmons did mention that she wasn't this ill with either of her other two pregnancies though, and as she's a good deal older now I'd like to run some other tests. I'll get a nurse to bring in some pamphlets about Jody's condition and also some information on the tests I'd like her to have in the next few weeks."

"Okay."

"We'll get her up and going again before we do anything more though. I can tell you the ultrasound showed everything is otherwise progressing normally for a three week fetus."

"Thank God," Dan breathed the words out in a rush of air.

"This extreme form of morning sickness can be very frightening, but I assure you she and the baby will be fine as long as we control the nausea and make sure she'd keeps up her fluids and nourishment."

Dan held out his hand. "Thank you."

Doctor Moore shook Dan's hand. "I take it this is your first?"

"Yes." Dan smiled. "Does it show?"

"A little." The doctor smiled and stepped around Dan to check Jody's IV. "All looks good. I'll come by once they move her up to her room to make sure she's settled in."

"Do I need to fill in any paperwork?"

"Not now. I'll get the nurse to bring it to her room later."

"Thanks." Dan turned back to Jody. She'd slept through the whole exchange, and even though they hadn't been here long, he swore some color was returning to her face. It was the most welcome thing he'd ever seen.

19

———

Something tugged at the back of Jody's hand when she tried to roll over.

"Hey, hey, careful now."

Dan's soothing voice filled her ears and she turned her head in his direction. Her eyelids felt heavy but she forced them open to see him standing beside her. "Where...?" She scanned the room around her.

"The hospital. You don't remember?"

"No." She licked her lips. "How did I get here?"

"You don't recall me finding you on the floor at your house?"

Jody shook her head, but the action brought on a wave of dizziness that made her moan and her stomach roll. "N-no."

"Well, that might be for the best. What's the last thing you do remember?"

She thought about it for a moment. "Sending the girls to school?" Was that this morning? What day was it? Jody could see through the window that it was dark outside.

"Today, yesterday or Wednesday?"

"It's Friday?" Jody tried to sit up only to be forced back by her spinning head and her pitching stomach.

"Take it easy." Dan stroked her hair back from her face with the fingertips of one hand while he held her hand—the one with the tube snaking out from under a bandage—with the other. "Yes, it's Friday, and from what I can gather you've been sick since I left Tuesday night."

A horrible thought occurred. "The baby?"

"Is fine. You have hyper-something or other. Severe morning sickness. It has a fancy name but I don't remember it, and even if I did I probably couldn't pronounce it correctly. The doctor said he was going to give us some leaflets that explain what's going on and how to help make it more bearable."

"So I am pregnant?"

"Yep. Three weeks according to the ultrasound they did when I brought you in earlier."

"I guess there's no denying it now."

"Nope. We're going to have a baby."

Dan grinned at her like it was the best thing in the world, and she supposed for some it would seem that way. But right now all she could think was she hadn't planned for this—hadn't wanted to find herself in the same situation a second time in her life. But she'd learned a valuable lesson the first time. Forcing two people together for the sake of a baby was the worst possible way to begin a relationship of any sort, especially marriage, and Dan had been adamant that they get married if she was pregnant.

"I won't marry you," Jody blurted out.

He jerked back, his eyes widening, his eyebrows shooting up into his hairline. "Wow. Okay. How about we leave that discussion for later, when you're better and home."

Why was he being so accommodating? What happened to giving their child security and family? "I won't change my mind. I'm not going through that again."

"Jody." Dan sighed. "I understand you're frightened by what's happening, but I swear I'm not going to treat you the way your ex has."

"He was fine in the beginning too. Then when reality set in it all changed." She folded her arms around her waist, hugging herself tightly. "I can't do it again. I *won't* go through that again."

"Stop." He stepped closer and leaned over the bed until their faces were inches apart. "I don't want you to work yourself up. It's not good for you or the baby. We'll talk about this more later, when you're back on your feet and not lying in that bed looking like you're at death's door, because I have to tell you I feel partly responsible for that look and it's killing me to know that carrying my baby—our baby—has put you through this."

"But—"

"No buts. Just rest. Get better so we can argue later when it won't feel like I'm kicking a sick puppy." He stroked her face with a fingertip, back and forth across her cheek. "I don't like this Jody. I like the one who fights with me. The Jody who doesn't look like she'll fall over if I breathe on her."

Jody didn't want to talk about the baby or the future or them any more than he did, so she changed the subject and felt a slam of guilt for not thinking to ask before now. "Where are Leigh and Amy?"

"Luc has them with him. He and Cassie will keep them overnight, and if they let you go home tomorrow then you can all stay with me or I'll stay with you." He held up a hand. "And don't even think about arguing with me on that one. It's not negotiable. You're going to need someone to take care of you until you get better."

She wasn't stupid enough to open her mouth this time. She'd wait until he went then she'd ring her brother and organize for their mum and dad to have her and the girls at their place until she got her strength back. They'd happily taken them in when she'd separated from Colin and they'd been sad to see them move out into their own place, so Jody was sure her parents would be more than pleased for the three of them to move back in indefinitely.

"What are you smiling about?" Dan asked.

"Was I smiling?"

"Yes. And I know that smile. It's the one you get when you're planning something."

"I have no idea what you mean."

"And why do I not believe that?"

Jody really did smile then. "You've got a suspicious mind?"

"Me? *Ha.* I'm not the one thinking the worst of the other every step of the way." He stood back and crossed his arms over his chest.

Her smile faded. He was right. She thought the worst of him a lot. And if they were having a baby together that had to change. It wasn't fair to him or their baby if she continued to expect him to let her down or turn away. But the lessons of a lifetime were hard to unlearn, and Jody knew there was no way she'd be able to open herself to him. She'd locked a part of her heart away when Colin had sliced into it with his indifference, and she wasn't about to let any other man have the same opportunity to hurt her.

Dan met Luc on the street in front of the hospital. He'd asked him to bring some of Jody's clothes over so she'd have something clean to change into after her shower. They'd seen the doctor this morning and he'd told them Jody could go home this afternoon as long as she kept her breakfast and lunch down. Doctor Moore was more than happy with her progress, which pleased Dan because even though he could see a marked physical difference, having the doctor's reassurance made him breathe easier.

"How is she?" Luc asked as he handed over a backpack.

"Tired still. Grumpy about being here even if it is for just a few more hours and pissed at me for not fighting with her when she's clearly spoiling for one." Dan ran his fingers though his hair.

"And what does she want to fight about other than the fact you got her pregnant?" Luc asked.

"First, *we* got her pregnant. It takes two. And second, she's feeling trapped." Dan shrugged. "Nothing I can do about that. I want to get married, she doesn't. We're at a stalemate."

"You asked her to marry you?"

"Ah, not in so many words…"

"Oh my God. You didn't?" Luc laughed. "You did." His laughter got louder.

Dan crossed his arms and waited him out.

"Sorry." Luc sucked in a breath. "Man, you really fucked that up, didn't you?"

Dan sighed. There was no avoiding it. "Yeah. I might have fudged the delivery of my proposal but my intentions are serious. She thinks it's because of the baby, and she's partially right, but the baby isn't the only reason I want to marry your sister."

"Does she know the other reason?" Luc asked. "Do you?"

"You know I do."

He wasn't about to declare his love for Jody to her brother. No. The first person to hear those words from him would be the woman he'd fallen in love with. Only she wasn't ready to hear them.

"Look, I know I've got some ground work to do and not all of it is to repair the damage I've done. In fact, most of it is because some asshole took her love and her trust and crushed them under his feet as he was walking out the door. Is that fair? Fuck no. But it's the way it is and it's my reality and hers. Now I have to work out how to show her I'm serious and ready to stand beside her every step of the way, so what I need from you is support. As a friend and her brother. Can you do that?" Dan asked.

"All I want is for Jody to be happy. If that's being with you then I'm all for it, but I don't see how I can help you prove you're serious about her. I couldn't convince her not to marry Colin all those years ago, so even if I want her to marry you—which I will admit I'm leaning toward—she isn't going to listen to me sprouting off your virtues."

"Okay, maybe support is the wrong word." Dan scratched his chin. What was he asking Luc for?

"How about I agree to stay out of it?" Luc asked. "I won't offer advice to either of you or interfere."

"Thanks." Dan held out his hand. "I appreciate your understanding. We need to work this out between the two of us."

Luc shook his hand. "I'll be honest and tell you I think you're good for both her and the girls. And you're a thousand times a better man than Colin is or was. As stubborn as my sister is, my money's on you."

Dan smiled. "Let's see if you still think that way in a few weeks." He turned to go but then remembered something he wanted to ask. "Hey, you didn't tell the girls about the baby did you?"

"And risk my sister removing any future chance of me having babies of my own? Not on your life." Luc shuddered.

Dan had to laugh. The idea of this six-foot-five-inch solid wall of muscle being frightened of his much smaller sister was ludicrous. "Good. Although I'm not happy with her decision to keep quiet about the baby, I see her point in not telling anyone until she's further along."

"Me too. But they're asking questions—lots of them—so expect to be subjected to their brand of the Spanish Inquisition the second I bring them home."

"We'll let Jody handle it. I'll let you know when we're back at her place. I'm expecting around five, so if you guys want to stick around we can order pizza for dinner."

"Sounds like a plan. I'll see you then." Luc waved before he headed across the street to where he'd parked.

Dan waited until Luc was out of sight before heading back inside. He'd left Jody's room about thirty minutes ago. She'd been napping on and off all morning, and he wasn't sure how she thought she was going back to work on Monday, but he'd let her think whatever made her happy for now. Cassie had already decided she wasn't going in. Of course, Dan had to be the bearer of that news flash. He figured he'd wait until Sunday night to let that piece of info out.

When he made it back to the room, Jody was out of bed, the IV had been removed and a nurse was helping her get ready to shower.

"Looks like I made it back just in time," he said as he walked over with the bag of clothes. "Here, I got Luc to bring you some clean clothes."

"Really?" Jody's face lit up and the smile that stretched her lips made him smile in return.

"Yep. I didn't check what he brought, but anything would be better than what you came in here wearing yesterday."

"Oh my God, yes. I was contemplating going home in a hospital gown. The idea of re-wearing the clothes I'm sure I wore for three days straight is too repulsive to think about, never mind do."

He leaned over and planted a kiss on her forehead. "Good thing you've got me around to think of these things then, isn't it?"

"I wish my man was so thoughtful," the nurse said. "Come on. Let's get you in the shower so you can go home with that gorgeous man of yours."

Jody frowned but Dan smiled. He couldn't have paid the woman to sing his praises better. Now all he needed was for Jody to see those good points and realize they weren't booby-trapped.

Jody wasn't ready to go home with that gorgeous man of hers. For a start, he wasn't hers. And *he* was the reason she'd ended up in here. Okay, that wasn't fair. If anyone was to blame for this accidental pregnancy, it was her. He'd accepted in good faith that she was safe and look where that had gotten him. A father-to-be. She was the one who'd proven untrustworthy, and yet not once had he uttered a word of blame in her direction.

The nurse made sure she was all right before leaving her in the bathroom to shower. It felt good washing away four days of sweat and sickness. She remembered showering Tuesday night after Dan left, but everything else was a blur except sending the girls off to school on Wednesday morning. Lord knows what they'd been doing while she'd been so sick. Or what they'd been eating. Another wave of guilt swamped her. She'd left the girls to fend for themselves. Anything could have happened to them while she'd been out of it.

She ducked her head under the water to wet her hair then grabbed the little bottle of shampoo the nurse had left her. It didn't smell the best, but anything would be better than the foul odor emanating from her hair right now. Lathering up, she scrubbed at her scalp with her nails before rinsing and repeating. A palm-full of conditioner left her hair silky smooth and she made quick work of washing the rest of her body. She'd been in here a while and the last thing she wanted was for Dan to come in to check on her.

Jody stepped out and used the scratchy hospital towel to dry off then pulled out the clothes Luc had brought over. She was surprised her brother hadn't come in to see her. Then again, he probably didn't want to for fear they'd end up in an argument about being stupid and getting pregnant again. When she'd conceived Leigh he'd been so angry, but that had been nothing compared to when she'd told him she was marrying Colin for the sake of their baby. He'd exploded. They'd had a huge argument and the result had been months of not speaking to each other. Jody could only imagine how pissed off he was that she'd managed to do it again.

Shaking off the memories, she got dressed, gathered her things and left the bathroom. Dan waited in the chair next to the bed. He was flicking through a magazine he'd picked up for her last night. Jody didn't think there was anything appealing in the gossip mag for him to read, but there wasn't anything else for him to do while he waited for her.

He glanced up. "Ready? The nurse dropped off your paperwork." He pointed at the bed.

She picked up the bundle of papers and tucked them into the backpack. "So I'm clear to go then?"

"Yep. We just have to buzz the nurse and she'll bring a wheelchair in."

"A wheelchair? I can walk." The idea of being pushed out of here grated. She wanted to walk out. Probably a trivial thing, but she needed to be in control of something right now.

"You can argue with the nurse over it." Dan leaned over and pressed the call button.

A nurse arrived within a minute, a wheelchair leading the way.

"I'm not getting in that thing." Jody didn't wait for the woman to get all the way in the room before voicing her protest.

"You think you're up to walking out?" the nurse asked.

"Yes."

"Okay, but I'll still have to come down to street level with you. Hospital policy." She pushed the wheelchair off to the corner.

"Let's go then," Jody said.

"In a hurry?" Dan asked.

"Aren't you ready to get out of here? And you didn't even have to stay. You chose to be here overnight." Jody shook her head. She still couldn't believe he'd spent the night in the recliner in her room. And now that she looked at him, she realized he looked a little worse for wear. "You need a shower."

Dan laughed. "Thanks. I'll grab one when we get home."

Her heart skipped a beat. Going home with Dan was the last thing she wanted. She wasn't ready to face the future. The stay in hospital might have been uncomfortable—and annoying—but at least she'd been able to avoid the whole Dan and baby situation to a certain degree.

"C'mon, I thought you wanted out of here?" Dan stood in the doorway, the nurse already out in the hall.

Jody had been too busy thinking about something she had no power of stopping instead of paying attention to what was going on around her. "Sorry. I was just wondering what to cook the girls for dinner," she lied.

"Already sorted. We're ordering pizza when Luc and Cassie drop them off."

He held out his hand, and without thought she closed the distance between them and slid her hand into his, weaving their fingers together instantly. And didn't that say it all about their relationship. When she didn't think, when she went on gut instinct, she walked straight to him. It was only when her brain—her wounded heart—got involved that she ran in the opposite direction out of fear.

20

"**D**an!" West clicked his fingers in front of Dan's face.

"Shit. Sorry. What?" He'd been doing that a lot in the last few weeks. Ever since he'd taken Jody to the hospital, he'd pretty much spent twenty-four hours a day awake.

"You look like crap man. Are you sleeping at all?" West's face creased in concern.

"Yeah, a few hours a night."

"You can't keep this up. Something's got to give."

Dan agreed. "I know, but Jody's barely tolerating me as it is. The only way to get more sleep is to leave her to take care of herself and the girls every night after she's been at work all day. And there's no way I'm doing that."

"Running yourself into the ground won't help anyone either," West protested.

"I know, and I'm working on solving the problem." And he was. It was just taking a lot longer than he thought it would to win Jody over.

"Jody seems to have taken Cassie's change to her hours okay."

Dan laughed. If only. "Ah, yeah, no. I thought Jody was going to pop a blood vessel when Cassie said she was changing her to nine to five, Monday to Friday. Of course, Jody blamed me for that and let me know it."

"Surely she's happier not working weekends. She gets to be at home with her girls. Which reminds me, does anyone know she's pregnant yet?"

Dan had confided in West weeks ago, but other than Cassie and Luc, Jody's pregnancy was still a state secret. He shook his head. "No. She wants to wait until the twelve-week mark to tell Leigh, Amy and her parents. Of course, that means I haven't been able to tell my family either. I'm not looking forward to the ear bashing I'm going to get over that."

"They'll get over it. C'mon, let's get this food loaded so you can get on your way."

Glancing at his watch, Dan saw he'd be late if he didn't get a move on. "Shit. I seem to be constantly running five minutes behind."

West smiled and handed him a cooler box of food. "Better late than never."

"Can't be late. This stuff has to be there by eleven-thirty ready for lunch."

"You've got plenty of time. Traffic isn't bad this time of day. You'll be across town and back again before one." West picked up a crate of drinks.

"I know, but I was hoping to have enough time to duck home to Jody's and check on her before I came back to the warehouse."

"Everything okay? She's not sick again is she?"

"No. She's doing really well actually, but that's what worries me. Yesterday I found her up a ladder dusting the ceiling fans." Dan shook his head. "A picture of her sprawled on the floor flashed in my mind and I yelled at her, which of course made her start and the ladder wobbled...took ten years off my life."

West frowned. "She's pregnant, not a cripple. Surely she's capable of climbing a ladder and cleaning the fans."

Dan slid the cooler into the back of the van with a sigh. "Yeah. She is. It's me that isn't capable of seeing her do it."

"Ah, I see. You need to go home because you're in the dog house again."

"I'm always in the dog house." Dan laughed as he headed back to the kitchen for the second cooler of food. "But I figure if she's seeing me she can't forget about me."

West chuckled. "I doubt that's possible, mate. She's carrying your kid. Kind of hard to forget you when she's feeling sick every day."

One more strike against him as far as Dan was concerned. Jody had told him she'd breezed through her other pregnancies without so much as an up-chuck. His baby, however, was determined to make his mother throw up every damn day. At least she was only sick first thing in the morning now. And once that initial wave of nausea passed, it was smooth sailing for the rest of the day.

"Not exactly an endearing effect though," Dan said.

"No. I guess not." West grabbed the second crate of drinks while Dan picked up the cooler. "But look on the bright side."

"There's a bright side?" Dan arched an eyebrow.

"Hell yes. You're gonna be a dad."

Dan grinned. "Yeah, that is definitely one of the highlights of this whole thing."

"One of?"

"Being connected to Jody for the rest of my life is another. And Leigh and Amy. They're a bright spot in all this."

"I can't believe they haven't worked out their mother is having a baby."

Dan frowned when he remembered the conversation he'd had with Leigh yesterday. "I think Leigh is suspicious, but she hasn't outright asked me or her mother yet. She's a smart kid. I think she's biding her time. I just hope Jody's the one she asks and not me. I won't lie to her if she asks me directly if her mother is pregnant."

"I'll cross my fingers for you."

They loaded the rest of the food and beverages without further conversation, and Dan was soon moving through the congested streets of Sydney's CBD. He parked in the loading zone outside the office building where Maggie was running today's corporate event.

She met him in the lobby with a couple of guys she'd roped into helping and Dan didn't even have to leave street level to deliver lunch, which meant he was back on the road and heading for Jody's with plenty of time to spare before his job this afternoon.

He glanced at the dashboard clock and figured they wouldn't have had lunch yet. Dan pulled over and reached for his phone. He'd give Jody a call and see if she was okay with him picking up something. Leigh answered on the fifth ring. "Hey, Leigh, where's your mum?"

"Outside in the garden with Amy. They're trying to grow herbs or something." Dan could image her rolling her eyes.

Dan smiled. They'd picked up the seeds and pots for Amy's herb garden last weekend and he was happy to know Jody was up to helping her daughter plant the seeds. "Okay, tell her I'm on my way through from one job to another and I'll drop off some chicken and salads for lunch. Sound good?"

"Yes. I was just looking at the fridge thinking we need to go shopping again."

"We can do that tomorrow. Do me a favor and write a list for me."

"Sure. See you soon."

Dan hung up then pulled back into traffic. He'd stop at the little shopping center near his place for the charcoal chicken. The place near Jody's wasn't nearly as nice and often didn't have a good selection of salads on hand. Distracted by his thoughts, Dan didn't see the truck speed through the red light until it was too late. Squealing tires and shattering glass filled the air just before the airbag exploded in his face and everything went black.

Jody fumed as she paced the kitchen. She should have known she couldn't trust him. Except he'd been so attentive in the two months since she'd been admitted to hospital that she'd softened. He'd been so good with her and the girls that she'd looked forward to his visits—to his care. Still, she should have known better than to get sucked in by his kindness. Dan couldn't be trusted any more than Colin could.

It had been three hours since he'd called Leigh and told her he was bringing lunch, and he wasn't answering his phone so Jody couldn't even give him a piece of her mind. The doorbell rang and she hoped it was him with some flimsy excuse so she could slam the door in his face without a word. She stormed down the hallway and flung the door open to find Luc and Cassie on her doorstep.

"Oh, hey, I wasn't expecting you guys." Jody moved out of the way to let them in. "Come in."

"Thanks, but I can't stay, I'm just dropping Luc off," Cassie said.

"Huh?" Confused, Jody studied them more closely and the look on Luc's face registered. Narrowing her eyes as she moved in front of her brother she said, "What's going on?"

"Let's go sit down."

"No." Jody knew this wasn't going to be good. "Whatever it is, just tell me."

"Jody."

"Don't you Jody me. Tell me, Lucas. Now." She crossed her arms and barred the entry. Not that she'd be a barrier to him if he really wanted to get in.

"It's about Dan."

Jody held up her hand. "I don't want to even hear his name. He's proven I was right and shouldn't have trusted him."

"What the hell are you talking about?" Luc asked as he pushed his way into the house, Cassie following behind.

"I thought you were just dropping him off?" Jody looked at Cassie.

"I was, but I don't think I want to miss this. Why are you mad with Dan now?"

"Mad? I'm not mad, I'm furious. He comes here and takes over, does things, looks after us and makes it easy for us to rely on him—to care about him. Then he just doesn't show up. Says he will but doesn't. And he's not answering his damn phone or I'd tell him to never step foot in my house again." Jody couldn't believe how angry she was. She'd never gotten this upset when Colin let her down. Never felt this gut-deep burn of rage.

"Jody." Luc grabbed her shoulders and held her still. "Dan's been in an accident."

Cold settled over her. It started at her head and sank lower as though she was diving into a pool of liquid nitrogen headfirst in slow motion until every inch of her between scalp and toenails was frozen solid. "Accident?"

Luc nodded. "He was hit by a truck."

Bile rose in her throat. "Oh God." Jody slapped a hand over her mouth and ran for the bathroom.

The cheese toast she'd eaten not thirty minutes ago hit the toilet bowl as Cassie slipped into the bathroom behind her.

"Go away."

"Not on your life, Jody."

Water ran then Cassie was pressing a wet towel to Jody's forehead and pushing her hair off her face. She wanted to push Cassie away but the cool cloth felt wonderful against her hot, sweaty face. "How bad?" Jody got the question out around another wave of heaving.

"He's okay. Wait until your stomach settles and then we'll talk."

Jody cried then. Big fat horrible body jerking sobs. Cassie waited through a few before wrapping an arm around her waist. "C'mon, I think you've finished being sick. Luc!"

"No." Too late. Jody found herself being lifted against her brother's chest.

He carried her out to the lounge room where the girls were waiting, huddled together on the couch. "Leigh, can you go grab your mum a glass of water, please?" Luc asked as he sat down with Jody in his lap.

"Is Dan going to be okay?" Amy asked.

"Yes, sweetie. He's got a concussion, a couple of bruised ribs and some minor cuts, but other than that he's fine," Cassie explained.

"Fine? That doesn't sound fine." Jody pushed out of Luc's arms. "Let me go. I have to go see him."

"Hang on." Luc held her tight. "I'll drive you to him in a minute, but first calm down."

"I don't want to calm down until I see for myself that he's okay." She yanked out of her brother's hold and headed for the kitchen and her car keys.

"Jody." Cassie stepped in her way. "Wait."

"Why?"

"Because you need to think about this."

"Think about what? Dan's hurt and I need to go to him."

"Why?"

Why? "Because he's hurt, that's why."

"And?"

"And? And? And I have to see he's okay." Why was Cassie trying to stop her? Jody had no clue what her boss was getting at and really didn't care. She brushed past her and ran to the kitchen.

"Stop!" When Jody turned around Luc stood in the doorway. "Why are you racing off to a man you were angry at only minutes ago?"

"Angry?" Why was she mad at Dan? "I don't know what..." But she did know what Luc was talking about. Dan hadn't shown up with lunch and she'd put him right in the untrustworthy box beside Colin. Jody hung her head forward on a groan.

Luc's shoes came into view just as he tipped her chin up with his hand. "Why are you racing off to check on Dan?"

Jody met his gaze and her eyes blurred. She'd been an emotional wreck the last few weeks because of the pregnancy hormones, so the urge to cry didn't surprise her, it was the reason she wanted to cry that did. Oh God. She was in love with Dan. Even with all the barriers she'd thrown up, with all the lectures and reminders of what had happened last time she'd agreed to be with the father of her unplanned baby, she'd still opened herself up in a way that could tear her apart if it went wrong. It would destroy her if Dan walked away.

Luc pulled her into his arms and held her against his chest. "Let it out, Budgie."

The childhood nickname worked like a switch. She cried into

Luc's shirt until her eyes were dry and her throat sore. And still she stayed in the safety of his arms for a few more minutes. Pulling away, she snagged a handful of tissues from the box on the kitchen counter and dried her face. "What am I going to do now?"

"I'm thinking that was meant as a rhetorical question, but I'm going to answer it anyway." Luc turned her around to face him. "Marry him."

"What?" Jody's mouth dropped open.

"He's the best damn thing to happen to you in forever, Jody. Even mad at him and fighting, you're the happiest I've seen you in years. And the girls are thriving. If you're not ready for marriage then at least let the guy in here." Luc tapped her chest. "Try to make it work because it's obvious to everyone but you that you're in love with each other."

"What?" Jody couldn't get over the fact her brother was telling her to get married this time. "But last time this happened you tried to talk me out of getting married."

"Because Colin was and is a loser who never deserved you."

"Oh."

"I know you're still carrying the scars from your first marriage. And I know the idea of going through that again terrifies you. But, Jody, this is Dan. You said it yourself earlier. He's been here every day. He's taken care of you and the girls, and if you're honest you'll admit he was doing it before you found out you were pregnant."

Jody nodded. Luc was right. Dan had been there for her when Colin had shown up all enraged about her and the girls moving on with their lives. She closed her eyes and sighed. She'd been so wrong to expect Dan to behave the same as Colin. To watch for every little sign that he would treat her badly. Her fear of being hurt again had blinded her to the good man Dan was, and she'd be lucky if he forgave her for the slight she'd shown him.

She opened her eyes and stared at her brother. "Take me to see him."

Luc smiled. "That's my girl."

"Is he really okay?"

"Yes. The airbag knocked him out for a few seconds and he's got bruises from the seatbelt and steering wheel, a couple of minor scratches from flying glass. Nothing major at all," Luc reassured her.

"Why didn't he ring me?" Did Dan think she wouldn't want to know he was hurt?

"His phone is trashed. A bystander called Are You Game? to let them know the van had been in an accident, which is how Cassie found out. She rang me because she thought you'd want to hear it from me in person instead of over the phone."

Jody smiled. "Thank you, for that and putting up with the crazy pregnant woman."

"Hey, it's easy when you're crazy all the time." Luc grinned and ducked out of the way of Jody's fist.

"Smartass." She poked her tongue out. Turning around, she located her handbag on the counter and grabbed the handles. "Can we go now?"

"Sure. But you might want to put some clothes on."

Jody glanced down at her pajamas and groaned. Not only had she not dressed this morning, but her top and pants were smeared with dirt from when she'd helped Amy pot her herb seeds earlier. "Give me five minutes to change."

"Don't rush. I'll get the girls ready to go while you change." Luc called after her as she made a dash for her bedroom.

Jody made it back to the living room in three and a half minutes to find Luc waiting for her. "Where's Cassie and the girls?" she asked as she slipped her feet into her sneakers.

"Cassie took them to work with her. She said she's giving them a crash course in event management."

Jody's gaze darted up to meet Luc's. "What?"

"I'm kidding. I think she's making a cake or something for tomorrow's baby shower. She said the girls can hang with her until you find out if Dan has to stay in overnight or not."

She sucked in a breath. "You said he was okay."

"Relax." Luc placed his hand on her back and steered her to the front door. "It's just a concussion. You know how careful they like to be with head injuries no matter how minor."

As far as Jody was concerned, no head injury was minor. A ball of lead sat on her chest and her tummy started churning. God, she hoped she didn't throw up again. She was getting tired of living in the bathroom with her head in the toilet. Mind you, she'd rather be making a dash to the loo instead of one to the hospital.

21

D an sat up in bed and cursed the idiot who'd phoned his mother. "I'm fine, Ma." Then he cursed himself for still having her listed as his emergency contact.

"You don't look fine." She leaned over and poked at the bandage near his temple.

"Shit! Keep doing that and I won't be fine." He batted her hand away.

"Daniel O'Conner. Language."

He rolled his eyes. "Why don't you get Reagan to take you home now? You don't need to be here and you've seen that I'm okay." Dan turned his gaze to his sister, pleading with his eyes to get her to take their mother out of here before Jody showed up.

"C'mon, Mum. We can't do anything for him and you've already spoke to the doctor and know his injuries aren't life threatening." Reagan placed her hand on their mother's arm. "Besides, you know as well as I do that Dan has the hardest head in the world."

"Who's going to watch him for complications? He lives alone. He could die in his sleep," Ma argued.

The gasp from the doorway had all three of them turning in that direction.

"D-die? But they said..."

Shit. Jody and Luc stood just inside the room. "Jody." Dan held out his hand. "My mother is exaggerating as usual. I'm not going to die."

To his surprise, she came forward and took his hand. He'd expected to have to coax her into the room.

"You're really okay?" she asked as she wove their fingers together and squeezed them in a death grip.

Dan gave her hand a gentle squeeze in return and tugged her closer. "I'm fine. One more set of observations and they're letting me out of here."

"Really?" she murmured, her voice shaky with uncertainty.

He smiled at her. "Honest. I tried to ring you, but my phone got broken in the crash and I couldn't remember your number."

She brushed his hair away from his bandaged head. "Does it hurt?"

"No. The headache is gone and the pain in my ribs is bearable."

"Ahem."

Dan's gaze darted to his mother. Shit. "Um, Jody, this is my mother and sister, Susan and Reagan O'Conner."

Jody turned with a smile. "Hello. I wish we were meeting under better circumstances." She let go of his hand to offer it first to his mother and then his sister.

Dan avoided his mother's questioning look. A complete change of subject was in order. "Hey, Luc, how's the van?"

"Totaled according to the tow-truck driver, but Cassie said she'll wait until the insurance assessor takes a look. She's organized a rental for Monday."

"You wrecked the van?" Jody asked turning back and taking his hand again.

"No. The idiot who ran a red light wrecked the van."

"You're lucky a few bruises and a concussion is all you got." She stroked her fingers through his hair and he closed his eyes.

"That's what the policemen, the paramedics, the nurses *and* the doctor said."

"Are you supposed to go to sleep with a concussion?" Reagan asked.

Dan opened his eyes. "I'm not sleeping, I'm resting. Doctor's orders. So you can all leave now." He pointed at Jody as he pulled her right up to the side of his bed. "You stay."

"Dan," Jody gasped.

"What? I'm grumpy and all I could think about was not being able to tell you I was going to be late and knowing you were going to get angry with me when I didn't show up with lunch." He used the hand he held to pull her closer until her face was near his. "Kiss me so I know I'm not having a drugged-up dream. Remind me I'm the luck-iest man alive to walk away from that crash with nothing but bruises."

Her eyes darted to the side and he realized no one had left. But Dan didn't care who saw. He was done pretending he didn't love her. Wrapping a hand around her neck, he tugged her down the last few inches and pressed his mouth to hers.

He forgot about everyone else. Nothing mattered except Jody and the way she surrendered to his kiss. Her lips were soft and warm and such a welcome touch. Their tongues tangled and their breath mingled and a part of Dan that had been wound tight since the acci-dent unfurled. He'd thought of nothing but her since he'd regained consciousness sitting in the mangled wreck, the airbag deflating around him.

Dan pulled back, separated their mouths and leaned his forehead against hers. "No more. I can't fight this anymore, Jody. I want to marry you, and not because of the baby. I want to spend my life with you because you're the light in my days and the dark in my nights. You're everything I never dreamed I wanted and I can't take another day—another minute—without knowing you're mine."

"Dan." She breathed his name against his lips and the tightness in his chest eased.

"You. The girls. The baby. Are my life. My future. And I want it to start now." He locked his gaze to hers. "I love you, Jody Walsh. Marry me."

J ody couldn't believe he'd blurted all that out in front of everyone. But she couldn't worry about it now. Not when he was kissing her again. Kissing her like she was the breath that would save his life. She lost herself then. Lost herself in him. Lost every last shred of wall between her and this man. He'd said he loved her. She'd thought—hoped—his feelings ran deep, knew hers did, but she'd never once believed it was possible to love this completely.

A clearing throat pulled them apart, but Dan didn't let her go far. He tugged until she sat on the edge of his bed. Jody turned to find a very familiar man in a white coat standing before them.

"Hi, Doctor Moore." Jody smiled at the man who'd treated her weeks ago.

"Well, I must say it's a pleasure to see you up and about. Can't say the same for your young man though." The doctor tipped his chin in Dan's direction. "I could have done without seeing him come in on a stretcher."

She shuddered. "I glad I didn't see that."

"So how are you feeling now? Keeping things down?" he asked as he picked up the chart from the end of Dan's bed.

"Yes. Things are going well and my doctor has scheduled those tests you requested."

"Good. Well, let's get to today's patient shall we?" Doctor Moore walked around the other side of the bed and checked Dan's pulse. One by one, he made his way through blood pressure, temperature and a quick listen to Dan's chest. "Well, young man, you're free to go home as long as you have someone who can be with you for the next twenty-four hours."

"I do."

"He does."

Dan and Jody spoke at once, drawing a chuckle for the older man.

"All right then, you can leave whenever you're ready, no paperwork as you weren't admitted." Doctor Moore pulled a card from his pocket and handed it to Jody. "Ring me if you're worried, but I doubt there'll be any problems. And I don't want to see either of you again until it's time to deliver that baby."

There was a split second of stunned silence before Dan's mother exploded with the kind of lecture only a mother can give. Jody tried to interrupt but the woman was a force she had no hope of stopping. In the end, Dan had to lean over and cover her mouth with his hand.

"Be quiet and listen for a minute." Dan indicated Jody should say what she had to.

"Please don't blame Dan for not telling you. I asked that he keep things between us until the twelve-week mark. I have two other children and I wanted to be sure everything was okay before I upset their world by telling them about the baby." It wasn't a complete lie, but Jody didn't think telling the truth would make a good first impression.

"You have other children?" Susan asked.

"Yes, two girls, they're thirteen and fifteen."

"And you are going to marry my Daniel, yes?"

It suddenly dawned on her that she'd never answered him. Spinning around she met his gaze. "Yes. Yes, I'll marry you."

He grinned then pulled her in for a kiss.

"Right, where are these granddaughters of mine?" Dan's mother brought them back to the here and now.

"They're with my brother's girlfriend, Cassie," Jody said a little breathlessly.

"You work with Dan?"

"Yes. And Cassie is dating my brother, Luc." Jody pointed to Luc leaning against the wall in the corner of the room.

"When can I meet them?"

"Ma, c'mon, give us a minute, would you?"

Jody watched mother and son stare each other down until Dan's sister stepped in and ushered their mother from the room with a promised return in five minutes. Luc pushed off the wall and walked to the door where he kicked the doorstop out of the way.

"I'll wait out here and hold her off as long as I can." He waved his phone. "I've got pictures of Leigh and Amy I can bribe her with."

The door whooshed close and Jody breathed out with a rush. "Oh my God. Did I really just meet your mother?"

"Yep. Now come here and kiss me again. Actually, better yet, use those lips for something else. Say it." Dan held her face in his hands. "I need to hear you say it."

She knew what he wanted. He'd told her, but she hadn't said the words yet, not to anyone but herself. She wasn't sure if she could, but for him—for them—she'd force aside the fear that was still an automatic reaction. "First, I need to say I'm sorry. For everything I've put us through but mostly to you for what I've made you put up with."

"Hey, Ma always says nothing worth having is easy. And you—" he tapped her nose with his thumb "—are the least easy person I know. And you're worth every painful second of it." His smile softened the blow of his words.

Jody smiled in return. "I love you," she whispered before pressing her lips to his.

Dan leaned back. "Again."

"I love you."

"Good, because I plan to love you for the rest of my life." He kissed her this time. Only he didn't keep it light. He took them deep. Fast. And it wasn't until his mother cleared her throat from the doorway that they came up for air with matching grins on their faces.

"Enough for now, I want to meet these granddaughters I plan to spoil." Suzan O'Conner spun around and disappeared out of sight.

Reagan stuck her head in the door. "I'll detour as much as I can, but you better give me an address of where she can meet those two beautiful girls we just saw on your brother's phone or Dan will need more than a few Band-Aids and rest to recover."

"What? Tonight?" Jody squeaked.

"Yeah, there's no stopping her when she's on a tear, and she's definitely on one," Reagan looked to the side. "Yes, I'm coming."

Dan laughed. "My place at six for dinner."

"See you then, big brother." Reagan disappeared.

"I think we better get going. We've got lots to do before my mother turns up and lets the cat out of the bag about the baby."

"Oh no. I didn't want to tell the girls yet."

"It'll be fine. Besides, you know you were keeping it a secret as much to keep me at a distance as to protect them."

Dan helped her off the bed and stood. Jody turned and was struck speechless by his state. "Oh my God. Look at you." His clothes were torn in several places and splattered with blood in others.

He shrugged. "Not much I can do about them until we get home."

Jody liked the way he put home and we together. It had been a long time since she'd thought in terms of home as anything except her, Leigh and Amy. Now, the thought of home brought images of Dan to mind.

She put her hand in his and pulled him toward the door. "C'mon, let's go home."

EPILOGUE

"**D**on't you dare lift that!" Dan yelled as he walked into the bedroom and saw Jody attempting to put her suitcase on the bed.

"It's not that heavy," she protested as she heaved it off the floor a couple of inches.

He raced over and replaced her hand with his and swung the bag up on the mattress. "There. Next time just ask."

She pouted. "But you were busy with the girls."

"I'm always busy with the girls. They find something they want me to do every other second." Not that he was upset by their constant need for his attention. In fact, he loved it.

"You shouldn't have told them they could do whatever they wanted in the house then," Jody said as she unzipped the bag and threw open the top.

"I want them to feel at home as soon as possible. I want you all to feel that way." He wrapped his arms around her thickened waist and splayed his hands over her protruding belly. "Is he moving?"

"*She* is asleep. For now." Dan could hear the smile in her voice.

They'd decided not to find out the sex of the baby, but each of them had their own thoughts on what was growing inside Jody's rounded stomach. "I love touching you like this."

"You just like touching me." She laughed.

"Well, yeah, I am a guy. But like this." He smoothed his hands over her curves. "It brings a lump to my throat and tears to my eyes. There's a part of you and me growing in here."

"Don't I know it." Jody cupped her hands over his and moved them lower. "She's kicking."

"I'll never get over how amazing that is."

He followed the movement with his fingertips. Their baby was so tiny. With less than three weeks to go, he worried their child wouldn't be big enough to survive. It didn't matter how many times the doctors told him everything was progressing normally, he wouldn't believe it until this little person was in his arms and breathing. Jody's stomach tensed beneath his hands.

"Whoa. What was that?" Dan's own stomach tightened.

"Mmm..." She leaned back against him and hummed out a breath.

"Jody?"

She dug her nails into his forearms as she hissed out a breath.

"Jody?" She had him worried now.

"Can you ring whoever drew the short straw for coming to sit with the girls while we're at the hospital?" She let go and stepped from his arms like she was doing nothing more than getting a drink of water.

"It's time?" Did his voice just go up two octaves? "It can't be time."

"Babies always have their own timetable. Ours has chosen today."

"But..." He watched as she pulled some things from her suitcase and piled them on the bed. Why was she unpacking now? "What are you doing? We have to go."

Dan wasn't proud to say he was beginning to panic. What if she had the baby before they made it to the hospital? He moved next to her and grabbed her hand.

"Jody. Talk to me. I'm freaking out here."

She patted his cheek. "Relax, these things take a whil—" The word was cut off by a gasp and she doubled over just as water splashed over his bare feet.

"Fuck."

"Okay," she panted. "Maybe this won't take so long after all." She gripped his arm and dug her nails in so hard he had to clench his jaw to keep a cry of pain from escaping.

"Leigh! Amy!" he yelled.

Both girls came running and skidded to a stop in the doorway.

"Get the phone. Call 000," he ordered as another pain ripped through Jody.

"Is Mum having the baby now?" Leigh asked. "She can't have it now. It's not time."

"Try telling him that."

"Her," Jody got out through gritted teeth.

Dan eased her toward the bed.

"No. Not on the bed. I don't want to ruin the bedding or mattress."

"Screw that." Dan scooped her up into his arms and placed her on the bed. "We'll buy new ones if we have to."

"Dan." She grabbed his arm. "This is happening too fast. We aren't going to make it to the hospital."

"Clearly."

"Ring doctor—argh..." Jody gripped her stomach and groaned through the next contraction.

"How close are they? I haven't been keeping track." Dan glanced at the alarm clock, noting the time. "Where's the phone?"

"They're on the way," Leigh said.

Dan turned to see his stepdaughter with the phone to her ear.

"The lady wants to know how close the contractions are."

Dan looked back at Jody just as another pain gripped her midsection. "Shit. Less than a minute."

Leigh relayed the information and then disappeared down the hall calling out, "I'll get Amy to direct them in."

The next few minutes were a blur of Jody's pain and Dan's panic. When the paramedics rushed into the room, Dan wasn't sure which one of them breathed the bigger sigh of relief. It didn't take them long to determine the baby wasn't waiting for a trip to the hospital to enter the world. He followed directions. Tried to remember the breathing from class but he couldn't, and when one of the paramedics said the baby was crowning, his whole existence boiled down to this monumental moment.

Leigh and Amy hovered near the door and he wondered if he should shoo them away or urge them closer. He sat on the bed behind Jody, propping her up so that she could concentrate on bringing their child into the world. And with the very next contraction, she did.

The hearty wail of a newborn filled the room and tears slid down Dan's face. It didn't matter what they had as long as the baby was healthy and his wife of three months didn't kill him for making her go through this. His world was complete.

"It's a boy. Here you go, Mum and Dad."

The paramedic passed the slippery bundle of squirming arms and legs. For a second, Dan's heart stopped. But he wasn't about to miss this catch. And with his son firmly in his and Jody's grasp, he placed a kiss on his wife's head.

RED LIGHT, GREEN LIGHT

ARE YOU GAME? BOOK 3

DEDICATION

For those of us with fond memories of childhood games.
And for Mr. Summers for his advice and Eden Summers for asking.

1

West's gaze connected with the woman across the room for what seemed like the millionth time in the last hour. Since he'd arrived, she'd avoided him with everything except those mesmerizing eyes of hers. It wasn't the first time they'd played this game. Only lately, he'd grown tired of playing—their constant game of red light, green light felt anything but fun. Especially when the light was red more than it was green.

He'd walked away from her once. Young and stupid, he hadn't really thought about what he was giving up when he didn't make a move beyond their one night. And by the time he *had* figured it out, he was too late. She was dating someone else. That was one mistake he didn't need to repeat to learn from.

"Shit, man. Tell me you are not seriously thinking of going there?" His best friend elbowed him in the ribs.

Bringing his beer to his mouth, West took a sip—his eyes still locked on Kelsey—before he turned to face Zac. "Going where?" He'd play dumb if he had to.

Zac arched one eyebrow. "Dude. I know that look. It says, 'I wanna fuck you'."

West grinned. "Thanks, but no thanks. You know I don't swing that way."

"Fuck off." Zac elbowed him again, this time with a little more force. "You know I'm talking about Kelsey. You don't wanna go there."

Too late. Been there, done that. Should never have moved on.

But West wasn't about to tell his best friend that train had already departed. Ten years ago. Turning back to look at Kels, West caught her eye once more and sent her a wink.

"Shit. She's giving you the look now." Zac took a swig of his beer and choked. "Fuck." He wiped his mouth with the back of his hand. "That's not the I-want-to-do-you look. That's the I've-done-you-and-I-want-to-do-you-again look." Zac rounded on him and got in his face. "What the fuck, West?"

Crap. West took another sip of beer as he turned away from the woman of his dreams to lean his elbows on the bar. He had to be careful. Too many words would reveal something he didn't want anyone, including his best friend, to know. Too little would prompt questions he had no intention of answering. "What? She's hot. I'm not dead and it's not like there's a law against looking." He shrugged and tried to portray a nonchalant attitude when he felt anything but indifferent when it came to Kelsey.

"Yes, there is." Zac got right in his face again. "She was married to Bry."

"*Was* being the operative word." And West didn't need to be reminded. He'd spent three years of his life living that particular nightmare. Not to mention the three Kelsey had dated Bryan before becoming Mrs. Newman.

"Jesus. Are you for real?" Zac glanced around before lowering his voice. "You've already gone there, haven't you? Are you the reason she filed for divorce?"

Shit. He wished. No, Kels and Bry had done that all on their own without outside help. And from what Kelsey had told him—and what seemed to be common opinion among their group—it had been a long time coming. West was the first to acknowledge they never should have gotten married. Not when he knew Bry didn't want

Kelsey the way he did. No one could want her on the level West did. His bones ached he wanted her so badly. Of course, he'd had her.

Once.

Okay, more than once, but it had only been one night. One night of absolute pleasure his body had spent the last ten years craving a repeat of. He shook his head clear of memories that had the power to bring him to his knees and focused on the present.

"C'mon, Zac, you have to admit she's smokin'." West took another swig of beer.

"Sure. But which one of our group isn't? Every woman we went to school with is hot enough to melt the South Pole. Must have been something in the water that year." Zac grinned and West joined him, hoping he was pulling off the blasé attitude of a guy checking out a passing woman.

Heat and movement behind him had West glancing over his shoulder then jack-knifing upright and around, tightening his fingers on the bottle in his hand.

Kelsey.

"Hey, Kels, how ya doing?" West played it cool like he always did when he was around this woman.

"Good." She smiled and West's insides clenched, his pulse racing with heated blood.

He'd had those lips wrapped around his cock. Knew how hot and wet her mouth was. How hard she could suck.

"Thanks for helping me move my stuff the other day."

Her words brought him out of the past and back to the crowded bar. "Oh, right. No worries. Any time."

He was conscious of Zac standing statue-still beside him. Silence settled between the three of them and West knew he needed to say something to break the tension before the moment turned awkward. His gaze landed on Kelsey's empty wine glass and he latched on to the diversion. "You want another drink?"

Kels looked at the glass in her hand and shook her head. "No, I've already had too many. I'm going to have to leave my car in town as it is, don't need a hangover tomorrow to add to the inconvenience."

West put his bottle on the bar behind him. "I'll drive your car home if you want. I've only had one and I caught a ride in with Zac." He took the glass from her hand. "Consider me your designated driver."

"Really? That would be great. I've got an early class tomorrow so I was going to have to get a cab back into town at some ungodly hour." She smiled up at him and West's insides did that whole clenching thing again. Only this time, his groin tightened to the point of pain.

"You still teaching those community-college classes?" Zac asked. It was the first words he'd spoken since Kels had come over and West had pretty much forgotten he was there.

"Yeah. Tomorrow is budgets for the elderly. I think the youngest member of class is sixty-five." She smiled.

Kels had been working at their local community college since the day she'd received her accounting degree. She did it for free, and West knew it had been a bone of contention between her and Bry their whole married life. He was glad she hadn't bowed to Bry's demands to either be paid or stop giving the classes. Another reason he'd known the two of them were wrong for each other. Bry just didn't get Kelsey's need to help those without the means to help themselves.

"Oh, there's Coop. I wanna catch him before he leaves." Zac was gone before either of them could say a word.

"Did I scare him off?" Kels asked.

"No. He was a little uncomfortable with our exchange of glances earlier." West shrugged. "Not our problem."

"Did he say anything?" Anxiety pinched her mouth and turned her blue eyes a shade darker than normal.

"Nothing you should be worried about."

She narrowed her eyes at him.

"Honest, Kels, its fine." He brushed his hand against the back of hers.

Kelsey jerked away and, eyes wide, glanced either side of them to see if anyone had noticed the intimate caress. "Um, I'd like to get out of here early, if that's okay? Would you mind leaving in about thirty minutes? If not, I can go back to my original plan and get a cab home."

West sighed. Just like that, they were back on the friend's side of the fence. He couldn't count the number of times they'd skirted the line of friendship in the last three years. He'd hoped to be closer to her by now. Hoped they'd have found a way to cross the line from friends to lovers now that she was free. "Whenever you're ready to go," he said with a tight smile.

She returned his smile with one that didn't quite reach her eyes. He hated that smile. It was the one she used when she was trying to pretend everything was okay when it wasn't. He'd seen that facade far too many times in the past and he couldn't stand to see it right now. Not aimed at him.

"I'm gonna go sit with the guys." West indicated the table where Zac had run off to. "Come get me when you're ready to leave."

West didn't run, but he may as well have. He needed to think. Kelsey had been the girl he'd lost his virginity with. The one he'd let walk away and hook up with a friend. He'd wanted her to be happy and thought Bry might be able to do that. Except Bry hadn't, and West had spent ten years of his life sitting on the sidelines while the woman he loved wasn't really happy. It'd cut him to the core to stand back and do nothing. It still did. But he was done with the sideline.

He glanced back in Kelsey's direction. He was getting in the game.

West wasn't sure how or when he made the decision, but he was going after Kels and was prepared to break every friend code there was to claim her as his.

———————————

Kelsey leaned her forehead against the stall door as she turned the latch. It was getting harder and harder to control her reactions around West. She'd snuck away from the group to hide out in the bathroom for a much needed breather. He didn't need to touch her to get her motor revving. Just one look from those stormy-gray eyes sent her pulse racing and her nerves into a frenzy. But the second he'd run his fingers over her skin... God, she'd almost melted at his feet.

The outer door opened and voices echoed as heels clicked over the tiled floor. She straightened and stepped back, glancing over her shoulder to check the toilet lid was closed before taking a seat. Leaning her elbows on her knees and propping her head in her hands, she stared at the floor.

What the hell was she going to do about West? They couldn't keep this up. *She* couldn't keep it up. At some point, she'd break, and as much as she wanted to cross that line with him, she equally feared it.

She'd tangled herself up with West before and all she'd gotten was a night of unforgettable pleasure and a broken heart. It had taken her a year to get over West's rejection. They'd never discussed what had happened between them. Not once in all the years since had he brought it up. Then again, neither had she. And yet their sizzling chemistry had continued to bubble beneath the surface of their platonic friendship even during her ill-fated marriage to one of his best friends.

She groaned. God she'd made a mess of her and Bry's marriage. She'd loved Bryan. Still loved him. But not the way a wife should. Not with everything she was. How could she when she'd given a huge piece of her heart to the boy she'd given her virginity to? If she were honest—and she should be, at least with herself—West had owned her heart long before they'd made their pact to divest each other of their virginity.

Kelsey had no one to blame but herself for the hurt she'd suffered afterwards. She'd gone into that night with her eyes wide open, but like every other teenage girl with stars in her eyes and dreams in her heart, she'd thought loving him physically would unlock his heart and he wouldn't be able to live another day without her. She shook her head at how naive she'd been. How she'd allowed visions of fairy-tale-style happy ever after to cloud her mind and render her defense-less—vulnerable.

After their night, West had ignored her to the point that Kelsey had thought she'd done something wrong—something to turn him off. For months, she'd gone over and over every second she'd spent in his arms until she'd come to the only conclusion she could. He didn't want *her*. It wasn't as though he'd jumped straight from her bed to someone else's. He'd been without a significant other until long after she'd begun dating Bry. Not that she'd really seen much of West in the year following their one night.

They'd both been busy with university and work. Kelsey knew she'd avoided more than one event West had been at because seeing him and not being able to touch him had cut so deep she'd struggled to keep tears at bay. She'd skipped out early on a lot of their friends' birthdays in those first few months.

"Hey." The door rattled as someone thumped on the other side. "You about done in there?"

"Give me a sec," Kelsey called out as she pushed to her feet. She turned around and flushed the toilet even though she hadn't used it. Unlocking the door, she kept her gaze lowered and made her way to the sink where two women were in the middle of a whispered discussion.

Kelsey froze when she overheard Zac's name, but when she tried to inch a little closer to hear more clearly, they turned her way. She quickly leaned towards the mirror and fluffed her hair, pretending she was oblivious to them and what they were saying. Getting caught eavesdropping on what was intended to be a private conversation wouldn't be the best of circumstances. When the woman closest to her stepped in her direction, Kelsey figured she'd managed to put herself in that exact situation.

"Oh, hey. Don't you hang out with Zachary Moreland and that group of hunks?" the woman asked.

Kelsey turned and had to stifle a gasp. Had she thought they were women? Neither of them could be a day over nineteen. They had to be at least eighteen to get into the bar, but Kelsey had a suspicion they'd barely scraped past that milestone. "Um, which guys?" Stalling seemed to be her best option.

"The one's hanging out in the back of the bar. I saw you talking with Zachary and another one earlier." Blondie nudged her equally blonde friend. "You did too, right?"

Kelsey sighed. If she had a dollar for every time some strange female asked her about one of the guys, she'd be richer than Midas. "Yeah, I know them." She turned to leave.

"Could you introduce us?"

Kelsey's eyes popped wide and her mouth dropped open as she spun back towards the teenagers. Well, that was a first. No one had been brave enough to ask for an introduction before. "I don't think so. For a start, I don't even know who you are."

"I'm Candy—" the blonde who'd done all the talking so far waved at her friend, "—and this is Missy."

What kind of names were those? Kelsey shook her head. "Sorry. No can do."

Before either of them could say another word, Kelsey strode around them and out the door. She'd taken no more than five steps along the dark hallway when a large shadow pushed off the wall into her path. A shaft of fear shot up her spine before she recognized West.

"Oh, it's you." She placed a hand on her chest over her thumping heart.

"Hey, you okay?" He stepped in front of her, the tips of his shoes bare inches from hers. "You were in there a long time."

West was right. She had been in there a while, and Kelsey shouldn't be surprised that he'd come to check on her. Regardless of their strained friendship, he'd always watched out for her. Then again, maybe it was just her who felt the tension between them. "I'm fine."

"You sure? We can head out now if you're feeling under the weather." He bent forward so he could look directly into her eyes.

Kelsey smiled. "Is that a polite way of asking if I've had too much to drink?" She and every one of her friends knew she was a light-weight when it came to alcohol.

West moved closer, his white teeth flashing as he smiled down at her. "You and I both know it only takes a couple of glasses to put you under the table."

Returning his smile, she was about to reply when someone slammed into her from behind, shoving her against him. Kelsey threw her hands out to catch herself. They landed on his chest as he spanned his hands around her waist to steady her.

"Thanks for nothing, bitch," Candy muttered as she and Missy pushed past in the narrow corridor.

"Hey!" West glanced over his shoulder as the women disappeared out of sight. Turning back to Kelsey, he asked, "What was that about?"

"You don't want to know." He arched one eyebrow. Then again, maybe he did. "Fine. But don't let it go to your head. They wanted me to introduce them to our group. Well, you guys anyway."

His other eyebrow shot up his forehead. "Why? Who are they?"

"I haven't a clue who they are, and isn't it obvious why?" Kelsey would never understand how none of the guys had figured out their appeal to the opposite sex and used it to get laid. In fact, she couldn't recall any of them having anything other than serious relationships. All of them were standup guys who didn't indulge in one-night stands. Unless they'd managed to keep their sexual exploits well hidden, but she didn't think so. While they weren't inclined to share their conquests with her, she'd never overheard any of them bragging about women and never seen them hook up whenever they were all out together.

"You don't know them?"

She shook her head. "Nope."

"Wow. That takes balls."

Kelsey laughed. "I think it was balls they were after."

"Jeez." He let go of her waist and cupped one elbow. "C'mon, let's get back to the table to warn everyone."

"Why warn them? They're big boys, I'm sure they can take care of themselves." Kelsey tugged her arm from his grasp and moved a step in front before they entered the main room of the bar.

"A couple have had a few too many, and with vultures like that hanging around, someone's bound to get themselves in trouble."

West placed his hand on her lower back and steered her through the crowd. The place had gotten busier while she'd been hiding in the bathroom. It didn't help that their group had taken up residence all the way in the back of the room.

"Hey, we're heading out now. Anyone want a lift?" West asked when they reached the table. After a no from everyone, he scanned the area, spotted the two women from the bathroom and nodded his head in their general direction. "Blonde and blonder in the far corner are on the prowl. Don't anyone be stupid."

Zac glanced over and paled. "Shit. Again?"

"You know them?" Kelsey asked.

Zac let out a gush of air and slouched down in his seat. "Yeah, worst luck. Blonder—I think her name is something stupid like Lolli —is the younger sister of that footballer who was in the papers a few months ago. You know the one up on assault charges."

Kelsey laughed. "It's Candy, but I guess Lolli is close."

"What?" Zac asked.

"She introduced herself in the bathroom when she recognized me as someone who'd been talking to you."

Zac's mouth hung open.

"How the hell do you know her?" West asked Zac.

"She came into the office with her brother every damn time he met with his lawyers. Barely legal and on the hunt for a sugar daddy that one."

By now, all the guys had craned their necks for a better look, and Kelsey wasn't surprised when Blonder—Candy—headed in their direction, her friend trailing behind.

"Shit," West muttered when he saw what Kelsey was looking at. "We're outta here. Catch you all later."

Kelsey barely managed a goodbye over her shoulder when West spun around and towed her across the room.

2

West pulled into Kelsey's driveway and killed the engine. The drive had been filled with mundane chatter about work and of course her usual nagging about his need for an office manager. He'd been fighting her on that for months now, but truth be told, she was right. He needed someone in the office fulltime because the hours he put in on paperwork around everything else he did weren't cutting it anymore. But if he had to have anyone poking around the innards of Weston's, he wanted Kelsey. And she refused to take the job.

He slipped the key from the ignition and opened his door. He had one foot on the ground when Kels grabbed his arm and stopped him from getting out.

"What are you doing?" she asked, her voice a little high—a little tight.

"Getting out."

"Why?" She dug her fingers into his forearm.

Okay. This was interesting. "Um, because we're at your house?"

"Yes, but you don't have to come in."

West arched an eyebrow at her obvious horror at the thought of him coming inside. "I wasn't planning to come in, Kels. But I don't plan on sitting in your car all night either."

"Oh. Right." She licked her lips and West was hit with the urge to lean over and follow her tongue with his. "Okay. I'll see you later then."

Before he could make sense of the conversation, or her fear, she was out of the car and hurrying along the footpath. "What the hell?" he mumbled as he climbed out of the car and, shaking his head, shut the door behind him. Unlike Kels, West took his time walking to her door.

She'd stopped on the path, her hand stretched out in his direction, her gaze directed at the ground. "I need my house key."

He'd figured as much, but she'd jumped out of the car before he could hand over her key ring. West wasn't sure what had her so flustered, but she was as twitchy as a cat in a room full of rocking chairs.

He held out her keys.

She snatched them from him before she turned on her heel and launched herself up the step. Except her shoe clipped the edge and she tipped forward, quickly on her way to meeting the floor with her face. West lunged for her and managed to grab her shirt. In a split second, he realized he couldn't stop her fall with his limited hold. With a hard yank, he pulled her towards him. The action spun her around and brought her close enough for him to wrap his other arm around her waist.

He pulled her against him. Bracketing her torso with his arms, West hauled her up until her chest was flush with his and her feet dangled above the ground. Her body went taut as air rushed from her lungs like a punctured balloon. In this position, they were eye to eye, and he took in her expression. Fear and shock filled her gaze before another emotion overtook them. She sucked in a deep breath and her breasts rose to press against him. West didn't miss the hard points of her nipples digging in to him.

"Kels." Her name was no more than a breath, and in the next second, he ditched all common sense and slanted his mouth over hers.

She didn't fight him like he expected. Instead, she melted into him. She thrust her tongue out to stroke over his and he took the unspoken invitation to explore. Memories bombarded him. Images of her naked beneath him. Of his mouth and hands searching out every sensitive spot on her lithe body. Except she wasn't the same as before. There were new curves, new slopes, and West struggled to control the need to rip her clothes off and discover every one of them.

West moaned when she slid her hands over his shoulders and up his neck until her fingertips tangled in his hair. It was a little long, in need of a trim, but right now, with Kels tugging on the ends, West vowed to never cut it again if she just kept up the sexy pull. His groin throbbed as blood rushed to fill his cock with heat. The sweet ache he always felt around Kels exploded into a blinding flash of pain that singed his insides.

He had to have her.

Had to bury himself so deep nobody could tell them apart.

A growl rumbled in his chest as he gripped her ass and pressed his hard length into her. The way he held her meant they were lined up perfectly, and he took the single step to her porch without looking. He kept going until he had her trapped between his body and her front door.

Timber rattled and Kels tore her mouth from his. He saw the second the lust haze cleared. The second she realized what they were doing and where they were doing it. He'd never forced himself on a woman, and he wouldn't be starting with this one no matter how much he craved her. So when she shoved her hands against his shoulders and wiggled in his arms, he slipped his hands to her hips, took a step back and lowered her to the floor. It took strength he didn't know he had to let go of her completely.

Her mouth worked. Opened. Closed. Only nothing came out, and West couldn't think of one damn word to say either. Well, none that weren't about getting naked and continuing inside. It took him a moment of dragging in deep breaths to clear his head, but once he did, he knew there was no way they were going to finish what they'd started. He could see the big red light she'd turned on. Kels didn't need to say a word, it was written all over her face, blazed in her sky-blue eyes.

That one taste was all he was getting tonight, and unless he wanted to start an argument and push her farther away, he had to suck it up and keep his raging lust in check. Glancing at her hands, he saw she no longer held her keys. He turned around and spotted them lying on the path. She must have dropped them while they were locked at the lips. With a grimace of pain, West leapt off the single step and bent to scoop up her key ring. The tight fit of his jeans wasn't kind to the full-blown hard-on he sported.

Hiding his discomfort behind a smile, he turned and headed back to her door. He made quick work of sliding the key into the lock and swinging the door wide before pressing the keys into her hand. If he was going to do the right thing and leave, he had to do it now.

"I'll catch you later." He gripped her elbow and urged her inside. West tried not to laugh at the shell-shocked look on her face, but he couldn't hold back the smile curling his lips. "See you Monday."

"M-monday?"

"Yep. Tax time, remember?" The look of horror that passed over her face made him chuckle. "Does that look mean I'm in for a bill other than yours?"

"What? Oh no. I'd forgotten all about our meeting, that's all."

He'd just bet she had. After that kiss, West was lucky to remember his name. He smiled and leaned into the house, making her jump back a step. But she needn't worry, he wasn't about to touch her again. Not tonight. "Lock the door."

West pulled the door closed and waited for the deadlock to click into place before he left. Good thing it was a ten-minute walk home. He thought about running the distance to disperse some of the energy buzzing in his veins. But a walk in the cold night air would help cool him off. Plus, he had a lot of thinking and planning to do. She may have been on board with their kiss, but the second sanity had returned, she'd backed right away without moving a step. They'd been building up to that kiss for months. Every time he'd gotten close, she'd managed to pull away.

But tonight she'd given him a green light. The first. She'd opened up and let him in, and he'd be damned if he let her throw up that red light permanently. West had no doubt he was in for a bumpy trip in his pursuit of Kelsey, but as long as he got to the destination he was aiming for, he'd put up with a few stop-starts.

Kelsey took a deep breath and got out of the car, lugging her briefcase over the console behind her. She'd been dreading this meeting since Friday night when West had left her breathless and confused with her door closed between them. And frustrated. God. He'd left her so sexually wound up that she'd resorted to taking care of things herself every night since. Three times and she still walked on the jagged edge of arousal.

She'd barely made it through the weekend without tearing her hair out. Or driving over to West's place to demand he finish what he started. The smoldering desire she'd lived with for years had turned into a blaze with only a kiss. Then again, her body knew what he could do when he set his mind to it, and surely he'd improved his skills over the last ten years. She shivered. Lord, just the thought of what he'd learned had her pulse skipping and her insides melting.

He'd had serious talent as a novice, and he hadn't been afraid to try something new or push for more all those years ago either, so he was bound to have gotten better. Another shiver skipped over her skin, pulling a wave of goose bumps behind it. Her stride faltered as the door to West's building opened and the man himself stepped out.

"Hey, I've been waiting for you." He came towards her, his hand outstretched. "Let me take that for you."

She let him take her bag more because she didn't have the brainpower to protest than anything else.

"Tough day?" he asked as he placed a hand on her lower back and guided her towards the door.

"What? Oh, no, not really. But it's been a full one." Kelsey wasn't about to tell him she hadn't slept well since their kiss. He already had enough power over her without giving him that piece of information.

"Have you eaten?" West reached out to open the door. "I can make you a snack if you're hungry."

"No. I'm good. I grabbed a burger for lunch." As soon as the words left her mouth she knew she was in trouble.

"A burger?" He pulled her to a stop. "Please tell me you are not referring to one of those things they serve at the Golden Arches."

Kelsey ducked her head. "Then I won't."

"Jeez, Kels, you can't live on that crap."

"I don't. I eat other stuff."

"Frozen diet meals don't count in the not-crap column either."

Damn. He knew her so well. "Fine. I promise to eat better if you promise to take my advice and hire a fulltime office manager." Kelsey wasn't above using her capitulation to get something she wanted. It didn't matter that it was something West needed desperately.

"Deal. When do you start?"

"I'll start by making a healthy chicken salad for dinner tonight."

"I'm talking about work."

"What?"

"I'm happy for you to continue seeing your regular clients out of here if that makes things easier." West steered her into the small windowless room he used as an office.

"Wait. What?" Had she missed something he said? She must have, because she was completely lost in this conversation.

"Sit. I'll get you a drink." He pushed her into the chair behind his desk and left the room before she could blink.

What the hell had just happened? Kelsey ran back over every word they'd spoken, and even though she thought she had a handle on it, the outcome didn't make any sense. West was talking as if she'd agreed to be his new office manager. It wasn't the first time he'd suggested it, but she'd never believed he meant it as a real possibility. He couldn't be serious. Could he?

She mulled over the idea while pulling files out of her briefcase. Spying a folder overflowing with invoices, Kelsey tried not to panic at the thought of all those numbers not being entered into the relevant spreadsheets she'd set up for West's business. With a sinking feeling, she began leafing through the paperwork on his desk. She'd just booted up his computer when he came back in.

"Here. This will go a long way to repairing the damage that processed burger is doing to your system." He placed a bright-green drink in front of her.

"What the hell is that?" Kelsey leaned over and took a sniff. "Banana?"

"Yep, with some extra nutrients thrown in."

Oh God. He was feeding her one of those super smoothie things his sister made. Kelsey scrunched up her nose as she took another sniff.

"Just drink it. It won't kill you." He flopped into the chair on the other side of his desk.

"But it's green."

"It's only kale and spinach. Nothing sinister, I promise."

Kelsey eyed the glass as she picked it up and brought it to her lips. She took a tentative sip and was surprised by the sweet banana flavor that burst across her tongue. Taking a bigger drink, she tried to determine what else he'd added to it.

"Good?" West watched her with a grin on his face.

"It's okay." Kelsey wasn't about to admit the damn thing tasted yummy. She took another drink before she put the glass down and opened the file that held West's tax documents. "Now if you'll pull up the spreadsheets for me, I'll get started."

"Ah, yeah, about that…"

She glanced up, eyebrows raised.

"I kinda, sorta haven't gotten to those." He lifted his chin in the direction of the overflowing folder.

"Dammit, West." This was going to take so much longer than she'd thought—hoped. With a sigh, she leaned back in the chair. "You promised me this year would be different."

"I know. And it would have been. But time got away from me, and today I got caught up in the kitchen."

Kelsey held up her hand. "I don't want to hear excuses. This is why you need an office manager."

"I know."

"Then hire one."

"I want you."

The words hung in the air between them. He'd said those exact words numerous times before when they'd talked about his need for a fulltime manager, but after Friday night's kiss, those three simple words took on a whole new meaning.

From head to toes, everything tightened, warmed and tingled, and a full-body shiver rolled over her. His eyes went dark, his gaze laser-like in its intensity, and Kelsey's breath hitched. She licked her lips, her tongue sticking on the dry surface. West's hands fisted on his thighs and her eyes were drawn to the bulge in his pants. He didn't hide from her, and if she was reading him right, he wanted her to know exactly what he wanted her for.

"West." His name was a plea on her lips, but Kelsey had no clue what she was asking for.

"Take the job, Kels." The words came through clenched teeth.

"I have a job. A business."

West sucked in a deep breath and let it out slowly. As she watched, his shoulders relaxed and his hands opened. "Yes, and we both know that things are going to get slow now that tax season is coming to an end."

"I still have clients," she argued.

He nodded. "And I'll bet you next year's profits that you can manage those as well as Weston's. With your hands tied behind your back."

Kelsey opened her mouth to argue further, but she couldn't come up with another excuse to refuse the job. Not without revealing her feelings, and she wasn't ready for West to know how deep those went. Besides, her business was about to shrink, and with it her income. Not that she was in any danger of going broke. Tax time might be exhaustingly busy, but it was also extremely lucrative. She closed her eyes and leaned her head back against the chair.

Leather creaked, but she kept her eyes shut, not wanting to see him just now for fear one look into those storm-cloud eyes would seal her fate. His feet brushed over the concrete floor as he moved around, and it only took a moment to work out he was walking around the desk towards her. She heard him crouch down beside her, felt the light brush of his hand over her denim covered knee.

"Kels. Look at me."

She swallowed, her constricted throat aching as the muscles worked. Slowly, she raised her eyelids and turned her head to meet his gaze.

"Give me a year. One year to make it work for both of us."

She wanted to say yes. God, did she. But there was more at stake than their perspective businesses. If she said yes, she'd be in West's presence every day. There'd be no hiding from her feelings and certainly no stopping them from growing deeper. Day in, day out, Kelsey would be faced with her biggest weakness.

Weston Mann.

3

West held his breath. He could see Kelsey wavering. Could see she wanted to say yes, but something held her back, and he had a sinking feeling it was what lay unspoken between them. They'd never talked about what they'd done, and he couldn't decide whether he should bring it up now or let it lie. His gut told him opening up that topic might destroy any chance he had of building a future with her, and he wasn't prepared to risk that. Not yet. First, he needed to convince her to take the job so he could spend more time with her.

"C'mon. You and I both know you can do the work with your eyes closed. Plus, you already know the system inside out. It's yours after all." He hoped a little flattery would sway her.

She let out a harsh breath. "Fine. A year. But if at any time between now and then, I can't keep up with my existing clients, the deal's off."

Before she could change her mind, he thrust out his hand. "Deal." Kelsey put her hand in his and it took considerable control he didn't think he had not to pull her from the chair and into his lap.

"Don't think for one second me taking the job gets you out of inputting all those invoices," she said as she untangled her hand from his.

"Isn't that your job?"

"Yes. But not until next Monday. I'll need the rest of this week to get everything figured out if I'm going to run my business alongside yours. We don't want—or need—any glitches in the transition." She pushed the chair back and stood. "Have at it."

He shot to his feet. "Where are you going?"

Kelsey jerked back, one eyebrow arching almost to her hairline. "To the bathroom?"

"Oh. Right." West took a deep breath and moved out of her way. "I'll, um, get started on these then." He indicated the overflowing folder on his desk.

She gave him a smile that was more a grimace before edging past him and leaving the room. West shook his head as he dropped into his chair. He really needed to get a hold of himself. No one and nothing could rattle him like Kelsey. It had been that way since high school when he'd secretly lusted after her. Of course, he'd been a juvenile idiot back then. Proof being the way he'd handled the whole sleeping-together thing. He'd fucked it up royally and had thought any chance to be with her had disappeared the day she'd said I do to his friend.

And now, three years after Kels and Bry had parted ways, he couldn't hold back his desire or his need to be with her. He had a plan, he'd come up with it over the weekend, and she'd just said yes to the first stage. She'd given him a year, but West didn't think he'd need that long to get what he wanted. He'd seen the heat in her gaze —felt it in the bone-melting kiss they'd shared last Friday. He knew she wanted him and their attraction went both ways. But would she act on her feelings?

Jesus, he hoped so. Hoped with every fiber of his being. Not wanting to be in her bad books before they even got started, West flipped open the folder of invoices he'd neglected and brought up the spreadsheet Kelsey had made for him to enter his business expenses. He wasn't the smartest when it came to computers, but he prided himself on being a quick study. Unfortunately, the complicated charts that Kels had first given him had proven idiot proof. He'd been the biggest idiot in the bunch, so she'd put together something more his speed.

By the time Kelsey returned from the bathroom, West had punched in the numbers on four invoices and was working on the fifth. He tried not to be distracted when Kels sat on the other side of his desk. Tried not to watch her slender fingers tapping over the keys of her laptop. Or the way her reading glasses kept sliding down her nose. But it was hard when her perfume—something sweet smelling like one of the sugary desserts he made—floated around him, reminding him of her taste.

With a groan, he deleted the wrong figures. Again. That made three times he'd attempted to enter the same fucking number.

"Something wrong?"

West glanced up to find Kelsey leaning across the desk in an effort to see his screen. She wore a simple tee. Nothing fancy or revealing or sexy. But her lower arms were resting on the desktop, the upper section pressing into her sides and pushing her breasts together in a way that made the V-neck of her top gap open to reveal a cleavage of smooth, tanned skin. He swallowed. Hard.

He licked his lips and opened his mouth but only a garbled croak came out.

She raised her eyebrows. "You okay?"

Nodding, he spotted the smoothie he'd made her and reached for it. He took a mouthful to wet his parched mouth and throat. "Yep. I'm good."

A smile kicked up one corner of her lips. "I guess I know why you're always avoiding doing your books."

"Huh?" West took another sip of her drink before putting it down.

"Obviously, your creative brain can't handle numbers."

"Creative?"

"You don't consider yourself creative?" she asked as she picked up the glass and brought it to her mouth.

He shook his head. "Ah..." Jesus. She was going to put her mouth right where his had been. Why that should send a burst of lust through his system, he hadn't a clue, but that's exactly what it did.

Blood rushed south to fill his groin, making his jeans tight, and he cursed the fact he'd had to go commando this morning because he'd forgotten to do his washing again. His cock pressed into the thick denim of his zipper and West shifted in his seat in the hope of giving himself a little bit of room. It didn't work.

Kelsey watched him closely over the top of her glasses and he stopped squirming instantly. The last thing he wanted was for her to figure out how worked up he was having her sitting across the desk from him. She'd retract her acceptance of the job and head out the door in a second if she thought he couldn't control himself around her. He picked up the invoice and turned back to the monitor to focus on the numbers in front of him and not the pain in his groin or the urge gnawing at his insides to throw her on his desk and take her hard and fast.

———————

Kelsey couldn't believe she'd agreed to take the job as West's office manager. She had no one to blame but herself for giving in though. He'd looked at her with those stormy eyes and she'd folded quicker than a house of cards in a light tropical breeze. They'd been at his desk working for over an hour now. She'd been done in half that time but had worked on a to-do list for making the transition to working at Weston's while she waited for him to finish keying in his invoices.

It probably would have been more expedient to do them herself, except she didn't want West to think he could get away with pushing them off onto her again. He'd done it every year since she'd taken Weston's on as a client, and regardless of whether she minded or not, it didn't sit well with her knowing she'd given him special treatment because of their friendship. She would never allow any of her other clients to get away with it.

She sighed. But then West wasn't just any old client.

West slapped the last sheet on top of the pile, making her jump.

"Done." He flopped back in his chair as though he'd run a marathon.

She couldn't help it. She burst out laughing.

"Hey." He scowled at her.

"C'mon, it's not that bad." Kelsey reached over for the invoices, stood them up, and tapped them on the desk to straighten the pile. "Pass me a paperclip."

West opened his top drawer and rummaged around inside for a minute. When he slammed the drawer closed and opened the second, Kelsey smiled.

"Never mind. I've got one." She unzipped the side pocket on her briefcase, slipped her hand inside and came out with a handful of clips. "Here, throw the rest in your drawer."

"It's your drawer now."

Kelsey grinned. "Not until next week it's not."

West's forehead creased and she could tell he was contemplating something serious. Instead of asking him what as she normally would, she busied herself with setting out her paperwork for his tax return.

"Can you put your spreadsheets on this for me?" Kelsey pushed the memory stick she used for Weston's financial files towards him.

"Sure."

She waited for him to load the USB and pass it back. Once he did, she plugged it into her laptop and got to work.

"Anything else?"

Focused on her screen, she shook her head and continued to combine the information he'd given her with the year's spreadsheet. She was surprised to feel a release of tension in her shoulders a few minutes later and glanced up to discover West had left the office. The fact she noticed his departure on such a cellular level worried her. He was more than under her skin and always had been. And with her taking on a more permanent role in his business, she wondered how long it would be before she gave in to her desire and fell into bed with him.

The muffled sound of her phone chirping came from her briefcase. She was waiting to hear from Shaye, so she leaned over to retrieve it from her bag. Kelsey laughed out loud when she read the text.

OMFG! Get me out of here!

Kelsey hadn't even hit reply when the thing vibrated and chirped again.

GIRLS' NIGHT! Your place at 7!

Uh oh. For Shaye to want a girls' night on Monday, things obviously hadn't improved at work since last week. Kelsey quickly fired back a reply.

Things no better?

It was a while before her friend texted back, and Kelsey had started to worry. That didn't improve at all when Shaye finally replied.

Worse! Talk later.

"Shit."

"What's the matter? Am I in for a bigger tax bill than we projected? I know this last quarter's income went beyond expected." West put a plate of sliced fruit on the table in front of her.

"Ah, no." She held up her phone. "Shaye just texted me."

"Still problems with her boss?"

Kelsey sighed. Shaye had told everyone on Friday night that her boss had started making inappropriate comments and suggestions. She'd been hoping Zac would have some advice on how to handle it seeing how he was a lawyer. Unfortunately, he'd only repeated what Kelsey had already told her. She needed to go to HR and report the man. "See for yourself." She handed him her phone.

"Wow. She really needs to report him."

"She can't afford to lose her job."

"If she lost her job over that, she'd have grounds to sue the company." West handed her phone back. "Want me to throw together something for you guys to have for dinner?"

Kelsey knew he would in a heartbeat, but she didn't want to put him out or let him in to her life anymore today than she already had. "Nah, but thanks. We'll order pizza."

He shuddered and pulled a face, making Kelsey laugh.

"What?" he asked.

"There's nothing wrong with pizza."

"No, but I can send you home with a nice homemade lasagna to go with the alcohol you're both liable to consume while Shaye bitches about her boss."

Her mouth watered. She glanced at the time on her laptop. "You can make lasagna in an hour?" Kelsey couldn't believe how tempted she was.

"Sure. It'll only take me thirty minutes tops, and all you'll have to do when you get home is stick it in the oven on one-eighty for about the same."

Damn, she was tempted. So tempted. West made the best lasagna Kelsey had ever tasted, and it had been weeks since she'd had some. "Are you sure?" she asked.

"Consider it done." He walked around behind his desk and dropped into his chair. "Now what can I do to help get this tax return done?"

"Nothing. I just need to finish generating the yearly reports off the spreadsheets and then enter the info in your return and we're done for another year." Kelsey smiled.

"Really? Are you sure there's nothing I can do?"

"Positive."

"Okay." He pressed his hands on his desk as he stood up. "Then I'll go get that lasagna started."

"Okay, but if it's too much trouble or you have something else to do, we can just have pizza." Kelsey didn't really want pizza now that West had her thinking about his lasagna, but she didn't want to put him out either.

"No trouble. I have to whip up a batch of curry anyway." He started around his desk. "If I'm not back before you finish, come find me."

Once West left, Kelsey went back to work. It didn't take her long to have everything ready to file with the tax department, and because she did that electronically, she just had to give the forms one final read through and she'd be done. He was lucky. The business may have generated higher-than-expected earnings last quarter, but the staff, equipment and supplies he'd added in recent months offset that enough that he didn't owe that much more tax than they'd calculated at the beginning of the financial year.

West still hadn't come back by the time she was finished, so she saved her files and switched off her laptop. She'd print out his copies later. Of course, now that she'd be working for him, it would be her responsibility to file them away, so it wouldn't make a difference if he didn't have them until next week. He certainly wouldn't bother putting them away himself. She smiled when she thought about his aversion to office work. Probably a good thing she liked it seeing how she'd taken on the job to get Weston's organized.

With everything packed up, Kelsey walked around West's desk and closed all open programs on his computer before shutting it down. She thought about going through his office supplies and writing a list of what was needed but her phone buzzed, signaling another text. Glancing over, she saw it was from Shaye and reached over to pick it up. The message made her stomach tighten.

Do you still have a spare key hidden in the frog in your backyard?

Her spare key? Another message popped up.

I'm at your place now.

Kelsey glanced at the time with shock, but she quickly recovered to send Shaye a reply. *Yes. What happened?*

Quit!

What the fuck? Shaye had quit her job? Thumbs flying over the screen, Kelsey sent another text. *What did that asshole do?*

I'll explain when you get here. I'm in. :-)

Kelsey stared at her phone for long seconds before she snapped out of it and gathered her things together. She needed to head home now. Shaye wouldn't have quit over something minor. She'd been putting up with her boss's inappropriate behavior for months, so to Kelsey's mind that meant the man had crossed the line from inappropriate to downright indecent.

Briefcase in one hand, keys and phone in the other, Kelsey made her way out of the office and across the warehouse towards the kitchen that took up the back half of the building. She found West standing in front of the stove, stirring something that smelled absolutely divine. Her tummy rumbled.

"I have to go."

He turned her way. "What? Why?"

"Shaye just sent a text saying she quit."

"Quit? Her job? Why?"

She shrugged. "I don't know, but she's already at my place so I want to get there right away."

"Of course."

"I'm sorry about dinner. We'll just order pizza after all."

"Nonsense. I'll put this together and drop it off later."

"I can't ask you to do that," she argued.

"You didn't ask. Your place is on my way home, and all I have to do is wait for this sauce to thicken then put it together. No trouble at all."

"Are you sure?" She hated to put him out, but it did smell delicious and she really didn't have time to argue.

"Definitely." He took the saucepan off the heat but continued to stir. "Just about done now, but you go. I'll bring it by in an hour or so."

"Okay. Thanks." She turned to leave but only got a few steps when he called out.

"Kelsey. Ring me if you or Shaye need anything."

She looked over her shoulder and smiled. He was always ready to help her with anything. A sharp pang of longing stabbed her. West made her want things she shouldn't. Screwing up her marriage with Bry had left a fear she just couldn't shake. If she and West took their friendship farther—if they crossed that line again—she stood to lose far more than just her heart. Her split with Bry hadn't damaged any of the close friendships in their group, but if anyone found out about her and West's history—if they found out she'd loved him all along, they'd never forgive her.

Especially Bry.

4

____

West re-read the text message he'd just received.

Give job Shaye.

He thought he understood, but he hoped like hell he was wrong. Earlier, when he'd dropped the lasagna at Kelsey's, she'd been well on her way to being drunk. And from the look of Shaye, she'd barely gotten started. He hovered his thumb over the screen while he debated whether or not to reply.

"What are you doing?" Coop asked as he sat on the couch beside him, a fresh beer in his hand.

Without taking his eyes off the phone, West said, "Trying to decide if I should go over to Kelsey's and remove all the alcohol or ignore her."

"What the fuck is going on with you two?" Zac growled from the other side of the room.

West glanced up at his best friend. "Nothing. Shaye's over there. They're getting drunk because Shaye quit her job today." West looked back down and hit reply just as another text came in.

Wasted! :)

He laughed as he fired back a response. *Shouldn't have had that second glass. ;)*

Lifting his head, West met his best friend's narrowed gaze once more. "I finally convinced Kels to take the job today." Zac and Coop both knew what he was talking about. Hell, their whole group would know, he'd been talking about trying to get Kels to work for him for months.

"She agreed?" Coop shook his head. "Never thought I'd hear that."

"Tell me you haven't touched her," Zac demanded.

Coop shot forward in his seat as beer sprayed out his mouth and rolled down his chin. "What?" he choked out while wiping his jaw with the back of his hand.

Zac stared West down, but West held his gaze and didn't answer either way.

"You and Kelsey?" Coop's words held curiosity, not censure.

"West."

"What, Zac? What do you want me to say? Of course I've touched her. She's my friend."

"That's not what I'm talking about, and you know it."

West scrubbed a hand down his face and blew out a breath. He could lie or he could hedge or he could just tell his two best friends the truth. His phone vibrated in his hand and he glanced down.

Second bottle did it.

He couldn't hold back his laughter, which of course only got him another dirty look from Zac.

"What's she saying?" Coop asked.

"That she's wasted."

"So she's had two glasses then," Coop said with a grin, and Zac couldn't help but laugh even if he tried to cover it by coughing. Everyone knew how much of a lightweight Kels was.

West was relieved to see Zac loosen up on the whole Kelsey thing for a second. Lord knows he was going to blow a gasket when West came clean about his intentions.

"When did Shaye quit?" Coop asked.

"This afternoon. Don't know the details, but I did see a couple of messages she sent Kels this afternoon that hinted at things being worse at work." On Friday night, he'd wanted to find Shaye's boss and slam the man's head through a wall when she'd told them what had been going on, but after today, West thought putting the guy's head through a wall might not be enough.

"Anyone know where we can find the guy?" Coop's words were laced with a steel edge that had West and Zac staring in his direction. "What?"

West lifted one brow. "Shaye?"

Coop relaxed back against the couch and brought his beer to his mouth. He took his time taking a sip before answering. "Problem?"

West looked at Zac who was shaking his head, a scowl on his face. Turning back to Coop he said, "Nope. Not from me. Just surprised."

"Been thinking on it for a while. Trying to gage whether it's worth pursuing or not. But after the conversation Friday night, and my gut reaction to it, I've figured out I'd be stupid not to." Coop pulled his phone from his pocket. "Let's see if I can get some drunk texts too."

West watched his friends. Coop appeared relaxed, but Zac's body held a tautness that told him revealing anything about his intentions regarding Kelsey might cause some friction that West wasn't interested in dealing with right now. Coop's unexpected revelation about his feelings for Shaye should take some of the sting out of his own admission, but with Zac's next words, West knew he'd have to keep his mouth shut unless he wanted a fight with one of his best friends.

"What is it with you guys wanting to fuck with the group?" Zac shook his head, his forehead wrinkled. "It wasn't bad enough when things went south with Bry and Kelsey?"

"Bad?" Coop lifted his gaze from his phone to look at his twin. "What the hell are you talking about? Those two should never have gotten married in the first place, and you know it. Their friendship is just as strong now as it was when they were sleeping together, Zac."

"Coop's right," West added in a calm voice despite the less-than-calm emotions churning his insides at the thought of Kels and Bry together. "There wasn't any drama when they split, which says a lot about their marriage."

Zac frowned.

"Theirs was never really an overly passionate relationship," West said as razor-sharp jealousy sliced at his insides and threatened to spew from his chest on a growl.

"And don't forget Kelsey moved out before anyone knew about the split. Shit, I don't remember them ever having a fight," Coop added.

West had known. He'd known because he'd helped her move some of her things. Of course, he hadn't said a word to anyone. Kels had wanted it kept quiet until after she'd filed the divorce papers and, as was West's usual MO when it came to Kelsey, he'd done whatever she asked.

West's phone buzzed. *I don't feel so good.* "Uh oh, Kels isn't going to last much longer."

Coop's phone went off and he burst out laughing when he read the text.

"What?" Zac asked as he got out of his chair and headed towards his brother. "Show me."

"You sure you want to see what we're saying, little brother?" Coop teased.

"Two minutes, for fuck's sake."

"Yeah, but those two minutes put you a whole day behind me." Coop grinned. The long-standing taunt got the usual reaction from Zac.

"Give me the phone." Zac lunged at Coop and the two of them wrestled on the couch until they rolled to the floor at West's feet.

Zac finally yanked the phone from Coop's hand. He scanned the screen quickly. "Jesus. Are you for real?"

West leaned over and grabbed Zac's wrist to keep the phone still so he could see the exchange between Coop and Shaye.

So my buddy is getting some text messages from your drunk friend. Wanna play too?

I'll play with you anytime, stud. ;-)

"Holy shit!" West said.

Coop grinned. "Yeah. I think I'm going to see if she needs a ride home."

Zac tossed the phone at his brother as he climbed to his feet. "You two are sick."

"What the fuck is up your ass, Zac?" Coop sat up.

"Nothing." Zac bent to retrieve his keys and phone from the floor beside his chair. "I'm outta here. Catch you dickheads later."

Before either of them spoke, Zac was gone. West turned to Coop. "What's going on with him?"

"Hell if I know. I was planning to ask you. He's been weird for a while now. Ever since he helped Cassie out with that party a few months back." Coop shook his head. "And before you ask, neither Cassie nor Dan can remember anything happening that night. I already asked. Maybe something's going on at work?"

"Hmm…" West had an inkling of what might be going on with Zac, but he didn't want to bring it up with Coop yet. He'd have a chat with Dan next time he saw him and double-check his suspicions. "Enough about grumpy. Are you really going to play with Shaye?"

"Don't see why I shouldn't, in spite of Zac's objection."

"You're not worried about what it'll do to the group dynamic if things go south?" West asked. It was something he'd considered when contemplating him and Kelsey. Although at this point he'd decided he didn't care how the group was affected.

"If I went into every relationship thinking it was going to end, it wouldn't be worth bothering, would it?" Coop shrugged. "Besides, I'm not about to let something that could be great pass me by just because it might upset some of my friends."

"Guess you have to weigh up whether the possible outcome is worth the risk."

"Oh, she's worth it." Coop grinned as he began poking at his phone again. "Now if you'll excuse me, I'm going to offer my services as a designated driver."

"Is that the only service you're offering?"

Coop laughed. "I'm game for anything with Shaye."

West stood up as Coop's phone beeped. "She say yes?"

"Sure did."

"Do me a favor? Check on Kels when you pick Shaye up. Make sure she isn't going to be sleeping in her own vomit."

"What do I look like? Your slave boy?" Coop pulled his keys from his pocket. "If you're that worried, head over there and check on her yourself."

West frowned. He wasn't sure going around to Kelsey's was a good idea, but he wanted to make sure she was all right. If she wasn't lying about the two bottles of wine, she was going to be one sorry woman come morning unless she flushed her system with water now. A couple of aspirin wouldn't hurt either. "Just send me a text telling me how trashed she is."

"Fine. But avoiding her isn't going to fix your problem," Coop said as he pulled West's front door open.

"What's that supposed to mean?"

"Man up, West."

"Hey!"

"Don't give me that shit. You might never mention it and think you've managed to keep your feelings for Kelsey secret, but you're forgetting who you're talking to. I know you. I remember the crush you had on her back in school."

"That was then." West tried to brush it off.

"Yeah, and this is now, and she's no longer trapped in a passionless marriage with one of our closest friends." Coop clapped his hand on West's shoulder. "Don't let what Zac says, or what anyone else, especially Bry, might think stop you from going after what you really want. She's worth the risk."

With those parting words, Coop left him standing in his foyer, wondering if his friend was the only one who'd seen through his facade to the deeper emotions for Kelsey lurking beneath. Zac had certainly picked up on it, but then out of the two Moreland twins, West and Zac were closest, so that was to be expected. Sighing, he reached over and flipped the deadlock before heading back into the lounge room and picking up his empty bottle. He'd dumped it in the trash and put away the leftover food before his phone buzzed with the text he was waiting for.

She's already driving the porcelain bus. Get your ass round here now. We'll wait until you're here before we leave.

"Shit!"

It didn't matter how much he thought he should stay away from Kels right now, there was no way he was going to let her suffer alone. Figuring he'd be spending the night at her house, West threw a change of clothes and his toiletries in a bag before racing out the door.

———

Kelsey's stomach hurt. Her head hurt. Even her butt hurt where she was sitting on the cold tile floor. And her mouth tasted like shit. Not that she knew what shit actually tasted like, but she thought it was probably close to the ghastly flavor coating her tongue and teeth.

"Oh God," she moaned as another wave of nausea squeezed her belly, only she'd already emptied out her stomach. That included the lining. Or at least that's what it felt like.

"Here, put this on your forehead."

West.

"Go away." Kelsey wasn't sure if he understood her. Her tongue kept sticking to the roof of her mouth and her lips were so dry it felt as though they'd shrunk three sizes. *Do lips come in sizes?*

"I'm sure you'd like that, but it's not happening."

Her head spun when West scooped her up off the bathroom floor and carried her from the room. "Where...?" She couldn't manage the rest of the sentence. Her brain was too busy impersonating a merry-go-round on speed.

"Easy, there."

"Dizzy."

"Keep still and it won't be so bad."

He placed her on her bed. She knew it was her bed because she could smell the scented candle she had sitting on her bedside table and the softness of her mattress cradled her hurting body. "Damn Shaye."

West chuckled. "Yeah, well, you should have known better than to try to keep up with her."

"She needed me."

"I don't think she needed you to make yourself sick." He slid his hand under head and lifted. "Here. Try to get some of this down."

Cool glass was pressed against her lips. She opened her mouth and took a few sips, but her coordination wasn't the best and some of the water spilled over her lips and down her chin.

"Slow down." West pulled the drink away and eased her back against the pillow.

His warmth disappeared and Kelsey reached out blindly. "Don't go."

"I'm not going anywhere." He wiped her face. "Do you want anything else?"

"You."

"I'm right here."

"'Kay." His fingers brushed the hair from her face and she moved into his touch. "Feels nice," she murmured.

"Mmm."

"Don't stop." Kelsey snuggled into the bedding. "Don't ever stop."

Her stomach continued to churn and her head was all floaty, but the soothing rhythm of West's gentle strokes across her temple soon had her drifting in and out of sleep.

Kelsey wasn't sure what disturbed her, but she knew exactly what it was that catapulted her out of sleep. There was someone in bed with her. And not just *any* someone. West. She'd know his scent anywhere, and it was definitely him she was currently wrapped around like white on rice. Oh my God. What had she done? She remembered coming home to find Shaye already into the first bottle of wine. Then they'd opened a second...

Damn. She couldn't remember beyond that. Gingerly, Kelsey tried to untangle her legs from his, but she'd managed to get herself well and truly pinned by one of his legs. They were lying on their sides, her face smashed up against his chest. At least he had a shirt on. And if she was right, they both had pants on too.

"Stop freaking out and go back to sleep."

Kelsey jolted at the sound of West's voice.

"Unless you need to go to the bathroom or want a drink stay right where you are."

"But—"

"Not listening." He tightened his arms around her. "Go back to sleep."

She lay there with thoughts bouncing around her head. When had West come over? And when the hell had they climbed into bed together? Why had they gotten into bed if they still had their clothes on? Kelsey could only think of one reason to crawl into bed with West, and it wasn't to sleep.

"Kels, quit worrying this to death. You were drunk. I held your hair out of the toilet and made sure you got to bed, at which point you ask me to stay. I did. End of story. Now go back to sleep. We have to be up in a few hours."

"I can't remember what happened after Shaye opened the second bottle." Kelsey hated admitting her lack of memory, but she knew West would be honest with her regardless of how bad the truth was, and she really, *really* needed to know what had led up to him being in her bed.

"Nothing happened, if that's what you're worrying about." West slid his hand up her spine and cupped her nape, moving his thumb and fingers in circles on either side of her neck. "I'd never take advantage of you like that."

She sighed. Of course he wouldn't. Worst luck. If he did, she wouldn't have to worry about making the decision to go there again. It wouldn't be her fault.

West chuckled. "You don't really want me to make it that easy for you, do you?"

"W-what?"

"I know you. You're thinking if I took advantage of your drunken state to get you naked underneath me you wouldn't have to take responsibility for your actions." He tangled his fingers in her hair, massaged the back of her head with hypnotic pressure. "When you find yourself under me again—and make no mistake, you will some-time soon—you'll know exactly what you're doing. And you'll remember every damn second of it."

"Oh."

5

West leaned against the counter and rubbed his eyes with his thumb and index finger. They were dry and gritty from too little sleep. It was barely ten a.m. and he was ready to crawl back into bed, and for once he wasn't thinking about Kelsey being under him in it. He'd had her there last night. All soft and malleable and smelling like a brewery. He smiled. If she ever found out some of the things she'd said in her drunken stupor, she'd die of embarrassment.

Good thing he'd been the only one around and had no intention of telling anyone what her loose tongue had revealed. She'd mumbled plenty while she'd drifted off to sleep. From how good it felt when he touched her to how good he smelled. How much she'd missed him. Which seemed weird when they'd never lost touch. And, of course, the big one. She loved him. West didn't think he could hold her to that confession, but he was going to take the thrill that had coursed through him at her words and run with it.

He'd give anything to hear those words pass her sexy lips while she was stone-cold sober. He figured he'd be waiting a while though. The phone at his hip rang and he unhooked it from his belt to see who was calling now. It had been a morning of one thing after another. That was why he was working in his back-up kitchen at Are

You Game? He wanted to avoid people at all costs this morning. Didn't help that he'd rather not have come to work at all, especially when he'd had to crawl out of bed where the woman of his dreams was sleeping beside him.

Seeing Kelsey's face and name illuminated on his screen sent a flurry of emotions through him. A little excitement, a bit of relief and a good dose of anxiety tangled together to have him staring at the device through five rings. Fear of her hanging up or the call switching over to voicemail had him sliding his finger across the screen to answer.

"Hey."

"You lied," Kelsey groaned.

West chuckled. She sounded horrible, and if he didn't know it was self-inflicted misery, he'd be more sympathetic. "About?"

"I'm not feeling any better than when you left this morning."

West could hear the whine in her voice and imagined her lying on her bed with one arm thrown up over her face. "Take some more aspirin."

"Did."

"When?"

"Now."

He laughed. "Give them a chance to work."

"I feel like my head is going to explode."

"I promise you it's not."

"Cross your heart?"

"Yes. Why don't you go back to bed for a few more hours?"

"Can't. Gotta work."

"Kelsey, you work for yourself, you can take a few hours off and catch up later."

"I'll be dead then."

He smiled at her melodramatic performance. It wasn't like her to complain. Then again, it wasn't like her to tie one on either. "You better not be dead. You have to be in the office at nine a.m. sharp Monday morning."

"About that..."

West could hear the words before she said them. "Don't you dare go back on our deal. You promised me a year."

"That was before."

"Before what?" He knew what she was thinking. They'd wound up in bed together, and while the night had been innocent, the temptation had been there. If he wasn't such a stand-up guy, he'd have made a move on her. They both knew it.

"*West*." His name came down the line on a sigh.

He wasn't about to let her back out. "Here's the thing. There's something between us. There always has been, and we need to work that out. But right now, I need you in my office more, so you stick to your end of the deal and I promise I won't push you on a personal front." Jesus. What the hell was he saying?

"God. My head hurts too much to think straight," she murmured.

"Then don't think about any of it for now. Go back to bed and I'll be over later to check on you and bring some food." Maybe she'd forget his stupid words by then and he could continue with his original plan of slowly seducing her into his bed. His life.

"You can't keep feeding me."

"Why not?"

"Because you can't, that's why." Her voice rose slightly. "Oh, God," she moaned, and he could picture her holding her head.

"Go back to bed. We'll talk about it later."

She was silent for so long, West thought she'd hung up. He even pulled the phone away from his ear to check.

Bringing it back to his head, he said, "Kels? You still there?"

"Yeah, I'm here." Her heavy sigh filled his ear. "I don't know if I can do this."

He wanted to reassure her, but she wasn't the only one worried about what would happen, and he couldn't find the words to appease either of them right now. All he knew was he couldn't walk away. Not again. "Get some more sleep. I'll see you later."

"Okay," she whispered, a second before the line went dead.

West dropped his arm by his side and hung his head until his chin hit his chest. He had no idea what they were doing. He'd had a plan, but in light of last night he didn't think it would work as it stood, and he certainly hadn't factored in Kelsey's drunken ramblings. After those revelations, there was no way he was giving up. If anything, he wanted to race towards the finish line. Suppressing the urge to rush was going to be hard, but for the sake of all that was at risk, he'd do it.

He slipped his phone back onto his belt and pushed off the counter. It wouldn't matter how much he stressed over the situation. They'd just have to find their way one step at a time.

K elsey sat on the edge of her seat. Literally and figuratively. She'd been waiting hours for West to show up. During the endless afternoon, she'd gone over her speech a million times. She'd prepared it as well as she had any of the debates she'd participated in back in high school. There wasn't a box of trophies in her parents' attic for nothing. All she had to do was stick to the argument. Except she had a sneaky suspicion that with West right in front of her, every solid, reasonable justification of why they shouldn't get together would be swept aside as nothing more than flimsy excuses.

A rush of air left her lungs as she slumped back on the couch. She closed her eyes and hoped for strength. But she had the horrible feeling that nothing short of a miracle could save her from her own heart. That traitorous organ had been firmly on West's side for as long as she could remember. Add in the one night she'd spent in his arms and Kelsey didn't think she stood a chance of stopping this thing between them developing further.

The sound of a car pulling up outside had her eyes springing open and her body bolting upright. On her feet, she twisted her fingers together and toyed with the idea of pretending she wasn't home. Only her car was in the driveway where she'd left it and West knew she'd never risk getting behind the wheel if there was even a slight chance she still had alcohol in her system. Taking a deep breath, Kelsey screwed up her courage and headed for the front door.

After waiting what felt like an eternity for West to ring the bell, Kelsey moved to the side of the door to peek through the front window. Cracking the blind a tiny bit, she peered out into the fading light of day and discovered no car on the street or in her driveway other than her own. Laughter bubbled up her throat, the slight hysterical edge only making her laugh more. She was such an idiot.

Light flooded the road right before West's familiar four-wheel drive appeared and turned into her driveway to park beside her small hatchback. The laughter of moments ago turned into a choked sob and Kelsey whipped her hand away from the blind and took several steps back, only stopping when she collided with the wall behind her.

"Oh God."

She brought her hand up to cover her mouth, her fingers trembling. Fear? Anticipation? Kelsey couldn't decide what set her nerves to shaking, but she couldn't deny that West did one thing that had been missing for years. He made her feel deeply, made her yearn for something she thought she'd found only to discover it was a poor substitute for the real thing.

"Oh my God."

Was that it? Was what she felt for West the real thing?

Kelsey had known all along she didn't love Bry the way she loved West, but she'd never thought too much about the differences in the two sentiments, figuring her mind had blown her youthful love out of proportion, and what she had with Bry was the grownup version. Yes, Bry was her friend, one of her best friends still, and she loved him. But with hindsight, she knew she hadn't been *in love* with him. She hadn't wanted him with the same need she'd always wanted West. A bone-deep ache that had never gone away.

Guilt filled her chest, making it hard to draw a breath. She'd let her wounded heart be soothed by the easy love Bry had offered in those first few years after West's rejection. She'd accepted Bry's proposal of marriage because she'd wanted a home, a family, but not with the enthusiasm of a blushing bride. It had just seemed like the logical next step in their relationship.

God. She'd cheated both herself and Bry of so much. She should never have agreed to get married. Should never have waited—hoped —so long for their love to grow—deepen. Kelsey leaned against the wall and closed her eyes as a lump of regret lodged in her throat and tears stung her eyes.

"Kels? You okay?"

Her eyes snapped open as a scream ripped from her chest.

"Hey, hey, it's just me." West stepped forward, letting the front door close behind him.

"H-how'd you get in?" she asked to the accompaniment of her pounding heart.

West held up a key. "You gave it to me for emergencies, remember?"

"Oh, right." She'd forgotten all about giving him a spare.

"Are you still feeling sick? You don't look too good." He cupped her shoulders and bent so they were eye to eye. "Why aren't you lying down?"

She couldn't tell him what had put the sick look on her face. Not without revealing she'd carried—still held—a torch for him all these years. "Just a little lightheaded. Must have got up too quickly or something." Kelsey forced a smile and moved out of his grip.

He eyed her warily for a moment longer before bending to grab the bag at his feet she hadn't noticed until now. "Hungry?"

"Um, sure." Kelsey turned and led the way to her kitchen. She could feel West's eyes on her with each step she took, and she tried to keep her steps smooth and even but feared he could tell she was ready to shoot through the roof at the slightest provocation.

When they reached the kitchen, Kelsey had no idea what to do or say, but obviously West didn't have that problem. He went straight to the island counter where he proceeded to remove food from the bag he'd brought in.

"Thought I'd put together a stir-fry," he said.

He appeared at home in her house. Without pause, he knew where the pans were kept, where to find the utensils necessary to put their meal together, and Kelsey wondered when it was that he'd become so familiar with her home. "Do you need help?"

"No. I've got it." He glanced up but continued to dice an onion at a thousand miles an hour without missing a beat. "Why don't you go sit down? Watch some TV?"

She'd love nothing more than to leave the room. To hide somewhere in the house away from all the conflicting emotions West stirred just by being West, but she knew she wouldn't. As much as she wanted to avoid him—to stick her head in the sand and pretend there wasn't a big fat white elephant in the room—she wanted to be near him more.

With a sigh, Kelsey pulled out a stool at her small corner table and sat. "I'm good here. Are you sure you don't want a hand?"

"Nah, almost done." West grinned at her with that knee-wobbling smile that never failed to send her into a restless, flustered state. Oblivious to her reactions to him, he skillfully prepared their dinner.

Tense beyond tolerable, Kelsey tried to think of something to talk about that would relieve the strain. Something that wouldn't lead to awkward questions. "How was work?"

He looked up with a frown and shrugged. "The usual."

"Oh. Right. Good." She couldn't keep eye contact. Not with all those questions she didn't want to answer, or even hear, lurking in his piercing gray gaze.

"Kels."

She reluctantly met his gaze once more, but there must have been something in hers—some desperate plea in her expression—because he shook his head and turned to the stove where he lit the burner under the pan.

Kelsey leaned one elbow on the table and propped her chin in her hand while she watched West move around. For as long as she'd known him, he'd loved to cook. One of the few boys in their year to take cooking in high school, it had been a part of him from the beginning. And now, having a front row seat to a grownup West using his culinary skills, she had to admit it was totally hot. And she wasn't referring to the stove.

He moved with fluid grace and a confidence that spoke volumes. She'd never felt that confident about anything. Not even her job gave her that level of self-belief and she was a damn good accountant. It just wasn't enough. What would it be like to feel complete satisfaction in anything? Kelsey had never known that feeling. No, that was a lie. Once. Once she'd felt the glow of contentment so enormous she'd floated on a cloud for weeks. Until it had all come crashing down in the face of West's lack of interest.

"Hey." West clicked his fingers in front of her. "You still with me?"

"Sorry. What?" She blinked and brought her focus back to the man before her.

"I asked if you wanted to eat in here or out in the living room."

Kelsey stood up. "The living room will be more comfortable." It would also offer a distraction in the form of her TV.

"Here." He held out two plates filled with a yummy-smelling noodle stir-fry. "You take these and I'll grab drinks and cutlery."

She took their meal and headed towards the front of the house. She'd bought an older place when her divorce was final with the hope of doing it up. But so far, in the not quite two years she'd lived here, she'd done nothing more than line the cupboards with paper.

Putting their plates on her garage-sale coffee table, she sat on her worn secondhand couch and questioned why she was living with hand-me-down furniture when she could afford to purchase new. The only new things in the house were the TV and her bed. Everything else had been picked up cheap or given to her.

"Water good?" West asked as he put two glasses on the table in front of her. He held out a fork. "Dig in before it gets cold."

Kelsey stared at the scratched and scarred fork. Oh my God. Even the cutlery was secondhand. She raised her gaze to find West watching her with one eyebrow arched in question.

"Everything is old," she murmured.

Wrinkles creased his forehead as he sat beside her still holding the fork out to her. "Huh?"

"All my stuff. It's old and used and I have no idea why."

"*Okay.*"

"Don't you see?"

He shook his head. "No, I don't understand what you're talking about."

And then it dawned on her. She'd walked away from Bry with nothing. She let him keep their house, their furnishings, even her car. Sure, he'd paid her half the value of everything they owned in the divorce settlement, but before that she'd left with her clothes and half the money in their savings account. Why would she do that? It didn't make any sense. She'd always had secondhand belongings growing up and she'd vowed never to settle for second best again once she moved out of her childhood home.

Her gaze travelled around the room. Jesus. Even the blinds were used. She'd picked them up at the same garage sale as the coffee table, thinking they'd do for a few weeks until she bought new ones, only she still hadn't replaced them.

"Kels?" West put his hand on her knee, drawing her attention back to him.

Knowledge slammed into her like a punch to the stomach. She'd not only settled for second best when it came to her possessions. She'd settled for the love she felt for Bry instead of putting her heart on the line and going after the man she'd really wanted all those years ago.

6

West leaned back and extended his legs out in front of him. He laced his fingers together and rested them on his stomach as he settled his gaze on the TV. He'd wanted to talk to Kelsey. Wanted to get things out in the open, but he knew that would probably cause distress. For the moment, he was enjoying sitting together, relaxing while some sitcom played out on the screen before them.

The meal he'd cooked was gone, and he was pretty sure Kels was dozing off beside him. Another reason not to bring up the topic neither of them seemed to want to deal with. He hoped she drifted off to sleep so he could sit beside her for a few hours without the usual turmoil. No pressure. Lately, every time they saw each other the tension between them was so thick you could cut the air with a knife. But if she were asleep, those barriers she always erected when he was around would be down and he could drop his guard too. Not worry about every little move he made or word he said.

He yawned and did something he hadn't done since he was a teenager. Stretching his arms over his head, he rolled his shoulders before he brought his arms down to lie along the back of the couch. West grinned when Kelsey didn't flinch. If he was in luck, she was already on her way to the land of nods and wouldn't even notice his juvenile move.

A few minutes later, a soft snoring came from beside him and he leaned forward to get a look at her face. Sure enough, she'd fallen asleep. She was probably still feeling the draining effects of last night's binge. He always slept like the dead for the next few days after getting rolling drunk, and Kelsey's body wasn't used to consuming large amounts of alcohol so she was liable to feel it for a long time yet.

West thought about moving her to bed where she'd be more comfortable, but he figured she'd wake up and send him home, and he wasn't ready to leave yet. Wrapping his arm around her shoulders, he nudged her closer against his side and was pleased when not only didn't she protest the move, but she snuggled in. She turned towards him and nestled her head into the crook of his neck, splayed her hand over his chest.

You couldn't have removed the grin from his face with a crowbar. He continued to watch TV, but if someone asked him what was on he couldn't tell them. The woman beside him held his complete attention and he gave in to the urge to look at her. Her features were so delicate—high sculpted cheekbones, long, feathery lashes, her slender nose drawing down to an up-turned tip. And her lips... They were plump, but not that bee-stung look some women were into these days. No, Kelsey's were just right as far as West was concerned. He'd love to lean over and lay his mouth on hers, but he wasn't stupid and really didn't want her to send him packing just yet.

He ignored the TV and continued to stare at Kels. He'd been shocked when she'd cut off her long hair a few years back, but he understood it was a cleansing of sorts for her. She'd left her husband and was starting a new life, so it had seemed only fitting she should have a new look. And West had to admit he loved the shorter length. There was still plenty of hair to get his fingers tangled in, and the way it floated around her face giving her a just-out-of-bed look always managed to get his engine revving.

Not that he was ever idle when Kelsey was around. He'd spent years living with the low buzz of arousal where she was concerned. Amazing how she could get him worked up without trying, and it took concentrated effort by other women to even pique his interest, never mind get him off. He hadn't been a monk or anything like that. He was a healthy guy after all, but he hadn't been one to indulge in one-night stands.

His longest relationship had lasted a year. But he usually found himself losing interest long before that, and if he were honest, he'd have to admit the woman currently lying in his arms was the reason. Even when she'd been off-limits he'd held out a tiny bit of hope that he'd have her one day in the future. And didn't that make him a prick of a friend.

He scrubbed his free hand over his face. All this self-examination was doing his head in. Closing his eyes, he concentrated on the feel of Kelsey against him and the steady rush of her breath warming his skin through his shirt as she slept in his arms.

West woke with a pain in his neck and an elbow in his ribs. The neck ache was due to his head flopping forward in his sleep and the elbow belonged to the woman currently cursing under her breath and trying to crawl off him.

Kelsey.

He sucked in a jagged breath when her knee came dangerously close to his goods.

"Kels," he warned.

"Shit." West cracked one eye to see her glaring at him. "Don't do that!"

"Don't do what?" he grumbled. "I'm not the one inflicting grievous bodily harm."

"What?"

He glanced down at his groin where her knee was still firmly wedged between his thighs only centimeters from his balls.

"Oh my God." She planted her hands, fingers splayed, on his chest and pushed back. "Sorry. I didn't mean…"

Her words ground to a stop when she noticed things weren't exactly quiet down there. His usual morning woody was helped along by the fact she'd been plastered against him in all her curvaceous glory not five minutes ago. And while his jeans weren't skin tight, they certainly didn't offer enough room to hide eight inches of hard flesh from view.

"I...um..."

West kept his eyes on her face, so when she stammered over her stuttered breath and licked her lips, he all but burst from the zipper in his pants. "Kels." He wasn't sure what he was saying other than her name. Need rocketed through him, and if she didn't take her delectable ass off his lap in the next five seconds he wouldn't be responsible for where she ended up. Or down. He'd like her down. On her back, legs wide, waiting for him to plunge deep.

Kelsey's gaze slowly travelled up his torso until she met his eyes with ones swimming in emotion. West could see the struggle, knew his own gaze reflected the same desperate war of advance or retreat. In the end, it was need that won out.

He wasn't sure which one of them moved first. It didn't matter. Their lips fused in a kiss so hot, so wet his mind switched off and his body took over. Every nerve sparked with awareness until he felt like a livewire in urgent need of discharging latent energy. She slid her hands up his chest and scrunched her fingers in the fabric of his T-shirt as they took the kiss deeper.

She opened for him. Let him tease and take at his will. Her surrender fired his blood, filled his already hard cock with pounding heat. He shoved his hands into her hair and pinned her head in place so he could devour her mouth more. God, he wanted so much more. The whimper that slipped up her throat was sucked down his, and West knew if they didn't stop now, they wouldn't. And as much as he wanted to overwhelm her with desire to get what he wanted he couldn't.

Pulling his mouth from hers, he moved his hands to cup her face and waited for her eyes to open. Her eyelashes fluttered, slowly rising to reveal eyes gone black with arousal. A small outer rim of blue was the only glimpse of her normally clear-blue gaze. When her tongue peaked out and swiped across her kiss-swollen bottom lip, he wanted to dive right back in again. But he couldn't. Not without her full agreement.

"If we're going to stop it has to be now," he growled through clenched teeth. "If you want to keep going then we're moving this party to your bed where I can spread you out and take my fill before starting all over again at the beginning."

Kelsey's breath hitched and she curled her fingers into his shirt tighter as her eyes dilated farther. "I…"

West waited for her to finish. She glanced down, air whistling through her teeth as she flexed her fingers on his chest, digging her nails into his pecs. He knew she was looking at his cock. Regardless of the thick denim of his jeans, his width and length were clearly outlined. "What's it gonna be, Kels?"

Gaze still lowered, she shifted forward, kept moving until her sex sat snug against his. He dragged in a breath, clenching his fingers as he used his grip to tilt her face up. Her eyes were alight with lust and a dark swirl of need lanced through his belly and exploded in his groin. He'd given her an out. Done the right thing by giving her a choice, but with that move, with the way she was grinding herself against him…

He pulled her head to his and slanted his mouth over hers. Any answer she might have given was erased by the swipe of his tongue. She met him stroke for stroke. And when he slipped his hands down her neck and over her chest, she tore her mouth from his and arched back.

"Don't stop," she panted.

It was all the invitation West needed. He surged to his feet and, gripping her ass cheeks to keep her wrapped around him, strode from the room.

Kelsey's heart beat in her chest so hard she thought her ribs might crack. Her stomach fluttered, dipping and rolling, as West carried her down the hall to her room. She knew there were reasons they shouldn't do this. Knew this would complicate their already confusing relationship, but for the life of her she couldn't deny herself the pleasure of being with him again.

He dropped her to the bed and followed her down, draping his hard body over hers and pressing her deeper into the mattress. His weight was a welcome burden. One she'd craved with a secret yearning for years. And now she was here. Beneath him once more.

"Kels."

Her gaze met his.

"This is your last chance. Yes or no?"

His eyes searched hers, the need and desire flaring in the deep-gray gaze she knew so well only reaffirmed her decision. "Yes."

West took her mouth then. But this time he didn't ravish—he cherished. With liquid strokes and barely there caresses, he drove her out of her mind with need. She wanted them naked. Wanted to be under him skin on skin, hard on soft. His mouth left hers to trail over her chin and along her jaw until his lips toyed with the delicate skin beneath her ear. He licked and sucked and nipped with his teeth, drawing unintelligible words from her throat.

Growling, West dragged his teeth across her flesh and latched onto her earlobe. Sucked it between his lips and flicked it with his tongue. A shiver skipped down her spine.

"I want you naked. Now." The gravelly need-drenched tone sent a shudder shaking her from head to toe.

He sprang from the bed and Kelsey watched, unable to move as he put his arms over his head, grabbed the back of his shirt and tugged it off with one swift yank. Her mouth watered. His chest was a work of art. She'd felt his sculptured contours earlier, but seeing them uncovered did extraordinary things to her insides. She tightened and loosened all at once. Slick heat filled her core while the rolling clench of her pussy was a reminder of how long she'd gone without the pleasure of a man between her thighs.

West tipped his chin towards her as his hands worked at the button on his pants. "Get naked, Kels, or I'm ripping those clothes off you."

She had no doubt he'd follow through on his threat, but suddenly the idea of being exposed to this man delivered a sharp blade of fear she had no hope of squashing when faced with such masculine perfection.

"Kelsey?" West's hands were clenched at his sides, his jeans open but still up, and she brought her gaze up to meet his. "Second thoughts?"

She sank her teeth into her bottom lip as she shook her head.

"I'm hanging on the edge. You're either in this with me, all the way, or you're not."

"You're beautiful." The words left her mouth without consent and her cheeks filled with heat at her wayward tongue.

He grinned and pushed his pants down his hips, revealing his erection. "Oh no." West kicked his pants aside and put one knee on the bed. "We haven't even begun to uncover beautiful yet."

And then he began to undress her. He started with her top. Inching it up her body to reveal a centimeter at a time, he took long seconds to kiss each new section of skin he exposed.

"Here."

He kissed the curve of her waist.

"And here."

Another kiss just below her belly button.

"Mmm, here too."

More kisses were trailed across her stomach until she quivered with anticipation of where he would lay his lips next. It seemed to take forever for him to reach her breasts. But when he did, the attention she was expecting never came. Instead, he trailed his fingers over her, dragging her top with them, up to her collarbones. She trembled as she waited to see what he would do.

"I think we need to get rid of this." West tugged on her shirt, urging her to lift up and raise her arms so he could whisk the fabric away. "Ah, there. See, now that's what I call beautiful."

He stroked his fingers along the lace edge of her bra, his thumbs a whispered caress over her taut nipples where they pressed against the silky barrier that remained between them. Her breath hitched and she held still, every nerve waiting for the next touch, the next word.

"So, so beautiful," he murmured as he lowered his head to press his lips to the upper curve of her breast.

"West." Kelsey wasn't sure what she wanted or how to say it, she just knew she needed him to do more. Yes. "More."

His mouth found hers and he spoke against her lips. "Don't worry. There's definitely going to be more. But first..." He sat up and moved lower on the bed. "These have to go."

He slid his fingers into either side of her sweat pants and tugged them down her legs. She held her breath as he stared down at the sheer white panties she wore. They were one of her nicest pairs and she briefly wondered if she'd put them on yesterday with this in mind.

"God. Kelsey."

Her fears of earlier evaporated under his gaze, in the echo of his words. In that moment, she believed he saw her as beautiful whether she saw herself that way or not. She curled her hands around his biceps and pulled him closer as she lifted up to meet him. When her mouth met his, she nibbled on his lips, licked at the seam and pressed inside to taste him again.

He let her have her way, held perfectly still while letting her lead him into the sweetest kiss she'd ever known. As the seconds ticked by, Kelsey's need grew until kissing him wasn't enough. She had to have it all.

7

West pulled in a sharp breath and stared at the woman laid out before him. She'd been gorgeous as a teenager but now...with all the curves the years had added, Kelsey was a mouthwatering, mind-numbing dream come true. *His* dream come true. He wanted to devour her—gobble her up whole—and slake the lust burning in his bones. Except he didn't want to rush—didn't want this to be over too soon. Like their first time, he wanted to take his time, imprint every second of being with her on his memory for all eternity.

He traced a finger along the edge of her underwear. Back and forth. Back and forth. When he dipped beneath the flimsy fabric, she sucked in a breath, her stomach rippling, as he teased the skin hidden but not. The sheerness of her lace panties really didn't conceal a thing. Her dark cleft was easily seen and the moisture seeping from her body rendered the crotch area completely transparent. But even with so little of her covered, he wanted to see more.

"Let's get rid of these." West slipped both hands into the sides of her underwear and dragged them over her hips and down her thighs. "Jesus."

If he thought the sight of her wet panties was a turn on, it was nothing compared to the glistening flesh he'd revealed. His hands shook as he pulled her pants the rest of the way off. He tossed them over his shoulder, uncaring of where they landed, and then he reached for her hands and tugged her up until she sat before him so he could get rid of the last barrier between them.

"And this." With one flick, he had her bra undone. The straps slipped from her shoulders and he didn't waste a second removing it from her body and throwing it aside. "Jesus. You're so beautiful."

He pushed her back onto the bed as he leaned over and dropped a kiss on her stomach, just below her belly button and the cute little belly ring he'd had no idea she'd gotten. With his tongue, he toyed with the dangling stone and watched as goose bumps rose in a wave over her skin.

"When did you get this?" he spoke while continuing to tease her with his lips, his tongue and finally, his teeth, giving the tiny silver chain that held the sparkling purple stone a tug.

"A-ages. Ago." Her words came out around her stuttered breath and West smiled against her skin as he nuzzled his way higher.

"I like it," he murmured against the underside of her breast. "A lot." He nipped her smooth skin.

Her breath hitched, her chest rising and offering him the perfect place to feast. He didn't need to be enticed by her curves though. He was already well aware of—and wanted—every part of her. He'd waited so long to get her here. To be hovering over her while she quivered beneath him. And as much as he wanted to take his time, his patience to have her was running out. Fast.

West ran his tongue up between Kelsey's breasts until he reached the hollow at the base of her throat. Her pulse beat frantically beneath her skin and he figured if that was an indication of her arousal, she was right there with him. On the verge of going over the edge with little encouragement. Did she want him as badly as he wanted her? God, he hoped so. Because at this point, he wasn't fooling himself any longer. He had to have her and have her now.

"Kels." He spoke her name but he couldn't decide if he was asking for something or just reminding himself of who he was with—that this wasn't a dream like so many times before.

"West. Please."

He pulled back enough to look at her face, to see her eyes and the need and the want swirling in her gaze. To confirm in his own mind that he wasn't the only one being driven crazy. "Tell me what you want?"

West wasn't sure why he asked her, because he didn't think he could last much longer. If she didn't want what he did…

Kelsey cupped his face with both hands and pulled him towards her until their mouths were a breath apart. "You. I want you."

Her words were exactly what he needed to hear. With a slowness that almost killed him, West lowered his body to hers. From toes to chest, he pressed himself against her. His cock found the soft cushion of her pussy and the heat and wetness that surrounded his throbbing flesh dragged a groan from his throat.

"I want you now. *Need* you now."

"Yes," she breathed against his mouth before her lips met his.

The kiss started out soft—sweet—but soon their tongues tangled and their teeth bumped as they ate hungrily at each other. West rocked his hips, his intentions clear, and when Kels arched up to join him in their intimate dance, he knew he'd reached his limit.

He tore his mouth from hers. "Protection?"

"I'm covered and clean." She chewed the corner of her mouth and West's balls throbbed.

"I'm clean, but I have a condom in my wallet if you want me to get it." He had to give her the option. She had no reason to believe him, and while he hadn't been with a woman since he'd heard her and Bry had split, Kels didn't know that, and West had no intention of telling her. Yet. Giving her that kind of power over him when this thing between them was so fresh didn't feel right.

Her eyes searched his and West thought she might have been having second thoughts about the whole thing. In a split second, he made the decision for her. As much as he wanted to take her bare, he wanted her to want that too, and right now he wasn't sure she wanted him to keep going never mind come inside her.

"I'll grab the condom."

West jumped off the bed and raced from the room, cursing under his breath the whole way to the kitchen for taking his wallet out of his back pocket. He found his keys on the counter but no wallet. He could have sworn he'd put them down together. Spinning around, he was about to make his way to the living room when he kicked the missing wallet across the floor. It must have dropped off the counter at some point last night.

He scooped it up and ran back to the bedroom. It probably looked odd, a naked man sprinting through the house, but at this point West didn't care. All he was worried about was getting back to Kelsey before she changed her mind. Flipping his wallet open, he pulled out the one condom he kept on hand and prayed it wasn't past its use-by date. Although she said she was covered, he still didn't want to deal with the stress a broken condom would cause when they already had enough tension in their relationship.

"Got it." He held it up as he re-entered Kelsey's room, stopping short when he caught sight of her.

She hadn't moved. Her legs were stretched out, slightly parted and her hands rested on the pillow beside her head. She really was his dream come to life, and with everything he was, he would make sure he didn't fuck things up this time.

Forcing himself to move, West made his way back to the bed, dropping his wallet and tearing open the foil packet as he went. He stood at the foot of the mattress looking up at Kelsey, his gaze locked on hers as he fitted the condom over his cock. Covered, he placed a hand either side of her legs and slowly climbed onto the bed and up her body until his mouth hovered over hers.

"You still with me?" He wanted to kick his own ass for giving her another out, but he needed her with him. All the way with him.

"Yes." She placed her hands on his chest and trailed them down his torso until he shuddered with anticipation of her fingers wrapping around his hard length. Except she didn't grab him. Instead, she slid her hands to his hips and, digging in her fingers, urged him down.

He complied because he had no choice. His mind was one step behind his body. Slipping a knee between hers, West nudged until Kels parted her legs farther and gave him the room he needed to settle over her completely. They fit perfectly. At least it seemed that way to him. Then again, he'd waited so long to be with her he wouldn't care even if they didn't match in all the right places.

When they finally connected, skin to skin, from chest to feet, he held still. He wanted to take one second—only one—to savor the feel of Kels beneath him. She was soft where he was hard, and the silkiness of her skin where it pressed against his made him think of warm honey. Why, he hadn't a clue, but think it he did.

This woman did things to him no one else ever had. It wasn't just his body that reacted to her, his mind did too, thoughts and ideas inspired by nobody but Kelsey always filled his head when she was around. And when she wasn't. He'd never wanted to do better, *be* better, for anybody but her. If she'd only give him a chance, he'd spend the rest of his life being the best at everything for her.

Kelsey didn't think she'd drawn a full breath since West had taken off her clothes. The way he'd cherished each new section of flesh he'd uncovered and those teasing tugs on her belly ring had stolen her ability to think as well as breathe. He made her feel sexy and beautiful and desirable in a way Bry never had. Not that she should or was comparing them. They were so different and not just in the way they made her feel.

Bry was safe, comfortable, like slipping on a pair of old running shoes. Whereas West was daring, sexy beyond belief and a little disturbing, like wearing a pair of five-inch red stilettos. Except there were moments when West made her feel so content to be near him that she had to wonder if he couldn't give her what she'd sought from Bry all those years ago. Why she was thinking any of this while they lay skin on skin for the first time in over a decade was anyone's guess.

She didn't need to worry about thinking anymore when West bucked his hips and distracted her with the hot, heavy slide of his cock over her sex. Her muscles contracted and moisture coated her folds as the area throbbed with need. She'd never felt this close to coming with so little stimulation. It always took concentration on her part—concerted effort on her partner's—to get her there.

Except with West.

With him, all it took was a look. Kelsey didn't know whether to be embarrassed by how easy she was where he was concerned or thrilled that he could give her pleasure without thought or effort. Not wanting to be the only one experiencing this almost overwhelming rush to the finish line, she set her hands and fingers in motion. She started with his back and explored the smooth contours of muscle over bone, the broad sweep of his shoulders and then down his spine to the taut globes of his ass.

"God. That feels so good. Don't stop, Kels. Touch me everywhere."

West's panted words urged her on. She wanted to stroke every inch of him, but the need pulsing between her thighs grew more demanding with each beat, and she knew touching him wasn't going to be enough. Not right now.

Kelsey rolled her hips, thrust up and down with an urgency that increased the more she did it. His legs slipped deeper between hers and the crown of his cock nestled its way inside her folds to nudge her opening. On reflex, her legs widened and her pelvis lifted, causing him to sink inside the barest of millimeters. But it was enough to send her into a need so frenzied her vision blurred, her hips bucked and her nails dug into the flesh of his ass cheeks.

"Kels. Slow down."

"No." She dug her fingers in harder, used her feet to brace herself against the bed and drove herself onto his length as far as she could.

"Fuck!"

It was the only warning she got before West plunged down and impaled her completely.

For a split second, they froze. Kelsey didn't even breathe. Then everything happened at once. West moved, withdrew on a slow glide that instantly picked up speed, then drove back in again. She rose to meet him, digging her feet into the mattress as she did. He surged in and out, each stroke harder and faster than the last until she had no choice but to just hold on for the ride.

She wrapped her legs around his hips, her arms around his shoulders, and bowed her back to lift her hips to his. The new position sent him deeper, and the change of angle meant his cock brushed over the sensitive spot inside that guaranteed she'd find release.

He rose onto his elbows and stared down at her with eyes gone black. His jaw was firm, a muscle twitched along the right side, and his nostrils flared wide as he drew in ragged breaths.

"I want you with me," he puffed out. "I can't last much longer."

Kelsey wasn't worried he'd come without her. The tightness in her lower belly and the pulsing tingle in her clit signaled she wouldn't last much longer either. And when West leaned to one side and slipped a hand between them to stroke the bundle of nerves gone taut with need, he barely had to touch her to send her flying.

The orgasm ripped through her. It wasn't a gradual wave of release. It was a full-body slam. Head to toe in one simultaneous discharge of energy. Her back arched as every part of her went rigid for a split second before she dissolved into a liquid heat so intense she lost touch with reality for a moment.

West's control seemed to snap in that instant. He grabbed the back of her thighs and pulled them wider as he pistoned his hips, plunging his cock in and out until he broke. His body jerked, his rhythm lost as he came. The growl he emitted through clenched teeth was one of pleasure and pain that she remembered from their first time.

Memories swamped her, and with her emotions so recently bombarded, Kelsey couldn't fight the tears stinging her eyes. They leaked from the corners even though she squeezed her eyes shut so tight she saw stars.

"Kelsey?" West's voice was hoarse.

She didn't open her eyes. Couldn't let him see the regret and longing—the guilt—she knew would be reflected there. Turning her head, she burrowed her face against his neck. He still covered her, remained buried inside, but he held his weight on his arms as he bracketed her head with his hands and forced her to face him.

"Open your eyes." His hands tightened, but not painfully. "Look at me. Please."

It was the please that got her. Slowly, she raised her eyelids and met his gaze.

"Did I hurt you?"

Kelsey shook her head.

"Then why are you crying? Do you regret what we just did already?"

Why did he sound like he expected her to regret this? Even if she had to wait another ten years, or worse, never touched him again, she'd never regret making love with West. "No."

"Then why the tears? Talk to me."

She wasn't sure herself so how could she explain to him the maelstrom of emotions currently turning her insides into a tornado?

---

est eased out of Kelsey and rolled to the side, taking her with him so she lay across his chest, her head resting on his shoulder. "Talk to me," he murmured into her hair.

He stroked his hands up and down her back, the action designed to soothe her and the sudden anxiety that he'd fucked up royally—again—ripping through his gut.

"Kels?"

She shifted, buried her face against his neck, drew in a deep breath and let it out in a rush. "I don't know."

Huh? "You don't know why you're crying?" How could she not know?

She shook her head, the soft strands of her hair tickling his chin, catching in his stubble.

"Something must have made you cry. Are you sure I didn't hurt you? I was a little rough." He'd been desperate at the end there, and he was afraid his need had caused him to take her too hard—push her too far.

"No. You didn't hurt me." Kelsey tried to pull away but he tightened his grip and held her close.

"Stay. Let me hold you a little while."

West held his breath until she relaxed against him. He didn't speak, didn't want to risk her bolting if he said the wrong thing. He'd wait her out. She'd talk to him eventually. At least he hoped she would.

The phone beside the bed rang, disturbing the strained silence surrounding them. Kelsey pressed her hand to his chest and pushed, but he didn't let her go.

"I should get that," she said, her lips moving over his skin and sending chills down his spine.

"Let your machine pick it up." West wanted to wrap his hands around the neck of the person on the other end of the phone. "It's barely daylight. Who the hell rings at this time of the morning?"

"Nobody. Which is why I should answer. It could be an emergency."

There was nothing urgent enough other than death to warrant a dawn phone call, but he conceded her point. "Maybe. If they leave a message and it is, you can get back to them. If not we can stay right where we are."

Kelsey's voice echoed down the hallway and into the room, her message short and to the point, followed by the beep and then the last person West wanted to hear today of all days spoke.

"Kelsey. Sorry to ring so early, but I knew you wouldn't mind. Mum had a bad night. She's confused and asking for you. She won't let anyone else near her. Do you think you can drop into the home and settle her down this morning? She doesn't recognize me or I'd calm her myself. If you get this in the next thirty minutes ring me." The house went as silent as a tomb when Bry hung up.

Kelsey had stiffened in West's arms the second Bry's voice had blasted through the machine, and West knew there would be nothing he could do or say right now that would do him any favors. So when she pushed out of his arms and turned away to fling her legs off the bed and stand, he let her go without a fight.

"I have to go." She didn't look at him as she made her way over to the bathroom.

"I know." He sat up, removed the condom hanging from his now limp dick and wrapped it in a tissue from the box beside the bed.

"Can you let yourself out?" she asked without turning around.

He'd been dismissed. And while that possibility had lurked in the back of his mind, to actually hear Kels say those words—to *see* her dismiss him without a second thought as she ran to help her ex—cut so deeply that West looked down to check there wasn't a gaping hole in his gut. She was the only person who could kill him with a few words or none at all.

"West?"

He glanced up and met her gaze. "Yeah, I'll let myself out."

There must have been something in his voice or his expression, because she came back to the bed and reached out to stroke her fingers through his hair. "I have to go. Marjorie needs—"

West reached up and placed two fingers over her lips. "It's okay. Go. I'll talk to you later."

"Are you sure?" She spoke against his fingers, the warmth of her breath caressing his skin sending a shiver down his spine.

"Yes." He removed his hand and used both hands on her hips to turn her around and point her in the direction of the bathroom again. "Go. Do what you have to."

She glanced over her shoulder once before nodding and making her way across the room again. When the door closed between them, West let out a breath and flopped back on the bed. He stared at the ceiling. This wasn't the way he wanted to end their first time together, but he couldn't demand she not go no matter how much he wanted to. He'd love to stay until she came out of the bathroom except he didn't think that would do his cause any good either.

With a sigh, he dragged himself off the bed and gathered up his clothes and wallet. He grabbed the used condom and headed to the kitchen where he quickly trashed the rubber, got dressed and scooped up his keys. His shoes were in the living room, and once he had those on he was out of reasons not to leave. Heart heavy in his chest, he made his way to the front door. But he couldn't resist one last glance down the hallway before he opened the door and walked out.

8

K elsey rushed into the nursing home where Bry met her before she'd taken more than three steps into the foyer.

"Thank God, you're here," he said as he reached for her hand and pulled her into a quick hug.

"How is she?" Kelsey asked as she slipped from his embrace.

"Not good." He led her down the brightly lit hallway. "They were going to sedate her if you didn't get here soon."

"I got here as quickly as I could." Guilt swamped her.

"Oh, I know, I wasn't having a go at you." Bry glanced at her. "Did I wake you?"

"Ah, no. I was up." Kelsey felt her cheeks heat as she recalled exactly what she'd been doing when he rang. "I was, um, in the shower."

"Right. Well, I'm just so grateful that you came." He stopped her outside his mother's room and Kelsey could hear the older woman calling her name from the other side of the closed door, but Bry grabbed her hand before she could push her way inside. "Wait a second. When was the last time you saw mum?"

She had to think for a moment. She'd meant to keep up her visits when she'd separated from Bry, and she had in the beginning, but with setting up her new life and the fact that Marjorie rarely remembered anyone now days, Kelsey had let those visits slide. "A couple of months." She winced. "Maybe six."

"Try not to be shocked by her appearance. She's deteriorated rapidly in the last few weeks. Her weight is down and her lucid episodes are more and more infrequent."

"Okay."

Bry sighed. "She thinks we're still married, Kelsey."

"Oh." The last time she'd seen Marjorie they'd spoken about the divorce and Marjorie had voiced her disappointment that Bry and Kelsey couldn't make it work. Maybe her lack of memory was a good thing. At least now her ex-mother-in-law wouldn't be sad to see her.

"I know it's a lot to ask, but could you pretend we are while you're in there? She doesn't recognize me, so it's not like you'll have to be all over me or anything like that," he quickly reassured her. "In fact, she thinks I'm a doctor who's going to give her some horrible medicine or do something heinous to her so I won't come in at all if that's all right with you."

Kelsey looked at Bry for the first time since she arrived. *Really* looked at him. His cheeks were hollow and the bags under his eyes were a deep, dark-blue-black that made him look as though he hadn't slept in weeks. He'd lost weight too. She placed her hand on his arm and gave him a gentle squeeze. "It's fine. I'll see if I can get her settled."

"Thank you." His smile was a bare stretch of his lips and failed to convey any real happiness.

She smiled a sad smile of her own as she let go and turned to face his mother's door. Taking a deep breath, Kelsey tried to calm her nerves and put a genuine smile on her face. With her emotions fortified and her game face on she pushed open the door and greeted the woman who'd been her surrogate mother for most of her adult life.

"Marjorie. I hear you're giving everyone a hard time."

"Kelsey? Where have you been?" Her former mother-in-law

demanded as she rushed towards Kelsey and threw her thin arms around Kelsey's neck.

Kelsey did the only thing she could. She slipped her own arms around Marjorie's frail body and pulled her close. Closing her eyes, she held on, comforting herself and the older woman for long moments.

When Kelsey opened her eyes, she saw the staff had left them alone at some point, and with care, she eased Marjorie out of her arms and over to the bed. "Come on. Let's get you back into bed."

"Where's that son of mine? Why isn't he here with you? I don't know why you ever married that no good fool, but I'm so glad that you did, because if it wasn't for you I'd never see anyone besides those horrible doctors and nurses who want to perform weird medical experiments on me." Marjorie complained the whole time Kelsey helped her onto the bed and tucked her in.

"They're not going to experiment on you. They're trying to make you feel better, not worse," Kelsey soothed.

"Hmph. That's what they tell *you*," Marjorie mumbled as she snuggled down under the blankets.

Kelsey smiled. Marjorie's memory might have gone, but her imagination was still as fanciful as when she'd been a young woman writing fiction novels.

"Want me to read to you?" Kelsey knew that was one thing that her former mother-in-law still enjoyed even in her deteriorated mental state. Well, at least she had when Kelsey had been here last.

"Oh. Yes. Read to me."

The book on Marjorie's bedside table had a bookmark sticking out of the middle. When Kelsey picked it up she discovered someone —probably Bry—had been reading Marjorie one of her own early works. Smiling, she dragged over the armchair and took a seat. "I'll start where you finished off."

She was barely a page in when Marjorie's eyelids started to droop. And by the time Kelsey got to the bottom of the third page, Marjorie was sound asleep. Not wanting to risk stopping too soon, she kept reading for a few more pages.

The door creaked open behind her and she turned to see Bry poking his head through the small opening. "She asleep?" he whispered.

"Yeah." Kelsey placed the bookmark back where she'd started to read, figuring Marjorie wouldn't remember her reading that part and stood. "We should leave her to rest."

Bry backed out into the hallway as Kelsey moved towards the door. With one final look over her shoulder to assure herself Marjorie was covered, Kelsey exited the room, making sure the door didn't make a sound as it closed behind her. Neither of them spoke as they made their way along the corridor to the family room set aside for residents and their guests.

"Thank you for coming," Bry said as he held the door open for her.

"Bry why didn't you tell me she was getting worse?" Kelsey hoped their divorce hadn't given him the impression she no longer cared about his mother. Or him.

He sighed. "I didn't want to impose."

"Bryan. For God's sake, she's more of a mother to me than my own." It hurt to think he hadn't wanted to share Marjorie's worsening state with her. They might be divorced, but they were still friends. At least she'd thought they were. "I didn't think the divorce had affected our friendship but obviously it has."

"It hasn't." He scrubbed a hand over his face. "I haven't told anyone she's gotten worse. Honestly, until today it was just more prolonged memory loss." Bry shook his head. "I don't know what this morning was about."

Kelsey watched as he dropped into a chair and, resting his elbows on his knees, cradled his head in his hands. She walked over and put her hand on his shoulder. "So what happened last night?"

He shook his head again. "I haven't a clue. The night staff said she went to bed at her usual time. Perfectly fine. Then around one she woke disorientated and calling for you."

She took the seat next to him. "Has something happened recently that might have triggered her memories of me? As I said before, it's probably six months since I've visited and she barely recognized me the last time I was here. I had to keep reminding her who I was."

"No, nothing that I know of. And she hasn't recognized me for the last month, although until today she was happy to sit and chat, let me read to her, but for some reason I'm the enemy now."

Bry sounded so dejected, so heartbroken, that it was only natural for Kelsey to lean over and wrap her arms around him. "I'm so sorry. It's horrible to see Marjorie in such a debilitated state. I can only imagine what it must be like for you."

His arms came around her and he pulled her closer until she was almost in his lap. The action felt so normal, Kelsey didn't think to protest, never mind hold back. She slipped into his lap and held him tight.

"I have no right to ask," Bry murmured into her hair. "But I'm going to. I can't do this on my own any more. I need you, Kelsey."

West dropped the knife after he narrowly avoided slicing his thumb for the third time. He really shouldn't be chopping onions when his mind wasn't completely focused on the job. He'd be lucky if he didn't lose a finger, never mind cut one. With a sigh, he left the knife where it had fallen and walked over to the cold room to grab a bottle of water. Bottle in hand, he headed for his office. The onions could wait. It was busy work anyway.

No one else was in yet, the quiet only broken by the hum of the refrigeration units, and he knew he had the place to himself for another couple of hours. Plenty of time to brood. Alone.

He'd gone home after leaving Kelsey's, but a shower hadn't calmed his agitated state so he'd headed in to work. Not that he'd fared much better here. He dropped into his chair and leaned back, closing his eyes. It wasn't even three hours since he'd left Kels, but he already craved the sight—the touch—of her again.

She hadn't called to let him know everything was okay. Then again, should he expect her to? Sure, they'd slept together, but did that mean they were supposed to check in now? He didn't think so. And if recent weeks—hell, months—were anything to go by, he'd be the one making the first move. Every time he'd gotten closer, she'd thrown up a red light to stop him. He didn't think the fact they'd finally tumbled into bed would make any difference either. His phone vibrated in his pocket and his heart skipped a beat in hope. Hope that was quickly crushed when he saw the message was from Coop.

Can't make tonight.

Tonight? West's mind went blank. He had no idea what Coop was referring to. He started to type a reply when it hit him. They were supposed to get together with Zac for a few drinks. He deleted what he'd already written and started again.

Cool. Works for me. You wanna text Zac or will I?

West held his phone and waited for Coop to reply. Instead, he got a message from Zac.

Don't tell me. Something came up for you too.

He stared at his phone. He could hear the censure in his friend's words. West thought about saying yes but decided he really needed to get whatever the hell was bugging Zac out in the open before it destroyed their friendship.

Nope. I'm still good. Usual time, usual place?

He'd just hit send when his phone buzzed again. Coop.

WTF is up with Zac!!

West smiled. At least he wasn't the only one on the receiving end of Zac's mood. Thumbs flying over the screen, West fired off a reply to Coop.

No idea but I plan to find out. Going ahead with tonight. I'll let you know what happens.

He didn't have a clue when he'd see Kelsey now. Mentally going over this afternoon's schedule, West figured he could get away a few hours early and catch her at home. If she *was* home. Glancing at the time, West decided to ring her and see if she wanted to grab an early dinner with him before he met up with Zac. His phone went off twice in rapid succession before he could open his contacts. The first was from Zac.

Sure. Same time, same place.

The second from Coop.

Good luck. Wear a flak jacket.

West grinned. Hopefully, he wouldn't need armor when he saw Zac. Although West had the feeling his heart could probably do with some protection when it came to Kelsey. He wasn't the type of guy to put things off except when it came to her. But he wouldn't let his irrational fear of all things Kels get the better of him. He'd made the decision to pursue so he'd man up and do what he had to. Hitting speed-dial one, he brought the phone to his ear and waited for Kels to answer.

It rang five times before she picked up. "Hello?" Her breathless voice whispered in his ear, reminding him of the way she'd breathed his name earlier when they were in bed and he was driving her—himself—crazy.

He swallowed to wet his suddenly parched throat. "Hey. How'd it go?" West asked about Bry's mother even though he wanted desperately to get to the more important topic. Them.

"Um, good. Can I call you back? I'm in the middle of something."

"Oh, sure." West bit his tongue to stop the question of when from popping out his mouth.

"I don't know how long I'll be." He heard someone call her in the background. "I gotta go. I'll call you."

Right before she hung up West heard the same voice calling out again and a ball of lead sank to the pit of his stomach. He didn't want to believe what his ears, and mind, were telling him, but even if it were true there had to be a perfectly good explanation as to what Kelsey was doing all out of breath with her ex-husband. Shame he didn't think even a legitimate reason for them being together was acceptable.

"Who was that?"

Kelsey spun around to find Bry had followed her into the kitchen. "Huh?"

"On the phone." He tipped his chin to indicate the device still in her hand. "Client?"

"Client?" Her mind still played the reel of memories hearing West's voice had conjured up, making it hard to focus on the conversation.

Bry ginned. "Obviously not a client if you're this flustered. Boyfriend?"

"Wh-what?" She choked on the breath she'd just inhaled. Her cheeks heated, making her bring her hands up to cover her face while she continued to hack and splutter.

Kelsey spun around and grabbed a glass from the cupboard. She quickly filled it with water and took a sip, trying to soothe the rawness her coughing fit left behind.

"Hey. You okay?" Bry came up behind her, placed his hands on her shoulders and turned her around. "Come sit down."

She let him guide her to a chair and dropped into it, relieved to not be standing on her shaky legs any longer. He'd thrown her with the boyfriend comment. They'd never talked about dating others. Actually, Kelsey had never even contemplated dating, either her or Bry. Now though, she could only conclude that if he thought she was seeing someone then it was possible he was.

The stab of jealously Kelsey thought she should feel never happened. All she felt at the idea of Bry moving on with someone else was relief. Which delivered a shaft of guilt. She should never have married him. Should never have promised to love above all others when she'd known she couldn't.

"Better now?"

His words snapped her out of her thoughts. "Oh, yes. Breathed the wrong way, I guess." She shrugged and took another sip of water.

"Are you sure? 'Cause I should get going, but I don't want to leave you if you're not all right."

"I'm fine. Go." Kelsey gave him a little push. "I have to get to work anyway."

"Thanks again for this morning." Bry leaned down and kissed her forehead. "And for everything else you've agreed to."

Kelsey smiled up at the man she'd married—the man she still held great affection for—and wished with all her heart that it could have been different between them. "No need to thank me, Bry. I'm more than happy to help out with Marjorie."

For the first time since she'd seen him this morning his mouth curved in a genuine smile. "You might be happy to but you're not obligated, so I still feel the need to thank you. Probably will forever."

Kelsey frowned. "It's really not necessary."

"I know. And that's what I love about you, Kelsey. You're always willing to go above and beyond." He stroked a finger down her cheek, but unlike West's touch, there was no firing of neurons. No zap of desire hitting her veins. "I'll see you tonight."

"Yep. Six o'clock." She pushed out of the chair and followed him out of her kitchen.

"I'll bring take-out for dinner so we can eat before we head over to see mum."

"Sounds good." Kelsey held the front door wide as Bry stepped outside. "Oh, and, Bry. Try not to worry too much. Marjorie is getting the best of care at the home and everything that can be done is being done to make her comfortable."

He glanced over his shoulder. "I know. Having you with me makes it all easier to cope with too."

A twinge of guilt hit Kelsey, tightening her stomach. She'd let him and Marjorie down with her neglect. She wouldn't do that again. "I'm here for whatever you need."

"Thanks." Bry waved as he made his way down the path to the kerb where he'd parked his car when he'd followed her home to talk about Marjorie's situation.

Kelsey watched until he'd driven down the street and out of sight. She closed the door and then made her way back to the kitchen and her phone. She'd left it on the counter, and as much as she wanted to put off the coming conversation, she couldn't. She had to return West's call.

9

Every muscle in West's body tightened when he glanced at his ringing phone. He stared at it through three rings with trepidation tugging at his gut.

Kelsey.

He'd anticipated this call with a mixture of excitement and dread. Surprise ricocheted through him at the sight of his shaking hand and he swiped his thumb across the screen with a little too much force, making him juggle it as he brought it up to his ear.

"Kels."

He heard her suck in a deep breath before the voice that had called out in pleasure only hours ago echoed in his ear. "Hey, I can talk now."

For a split second, West had the urge to say he couldn't, but the notion was quickly overtaken by the need that burned in his bones for this woman. "You okay?"

"Of course. Why wouldn't I be?" He could picture her scrunching up her nose in question.

"You sounded weird earlier. I thought something might be wrong, that's all." His gut clenched when he thought about how out of breath she'd sounded and how it reminded him of making her breathless with satisfaction this morning. He quickly changed the subject. As much as he wanted to know what had gone on between her and Bry, he didn't. "Anyway, I've got a few hours tonight before I have to meet Zac, so I thought I'd bring dinner to your place around six."

"Oh. I can't."

"Seven then?" He'd be pushing it to make it, but for Kels he'd risk Zac's wrath by being a few minutes late.

"Ah, it's not really a good night—"

"Don't cut me out again, Kels." West couldn't stand it if she avoided him like she had in the past.

Her sigh filled his ear before she said the words he'd longed to hear. "I'm not, but I've got stuff going on, plus you're expecting to see me in the office next week, and at this rate I'll never clear all my clients off my desk."

"I told you you could see them out of here." West didn't want to give her any reason to quit before she started. "There isn't enough work here to fill your days, so it makes sense to continue to run your business out of my office."

"West." Her exasperation came through loud and clear.

"What? Surely you can see this is a mutually beneficial arrangement." He leaned against the counter and rubbed his fingers back and forth on his forehead. "C'mon, Kels. You and I both know you can do the office managers job in your sleep. There's no need for you to rush any of your clients' work."

She sucked in a breath. "I really can't see you tonight."

That pulled him up short, making his back straighten and his heart sink. "Why?" He knew before she spoke, but he hoped—

"Bry is coming over."

When her words met his ear, he clenched his jaw and ground his back teeth together. "Fuck."

"It's not what you think." Her words rushed over each other.

"And what is it I think, Kels?" Jealousy and anger burned in his gut.

"We're deciding on how best to handle Marjorie's worsening health."

"*We?* Why the fuck is it *we?* You're divorced. I know you were with him for years, but you don't owe him or his mother any kind of loyalty." West could hear the words he was saying. Knew they were callous and heartless. But he didn't care. His hurt and frustration were blinding him to his selfish behavior. Just when he thought he'd made it past Kelsey's red lights, he found himself faced with another one.

"West, please understand. Marjorie gave me what my own mother has never been able to. Whether I owe her or Bry doesn't come into it. She's someone I care about. Someone I want to support during this difficult time. God knows how much longer she'll be with us, and if I can help make that time a little better I will."

Suitably chastised, he closed his eyes, took a deep breath and tried to reel in his chaotic emotions. If he didn't gain control, she'd push him away again. "I get that, I do. But you can't hold the fact I want to see you against me. You have to know this morning wasn't just about sex for me."

West gripped the phone tighter as he waited for her to say something. Silence stretched until he thought the connection had been cut off. On the verge of pulling the phone from his ear to check, she spoke.

"It wasn't just sex for me either."

Thank God.

"But I can't deal with this—*us*—today."

Damn. That wasn't what he wanted to hear. "How long?"

"I, I don't know. This thing with Bry isn't going to be a one-time deal. It'll be ongoing. I'm sorry. I *need* to do this."

He understood Kelsey's need to help others. It was her doing so above her own needs and wants that he couldn't wrap his head around. She was the least selfish person he'd ever met, always looking out for those around her. West knew it came from her childhood. Having to take care of her younger siblings while her mother hid in the bottom of a bottle had left a mark. All he wanted to do was take care of her, make sure she got what she needed—wanted. If she'd let him.

"Can I call you later? After you've dealt with your commitments."

West needed a definite time of when they'd connect next even if it was only by phone. He needed to have her with him on this or at least know where they stood, and to do that they had to talk.

"Sure. I'll text you after I'm back from visiting Marjorie tonight."

It was better than nothing, and really, he had no choice but to accept the small concession for now. He'd prefer in person, but at this point he'd take whatever the hell he could get. "We'll talk later then."

"Okay. Oh, and, West?"

"Yeah."

"Could we keep what happened this morning just between us?"

"I'm not about to brag about getting you into bed, Kelsey."

"I didn't think you were, but I'd rather no one know right at the moment. It's not like we know what it is we're doing."

And there it was. While Kelsey wasn't sure what was going on between them West had a crystal-clear view of their future. It involved white picket fences and happy ever afters. But the last thing he wanted to do was scare her off with his plans. "Fine. Just between us."

For now.

Kelsey tapped out a message to West. He wouldn't be happy when he read it, but there was nothing she could do about it. Marjorie was far more agitated than she'd been this morning, and even though they'd had to resort to sedating Bry's mother, Kelsey couldn't bring herself to leave her former mother-in-law just yet—or leave Bry to deal with it on his own. Bry had suggested she leave the room while they administered the medication so Marjorie wouldn't lose faith in the only person she seemed to trust in her confused world.

She could hear Marjorie calling for her and it took all the strength Kelsey had not to go back in there before the nurses and doctor came out. Poor Bry had been relegated to doctor again and therefore one of the bad guys. It saddened Kelsey to see the woman who'd loved her son dearly not recognize him at all anymore. Kelsey wasn't sure how Bry coped with the blank stare his mother now gave him. They'd had such a close relationship, especially after Bry's father had passed away.

Her phone vibrated in her hand. Opening the message, she braced herself for West's anger. But it never came. Instead, he gave her something she hadn't realized she needed. Acceptance.

Do what you need to. Ring me when you're done. Doesn't matter how late. I'll wait up.

It was already after eleven and Kelsey wasn't sure how long the sedation would take to work, but she didn't think she'd be home before midnight. She stifled a yawn as she replied.

It'll be after twelve.

Funny how she hadn't wanted to face West after this morning and now she wanted to cling to this connection with both hands.

I'll be here.

She closed her eyes and leaned her head against the wall. Exhaustion had dug its claws in hours ago, but seeing Marjorie in full-blown panic when they'd arrived and not being able to do anything to calm the older woman had ripped what was left of her energy away. Kelsey had to admit she was glad Bry had talked her into riding over with him. At least now she wouldn't be a hazard on the road on the way home.

"Kelsey?"

Her eyes popped open and she jerked away from the wall, turning in Bry's direction. "Is she okay?" She rushed forward—if dragging her feet could be called rushing.

He scrubbed a hand down his face. "Yeah. She's already drifting off. I was thinking it might be better if you don't go back in there."

"Oh?"

"You can just tell her you came back after getting a coffee and found her asleep. If we're lucky, she won't remember anything. She certainly didn't recall last night or seeing you this morning." Bry's shoulders sagged and Kelsey couldn't stop herself from reaching out to touch him.

"If you think that's the best way to deal with it." She gently squeezed his arm before letting go.

"Mr. and Mrs. Newman."

Kelsey glanced over Bry's shoulder to see the doctor she'd met earlier coming out of Marjorie's room. She almost stumbled over the stab of fear that sliced through her chest when she saw the concern creasing his face.

"Is Mum okay?" Bry asked as he turned to face the doctor.

"Oh, yes, yes, she's sleeping soundly now." The other man walked towards them, his steps no more energetic than Kelsey's had been. "I just wanted to remind you that Marjorie has a routine doctor's visit tomorrow. I'm a little worried about her recent increase in confusion and anxiety, so I'll be talking to her specialist in the morning about getting her in for a CT scan."

"Why? What are you looking for?" Bry asked, his posture suddenly alert.

Bry slipped his hand into hers and their fingers tangled together naturally. Kelsey tightened her grip to offer her support but didn't say a word. She might be here as his ex-wife and Marjorie's ex-daughter-in-law but she had no real right to ask questions or demand answers.

"I'm not sure. I just want to rule out a few things," the doctor explained.

"Like what?" Bry's grip grew painfully tight and Kelsey wiggled her fingers until he loosened it. "Don't keep me in the dark."

"I'd rather not say anything until I have some solid evidence either way, Mr. Newman."

"Cut the crap, would you? It's been a long day—a long few months—and I'd rather not be blindsided tomorrow."

Kelsey could understand Bry's need to know, but if the doctor was only running on a hunch... "Bry, the doctor's right. It's best not to worry until you have to."

"I can't possibly get any more worried, no matter what he tells me." The strain and exhaustion of dealing with Marjorie's condition were clear in Bry's voice.

The doctor let out a sigh. "Look, I'm running on a tiny bit of instinct here, and I wouldn't normally say a word to the family of a patient, but I know how difficult the last few months have been for you. It's possible, and I stress I'm not sure and won't be until we see medical evidence, but I think you're mother may have suffered a mild stroke in the last few days."

"A stroke? But she doesn't appear to have any symptoms," Bry pointed out.

"Not all strokes are obvious. Unfortunately, a minor one can lead to a major one, and again I'll stress, I just want to rule this out, but I have seen it in elderly patients before."

"What happens if she has had a stroke?" Kelsey couldn't stop herself from asking.

"Let's cross that bridge when we come to it. We're monitoring her closely, and if there's any change in her condition or if I, or one of the staff, are concerned at all, we'll have her transferred straight to the hospital."

Bry let go of Kelsey's hand and extended his to the doctor. "Thank you. And I'm sorry I snapped at you. It's been a tiring few days."

"Totally understand." They shook. "Go on home and get some rest. We'll talk tomorrow."

They watched the doctor walk away and it struck Kelsey as strange that she couldn't remember his name. They'd been introduced earlier, but for the life of her she couldn't recall the man's name. She covered her mouth to hide a yawn she was unable to suppress.

"C'mon. Let's get you home before you fall asleep on your feet." Bry tugged on her hand, pulling her away from Marjorie's room and towards the front entrance. "Thanks for coming tonight."

"Any time." Another yawn cracked her jaw. "Gosh. I really am tired all of a sudden."

"Sorry about tonight. I should have given in earlier and let them sedate Mum instead of spending hours trying to calm her down. Especially when she doesn't even recognize me."

"How long has her memory been this bad?" She didn't want to say it, but basically she was asking how long since his mum had forgotten him.

Bry pushed open the front door and ushered her through. "I had five minutes about two weeks ago. Other than that, it's been well over a month." He pressed his hand to the small of her back and steered her across the parking lot to his car.

"I'm sorry." The sentiment seemed inadequate even if it was genuine, but there wasn't anything else to say in a situation like this.

Bry remained quiet as he unlocked his car. He opened the door and held it while he waited for Kelsey to get settled before speaking again. "I think I have to face the fact that Mum is essentially gone now. The woman we both knew isn't coming back."

Kelsey had no chance to reply before Bry shut the door and circled around the bonnet. He slipped into the driver's seat and started the car without another word.

Talking seemed pointless, so Kelsey leaned her head back and closed her eyes. What felt like seconds later but had to be at least forty-five minutes, she was jolted from a light doze when Bry pulled into her driveway.

"Thanks again for tonight," he said as he put the car in park and pulled on the handbrake.

"You're welcome." She faced him in the dark. The only light came from the glow from the dashboard and it made his tired features appear even more haggard. Kelsey felt ineffectual in her limited support. "Do you want me to come with you to Marjorie's doctor's appointment in the morning?"

"No. And I know we planned for us both to go in tomorrow night again, but it might be better to wait and see what her doctor says."

"Oh, okay."

"I'll call you." He leaned over and kissed her.

It was a quick brush of lips. A kiss between friends, and Kelsey was reminded again of the lack of passion between them. They'd never fired sparks off each other, and the thought made her sad but also made her crave West in ways she'd never wanted her ex-husband. Uncertain in Bry's presence for the first time since their separation and subsequent divorce, Kelsey reached for the door handle.

"Ring me tomorrow if you need me," she said as she pushed the door open and swung her legs out.

"I seem to be saying it a lot, but thanks, Kelsey. You're more generous than you should be."

"Nonsense. This is what friends are for." She tried not to put emphasis on the word friends, but that kiss had set off some warning bells. Kelsey didn't think he had any ideas of them getting back together, but in the three years since they'd gone their separate ways, he'd never kissed her. Not on the mouth. It felt like a line had been crossed. Then again, maybe that was because a small part of her saw that kiss as a betrayal of West.

Before her chaotic thoughts got the better of her, she slipped out of the car and closed the door. Without looking back, Kelsey walked up the path to her house. She retrieved her keys from her pocket and slipped the key into the lock. Giving Bry a quick wave, she opened the door, ducked inside and locked up before making her way to her bedroom where she collapsed onto the bed in complete exhaustion.

West let himself into Kelsey's house. He knew he shouldn't. It was two o'clock in the morning. But she hadn't called him like she'd promised and she hadn't answered her phone the numerous times he'd rung in the last few hours either. No lights were on and he didn't bother with them as he made his way down the short hallway to her room. Moonlight streamed in through the open blinds illuminating the woman sprawled across the bed. She still had her shoes on.

Smiling, he shook his head as he put his keys, wallet and phone on her dresser and walked over to the bed. With care, he picked up one foot and eased her shoe off. She didn't stir so he repeated his actions with the other foot. Shoeless, Kelsey murmured something he didn't catch before rolling over onto her back. West eyed her jeans and debated whether or not to rid her of them. She'd be more comfortable out of them.

But she'd probably pitch a fit if she woke without her clothes, and while he didn't mind getting her riled up, that wasn't the kind of reaction he wanted from her. He dropped to his knees beside the bed. Using his fingertips, he brushed the hair from her face and studied her. In sleep, she looked younger than her twenty-eight years. She reminded him of the girl he'd fallen for in high school.

"Kelsey." He moved his hand to her shoulder and gave her a gentle shake. "Kels."

"Mmm."

"You need to get out of your clothes."

"Mm-kay."

West grinned when she reached for the hem of her shirt and dragged it up her torso. She didn't open her eyes, and while he was okay with receiving an impromptu strip show, he didn't think her intention was to tease him. Before he could say anything to stop her, she'd whipped her top off and went to work on the button of her pants.

"Whoa. Kelsey." He stilled her hands. "Let me get out of the room first." West might have seen her naked already, but it felt as though he'd be crossing a line if he stayed while she undressed. He didn't think she'd be too pleased about it once she was awake enough to comprehend what she'd done either.

"Ss-okay."

He thought she was agreeing with him, but when she continued to undo her jeans and shove them down her hips, he realized she'd meant something completely different.

"Kelsey."

"Can't." She tugged on the denim, revealing a pair of pink lace panties. "Help me." She opened her eyes and the slumberous blue depths met his.

"I…" West couldn't finish the thought never mind the sentence.

"Please."

God help him, he wasn't going to be able to refuse her. He hadn't come here for this. He'd been worried when she hadn't called and had just wanted to check she was all right, not get her naked. West gripped the waistband of her jeans and pulled them down her legs and over her feet while trying his best not to look at the miles of flesh revealed. When he glanced up, she was already working on the front catch of her bra. In the blink of an eye, all that stood between him and her lush curves was a single strip of flimsy pink lace sitting low on her hips.

West swallowed, his constricted throat making it difficult. "Kels." He wasn't sure what he meant to say, but her name fell from his lips a little too pleading for his liking. Clearing his throat he tried again. "Kelsey, you need to get into bed."

Her eyes drifted closed as she reached her arms out towards him. "You too."

"No. I should go." He managed to avoid her by standing, but that left her groping hands right near his groin—the one with the hard-on straining to get out of his pants. West grit his teeth when she grabbed a handful of his sweats—her fingers brushing along his length—and yanked.

Distracted by her touch and surprised by her show of strength, he lost his balance and toppled forward. Throwing his arms out, he caught himself on his hands before he crushed her beneath him. When he looked down, it was to find Kelsey staring at him with eyes soaking in need. And not the kind of need pumping blood into his cock either. What he saw in her eyes was a whole new level of wanting that he'd waited a lifetime to see Kelsey aim his way.

"Please, West. I need you to hold me."

He had no idea what was going on. Why the woman who'd avoided, ignored and rejected him at various points over the last few months suddenly wanted him on a level he'd craved, but he didn't care. His one weakness had always been Kelsey, and he could no more deny her this than he could live the rest of his life without breathing.

Toeing off his shoes, he let them drop to the floor before moving to the center of the bed, taking her with him. He turned her so she lay wrapped in his arms, her head cradled on his shoulder, and held her while she slid back into a deep sleep. West was pretty sure she'd regret this in the morning, whatever the hell this was. But for now, he'd bask in her acceptance. It might not be the confession of love he wanted—needed—from her, but he wasn't above taking whatever he could get.

10

For the second morning in a row, West woke tangled with Kelsey. And Kelsey attempting to make a quiet getaway without much success. Unless her aim was to inflict physical harm. Then she was definitely doing an okay job.

West moved his leg to shield his groin. "You're going to do some real damage if we keep this up," he murmured.

"Shit." Kelsey jolted. Her elbow grazed the side of his head and her knee dug into his thigh.

"Ouch." West grabbed her leg to hold her still. "Don't move."

"Oh, God, I'm sorry." She froze in place, saving him from certain injury.

"I'm not sure why you think you need to sneak away whenever you find yourself wrapped in my arms." He rolled to the side, taking her with him so they were lying face to face. "Why the panic?"

She wouldn't meet his gaze, so he tipped her head up with two fingers under her chin. She sucked in a deep breath before she raised her eyelids, locking her gaze on his. "I don't know what to do with you."

West laughed and waggled his eyebrows. "I can think of a few things."

Kelsey's lips twitched before turning upwards and West couldn't resist leaning over to plant a kiss on her sexy mouth. He expected her to pull back, to push him away. He never expected her to meet him halfway. Their mouths meshed, their lips clinging for long seconds before Kelsey slipped her tongue out and pressed against him, urging him to open. West wasn't about to deny this woman—or himself—anything. He let her in.

The kiss started slow. Not a frenzied dance of need, but a gentle waltz of two people who were comfortable with each other—who'd danced this dance before. He let Kelsey lead. Let her take them on the tempo of her choosing. His body—specifically his groin—might be screaming for him to dive deeper—go faster—but he knew she needed to be in control for now. He'd pushed her enough in the last few days and realized the best way to get what he wanted was to give Kels a turn at the reins. Let her come to him.

West tangled his fingers in her hair, his grip loose but firm enough for her to know he was there. He wanted her aware of who she was kissing. Wanted to be sure she wasn't thinking about her ex while her tongue was tangling with his. She moaned into his mouth and need rocketed through him—had him tightening all over including his grip on her hair, making him pull on the silky strands. Kelsey surprised him again by reacting to the slight tug in a way he never expected.

She clawed at his back, thrusting her hips against his while she drove her tongue deeper into his mouth. It was like he'd flipped a switch. One minute they were on a leisurely stroll down the path of seduction, the next they were at a flat-out run. Her hands were suddenly everywhere. In his hair. Sweeping down his back. Cupping his ass. The sweat pants he wore didn't deter her. With ease, Kelsey slipped her hand inside his pants, beneath his briefs, and wrapped her fingers around his straining erection.

West tore his mouth from hers. "Slow down," he panted.

"Don't want to." She squeezed him as she stroked up his length and his eyes crossed.

"Jesus."

Kelsey laughed as she set a mind-numbing rhythm. "Nope. Just me."

Before West could utter another word, Kelsey pushed him to his back and crawled over the top of him. Her face hovered over his, the blaze of desire burning in her eyes hot enough to incinerate any protest he might have. "Kels." He brushed his fingers down her cheek and cupped her jaw. He'd give her anything. Everything. "You do me in."

She smiled. "There is a certain part of your anatomy I plan on doing."

The smile on her lips turned downright devious as she moved down his body, her hand still working him. He'd have to be an idiot not to know where she was headed, and as much as he wanted to feel that mouth of hers wrapped around his cock, he had to stop her before she took him past the point of no return.

"Kelsey." West slid his hands under her arms and tugged her back up. When he had her face above his, he kissed her. He didn't let himself linger too long though. His hold on control was thin already. And there was still that hand wrapped around his dick. "We have to stop now. Before we can't."

"But I don't want to stop." She thrust her tongue between his lips before pulling back to nip at him with her teeth, while that torturous hand did its best to get him off. "I want to make you feel good. Want you to make *me* feel good. I don't want to feel sad anymore. Just for a little while, I want to forget. Make me forget."

What the fuck? She was sad? Wanted to forget?

This wasn't about wanting him. It was about finding oblivion from whatever had put that look in her eyes when she'd asked him to hold her. He wasn't about to let her use him like that. She'd regret it just as much as him after they were done. Grabbing her wrist, he pulled her hand out of his pants. In a second, he reversed their positions and pinned her beneath him. Cradling her face in his hands, he left her no choice but to look at him.

"Kelsey?"

Air rushed from Kelsey's lungs as the world turned upside down. Blinking rapidly, her eyes focused on West now looming over her with storm-gray eyes.

Oh God.

What did she say? He'd wanted to stop. She'd told him she didn't. That she didn't want to feel sad—wanted to forget…

Oh God.

"Kels?"

She closed her eyes and took a deep breath, but neither action stopped the pinch of anxiety from squeezing her stomach—her chest.

"Talk to me." West stroked the side of her face, the caress soft like his voice, making her want to lean into him—lean *on* him.

Kelsey couldn't avoid answering no matter how much she wanted to. Opening her eyes she met West's gaze and tried to divert his attention. "If you don't want me, just say so."

He laughed and rocked his hips against hers. "Does that feel like I don't want you? Me wanting you isn't in question, it never has been."

She licked her lips and fought for control of her careening emotions. On one hand, she wanted to lose herself in the pleasure that West could give—the bliss that would obliterate anything else from her mind. On the other, she wanted to curl up in a ball and cry for all her ex husband and mother-in-law had lost in the face of Marjorie's illness. Kelsey didn't think West would appreciate the last sentiment. Not when they were tangled together in her bed. Not when he'd had such an angry reaction to her helping Bry in the first place. She needed to change the subject before she revealed what was weighing on her mind. "When did you get here? How'd you get in?"

West's hands tightened on her head. "Stop trying to change the subject. Tell me what the hell is going on. You don't go from trying to sneak away before I'm awake to offering to give me a blowjob in a matter of minutes."

Kelsey shook her head, her movements limited by West's hold.

"Don't." He dug his fingers into her scalp. "Stop shutting me out."

"I'm no—"

"You are." His voice and body vibrated with the frustration he didn't try to hide. "You didn't ring when you got home like you promised. I was worried, so I let myself in with your spare key. And I can see just by looking at you that I was right to be concerned. *Talk to me.*"

"I..." She couldn't dump her baggage on him. Her past was something she needed to deal with on her own. And until she did, whatever it was they were moving towards couldn't happen—*shouldn't* happen. "I'm sorry."

West's gaze bore into hers for long seconds before he pushed himself up and off her. "This isn't just about sex."

"I know."

He climbed off the bed. "Do you?" he asked as he glanced around the floor.

"Of course." Kelsey suddenly became aware of her lack of clothing—that she only had underwear on. Feeling vulnerable, she reached for the blanket. She couldn't remember getting undressed. What else was she forgetting?

"Then you need to let me in." West shoved his feet into his shoes. "Trust me with more than your body."

"I do."

"You think so? When I say I want more than just sex, I mean I want everything. The good *and* the bad. Until you can give me that we're not sleeping together."

Kelsey wanted to pretend she didn't know what West was talking about—wanted to go back to forgetting everything while wrapped in his arms. She knew she held a part of herself back. But she needed to in order to protect her heart from the one person who had the power to break it. He'd done it before, whether on purpose or not didn't matter. West had left her heart bruised and bleeding once, and there was no way she was going to risk it happening a second time.

The fact he picked up on her reluctance complicated things. Sleeping together had been a big mistake. One she'd almost repeated.

"You're right. We shouldn't have slept together. It won't happen again."

West laughed—the sound loud and sharp in the morning quiet. "Oh, it'll happen again. You can bet on it."

Before she could get a word out, he leaned over and pressed his mouth to hers. Hard and fast, he kissed her and then spun on his heel and left the room. Clutching the blanket against her chest, she sat in stunned silence until the front door slammed closed. Startled out of her stupor, Kelsey glanced at her alarm clock.

"Shit." She threw the covers off and bounded out of bed. If she didn't get in the shower now, she'd be late for her nine o'clock appointment at the community college.

Showered and dressed in record time, Kelsey detoured through the second bedroom she used as her office to grab the relevant files before heading out the door not fifteen minutes after West had left.

West.

What the hell was she going to do about him?

About *them*?

West tossed his keys and wallet on the counter as he made his way to the coffee machine. He needed a shot of caffeine. Actually, he needed something a lot stronger to deal with the drama surrounding Kelsey, but coffee was all he'd allow himself this early in the day.

She was shutting him out, and while he wasn't sure she meant to do it, she definitely knew she was holding back. He was convinced it had to do with Bry and his mother. Maybe their past had a bit to do with it too. Oh, who was he kidding, he didn't have a clue what was going through her head.

Sighing, he dropped a pod in the machine and hit the button. As soon as the coffee was done, he'd grab a quick shower and head in to work. There was no point hanging out here stressing about the latest red light Kelsey had put in his way.

His coffee had just finished pouring when his phone rang. He thought about ignoring it in case it was Kelsey, but he doubted she'd be ringing him after the way he'd walked out on her. Glancing at the screen, he saw Cassie's smiling face staring up at him. Figuring it was work related, West answered.

"Hey, Cassie. What's up?"

"Um, well, there's been a small incident in the kitchen here at Are You Game?"

West could hear commotion in the background. "What sort of incident?"

"There was a small fire."

"Did you burn another cake?" West chuckled. Last time Cassie had forgotten about a cake in the oven, it was because her boyfriend Luc had distracted her.

"Ah, no, it was a little bigger than that."

He suddenly registered the nuances in Cassie's tone and his protective instincts kicked in. "Are you okay?"

"Oh, yes. No one was hurt." He nearly didn't catch the next words she mumbled into the phone. "Well, no one except your kitchen."

"How bad?" If someone had burnt down his new kitchen he'd be in trouble. *They'd* be in trouble. Both Weston's Catering and Are You Game? had full calendars over the next few weeks. "Tell me it's at least usable."

Cassie's silence said it all, and West took a deep breath and tried to focus on the fact no one was hurt.

"Okay. What's the damage?" He was heading out the door, his coffee forgotten in the face of this disaster. And that's what it was. He'd have to source another kitchen and get the repairs on this one started ASAP. "Never mind. I'll be there in fifteen."

He took the back streets and made it to the Are You Game? building in thirteen minutes. Two fire engines and a police car filled the parking lot and blocked the driveway so West had to park half a block down. When he reached the property boundary, a policeman stopped him.

"Sorry, sir. You can't go in there."

"I'm one of the owners." It was a small lie. A technicality really, because he *did* own the kitchen that had apparently burnt down—if not the whole building—if all the fire personnel were an indication.

"Name?" the officer asked with a skeptical expression.

"West. Weston Mann." The delay had him clenching his hands in frustration.

The cop stepped away to speak into his radio, but West didn't have to wait for someone to confirm his identity because Cassie came out of the building and headed their way.

"West. God, I'm glad you're here. I had to send Jody home because I didn't want to risk the baby breathing anything toxic, even though the firemen say it's okay. And Dan's out on a job and can't get back for at least another hour, so other than Kerry it's just me here." Cassie threw her arms around him, her body trembling slightly.

He held her close before pushing her to arms length. "Are you sure you're okay? Who was in the kitchen when it went up?"

She shook her head. "No one."

"Then how'd the fire start?"

"Come inside and I'll explain." She turned and headed back the way she'd come, the cop making no protest when West followed her.

The second Cassie opened the outer door, West could smell the smoke. It was a mixture of melted plastic and burnt timber. He tried to remember what was on today's schedule but the stench had him waving a hand in front of his face and concentrating on not inhaling too deeply.

"Electrical," Cassie said as they headed across the warehouse floor.

"What?"

"They said the oven shorted out." Cassie pushed open the door to the kitchen and West's eyes and nose stung from the smoke hanging in the air in spite of how clear it appeared. "They're trying to pump the air out the back door. We need to keep this one closed as much as possible so the smoke doesn't seep into the rest of the building."

"Too late," West muttered as he moved farther into the room, his shoes sloshing through the water left behind by the sprinkler system.

He could see the blackened stove and surrounding cupboards. Well, what was left of them anyway. "Who's in charge?" he asked Cassie.

"Guy in the red hat talking to Kerry." She pointed across the room. "She's giving her version of what happened. I already gave mine."

"Shouldn't they do that somewhere else? The air in here can't be good for our lungs."

Cassie shrugged. "Most of the smoke has gone now."

It might seem as though the smoke was gone, but the sting in his nose and eyes told him the air was still contaminated and they really shouldn't be in here. West strode across the room to where Cassie's employee and the fireman stood. He stuck out his hand and introduced himself. "Hi. I'm West Mann. Owner of this kitchen."

"Oh, right. Ms. Moreland said you'd be arriving soon. Station Officer Rhodes." He shook West's hand before turning back to Kerry. "That should do it. I'll be in touch if I need anything else."

West turned to Cassie's employee. "Kerry, why don't you and Cassie head out front away from—?"

"Cassie!" Luc's voice boomed through the building.

"Uh oh," Kerry mumbled.

"Who's that?" Rhodes asked.

"That would be Cassie's boyfriend, Lucas Wilhelm," West answered just as Luc came barging through the door with the cop from out front hot on his tail.

West watched as Cassie quickly sprang into action pacifying both Luc and the cop in few words. He marveled at how well his pint-sized friend wrangled her six-foot-five boyfriend with the simple batting of her eyelashes. As the trio headed back through the door with Kerry following, West turned back to Officer Rhodes. "So can you tell me what happened?"

"It looks like a straightforward electrical fire. Ms. Moreland had switched the oven on and left the room while it heated. Unfortunately, there was an exposed wire in the wall behind the unit."

"Are you sure? This kitchen is only a year old."

"Doesn't matter how new something is, exposed wires are a fire hazard waiting to happen."

"How long before I can get a crew in to clean this up and start repairs?"

"Ms. Moreland has an electrician coming in to check the rest of the wiring for potential problems. The ovens have their own circuit so I'd say it'll be fine, but best to be safe than sorry. Then your insurance company will want to take a look."

"I guess it really doesn't matter does it? The kitchen is out of commission indefinitely."

"Afraid so."

West's gaze travelled the room and landed on the pantry door. He nodded in that direction. "Do you think any of the food in there is salvageable?"

"The door remained closed during the incident so anything in sealed airtight containers should be okay, but if it's covered under your insurance I'd ditch it just in case." Officer Rhodes shook his head. "You can't afford to poison people in your line of work."

West ran his hand over the back of his neck and squeezed. "Great. Just great." He really didn't need this drama in his life right now.

"If you'll excuse me, I need to check in with my men."

West stared at the disaster in front of him for a few more seconds before heading in the direction of the back door. He needed fresh air and a plan. The fresh air was easy. The plan, not so much. First, he had to find a substitute kitchen. And fast.

11

Kelsey hung up the phone and took a deep breath. Letting it out in a rush, she slumped back against the sofa in relief. As much as she wanted to be there for Bry and his mother, she was glad he'd called to tell her not to visit tonight. In the mood she was in, she couldn't have put on a cheerful face for Marjorie and the woman didn't need any more angst in her life.

Her phone buzzed in her hand, making her jump. Glancing at the screen, she saw Shaye had sent her a message.

OMG! Did you hear about West?

She hadn't spoken to or heard from West since he'd stormed out this morning, so Kelsey had no idea what Shaye was talking about. Instead of texting back, Kelsey called. The phone barely rang when her friend answered. Before Shaye could say a word Kelsey's questions were tumbling from her mouth.

"What about West? Did something happen to him? Is he all right? He was fine this morning." She sucked in a big breath.

"Whoa. Slow down there, speedy. First, his backup kitchen caught fire. Second, he wasn't there, so as far as I know he's fine and no one at Are You Game? was injured either. And third, and most interesting I might add, *when* this morning did you see him?"

"I, um, the Are You Game? kitchen? But it's barely a year old."

"Coop said something about an electrical fault. And nice diversion. When did you see West?"

Kelsey could hear the smile in Shaye's voice. She didn't miss her friend's mention of Coop and wondered what was going on with them, but she wanted to steer clear of any type of relationship talk so didn't ask. Instead, she went with Shaye's recent lack of employment as her next attempt at distraction. "How's the job hunting?"

"Oh, complete change of subject. Nice try, my friend, but not good enough. When and where did you see the delicious Mr. Mann this morning?"

A sigh left Kelsey's throat before she could stop it.

"Tut, tut, tut. None of that. Spill." Shaye could be like a dog with a bone.

Thinking fast, Kelsey said, "He came over to talk about my new role as his office manager." That was plausible. Shaye knew she'd taken the job with Weston's because Kelsey had tried to talk Shaye into taking it instead now that she was unemployed.

"Oh my God! Did you sleep with him?" Shaye squealed in her ear.

"What?" Kelsey choked—stumbled over a denial. She couldn't lie to Shaye. Her friend would know straight away if she did so she went for another deflection. "Why would you ask that?"

"Oh, I don't know. The major freak out on your part about whether West was all right. The fact you saw him this morning when I know he was at Are You Game? *before* nine. That's awfully early to be at your place, don't you think?"

"H-he was passing by." Kelsey knew they were the wrong choice of words the second they left her mouth.

Shaye laughed. A deep, rolling laugh that went on and on, and Kelsey knew if she didn't get off the phone now, their secret would be out, because Shaye would pepper her with question after question until Kelsey caved and spilled her guts. She wasn't ready to talk about her and West yet. Hell, she couldn't get things straight in her own head, how would she explain it to her best friend?

"Look. I've gotta go. There's someone at the door."

"I didn't hear your doorbell, but by all means, runaway. I'll get the truth out of you soon enough," Shaye warned.

"Talk later." Kelsey hung up before Shaye said another word and then tossed the phone to the other end of the sofa. She knew her friend wouldn't let the subject lie as is and fully expected to get the third degree the next time they talked.

The room was quiet. The only noise was the chaotic thoughts racing around inside Kelsey's head. A minefield of emotions verse reasons verse memories that continued to plague her. Nothing was any clearer than it had been this morning when West had walked out on her. She didn't know what to do or think...

Her phone buzzed, and when she glanced over, she wasn't surprised to see a message from Shaye. Putting it off wouldn't make the text go away, so she leaned over and grabbed the phone, tapping the little envelope icon as she straightened.

You should really REALLY think about the way you felt when you thought something had happened to West.

Kelsey didn't want to contemplate her stomach-squeezing reaction to Shaye's first text. She knew her friend was right though. Knew she needed to sort out what was going on with her and West. To say she was terrified was an understatement. The man had the power to destroy her, and he didn't even have a clue.

Regardless of her reluctance to see or talk to him, there was no denying the urge to check everything was okay—check *he* was okay. He might need help organizing repairs on the damaged kitchen. She could help him coordinate the clean up and refit. Or she could supervise the rebuild while he got on with the everyday necessities of running Weston's Catering.

Flimsy excuses be damned. She wouldn't rest easy until she knew West didn't need her. It only took her a second to call him, but when his phone rang out and diverted to voicemail, Kelsey's earlier panic returned tenfold. She jumped to her feet and was across the room grabbing her keys and purse from the hall table on her way out the door before she thought about it.

Traffic was brutal. Then again, she didn't expect anything less at this hour of the day. Kelsey navigated peak hour—why it was referred to as an hour when the snarl of Sydney traffic lasted for at least five was beyond her—with little patience and a good amount of swearing as she headed to Are You Game? She soon discovered the place was locked up tight. Next, she drove a few minutes down the road to Weston's. The car park was full, but a quick scan of the vehicles told her West's four-wheel drive wasn't one of them. Pulling out her phone, she tried calling him again. This time, he answered on the first ring.

"Hey." He sounded tired, worn out in a way she hadn't heard before.

"Where are you?" she asked, her panic causing her voice to wobble.

"At home. Why?"

"I heard what happened."

"The group grapevine's alive and well I see."

"Do you need me to do anything?"

"Kelsey, what I need from you you're not willing to give."

"I, um…" Brakes squealed and a car blasted its horn, making her yelp.

"Are you driving?" West asked.

"No. I'm parked outside of Weston's." Kelsey wasn't sure she wanted to admit to her frantic search, except now she didn't really have a choice. She'd already revealed her whereabouts. "I was looking for you. You didn't answer your phone when I called before. I was worried."

"Kels," he sighed her name.

She could picture him frowning and rubbing his forehead like he did when something frustrated him. Until now, she hadn't admitted to anything that might overstep the friend's line. Her actions certainly spoke for her, but verbally she'd remained mute, even denied and fought against their connection. She'd been fighting a losing battle. One she'd been waging with herself for what seemed like forever. "Can I come over?"

"Careful. I might get the wrong idea."

He was right. It was irrational in the face of everything she'd said and thought, but she had to see him. Although he sounded tired, Kelsey had no doubt he *was* okay. Only she still couldn't shake the need to see with her own eyes. "Please."

There was a long silence before he sighed heavily into the phone. "No."

"No?" Her voice came out a croak as her throat closed up tight and her heart thudded inside her chest.

"I can't do it. I've got a lot of work to do if I'm going to keep Weston's from losing business in the next few weeks. I don't have the energy to fight with you too."

"Fight? What do you mean fight?" They were fighting?

West laughed, but the sound failed to convey any joy, just the opposite, and Kelsey's stomach felt hollowed out.

"Then let me help keep Weston's on track," she all but pleaded.

"You will be. Monday morning in the office."

"But surely there's something I can do now."

"Go home, Kelsey. If I need you before Monday, I'll call."

"But—"

"Night. Drive safe." He hung up before she could argue further.

"Fuck." She tossed her phone on the passenger seat. It bounced off the cushion, hit the dash and dropped to the floor with a thump. Not unlike her heart. He'd rejected her. This was exactly the reason she should never have gotten involved with him again.

***

West shoved his fingers through his hair and hoped he was strong enough to stick to his guns and that Kelsey wouldn't ignore his refusal to see her. He'd almost given in. When she'd uttered *please* in that whispery tone she used when they were tangling the sheets, his body had let him know instantly that it approved of her coming over. If she turned up on his doorstep against his wishes...well, his mind's wishes, his cock was all for a visit from Kelsey. The damn thing was rock hard and ready to go just from hearing her voice.

But he had to ignore his libido if he wanted to reach his end goal —Kelsey in his life on a permanent basis. And he wasn't referring to her role as his office manager. Getting her back into bed wouldn't be all that hard now that they'd fallen there. He knew neither of them could really fight their attraction after they'd spectacularly proven their chemistry was just as explosive as he remembered it being when they were teenagers.

He scrubbed a hand over his face and took a deep breath. There wasn't time to be rehashing the latest in the go-stop saga that was his and Kelsey's relationship. He'd brought home the schedules, list of venues and employee rosters for Are You Game? and Weston's. The kitchen he'd secured the use of was an hour away from Weston's, so he'd have to factor in the extra travel time for staff as well as delivery of product.

"Fuck." He had so much to do, and he wanted it done now. Wanted everything ironed out so his business would run smoothly. West pushed back his chair and headed for the kitchen and a cold beer. He'd allow himself one to take the edge off his crazy day. Maybe it would trick his blood pressure into thinking it was the weekend and he could relax. Every muscle was currently vying for the title of first to snap.

Lights flickered across the living room wall. Because of the position of his house on the block, the only way headlights could hit that particular wall would be if someone had pulled into his driveway. If he thought his body felt strung tight before, it was nothing compared to now. Detouring into the front room, he headed for the window. He stood off to the side in the hope of not being seen by whoever had come over. West shook his head. He didn't need to look to know who'd come calling.

Kelsey.

When West looked out the window, he saw her lights were switched off and he couldn't hear the engine and its irregular timing, but Kels hadn't gotten out yet. Her hands clenched the steering wheel at the very top, snug together, while her forehead rested on the back of them. West was conflicted. He didn't know whether to go out to her or stay where he was. He'd asked her not to come because he knew if he saw her he'd give in to his need to be with her and settle for whatever little scrap of herself she'd offer him.

Before he could make a decision either way, she moved. Jumping back out of view, he held his breath. She wouldn't see him, but now he couldn't see her either. He remained motionless for what felt like an eternity until an unusual ringing snapped him out of his frozen state. Glancing in the direction of the noise, West saw his phone vibrating on the dining room table. He quickly walked over to see what the hell it was buzzing for.

The phone was new and he was still getting used to the different ringtones and sounds it made. When he picked up the device, he discovered the reason for his confusion. Somebody was trying to video call him.

Kelsey.

West slid his thumb across the screen to accept. He debated what to say while the call connected. Her shadowed face appeared. Even in the dark, she took his breath. She was smoking hot, there was no denying that, but what was it about Kelsey that grabbed him by the balls—by the heart—and squeezed? He'd certainly seen prettier women—dated some even. None of them, in his opinion, held a candle to Kels.

"I'm sorry." Her murmured words snapped him out of his thoughts.

"For?"

"For not doing as you wanted."

"Which time?"

"I couldn't stay away. I'm in your driveway."

"I know." He sighed. There was no point lying. If he wanted her to be open and honest, he needed to do the same. "I saw your lights when you pulled up."

"I just wanted to see you're okay."

"You're seeing me now." Not that she'd actually made eye contact since the call had connected, which seemed impossible when her face and his filled their screens.

"I know...I just..."

"Just what?" West went back to the window and pushed the blind aside so he could see her sitting in her car. "What are you doing here? And don't rush to answer. Think about it for a minute."

He'd let her think on it while he went and unlocked the front door. He didn't try to disguise his movements. West wanted her to hear the lock disengage. The sound of her sucking in a deep breath echoed through the house, and he knew she didn't have any real idea —or was choosing to ignore it—about why she'd come. With everything he had, he wanted to go out there and get her. Pull her inside and tell her to look at him and tell him she didn't feel it. But he knew he couldn't.

She had to come to him.

"Kelsey?"

"I don't know."

"Yes, you do." He moved deeper into the house, away from the door—away from temptation. "You have to be brave enough."

"I'm sorry. So sorry."

"You keep saying that, but I have no idea what you're sorry for." West lowered himself onto his bed. He hadn't switched on the light, keeping himself in the dark deliberately.

"For everything. For not being enough. For Bry."

"You're more than enough."

"Then why did you never say anything? Why didn't you come after me?"

"Aw, Kels." He flopped back on the bed and stared into the darkness. "We were just kids. And I was stupid. So fucking stupid. By the time I pulled my head out of my ass you'd moved on."

"I never moved on." Her sharp gasp filled the room. "I didn't mean that. That's not what I meant to say."

West was on his feet and heading for the door. "You wouldn't have said it if there wasn't a kernel of truth in there." He was halfway to the front door when she stopped him.

"Don't come out! *Please.*"

He froze in place and dragged a deep breath in through his nose. Holding it, he counted to five and then let it out slowly. "Talk to me."

"You ignored me. I thought I'd done something wrong."

"Jesus—"

"No. Let me finish before you say anything."

"Okay." It was killing him not to have this conversation face to face. This stupid video call thing didn't count.

"You always made me feel too much. Good and bad. So when it went bad, it hurt so fucking much and I couldn't talk to anyone. We agreed we wouldn't. Then there was Bry. So easy. So simple. And he didn't make me feel so...open—so raw—when I looked at him. God." She sucked in a breath. "I promised I'd never let anyone hurt me like that again, West. *I promised.*"

"Come inside."

"No. I can't. Not now." She sniffed, and it killed him to know he'd done that to her. Again. "I should go."

"No. Just come in. No strings. It doesn't mean anything more than one friend comforting another."

"We're not friends. We crossed that bridge years ago."

He got what she was saying, but whether they were physically intimate or not didn't mean a fucking thing. She was still one of his closest friends, and he'd done the one thing he'd told himself he wouldn't. He'd hurt her.

Disregarding her instructions, he jogged out of the house and to her car before she realized he was coming. He flung her door open and reached in to unbuckle her belt, but she must have done it sometime after she'd arrived. With actions a little on the rough side, West pulled Kelsey from her car and wrapped his arms around her. She buried her head beneath his chin and slid her arms around his waist.

West couldn't say how long they stayed that way. How long she let him hold her close. How long she clung to him in return. But she finally pulled free of his embrace and took a step away, wiping her hands across her cheeks.

"I should go."

"I never meant to hurt you. Now or then."

Her gaze connected with his.

"I had no idea what I was doing. What I was walking away from." He had to make her understand that he regretted what had happen between them. "I'd go back and fix it if I could."

Kelsey gave a nod but didn't say a word. She turned toward her car.

West followed her, moved closer. "We're not done."

She threw a half-smile his way. "I know. But I need to go."

"Call me when you get home. Let me know you're safe." He tucked a strand of hair behind her ear, lingered along her jawbone. "It was never that you weren't enough, Kels. You were always too much."

Neither of them said another word as she got back in her car and closed the door. He waited until she'd started the engine and backed out of the driveway before he raised his hand to wave. Then he waited until her taillights were just a memory in the night before he went back inside.

12

————

Kelsey sat trapped in the corner. On her left were Coop, Joe and Nick, the empty chair belonged to James, who'd gone to the bar for another round of drinks. Shaye, Mel and Nikki completed their group on her right. There was no way she could get out except under. And crawling on the floor just didn't seem dignified no matter how badly Kelsey wanted to leave. She had no doubt Shaye had planned it that way. Her friend hadn't wanted Kelsey to have an easy escape.

It had taken Shaye over an hour to nag her into coming, and Kelsey still wasn't sure why she'd agreed. She'd spent a sleepless night after her discussion with West, and she felt as though she'd taken to her insides with a grater. She was raw and bleeding and she couldn't work out why or how to make the feeling go away. The group talked around her and Kelsey nodded on occasion to appear as though she were listening and involved, only she wasn't. Not until Nick said her name and she was forced to pay attention.

"Hey, Kelsey, I hear you've taken on managing Weston's," Nick shouted over the others who were having an animated discussion about what heinous thing to do to Shaye's ex-boss.

Kelsey smiled and nodded as she lifted her glass to her mouth.

West was definitely a subject she wanted to talk about as little as possible.

"When are you two going to come out?" Mel asked.

"Out?" Kelsey arched one eyebrow.

"Yeah. It's not like you guys can keep it hidden now that you'll be working together every day," Nikki added.

Kelsey shook her head. "I don't get what you mean. Keep what hidden?"

"I'll translate," Coop said. "They're asking when you and West are going to admit that you're a couple."

Cold water filled the back of her nose as Kelsey choked on the mouthful she'd just swallowed. "What?" She coughed and reached for a napkin.

Shaye patted her back while a big smile stretched her lips. "There, there, sweetie."

"But I thought..." Nikki murmured.

"Oh, you're not wrong," Shaye said. "Kelsey's in denial though."

"How can you deny it?" Mel asked. "You're either with someone or you're not. For instance, you're not with Bry anymore because you got divorced."

Kelsey's gaze darted from one friend to another. They all stared at her with varying expressions—from curious to surprise to smug—the last being Shaye of course. She sent her so-called best friend a dirty look. "We're not together. I don't even know where you got the idea from."

"The sparks," Nikki said. Beside her, Mel nodded and Shaye just had a smug try-to-deny-it-now look on her face.

"You and West always did have chemistry." Joe shook his head. "Never could understand how you ended up with Bry when you and West could light up a room."

"Who and West?" James asked as he put a tray of drinks on their table. "What have I missed?"

"Nothing." Shaye poked a finger in Kelsey's ribs. "Kelsey is remaining mum on the subject of her and West."

"Kelsey and West? But aren't you getting back together with Bry?" James asked, his forehead wrinkling in confusion.

"What? No!" Kelsey had no idea where all this talk was coming from. No one but Shaye knew something was going on between her and West, and even she wasn't privy to any details. As for her and Bry...where would James get *that* from?

"You're getting back with Bry?" Coop leaned in close and lowered his voice. "Does West know?"

She turned to Coop and whispered, "There's nothing to know."

He studied her a few moments before nodding. "Good. I'd hate for you to make the same mistake twice."

Kelsey gasped.

Coop leaned closer, his lips right next to her ear. "We both know you never should have married Bry." He smiled as he pulled away but it did nothing to calm the unease churning in Kelsey's stomach.

Instead of questioning Coop further, Kelsey focused on James and what he'd said about Bry. She needed to squash that particular kind of gossip before it went any further. "James, why would you think I'm getting back with Bry?"

James took his seat and pushed the tray around the table for everyone to grab their glass. "I know someone who works at the home Mrs. Newman is in. She said you guys have been in there together a lot lately. Said she saw you cuddled up in the visitors lounge one morning."

"We weren't *cuddled up*. I was comforting him after a particularly bad time with his mother. She's not been well. I'd do the same for any of you." Kelsey waved her hand to encompass the group. She didn't want to go into detail about Marjorie's condition. From what Bry had told her, nobody knew how bad things had gotten with her health, and Kelsey didn't want to reveal too much of his personal information, but she also didn't want anyone getting the wrong idea about her and her ex.

James shrugged. "Guess that explains it."

Kelsey didn't think he sounded all that convinced, but before she could say any more, Zac arrived. She was startled by the venomous look he threw her way. If looks could kill, she'd be six feet under. What the hell had she done? He'd been acting strange at recent get-togethers, and there was the weird vibe she'd gotten from him last Friday, but this was the first time he'd shown her any real outright hostility.

Coop leaned his shoulder into hers. "Ignore him. He's being a prick lately."

She glanced at Zac's twin. "So I'm not imagining things?"

Coop laughed. "Hell, no. Watch this. I'll show you it's not just you he's got a problem with." He leaned over her to tap Shaye's cheek. "Hey, hot stuff. We still on for later?"

Shaye's smile and eyes were full of sexual innuendo as she moved closer to Coop, the two of them all but in Kelsey's lap now. "Think you can handle me?"

"Oh, I'll handle you all right." Coop's gaze dropped to ogle Shaye's cleavage.

"For fuck sake." Zac slammed his empty glass down on the table. "I'm not hanging around to watch this shit."

Kelsey watched him storm off. Mouths hung open all around the table. Obviously, she wasn't the only one shocked by Zac's behavior.

"See. Told ya." Coop winked as he sat back in his chair.

"Did you just do that to piss your brother off?" Shaye asked.

"Yep." A smug smile curled Coop's lips.

"Why you—"

"*Shaye,*" Coop murmured.

To Kelsey's surprise, Shaye sat back in her seat, mouth closed. Kelsey couldn't believe Coop could silence Shaye so quickly. She'd seen the head of steam her best friend was building up. Normally, it took a good rant for Shaye to let it go, but Coop had managed to do what Kelsey had thought impossible, and by only uttering her name.

"Ah, is there something going on between *you two* we don't know about?" Nikki asked, her gaze bouncing from Shaye to Coop and back again.

"Nope." Coop picked up his beer and grinned. "Not yet."

Kelsey was happy for the conversation to head in that direction.

She leaned back in her chair and let her friends debate the Shaye-and-Coop development while she contemplated the situation with West. Now that she'd revealed so much of her inner turmoil, she wasn't sure where they stood. She'd called him to let him know she'd arrived home safe. They'd spoken only a few words before hanging up, and neither had mentioned what had been said during their video call. Or after he'd come out of the house.

Her phone rang, snapping her to attention. Fear and excitement warred inside her. The possibility of West being on the other end of the call delivered conflicting emotions. Kelsey was worried their conversation had left both of them with a bad taste in their mouths. She certainly regretted revealing the depth of hurt he'd caused her in the past, but there wasn't anything she could do about it now.

She scrambled to get her phone out of her bag before the call switched over to voicemail. Caller ID showed it wasn't West but Bry on the other end, and Kelsey instantly got a bad feeling in her chest. "Bry?"

"Mum had a stroke," he choked out.

"Oh, God, Bry. I'm sorry."

"It's bad. Can you—"

"Yes, yes." She shoved her chair back and nudged Coop with her knee. "I'll come right now."

"Thank you, Kelsey. I don't know what to do."

Kelsey could hear the tears in Bry's voice and quickly shuffled past the guys to get out. "I'll be there as soon as I can."

"She's in North Shore Private. Where Dad was." His voice cracked, the last words were murmured in a desolate tone that squeezed Kelsey's heart.

She didn't know what to say. How to comfort him over the phone when there were no words that could make the situation better. "I'll be there soon." She hung up and dug in her bag for her keys.

"Problem?" James asked as she looked up at the group.

"Bry's mum has had a stroke. I have to go. I'll catch you all later."

"Let us know if he needs anything," Nick said.

"I will." She turned to leave but Coop grabbed her arm.

Turning back, she found Coop eyeing her with concern. "Let West know where you're going. Don't let him find out from one of us."

"Ah, okay." Kelsey wasn't sure why Coop thought West had a right to know where she was going, but as one of his best friends—and a close one of her own—she valued his advice and quickly tapped out a text as she rushed out of the pub to her car.

West dropped the phone in his lap as he watched Kelsey's car wiz past. He'd just parked when he received her text and reading the words sliced him up in a way he couldn't explain.

On way to Bry.

He figured something had happened with Bry's mother, but with so few words and no real meaning behind them, no one would blame him for thinking the worst. The jealousy and anger that filled him each time Kelsey dropped everything to go to Bry only left him feeling like a jerk. But he couldn't help his reactions even knowing the state of Bry's mother's health. West opened his door, but he didn't get out. Suddenly spending a few hours at the pub with his friends held no appeal.

Not without Kelsey.

He couldn't really afford the time away from work either. He'd spent the day sorting out the details for the next few weeks, but he had to be realistic and accept it was possible his second kitchen would be out of action for months. The insurance company wasn't sending anyone out until late next week, and until then he couldn't touch the charred mess. Reaching over, he grabbed the door and slammed it shut. A night at home surrounded by paperwork wasn't exactly the most riveting Friday evening, but West could think of only one thing more interesting, and that wasn't an option.

West started the car, but before he left he sent a text to Coop, letting him know he wouldn't be turning up. He'd reversed out of his spot and was pulling out of the parking lot into traffic when his friend called.

Activating the integrated phone system with the button on his steering wheel, West answered. "Hey."

"Is she really the only reason you were coming?" Coop asked.

"No. Yes." West checked over his shoulder before changing lanes. "I wasn't coming until you dropped your not-so-subtle hint that Shaye was dragging Kels out."

"You know where she is?"

"Yeah," he sighed. "Do you know what happened to Bry's mum?"

"Stroke."

"Ah, shit." West could totally understand why Kelsey had gone running off to Bry now.

"Yep. And from what James has just been telling us, it seems that good old Bry has been keeping mum about Mum," Coop said.

"Huh? What do you mean?"

"James knows some woman that works at the home where Mrs. Newman is. She told him that the junior Mrs. Newman has been there with her *husband* in recent days and that the senior Mrs. Newman is not doing well and hasn't been for a while."

"Why the hell would he keep that from us?" West asked as he turned off the main road onto a side street. The conversation was getting too distracting to be navigating through traffic at the same time. He spied a parking spot about fifty meters down and pulled into it.

"Well, I don't know about you, but I haven't seen Bry more than two times in the last few months. He's skipped our usual Friday drinks for weeks."

West thought about it for a moment. "You know, I don't think I've seen him in over a month." He'd heard him though. Loud and clear through Kelsey's phone. Twice.

"Wonder what's up with that? It's not like there's an issue between him and Kelsey that would be keeping him away. They've never had any issues."

"If what James said about Bry's mum is true, then her condition might be the reason."

"Okay, we've danced around it long enough and you completely ignored my husband comment. Are you okay with Kelsey running off to him?"

West sucked in a breath. "Why wouldn't I be?" If Coop knew something he didn't...

"So you know she's not just standing beside him?"

"What?" West had no idea what his friend was talking about, but he wanted details. Fast. "What the fuck does that mean?"

Coop sighed. "This friend of James said she saw them in each other's arms in the visitors lounge at the home."

Whoa. That he wasn't okay with. West's brain told him Kelsey would never be with Bry after being with him, but his heart was a whole other story. It ached along with his gut as acid churned in his stomach.

"I'm taking your silence to mean this is news to you."

"I'm sure there's a reasonable explanation." There had to be.

"Oh, there is. And for what it's worth, I believe her."

West waited but Coop didn't elaborate any further. "Well don't leave me in the dark, man."

"She said she was comforting him after a bad episode with his mother like she would any one of us."

"And you believed her?" He trusted Coop's judgment.

"Yeah. I also think Bry is taking advantage of Kelsey's generosity. She's always been the bleeding heart among our group."

"Yes, she has." West scrubbed his fingers back and forth on his forehead. "I get why he would though."

"Doesn't mean you have to like it," Coop said.

"Oh, I definitely don't like it, but what can I do about? I can't exactly tell her not to go."

"No. I guess not."

West closed his eyes and leaned his head back against the seat. For long moments, neither of them said a word, only the faint crackle of the open phone line filled the car. He should hang up and head home. "Listen, I gotta go. I'll talk to you later."

"Want me to come over?" Coop asked.

A bark of laughter left West's throat. "What? This little deep-and-meaningful isn't enough? Now you wanna come hold my hand too?"

Coop laughed. "Nah, I was actually thinking I wouldn't have to pay for my beer at your place."

"Ha! Think again. My fridge is still full of the case you brought round Monday night."

"Actually, Zac paid for that." Someone yelled Coop's name in the background. "Okay, I'm being summoned by a hot chick. I have a feeling this is going to be my lucky night."

"At least one of us is getting some," West murmured.

"What?"

"Nothing. Catch ya later."

"We still on for tomorrow? You want me to look at the kitchen, right?" Coop asked.

West had forgotten he'd asked his friend to give him an estimate on repairs. "How 'bout we leave it until next week. The insurance guy isn't coming until Thursday, and I can't touch it until after he's been and given his seal of approval for the claim to go through." Not that he needed the insurance money to pay for the damage, but he paid his premiums so he may as well get his money's worth.

"Call me when you know when."

"Will do." His phone beeped signally an incoming call. "Gotta go, someone's trying to call. It might be Kels."

Before Coop could say a word, West tapped the screen on his phone to drop their call and pick up the new one.

"Hello."

"West?"

"Kels? You okay?" She sounded anything but okay, and when he heard her sob he bolted upright in his seat. "What's wrong, baby? Where are you?"

Her sobs echoed through the car for long minutes and West felt powerless to help her. He couldn't even drive to her. He didn't have a clue where she was.

"S-she's gone."

"Tell me where you are and I'll be there."

"I. Bry. He's devastated." Never mind Bry, West could hear the devastation in *her* voice.

"Tell me where."

"I don't think. Hang on." Sound was muffled and West figured she must have covered the phone with her hand for a moment. "I have to go. I'll call you later."

"Kelsey! Don't you dare hang up without telling me where you are."

"I'll call you later. Promise."

"Dammit. Stop shutting me out." West slapped his palm on the steering wheel.

"I'm not. Bry's not in any condition to see anyone right now."

"What about you?" Who was going to support her through this?

"Later."

The connection cut off before West could get another word out. He slapped the wheel again. And again. Pain radiated up his arm, but he didn't care. Frustration and anger burned a hole in his gut and the throb in his hand and wrist gave him something to focus on other than Kelsey's latest mixed signals.

If she didn't want him, why had she called? And what the hell was he supposed to do—to think—when she reached for him and pushed him away at the same time?

13

Kelsey let the car roll to a stop at the kerb. She switched off the lights and engine and sat in the dark, staring through the passenger window at the house. There wasn't a light shining in any of the windows, causing her to second-guess her decision to come here for the millionth time. It was after one am, and West was obviously asleep. In the end, her need for comfort made her grab her purse and climb out of the car. The last few hours had been a hellish nightmare. Doctors and reports and a soul-sapping sorrow she'd never felt before. Marjorie might not have been her mother, but the woman had given Kelsey more maternal love than she'd received from anyone else in her life.

She stumbled on the uneven path as she made her way to the house, the streetlight didn't illuminate this far into the yard and without a porch light to guide her, Kelsey took extra care not to trip on the steps. But when she reached the door, she hesitated, turned around and stared at her car. What if he wasn't home? What if he was and wouldn't let her in? She'd never needed anything the way she needed West's arms wrapped around her right now. Eventually, the desperation to feel connected clawing at her insides won out over her fears and she spun back around and pressed the doorbell.

The bell echoed on the other side of the closed door and she held her breath until she heard footsteps rushing over timber floors. When the door opened to reveal West in nothing but a pair of low-slung boxer briefs, Kelsey didn't know if it was exhaustion, grief or the naked masculine perfection in front of her that rendered her speechless.

Thankfully, West didn't need words to know what she wanted. What she needed. He reached out and grabbed her hand. Pulling her inside, he closed the door before wrapping his arms around her and holding her close. She gave in then. Let her purse drop to the floor at their feet and her tears fall to his chest. Kelsey had no idea how long they stood there. How long the wretched sobs racked her body. But when West slipped an arm behind her knees and lifted her up to cradle her against him, she was relieved—grateful that he was taking care of her when there was no way she could.

Without a word, he walked through the house to his room. Kelsey clung to his neck when he lowered her to the bed and tried to pull away. "No."

"I'm not going anywhere." He brushed his fingers down her cheek. "I just want to get you something more comfortable to sleep in."

She let her arms slip from around him and fall to her sides. "I should go home." Her protest was weak. She didn't have the strength to walk out to her car never mind the desire.

"You wouldn't have turned up on my doorstep at this hour if you wanted to go home," West said as he pulled the second drawer on his dresser out and grabbed a shirt. He came back to the bed and held out his hand. "C'mon, let's get you out of those clothes. Do you want a shower?"

For a split second, she thought about it. Thought about trying to wash away the smell of death that seemed to be clinging to her, but with her eyelids drooping and her arms and legs feeling as though they were weighted down with lead, Kelsey figured she'd end up in an exhausted pile at the bottom of the shower if she tried. "No."

"Okay. Straight to bed it is."

West undressed her with a minimum of fuss, and before Kelsey could come up with another feeble argument about going home, she found herself surrounded by the softest T-shirt she'd ever touched. He helped her beneath the covers before crawling into the bed on the other side. Kelsey wasn't sure what she expected, but it wasn't for West to pull her against him, his chest to her back, and just hold her. His comfy shirt wasn't the only thing she found herself enveloped in.

His warmth seeped through her skin to heat the cold that had settled in her chest since she'd arrived at the hospital to discover she was too late. He didn't ask questions—didn't press for any details—and Kelsey was so grateful to not have to relive those horrible moments if only for the rest of tonight.

She focused on his steady breathing, the beat of his heart against her spine. With each puff of air, each pulse of blood, she sank deeper and deeper into exhaustion, knowing that everything would be okay because West had her.

West was pretty sure he should be nominated for sainthood. He'd been lying here with an almost-naked Kelsey in his arms, her curvy ass snuggled up to his groin, for hours. And for hours, he'd had a hard-on he could do nothing with. Then again, a saint wouldn't think about sex at a time like this, half-naked woman or not. Self-recriminations for being such a deviant when Kels was clearly hurting bounced around his brain. She'd lost someone close —someone she cared about deeply—and his body wanted to roll her over so he could bury his cock inside her. Damn, he was such a selfish prick.

He glanced over at the alarm clock. Seven nineteen. The sun hadn't been up an hour yet, and with his room being on the southwest side of the house, it was still fairly dark. Hopefully, Kelsey would get a few more hours sleep before she was forced to face reality again. Pulling his arm out from under her, West eased away slowly so he wouldn't disturb her. She murmured something he didn't catch before rolling over and cuddling into the quilt. Satisfied she wasn't going to wake, he got out of bed and headed for the bathroom and a desperately needed cold shower.

Cold showers on winter mornings were not good. West shivered his way through, but at least he managed to get his hard-on under control, if not eradicated completely. The fact he had the woman of his dreams in his bed couldn't be ignored entirely. Slipping into jeans and a T-shirt, he headed for the kitchen and coffee. He checked Kelsey was still sleeping on the way and found her in the same position he'd left her. There was no denying the thrill that coursed through him at the sight of her in his bed. He'd waited years to get her there. Unfortunately, the circumstances weren't what he'd expected.

It had to be a good sign that she'd come to him in the middle of the night. She could have gone to Shaye, or even stayed with Bry, but instead she'd driven here. To him. That said a hell of a lot about the way she felt. Now, if he could only get her to be honest about those feelings when she wasn't in the pit of grief. West didn't delude himself though. He wasn't taking her arrival on his doorstep in the dead of night as a confession of anything. If she performed to her usual standard, she'd be denying and backpedalling and throwing up those damn red lights the second she woke.

With a sigh, West left the room and made his way down the hall. He spotted her bag on the floor by the door. She must have dropped it when he'd pulled her inside. West walked over, scooped it up and took it into the kitchen with him. He placed it on the counter next to his keys and wallet. Seeing Kelsey's bag—her personal belongings— beside his pulled him up short, and he stared at them. Wished it was something he saw every day.

He reached out to brush his fingers over the leather strap when her phone rang. For a second, he froze, but when the shrill ring blasted through the room again, he opened her bag and searched for the phone. When he saw who it was, it took him a heartbeat to decide whether or not to answer. Bry.

Taking a deep breath, West hit answer and brought the phone to his ear.

"Kelsey. I'm sorry to call so early after last night."

"It's West. Kels is still asleep." West might resent this man for a few things, but he did the polite thing and offered his condolences. "Sorry to hear about your mum."

"Oh. Um, thanks."

Silence filled the line, and again West was forced to do the right thing when all he really wanted to do was hang up on the guy. He was sure Bry only wanted to impose on Kelsey's soft heart again. "Can I help you with something?"

"Um, no, I just wanted to let Kelsey know our appointment at the funeral home is at eleven today."

"*Our* appointment?"

"Yeah, Kelsey said she'd come with me when I pick out Mum's coffin," Bry's voice broke over that last word.

And right there West felt like the biggest bastard on the planet. "I'll let her know. Does she have the address?" he asked.

"I was going to come pick her up."

"Oh, right. I'll let her know what time to be ready then. Do you need help with anything else?" It pained him to ask, but he had to. Had to forget this man had a connection to Kelsey that West envied— wanted to sever. One he wanted for himself.

"No. I can't do anything else until all the paperwork is dealt with. One step at a time. Funeral planning today." West heard Bry suck in a deep breath and let it out in a rush. "To be honest, I can't cope with thinking about more than that right now."

"I can understand that. Hang in there, and you know how to get me if you need anything. Same goes for the rest of the gang. We're all here for you." West wanted to be sure Bry knew Kelsey wasn't the only one he could call on. Maybe then he wouldn't demand so much from her. "Any time. Day or night."

"Thanks. I appreciate it."

"I'll make sure Kels is home and ready in time for you to pick her up." West couldn't stop himself from implying she wasn't there now.

He hadn't outright said she was at his house, but Bry would have to be stupid not to get the hint, and he definitely wasn't.

"Oh, I can pick her up from...wherever."

West smiled. No, definitely not stupid. "Nah, that's fine, she'll want to change out of yesterday's clothes anyway."

"Ah, right. Okay. Tell her I'll be there around ten-thirty to pick her up."

"Will do."

"Thanks." Bry paused but West didn't fill the silence. "Bye then."

"See ya, Bry. And don't forget. Anything you need. Any time."

"Yeah, okay. Thanks."

West waited for Bry to hang up before pulling Kelsey's phone away from his ear. He took note of the time and decided he'd make omelets for breakfast. There was no way Kels would let him go with her to help Bry, so he'd make sure she knew he was there for her in other ways. Ensuring she got sleep and ate properly would do for now.

***

Kelsey rolled over and stared at the unfamiliar ceiling. It took her a few seconds to remember where she was, but when she did, she was slammed with two things. Grief and guilt. The grief she could easily explain. Marjorie was dead. She might not have seen the woman in recent months, but for years their contact had been daily. The guilt came from a number of reasons. There were so many things she'd done she regretted—was ashamed of. Her biggest shame surrounded her.

She'd taken advantage of West by coming here.

He'd welcomed her unconditionally and she felt sick to the stomach when she thought about the way she'd treated him. She'd let him in only to shut him out then let him in again. Except she'd never let him get too close. And yet when she'd needed him, she hadn't thought about what that would do to their complex relationship. She couldn't deny it any longer. There was something between them.

Something that, even now, when she couldn't hide from it any longer, she didn't want to examine.

She could hear him at the other end of the house. He was in the kitchen, and if the aromas seeping into the room were a clue, he was cooking. Kelsey knew West cooked for the enjoyment of it, but also because he liked to feed people, her in particular. She'd lost count of the number of meals he'd turned up on her doorstep with over the last three years. Ever since she'd separated from Bry, she'd had the pleasure of eating one of West's meals each week.

Since she'd separated from Bry...

Oh God. She'd never thought about it before. But that was when West had started feeding her. He'd been the first to arrive bearing a housewarming gift to that tiny apartment she'd rented the first year. Then he'd helped her find her house, helped her fill it with used furniture and even showed her how to change fuses when she hadn't had a clue where to find them never mind replace them.

Had he been leading up to this? To them getting together? The more she thought about it, the more she remembered all the little things he did for her—little things that straddled the *friend's* line— the more she was convinced that West had been waging a slow campaign of seduction. She'd been blind. Stupid. Hurtful. Thoughtless. Without knowing it, she'd taken advantage of him. Except last night she'd known. All those second thoughts about coming over...

"Hey, sleepy head. Hungry?"

Jolted from her thoughts, Kelsey's gaze darted to the doorway where West leaned against the frame. He wore a snug dark-blue T-shirt and jeans so faded they were white in places. All the right places. "Um, I guess." Her stomach was hollow and she figured she could probably eat a horse if it was the only thing on offer, but after what she'd been thinking before he showed up, Kelsey wondered if it might be best to get out of here as quickly as possible.

"C'mon then. Up you get." He pushed off the wall and strolled towards her. "I've made omelets. And bacon."

Bacon. Her weakness.

He held out his hand and Kelsey did the only thing she could.

She slid her hand into his and let him pull her off the bed and to her feet. "I should get dressed..." She glanced around for her clothes.

"Nah, the shirt covers you and you've only got yesterday's clothes to put on."

She looked down. West was right. The hem brushed her lower thighs and the sleeves hit her elbows.

"Do you want coffee or tea with breakfast?"

Kelsey let him lead her from the room. "Coffee. I need the caffeine hit."

"You also need food. Did you eat dinner last night?" he asked as he ushered her into a chair at the table.

"A sandwich from the hospital cafeteria." She didn't add that it had been midnight when she'd gulped it down.

He exaggerated a shudder and pretended to gag, making her smile. "That's not food. In fact, I'm pretty sure they only serve nuclear waste in those places."

She laughed. "It wasn't that bad." The bread was a bit hard and the lettuce a little brown on the edges, but it had served its purpose and filled a hole.

"Well, this feast will be a definite improvement on your last meal." He disappeared into the kitchen only to return moments later with a tray loaded with their breakfast.

"Oh my God. How much food did you cook?" Kelsey eyed each plate as he set it in the middle of the table. There was a huge pile of bacon stacked on one and the biggest omelet she'd ever seen on another.

West shrugged as he handed her an empty plate. "I'll have the leftovers for lunch."

"And dinner, I think." She picked up a piece of crispy bacon and popped it into her mouth.

"Hey, I had my eye on that bit." He mock frowned at her.

Kelsey grinned as she chewed. It was perfectly crisp with just enough bacon grease to satisfy the sinful indulgence without clogging the arteries. Typical of West to try and make an unhealthy treat healthy—not that she cared either way. Bacon was bacon, and she'd eat it until there wasn't a slice left if she could.

"How much omelet do you want?" He held a knife in the middle of the egg-covered plate. "Half?"

"No. A quarter. That way I'll have room for more bacon." She grinned and reached for a second piece.

"A third." He didn't wait for her to agree. And before she could protest, he was putting a good chunk of the fluffy omelet on her plate.

"*West.*"

"*Kelsey.*" He mimicked her tone.

"I won't be able to eat all that."

"Fine. Don't finish it." He put the rest of the eggs on his own plate. "Serve yourself some bacon while I go get the coffee."

She did as she was told. Of course, she picked through the plate to find the crispiest pieces. By the time West put a mug in front of her, Kelsey had polished off another two slices and started on her eggs.

"Good?" he asked as he took his seat.

Kelsey covered her mouth with her hand and spoke around a mouthful of fluffy eggs. "You have to ask?"

He grinned and then scooped a forkful of omelet into his mouth.

Neither of them spoke for the next few minutes. It took no time for Kelsey to finish everything on her plate, and she stared at the empty surface with confusion. She would have sworn she wasn't that hungry when West served her that huge piece of omelet.

"You want more?" He indicated the few strips of bacon still on the plate between them.

Kelsey shook her head. "No. I'm good. Surprised I managed to finish what you served me actually." Then again, it was bacon...

"More hungry than you thought then." West picked up his mug and took a sip.

"Must have been," she said while eyeing those last couple of pieces.

West laughed. "Go on. You know you want to."

She looked up to find him grinning at her. Smiling sheepishly,

Kelsey reached over and snatched up the remaining bacon and dropped it on her plate.

"There you go. Not so hard, was it?" he asked.

"No. What'll be hard is the extra exercise I'll have to do to get rid of the fat these things are going to lay on my butt and thighs."

He put his mug down hard on the table, making everything rattle, and leaned forward. "First, you don't exercise on the best of days. Second, there's nothing wrong with your butt or your thighs. They're both perfectly sized and shaped, and I love running my hands over them."

Kelsey's pulse raced. Heat flooded her core and a tremor rippled through her. "I, um..."

West leaned back and picked up his coffee. He appeared calm. Except those penetrating grey eyes. His eyes were a firestorm of need and want and hunger, and Kelsey's body reacted to the blatant desire he aimed her way. She tightened—like one of those vacuum bags she stored her winter clothes in—shrinking until nothing but her bone-deep yearning for him showed.

It all came down to this. The all-consuming attraction she had for him. Now that she'd slept with him again, the walls she'd erected all those years ago were crumbling.

Crumbling quicker than she could deal with.

Quicker than she could patch them up.

"Finish your breakfast, Kels."

Instead of answering, she dug into another slice of bacon. The longer she could avoid examining her true feelings the better, because she wasn't ready for where this was going—where they were going. Wasn't ready to put her heart on the line again. She was popping the final bit of bacon in her mouth when West spoke.

"Bry phoned while you were still asleep."

Kelsey had to swallow carefully so she didn't choke at his words. "What?" Kelsey sat up straight, the bacon hitting her stomach like lead. "Bry rang here?"

"No. He called your cell."

"Oh." She pushed back her chair. "I should call him back."

"No need. He just wanted to let you know he'd pick you up at ten-thirty to go to the funeral home."

"You answered my phone?" Kelsey wasn't sure how she felt about that. Too many emotions were churning around inside her. Concern over what West might have said to her ex-husband about where she was definitely led the charge though.

West nodded. "I wasn't about to let it continue to ring and wake you up. You needed to rest."

"Oh." Kelsey didn't know what to say. Bry would have been surprised when West answered her phone, but hopefully the distress over his mother's passing would numb him to the strangeness of it. As far as she knew, the two men hadn't had any contact since her and West had fallen into bed together. She knew West wasn't comfortable with her supporting Bry as much as she did, and she hoped he hadn't said anything about it.

She also hoped he hadn't given away the fact she hadn't gone home last night.

14

Kelsey was dreading the next few hours. It had been an exhausting couple of days. Ones where she hadn't dared talk to West for fear she'd crumble completely. She had to be strong for Bry. As much as she knew it wasn't really her place to support him so fully, she also knew the man was falling apart. Without her to drive him around and help start the process of straightening out his mother's estate, he would still be standing in that hospital corridor where she'd found him the night Marjorie died.

Today was the funeral. And even though she knew she shouldn't go with Bry, she hadn't been able to refuse him when he'd asked. He'd looked so lost—so gutted—that every one of her heart's strings had pulled tight and threatened to cut off her blood flow. She'd been the one to notify all Marjorie's relatives and friends of her passing. To notify everyone of the time and place the service would take place. Bry couldn't even manage to shower, never mind coordinate a funeral.

The doorbell rang and Kelsey's stomach cramped. She hadn't eaten much in the last few days. She'd found a meal in her fridge with a note from West stuck to it each night, but other than that, they'd only had a handful of texts in the way of contact. He'd offered to come over every day since she'd left his house on Saturday, but Kelsey hadn't had the time or the energy to think about what was happening between them, and until she did she couldn't bring herself to lean on him. Not again.

Not if she was going to put a stop to whatever it was they were doing. And she had to. She didn't think she could risk her heart to him a second time, and it wasn't fair to either of them—but especially West—to continue seeing him unless she did.

With a sigh, she walked to the front door and opened it to find a pale and gaunt Bry standing on her front step. He really was a mess. He'd never get through today without her to guide him.

"The car is here," he said in way of greeting.

She glanced over his shoulder to see the funeral-home car waiting at the kerb. Taking a deep breath, Kelsey reached for the door to close it behind her. "I'm ready."

Bry held out his hand and then must have thought better of it, because he waved it in the direction of the street and the waiting car. "After you."

Kelsey smiled—more a grimace really—and moved past him. Leading the way, she glanced back to check he was following. She'd sent him home two hours ago to get ready and wait for the car. It was the first break, other than when she was asleep, that she'd had since he'd picked her up last Saturday to help chose his mother's coffin. He'd begged to sleep on her couch, and as usual, Kelsey found it impossible to refuse someone in need. They'd made a stop each day at his house for clean clothes, but other than that, Bry was basically living with her again. At least someone was benefiting from West's generous delivery of food.

Kelsey nodded at the driver when he opened the door for her. She climbed in and slid across the seat to make room for Bry. They'd be arriving at the church in about twenty minutes. One thousand two hundred seconds to brace herself for everyone's reaction. She was dreading it more than the funeral itself. Bry sat next to her and closed the door, but instead of offering him a reassuring smile like she'd been doing all week, she stared out the window and tried to focus on the passing houses.

They pulled up in front of the church all too soon, and Kelsey kept her gaze lowered as she got out of the car. She didn't want to face West or any of their friends just yet. Instead, she let Bry usher her inside to the pew reserved for immediate family and took a seat. There was no need for her to turn around, no need for her to make eye contact with anyone. She could feel more than one set of eyes on her. Their curiosity was understandable. It was the anger and confusion she was sure West would be feeling that she didn't want to see.

The service was simple—quick. Bry hadn't wanted anyone to speak, just the priest, and it didn't matter how much Kelsey had tried to convince him otherwise, he hadn't budged on that. Funny how he couldn't seem to make a decision about anything else but that he'd known with certainty. There were no pallbearers, only men from the funeral home dressed in black suits. Kelsey waited while the priest offered his condolences to Bry before they made their way out of the church behind the coffin.

She stood to the side and watched as the men loaded Marjorie in the back of the hearse for her final journey. Bry hadn't wanted a graveside service, instead opting for his mother to be lowered into the ground next to his father in private. He wouldn't even be there. He moved closer to her and despite her attempts to keep her distance as everyone came past to offer their sympathy, Bry kept including her in the conversations, kept pulling her closer.

Their friends waited until all other attendees had spoken to Bry before coming over. As much as Kelsey didn't want to look, her eyes sought West. She wasn't sure what it was swirling in those stormy-grey eyes, but she couldn't stop the catch in her breath nor the tears flooding her eyes and blurring her vision. She'd known seeing him would make her crack. Known the emotions she'd been holding at bay would come crashing down on her.

He stepped forward and pulled her into his arms, but she couldn't let him give her comfort. Not when she wouldn't be able to let go if he held her longer than a few seconds. She slipped from his embrace, avoided the eyes she knew would be filled with confusion and hurt, and turned to face the next of their friends. It seemed to take forever for the last person to come forward, for everyone to begin to move away and the driver of the funeral car to usher them back into the vehicle.

Kelsey slumped back against the seat and prayed she wouldn't lose it until after she got home. Until after she was alone and could let everything she'd bottled up run free. Bry didn't speak, and for that she was grateful. But her relief was short lived. When the car pulled up at her house and he exited with her, she knew she wouldn't be able to let go anytime soon.

West threw his keys across the counter and made a B-line for the fridge. He yanked open the door, pulled out a beer and cracked the top. But when he brought the cold bottle to his lips, he couldn't drink. His frustration and anger were a boiling, seething mass inside him, and he had to let it out. The only way to do that was to confront the person who'd caused it.

Kelsey.

God it had ripped him up inside to see her looking so exhausted. And thin. He didn't know if anyone else would notice but he could tell she'd lost a couple of kilos since he'd held her while she slept Friday night. Had it only been five days ago that she'd left his house after spending the night in his arms? He'd lost track of the days, what with Weston's being so busy and his worry over Kels, he didn't know what day it was.

Standing there, watching Bry be totally oblivious to Kelsey's pain and need had solidified something for West. If he couldn't have her completely, couldn't be the one to support her, he had to walk away. And by walk away he meant she couldn't work for him in any capacity. He'd have to find someone else to manage the books and his taxes. There was no way he could settle for the crumbs she'd been tossing his way.

Not anymore.

As he put the beer on the counter, he reached over and scooped up his keys. He slammed the front door on his way out. The small amount of satisfaction did little to appease his growing annoyance. West figured he was about to explode, and Kelsey was going to take the brunt of it. His fury may be an overreaction, but today had been the straw that broke the camel's back so to speak. He'd had enough of her pushing him away only to pull him close when it suited her and then push him away again.

He didn't remember the drive over. Couldn't say if he'd stuck to the speed limit or ran any red lights. His complete focus was on the coming confrontation with Kelsey. Slamming out of his car, West stopped to suck in a deep breath in an attempt to cool his jets some before he stormed into her house. With a little more control over his anger, he made his way up the path.

West thought about using his key but decided he better not. He should at least give her the courtesy of knocking, except when he reached the door, he found it open and Kelsey standing in the hallway with an armload of clothes. Men's clothes.

"What the fuck?" West didn't know he was going to open his mouth until his voice echoed off the walls.

"West? What are you doing here?" Kelsey's forehead creased and she looked over her shoulder.

"We have to talk," he said.

She turned to face him once more. "This isn't a good time."

"It's never a good time." He stepped closer, deeper into the house. "I'm tired of waiting for the *good time*, Kels."

"Please." She looked over her shoulder down the hall again before bringing her gaze back to his and then dropping it to stare at his chest. "Not now."

West had a feeling he knew why she kept glancing that way. He nodded towards the pile of clothes in her arms. "Want to explain that?"

She wasn't looking at him, so he doubted she saw his gesture, but she would have to be clueless not to know what he was talking about. "I...um..." Her struggled to find words didn't surprise him.

For the first time since he'd gotten there, West took his eyes off Kelsey and looked around. From where he stood, he could see into the living room. It was obvious she'd had company—still had company if he took into account the pair of men's dress shoes next to the coffee table. He'd seen hints of it this past week when he'd dropped off a meal each day, but he'd ignored it. He couldn't ignore it now. It was blatantly obvious Bry was staying with her.

"It's not what you think," she murmured.

He bought his gaze back to her. "You have no idea what I think or why I think it. You're too busy pretending nothing is going on and burying yourself in someone else's problems so you can avoid your own."

"That's not true," she argued.

"Isn't it?" He scrubbed his hand across his forehead.

"No. I'm helping a friend. Just as I would any other."

"Seriously?" West's mouth hung open. Did she actually believe that load of BS? "So you'd let any other *guy* friend stay over. Do his washing?"

"Bry's mother just died, West. What else am I supposed to do?"

"Support him without shutting out the man in your life for a start."

"The man in my life?" Kelsey lowered her voice. "We slept together once. It was a mistake."

He wasn't about to argue the number of times they'd slept together. They could pick that particular debate apart for hours. "Was it a mistake when you turned up on my doorstep in the middle of the night needing comfort too?"

"I—"

"Don't delude yourself. We're seeing each other. You wouldn't have had sex with me if you didn't feel something for me. And you wouldn't have knocked on my door after midnight just so I could hold you if you didn't feel it deeply. Stop lying to both of us."

"I can't deal with this now."

"Dammit, this has to stop!"

"What?"

"You shutting me out. Sneaking around behind closed doors like we're some fucking dirty little secret. Everything being on your terms."

"That's not—"

"Isn't it?" He stepped closer and she took a half-step back. "Who knows?"

"K-knows?"

"Yes. Who the hell knows we're seeing each other. And don't you dare fucking say we're not again. Do you have any idea how hard it was to watch Bry put his hands on you today? How hard it was not to give you the comfort I could see you needed? Any idea how much I wanted to pull you against me to hold you close—to claim your mouth in a kiss that would leave you with no doubt I'm here for you —leave no one in any doubt we're together?"

"I..." She shook her head.

"I know I fucked up before. But I'm not that boy any more. I know what I want. *Who* I want. And I know I have a lot to make up for, but I'm ready to do that and more, Kelsey. I just need you to meet me halfway."

"West," she whispered his name, her eyes glistening with tears, still shaking her head back and forth.

"Fuck." West couldn't do it. Couldn't stand here and argue with her when he knew full well she wasn't going to admit to a damn thing. Wasn't going to let him in and give him what he wanted. "I've had enough. I can't take it anymore. You either want to be with me or you don't. I can't keep doing this stop-start thing or continue to pretend I'm not so far gone on you that I can't see straight."

K elsey didn't know what to say. Couldn't think beyond the hurt, devastated look in West's stormy-gray eyes.

"Just as I thought." He dragged his hands through his hair. "I'm done pushing this. Done fighting for us on my own. When you're ready to be with me, *really* be together, out in the open for anyone to see, you know where to find me."

He spun around and stormed from the house. The slam of the door made her flinch, but other than that she didn't move. It wasn't until several minutes later that what had happened sank in.

"Oh God." He'd left.

"Kelsey?"

She turned to find Bry standing behind her. "Bry. I..."

"I should go," he said.

Oh God. Her cheeks filled with heat. He'd heard their argument. "I'm sorry."

Bry smiled. "You don't have anything to be sorry about."

"I do. You've just lost your mother. You need somewhere to recoup. Not somewhere with people arguing—"

"You should go after him."

"What?" She stared at her ex-husband.

"Go find him and fix it."

"I...it's not—"

He smiled. "Yeah, it is." Bry took a step closer.

Kelsey swallowed and confessed what was weighing on her heart before her mind could stop her tongue from forming the words. "I'm so, so sorry. I never loved you like I should have. Like you deserved."

He laughed and pulled her into a hug, the armload of his dirty clothes trapped between them. "We're both guilty of that."

She shook her head. "No. I—"

"Nope." He gave her a squeeze before letting her go. "No apologies necessary. We loved each other, still do, but it's not the kind of love you build a life on. And if we hadn't both been so intent on having that happy ever after, we might have worked out sooner that it was false walls we were putting up."

"Might have been better if we didn't like each other so much too." She gave him a tight smile. "I still feel guilty about all I cheated you out of."

Bry placed his hands on her shoulders and looked her right in the eyes. "I know what you can do to make it up to me."

Kelsey eyed him warily. "What?"

"Stop punishing yourself and West, and go after what *you* deserve."

Her eyes widened, her mouth dropping open, but before she could gain her wits, he was talking again.

"I've always known how you two feel about each other. And it shames me to admit part of my motive to get married was to stake a bigger claim on you than him." Bry smiled, but sadness and regret burned in his eyes. "So you see we both have things we're guilty of. Sorry for."

Kelsey stared at the man she'd married. He had been and always would be her friend, and yet she'd had no clue that he'd known about her feelings for West or that he'd felt threatened by them. "I don't know what to say."

"Tell me you're going to go find him. Tell me you're going to go fight for what you deserve. 'Cause you deserve a man who loves you to distraction and that man was never me. Would never have been me. West, on the other hand, he's that guy."

Her eyes and nose stung with the tears she held at bay.

"None of that." He tapped her on the end of her nose. "No tears. Not while I'm here."

Kelsey didn't argue when he took the pile of clothes from her arms. Or when he went into the living room and slipped his feet into his shoes. She still hadn't said a word when he came to stand in front of her again.

"Thank you, for going above and beyond." Bry leaned over and kissed her forehead. "You're more than I ever deserved, Kelsey."

With those parting words, Bry let himself out the front door and closed it quietly behind him. For a split second, she thought about going after him to offer him a lift. But the man was perfectly capable of calling a cab or flagging one down.

Bry was right. She'd gone above and beyond for him in the last few days.

Was West right though? Had she sunk herself into helping Bry so she didn't have to think about what was happening between them?

15

Kelsey had wanted to go after West on Thursday night, but she knew she had to be sure. If they were going to do this—if she was going to put her heart on the line again, she had to be one hundred percent certain it was what she wanted. So she'd taken a couple of days to think about it. *Really* think about it. She'd discovered some things about herself she wasn't proud of in the two days since he'd given her the ultimatum. He'd been right to call her on her behavior. She was ashamed to admit she probably would have continued to treat him the same neglectful way if he hadn't.

Once she'd decided she wanted what West offered. Wanted what they could have together, it was a matter of deciding how she'd go after it. Shaye had come over last night and they'd spent the evening plotting and planning. No alcohol. The one thing they both agreed on was that Kelsey had to do some grand public gesture. Well, as public as a show of her intentions in front of their friends. Today seemed to be the perfect choice for that.

Everyone was getting together at the Moreland house for Coop and Zac's birthdays. Kelsey had known the Moreland twins since kindergarten, and it still boggled her mind to think they were born on different days. Coop's birthday was today, while Zac's was tomorrow. It would be more bizarre if they were identical, but being fraternal twins meant the separate birth dates worked for them.

A horn blasted out front and Kelsey quickly scooped up her bag and headed outside. Shaye waited in her car—the cute little convertible she was going to have to sell now that she was unemployed.

"Hey," Kelsey said as she slid into the passenger seat. "It's a shame you're selling this thing. I'll miss our summer drives to the beach."

Shaye leaned forward to look through the windshield at the overcast sky. "Nothing like the long winter months and unemployment to show you the folly of driving a topless way-above-my-new-budget vehicle."

"You still haven't heard about those two jobs you went for this week?" Kelsey asked.

"It's Saturday. They're not going to call today even if they've made their decisions, and neither of them are being finalized until end of next week." Shaye reversed out of Kelsey's driveway.

"Oh."

"So. Are you going through with it?" Shaye asked as she whipped the little car around the corner.

"Yes."

Shaye grinned. "I can't wait to see this."

"Hey. You're supposed to be supporting me in my leap of faith."

"Honey, you don't need anyone for that. Doesn't matter what you do, West will catch you."

Kelsey hoped her friend was right. She'd never been this nervous about anything. Not even the night she'd given West her virginity had butterflies plagued her the way they were right now. Then again, she hadn't known what could go wrong then. How much it could hurt to totally open herself up to someone and have them reject you. And here she was planning to do it all over again.

It seemed to take no time at all to drive the thirty minutes to the Moreland family home. "Wow. That was quick," Kelsey commented as Shaye pulled up at the kerb.

"Yep. We got all green lights. I think it's a sign you're doing the right thing." Shaye grinned as she shut off the car and reached into the back for her bag. "Let's get this party started."

Kelsey swallowed, her throat tight with nerves and strained to the point of pain as she did so. She needed to take a breath, calm down and concentrate on what she planned to do, not what the outcome might be. Like Shaye said, she had to have faith that West would be there to catch her. If she didn't trust him to be there, she may as well turn around and head home now.

W est cursed a blue streak as he caught yet another red light. Story of his life. If he wasn't getting them on the road, he was getting them from Kelsey. She hadn't called him. Hadn't come into work and hadn't turned up on his doorstep in the middle of the night. He sighed. He had to stop obsessing over her. She'd need time to process what he'd said and then she'd need time to work up the courage to come to him.

If that's what she decided to do.

Determined to put Kelsey out of his mind, West concentrated on getting to Zac and Coop's parents' place without crashing. The Moreland driveway and the street surrounding it were packed with cars. He had to drive six houses down before he could park. Switching of the engine, he reached over for the two presents on the passenger seat. He'd bought them both the same thing. It was a tradition that had started back in primary school. The guys were so determined to be treated as two individuals that they'd refused all gifts that were identical.

He grinned. Last year he'd bought them matching T-shirts. This year he'd gone with hats. It was stupid, and their real presents— yearly subscriptions to magazines, different of course—would be turning up in the mail soon enough, but it was something he did every year. West stepped out of the car and pocketed his keys. The walk to the Moreland's gave him a chance to look for Kelsey's car. His heart squeezed when he didn't see it. Maybe, like him, she was late.

Or she's not coming.

West didn't want to contemplate that thought. Bypassing the front door, he walked to the open side gate. The hum of voices echoed between the fence and the house, telling him the party was well underway. Zac spotted him first. As usual, his best friend was manning the barbeque. Coop, on the other hand, was involved in a lively conversation with Shaye and Nikki. West worked his way over to Zac and handed over one of the gifts.

"Do I even bother opening this?" Zac asked with a grin. "Or do I just wait until Coop opens his to see what you got us?"

West extended his hand to Zac. "Happy birthday for tomorrow."

"Thanks." Zac leaned over and put the present on the table behind him. "You get that kitchen sorted yet?"

"Yeah, Coop ran up an estimate for me yesterday. It's not as bad as we first thought. Should be up and running in weeks not months, which is a relief."

"Speaking of my brother, he's heading this way with some liquid refreshments." Zac tipped his head, indicating over West's shoulder. "About time too."

"I heard that." Coop handed West and Zac a bottle each. "All you had to do was give me a shout little brother."

Zac shrugged and continued to turn the sausages sizzling on the hotplate.

"Are we still in a snit?" Coop asked.

"Fuck off."

"Ooo, definitely still snitty." Coop grinned.

West had had enough of Zac's attitude. It was time to find out what the hell was going on with him. "What gives man? You've been a prick for months."

"Nothing," Zac grumbled without making eye contact with either of them.

West sighed. He'd tried to get Zac to talk to him the other week with no luck. Today didn't appear to be any different.

"Let's leave pussy boy to sulk. C'mon, Cassie has something she's keeping secret, but I figure you should know."

"What? Cassie has a secret?"

"Shh," Zac hissed. "No one knows but us, and you if you can keep your trap shut."

What the fuck? West raised one eyebrow.

"I'm serious, man. She's not telling Mum and Dad until after the party because she doesn't want to take away from our day," Zac said with a roll of his eyes.

"Not that either of us give a shit about that, but it's what little sister wants, and you know if someone doesn't give her what she wants all hell will break loose. Besides, she's got that Neanderthal of hers who could crack heads just by looking at them." Coop faked a scared look but only managed to look like an idiot.

Before they could go find Cassie, she and Luc walked over. West didn't need to hear a word to know that whatever had put that glow on Cassie's face and the sparkle in her eyes was the best thing to happen to her since she took Are You Game? from a fledgling business to the successful company it was today.

"They told you, didn't they?" Cassie eyed her brothers.

"No. I know nothing." West grinned.

"As if," she scoffed.

"No, seriously. All they said was you had news."

Cassie crooked her index finger and urged him to lean over. West kept an eye on Luc. Last time he'd gotten too close to Cassie, the man had almost ripped his head off. Except the man was grinning like the damn Cheshire Cat.

With West bent forward, Cassie was able to whisper right in his ear. "I'm pregnant."

"What?" He bolted upright.

"Shh. Jeez, West, shut the fuck up, man," Zac growled.

He looked from Cassie to Luc to Coop to Zac and back to Cassie. "For real?"

"Yep." She nodded, her lips stretched from ear to ear in a smile.

"Oh Lord." West turned to Luc. Keeping his voice low so only their small group would hear, he said, "You better be ready to put a ring on her finger."

Luc reached over and tugged a gold chain out from under Cassie's top. "She's had the ring for months. Refuses to wear it."

"Oh." West looked at Cassie. "Why?"

She shrugged. "Wanted to be sure he was going to stick."

There was stunned silence and then all four men burst out laughing.

"Hey, what's so funny?" Cassie asked, her gaze bouncing between the four of them as she dropped the chain holding her engagement ring beneath her shirt once more. It was Luc she elbowed though.

They let Luc handle the explanation.

"I'm so stuck you'd need a surgeon to remove me. Even then I'd find a way to reattach myself."

West watched tough-as-nails Cassandra Moreland melt into a puddle of goo.

"Luc," she sniffled before launching herself at him.

His gut and chest ached with envy and he had to look away. He found Zac and Coop watching him, not their sister. "What?"

Zac tipped his head to the right. "She's over there."

West spun around to see Kels talking with Shaye, Mel and Nikki, but she was looking right at him.

"Her car wasn't—"

"She came with Shaye," Coop explained.

"If you're going over there, do it for the right reasons," Zac said behind him.

West turned his head, his eyes still glued to the woman across the yard. "Right reasons?"

"If you're going to go after her, and let's face it, you are. Make sure you mean it."

"What?" West snapped his gaze to meet Zac's.

"Don't play around like last time."

West stared at his best friend, his mouth hanging open. "You knew?"

"Of course I fucking knew. Half the time I know you better than I know him." Zac waved the barbeque tongs in Coop's direction.

"Why didn't you ever say anything?"

"Because I stupidly waited for you to work it out." Zac's gaze went in Kelsey's direction. "Then she hooked up with Bry and I wanted to kick your ass for letting her."

"You should have," West murmured.

"I will if you fuck it up this time."

"I'll help," Coop added.

"It's not me this time." West turned back to look at Kelsey, only she wasn't where she'd been. Scanning the yard, he spotted her walking his way. His gut cramped while every nerve came alive with the prospect of being close to her.

Nobody said a word as they watched her approach. West wasn't sure if he *could* speak. She was wearing a pair of skin-tight black jeans that displayed her gorgeous legs and a white jumper that hugged every curve of her torso. The neckline rolled in such a way that it drew his eyes to her breasts, which were showcased to perfection. His mouth watered and his groin tightened—throbbed.

"Close your mouth, West. You're drooling all over your chin," Coop murmured.

Zac chuckled and West made a mental note to beat them both up later.

Kelsey made it to his side and he dragged in a deep breath, filling his lungs with the smell of her. She licked her lips and it was all West could do not to groan at the erotic slide of her tongue on her glossy mouth. She'd obviously slicked some sort of shiny stuff on the plump red curves because they'd looked wet and tempting before she'd nervously flicked her tongue across them. And she was nervous. He could see it in the way she twisted her fingers together in front of her, in the way her eyes kept darting away from him.

Wanting to put an end to the awkward silence, West cleared his throat before speaking. "Hey."

"Hi. You were late."

She'd noticed his arrival? He'd take that as a good sign. Although she could have been dreading him showing up as much as anticipating it. "Yeah, traffic sucked and I think I got every red light between here and home."

"You've been getting a lot of those," Kelsey murmured.

West leaned toward her. "What?"

"Red lights."

"Red lights?"

"Yeah, you know. The opposite of green. You've had to stop a lot lately."

Was she referring to them?

"It would be nice to be able to move forward without having to stop, don't you think?" Kelsey's gaze held his.

She had to be talking about them. Surely this slightly bizarre discussion wasn't about traffic lights. "Um, yeah, it would."

"Maybe you won't get any more red lights."

Either he was getting his wires completely crossed or she was trying to give him a green light. He was done with cryptic though. He wanted everything out in the open, no more confusion or second-guessing or assuming. "What are we talking about, Kels?"

Her gaze darted either side of him before meeting his once more. "We start now. No more stopping."

West's heart stopped. Then it kicked back in at double speed. "Are you sure?" He pointed to Cassie and Luc who were locked in an embrace. Their gazes were glued to each other and that told anyone who looked they were together and deeply in love. "I want that, Kels. I want it all."

She kept her eyes on his. "I know."

"I'm not pussyfooting around this time. I want forever."

Kelsey licked her lips and swallowed. "I want that too. With you."

Everything inside him stilled. "Tell me what you want."

"I want to marry you. Make babies with you. Make a life with you. Grow old with you."

"Shit. Did she just propose?" Coop asked.

West grinned. "Yeah, I think she did." She'd surprised him and everyone else with her public declaration, but he wasn't about to leave her dangling. He reached for her hands and wove their fingers together. Pulling her in close, he said, "I've waited a lifetime for you. I want to spend the rest of my lifetime—our lifetime—making up for every second that we've missed."

Her eyes sparkled with moisture, but the smile stretching across her face told him they were happy tears. "You'll marry me?" she asked.

He laughed. "I'll marry you tomorrow if that's what you want."

"When doesn't matter as long as it's soon. I love you whether we're married or not."

It was all he needed to hear. He dipped his head and took her mouth with his.

West didn't let her up for air until he'd had his fill. He'd missed this. Touching her. Tasting her. And he wanted to be sure he never did again. Pulling his mouth from hers, he stared into her eyes. "Move in with me. Today. I don't want to wait another second to start. Not now you've given me the green light." He grinned.

Kelsey smiled, but they were surrounded before she could answer him. Everyone spoke at once, and West couldn't make head or tails of any of it, but he didn't care. In his arms was the woman he'd dreamed about—*wanted*—for half his life. Now he'd get to spend the next seventy years holding her close. He'd probably still dream about her only now he'd wake and reach for her and his hand would touch warm feminine flesh instead of cold night air.

"Say yes," he said over the noise of all their friends.

"Yes."

The grin on his face got bigger. "Again."

"Yes."

He leaned over and brushed his lips over hers. "Again."

"Yes. Yes. Yes."

Kelsey sat in West's lap, snuggled up close and watched the fire dance. Hours ago, Zac or Coop, she couldn't remember which, had dragged out the old metal drum fire pit they used to take to the beach for bonfire nights and lit it. A lot of people had gone home when the sun went down. All that remained were Shaye, West, herself and the full contingent of Morelands, including Cassie's fiancé Luc. It seemed she and West weren't the only ones getting married.

She still couldn't believe she'd asked him. Or that he wanted her to move in with him right away. Neither of those things frightened her the way they would have less than a week ago. Hell, two days ago, she would have been running for the hills. Now she was reaching for his hand. It was amazing how freeing it was to trust West—to trust what she felt for him.

"You okay? Not cold?" West murmured into her hair.

"No, I'm good."

"We can go whenever you're ready."

"I'm happy to stay as long as you want," she said, tilting her head back to look up at him.

"What I want is to take you home and toss you on *our* bed." He grinned and waggled his eyebrows, making her laugh.

"Another one bites the dust," someone sang from the other side of the fire.

"Yeah, they're dropping like flies. First Cassie, then Dan, now West." Zac scanned the people surrounding the fire until his gaze landed on Coop. "So who's next?"

"Not me," answered Toby, the next Moreland brother up from the twins.

The oldest Moreland, Damian, shook his head. "Don't look at me."

Adam, the brother between Damian and Toby, laughed. "I'd need to leave the office and actually lay eyes on a woman who, one, isn't employed by me, and two, isn't family."

Zac grinned. "My money's on Coop as the next to fall."

"You're going to bet on who finds love next?" Cassie asked, shaking her head at her brother.

"Yep. Who's in? I'm putting twenty on Coop," Zac said.

West chuckled. "I think that's a sucker's bet."

Everyone turned to look at Coop where he was leaning close to

Shaye, whispering in her ear. Kelsey had to agree with West. Coop and Shaye already seemed to be a done deal.

Coop turned towards them. "I'll put fifty on Zac. He'll be the next to fall."

"What?" Zac laughed. "What a croc of shit. I'm not interested in hitching myself up with a ball and chain."

"And you think I was?" Cassie asked. "Jeez, ask Luc what a challenge it was to get me to fall."

"It was worth every torturous second of it," Luc said.

"Brown nose," Zac murmured.

"You just wait. Take my advice and never bet against a heart my friend," Luc said.

"Yeah, everyone knows hearts are wild, big brother," Cassie added.

"You'd need one to bet against," Zac mumbled.

Kelsey was pretty sure no one but her and West had heard him, and she raised her eyebrow in question. West leaned forward to whisper in her ear.

"I think he's tangled with someone already. I get the impression she's not falling at his feet the way women usually do."

Kelsey looked back at Zac but the firelight proved too little for her to study him closely. Besides, it was getting late and she was starting to get cold. "As much as I'd like to dissect our friend's love life, and really, I don't, I think it's time we headed home."

"You're right." West got to his feet, Kelsey still held in his arms. "We're going to love ya and leave ya, people."

When West started to walk without putting her down, Kelsey wiggled and gave a token protest. "Put me down. I'm too heavy to carry."

"Kels, you're lighter than a pot of curry and I'm not stopping now. You gave me a green light and I'll poke my eyes out if I have to to avoid seeing another red one."

EPILOGUE
TWO MONTHS LATER

Kelsey sucked in a breath as she smoothed her hands down the front of her white dress and grinned at her reflection. It wasn't the satin and lace extravaganza she'd worn six years ago, but she'd known the simple sundress was perfect for the beachside wedding she and West had planned the second she'd laid eyes on it.

The bodice hugged her breasts, waist and hips, and the flowing skirt billowed around her ankles, a scalloped hem adding to the summery feel of their day. She turned around to look over her shoulder at the plunging back of the halter neck as the door opened and Shaye stuck her head in.

"You ready? Oh, Kelsey," Shaye said as she came farther into the room. "You look gorgeous."

Kelsey twirled around, the skirt swirling up. "You think so?"

"God, woman. West is going to swallow his tongue." Shaye grinned.

"That's the plan. Just because we're not doing this the traditional way, doesn't mean I can't knock my groom's socks off." Kelsey laughed and spun around once more.

"C'mon, I can't wait to see West's face." Shaye grabbed for her hand but Kelsey pulled away before she could get a good grip.

"Wait." Kelsey turned to the dresser beside her. "I have something for you."

They'd decided against bridesmaids and groomsmen, but Kelsey had wanted to give her best friend something special to mark the day anyway. Shaye had helped them pull everything together in record time and Kelsey wanted to say thank you. She just hoped Shaye liked the gift West had helped her chose. With the rectangular box in her hand, Kelsey faced Shaye again and held it out.

"What is it?" Shaye asked.

"Open it and see." Kelsey took a step closer and pressed the velvet case into Shaye's hand.

With a frown on her face, Shaye lifted the lid. Air rushed through her lips and her eyes widened—turned glassy. "Oh, God, Kelsey," she whispered.

"You've always admired mine and I thought..."

Shaye threw her arms around Kelsey's neck. "It's beautiful. I love it. Thank you."

Smiling, Kelsey hugged her back. "You're welcome. But it's me that should be thanking you. Without your help, today wouldn't be happening."

"Bullshit. But I'll take your thank you anyway. Help me put it on," Shaye demanded as she let Kelsey go.

Kelsey took the bracelet from the box and quickly secured it on Shaye's right wrist. "There." She brushed her fingers over the silver links. "It looks lovely."

"Lovely? It's gorgeous." Shaye shook her arm to make the charms jingle. "But enough with me. It's your day. Let's go."

Shaye grabbed Kelsey's hand and tugged her across the room.

Kelsey's stomach fluttered. The nervous excitement bubbling inside her was so different to what she'd felt on her first wedding day that she couldn't believe she'd gone through with marrying Bry back then. But she didn't want to think about that now. That was in the past and today was the first day of the rest of her life. Her and West's life.

"Is everyone here?" Kelsey asked as they made their way through the luxurious beach house they'd rented for the weekend.

"Yes."

"So we're ready to start?" Those flutters accelerated alone with her steps.

"We are." Shaye paused in the hallway and squeezed her hand. "Ready whenever you are."

Kelsey gave a nod. "I'm ready. More than ready." She grinned.

"Okay. See you in a few." Shaye's hand slipped from hers.

Kelsey watched as her friend disappeared into the large room that opened out onto the beach. Out there, standing on the sand, was the man she'd loved for most of her life. The man she was going to spend the rest of her life with. She couldn't stop the smile that spread across her face from growing bigger as she rounded the corner and got her first look at West.

He stood facing the house and for a split second, she saw the anxiety that wrinkled his forehead before he spotted her. The smile that curved his mouth when their gazes met sent a burst of arousal through her. She knew that smile. It was the one he gave her when he was peeling her clothes off.

Kelsey quickened her steps. She suddenly wanted this day to be over so they could get on with the rest of their lives. Marching over the warm sand, she reached West's side a little out of breath.

"Kels..." he murmured when he reached out to take her hand and pull her close.

She grinned.

"You..." He shook his head. "You're..."

Kelsey laughed and, pushing to her toes, planted a kiss on his lips.

West slid his arm around her waist and hauled her against his chest as he thrust his tongue between her lips and took the kiss deeper. He splayed a warm hand across her bare lower back and a shudder rolled over her. She melted into him, every part of her softening as she got lost in their kiss.

"Ahem."

The celebrant they'd hired to officiate cleared her throat, and

Kelsey remembered where they were and moved back, but West didn't let her go. He held her pressed against him. Their eyes met—locked. The look he gave her stole her breath. Everything he felt for her was in his gaze.

In that moment, Kelsey knew risking her heart on West again would be more than worth it.

West pulled Kels in against his side and nuzzled her neck. She shivered. "Cold Mrs. Mann?" His lips curled up at the sound of her new title.

"No." She leaned back and smiled up at him. "No chance of that with your roaming hands and lips."

He palmed her ass and tugged her closer so that every inch of her front was pressed to his. She couldn't miss his erection. The one he'd sported since the moment he'd first seen her in her dress. "Goes both ways."

"Will you two get a room," Coop yelled from across the patio.

West took his eyes off his beautiful wife—God, Kelsey was his *wife*—and glanced at his best friend. "We have a room. In fact, we have a whole house. It's full of freeloaders at the moment though." He grinned.

Coop held up his beer. "There's still beer and food, so you're stuck with us for a while yet."

Kelsey stood on her toes and whispered in his ear. "We could always go inside and lock the door."

His gaze collided with hers and he narrowed his eyes. "Are you serious?"

She laughed and slipped out of his arms. "No."

"Tease."

"It's only teasing if you don't follow through and, West—" she ran the tip of her finger down his chest until it reached the button on his pants "—I plan on following through. Just not yet."

He groaned as she strolled away.

"She looks so happy." Zac moved beside him.

West couldn't take his eyes of his wife's tempting ass as she continued to walk away from him. "Yeah."

"So do you."

He glanced at Zac and noticed the frown on his best friend's face. "And us being happy makes you sad?"

"What?" Zac's gaze met West's. "No. Jeez. I'm just as happy about you two getting together as you are."

West believed him, but something had been going on with Zac for months now, and no matter how often he or Coop had tried to get to the bottom of it, Zac remained stubbornly mute. Maybe now was a good time to press his friend on the subject. "What's going on, Zac?"

"Nothing." Zac took a sip of his drink. "Whatever you do, don't fuck this thing with Kelsey up."

Before West could say anything else, Zac strode across the patio to where Coop, Shaye and West's sister, Freddie, were sitting.

"Zac still brooding?" Kelsey asked.

West hadn't noticed her circle back around to him but was happy to pull her against him again. He turned her around so her back was to his front, his arms around her waist. "Yeah."

"You might not want to hear this, but I think I know what his problem is."

He glanced down at Kels. "You do?"

"I think so." She tipped her chin in Zac's direction. "Just watch."

It took a while, because West was a little preoccupied by his wife's warm body tucked against him to be sure he was joining the dots correctly. "Is he staring at Freddie?"

Kelsey nodded. "He's been doing it all day."

"What the fuck?" West loosened his grip ready to charge across the room.

"No, you don't." Kelsey spun around and grabbed him. "Don't. The staring has been going both ways."

"But—"

"West." She slid her hands up his chest and cupped his jaw,

brushing her thumbs over his bottom lip. "Wanna go lock that door now?"

His body instantly reacted. His heart raced, his pulse pounding in his ear—in his groin—and he couldn't stop himself from sliding his hands down her sides to cup her ass. "Are you serious?"

She rubbed her stomach against his throbbing cock. "That would definitely be a green light I see," she said with a grin.

He lifted her off her feet and grinned at her squeal. West turned on his heel and strode from the room.

"West!" She wrapped her arms around his neck. "We should say goodnight to everyone."

"You were trying to distract me from my murderous thoughts about Zac. Consider me distracted so completely I'm oblivious to the crowd of people on the patio." He tipped his head and dragged his teeth across her shoulder. "I can't wait to get you behind that locked door, Mrs. Mann."

Kelsey groaned and tilted her head to the side to offer him her neck. "Is it locked yet?"

West grinned. "Almost."

He moved through the house towards the master suite. He'd snuck away earlier to organize a surprise for his wife and he couldn't wait to see her reaction. West cleared the doorway, stopped just over the threshold and lowered Kelsey to her feet.

"Before we start and I get carried away, I want to say something."

She looked up at him with eyes full of love and his heart just about stopped. "What?"

He cupped her face and laid his forehead on hers. "I love you so much I can't think. Can't breathe. You are everything that makes me good. And I promise you, I will never let a day go by where I don't tell you I love you."

"West," Kelsey sighed his name and he couldn't resist pressing his lips to hers.

He'd intended it to be a quick peck, but as usual, Kelsey's mouth proved too tempting and they were soon lost in the hot, wet slide of a carnal kiss. West wasn't sure who started removing clothes first, but he soon found himself minus a shirt and Kelsey's dress was undone and hanging around her waist.

"Jesus. We haven't even shut the door." West reached over and flung the door closed, plunging the room into darkness. He backed her towards the bed, his eyes slowly adjusting to the lack of light.

"We need to get out of these clothes." Kelsey tugged on the button of his pants.

West put his hand over hers. "Hang on. I want the light on first."

He took her with him as he moved to the bedside table and the lamp he'd brought just for tonight.

"Let me switch...ah, there."

Kelsey's eyelids fluttered. Her eyes growing wide as the soft glow of his wedding present to them filled the room.

"What the hell?" She started down at the lamp.

"Happy wedding day, Kels." West tipped her chin up and kissed her softly.

"What?" She leaned away from him and blinked several times. "I haven't had that much champagne, but I swear that light is green."

He grinned down at her. "It is."

Kelsey shook her head a couple of times. "A green lamp?"

"No." Chuckling, he pulled her tighter against him. "It's our very own green light."

For a second, she stared at him, her mouth hanging open slightly, but then the confusion cleared from her eyes and she threw her head back and laughed.

For what's coming next, latest releases, sales and more, join

Rhian's Royal Readers
http://www.rhiancahill.com/contact/newsletter/

Curious about the party where Cassie met Lucas?

Read the Party Games series

Truth Or Dare

Sometimes it takes a daring heart to find true love

Even at an exclusive party, Miki Drummond finds herself retreating
to a safe corner. Watching life go by is something she does well,
especially after the hell of her collapsed marriage.
The last thing she expected to do was 'bump' into not one but two
blasts from her high school past.
Best friends, Grant Rogers and Dayne Pierce never forgot Miki—ever
—and a game of Truth or Dare seems like the perfect way to get
reacquainted. Except Miki repeatedly chooses to take a shot rather
than reveal her obvious pain, but neither man is willing to let her
hide in the past for long.
With Grant and Dayne, Miki is caught in an electrically charged
moment that offers her sweet torment and unimaginable pleasure.
But one night of pure fantasy is all Miki dares to take until her two
lovers dare her to accept the hard truth. Walking away is no longer an
option.

Note: If you find yourself sandwiched between two hunky men...it
might be worth taking the dare.

Spin The Bottle

The only rule is the rules always change

Modelling gave Lillian McDermott amazing experiences and enough

money to leave it all behind to start her own perfume and fashion label, but it didn't give her the man she's always loved—Mackenzie Harris.
Her brother's best friend, Mac only sees her as a surrogate little sister, except Lillian's success wasn't handed to her. She knows what it means to work hard and she intends to use the same single-minded intensity to rock Mac's world until ignoring her is impossible.
Best mates don't screw around with little sisters so no matter how tempting Mackenzie Harris finds Lillian McDermott it's hands off.
That doesn't mean he's ever been immune to her charms.
With one spin of the bottle Lilli turns up the heat and Mac's not one to back down from a challenge. And once that line is crossed, there's no turning back.

Note: A game of Spin the Bottle is hell on one's self control.

ABOUT THE AUTHOR

Rhian Cahill is the alter ego of a former stay-at-home mother of four. With motherly duties rapidly dwindling, Rhian is able to make use of the fertile imagination she used to keep herself sane for all those years of slavery. Years spent living overseas and visiting tropical climates have helped inspire some steamy stories.

Multi-published in erotic romance, paranormal romance, and contemporary romance, Rhian, with the help of Mr. Muse, spends her days and nights writing.

When not glued to the keyboard you'll find her, book or knitting in hand, avoiding any and all housework as much as possible.

For more on Rhian –

Website – http://www.rhiancahill.com/
Newsletter signup – http://www.rhiancahill.com/contact/newsletter/
FaceBook – https://www.facebook.com/RhianCahillAuthor
Instagram – http://instagram.com/rhiancahill/
Twitter – https://twitter.com/RhianCahill
BookBub – https://www.bookbub.com/authors/rhian-cahill
Goodreads – https://www.goodreads.com/rhian_cahill

LOOK FOR THESE TITLES BY RHIAN CAHILL

CONTEMPORARY ROMANCE

Everyday Heroes World

Flashback

Flyboy

Fallout

Winter Lake Series

Love Me Like You Do

Love The Way You Are

When You Love Someone

Let Me Love You

Wild Rush Of Love

Party Games Series

Truth Or Dare

Spin The Bottle

Pass The Parcel (novella)

Are You Game? Series

7 Minutes In Heaven

Catch'n'Kiss

Red Light, Green Light

Hearts Are Wild Series

No More Talking (novella)

Dare You To (novella)

Mad Love

Boys Of Summer

Bondi Beach Boys

Sand, Surf And Sunnie

Only You Series

All Of You

Holiday Romances

Christmas Wishes

New Year's Kisses

Valentine's Dates

Secret Santa

Frosty's Snowmen Series

A Touch Of Frost

A Kiss From Kringle

A Taste For Kandy

Secret Confessions

Sydney Housewives – Virginia

PARANORMAL ROMANCE

Coyote Hunger Series

Coyote Home

Coyote Wild

Coyote Whispers

Coyote Law (novella)

Coyote Lies

For a full list of available books visit

http://www.rhiancahill.com/books/

For what's coming next, latest releases, sales and more, join

Rhian's Royal Readers

http://www.rhiancahill.com/contact/newsletter/